THE WYRMLING HORDE

Fallion tried to remain quiet, but his throat betrayed him, and sobs issued from him in rapid succession, each a part cough, part moan.

'Serve me,' Lord Despair whispered, 'and I will release you from your pain.'

Fallion knew of only two ways that he could be free of such pain. Lord Despair could force it onto another, leaving Fallion an empty husk, emotionless and numb. Or he could kill the Dedicates who had granted their pain, thus breaking the magical ties that bound Fallion to his people.

He'll murder this family, Fallion realized. He'll do it in front of me and make me watch.

He hopes that in time, I will be evil enough to crave such a thing. For when I consent to the shedding of innocent blood, a locus will be able to make its home in me.

No, Fallion realized, Lord Despair wishes more from me than even that. He doesn't just want to make me a worthy abode for a locus. He doesn't just want to punish me – Lord Despair hopes that I will *become* him.

But I will turn the tables. I can never succumb. I can never let him beat me.

To Nichole, Danielle, Forrest, Spencer, and Ben — who have all helped their dad so much over the years.

THE WYRMLING HORDE

PROLOGUE

RUNES OF COMPASSION

This is Understanding's House,
I've seen these doors before,
Though when or where, I don't know.

In dusty rooms, like ancient tombs,
I studied endless lore.
For what or why, I don't know.

Yet soon I learned too much,
Like a child lost in war.
Lost in horrors
I hope you'll never know.

—A song of Mystarria

In all of his dreams, Fallion had never dreamed with such intense clarity. He dreamed that he was soaring above the Courts of Tide. He was not riding a graak, nor did he wear a magical wing. In his dream Fallion's arms stretched wide, holding him aloft, like some seagull that hangs motionless in the sky, its wingtips trembling as the wind sweeps beneath them.

Nothing below obstructed his view.

And so he glided over houses where the sweet gray smoke of cooking fires floated lazily above thatched roofs, and Fallion darted above a palace wall, veering between two tall white towers where a guard with his pike and black scale mail gaped up at Fallion in astonishment. Fallion could see each graying hair of the guard's arched eyebrow, and how the man's brass pin hung loose on his forest-green cape, and he could even smell the man's ripening sweat.

Fallion swooped low over the cobbled city streets, where fishermen in their white tunics and brown woolen caps trudged to their dank homes after a hard day working the nets; the young scholars who attended the House of Understanding stood on street corners arguing jovially while sipping tankards of ale, and a boy playing with a pet rat in the street gaped up at Fallion and pointed, his mouth an O of surprise.

'The king has come!' the child cried in surprise, and suddenly the people looked up in awe and rejoiced to see Fallion. 'The king! Look!' they cried, tears leaping to their eyes.

I must be dreaming, Fallion thought, for never have I seen the world so clearly.

There is a legendary stream in the land of Mystarria. Its icy waters tumble down from the snowfields of Mount Rimmon, beneath pines that guard the slopes, along moss-covered floors where huge marble statues of dead kings lie fallen. The stream's clean flow spills into forest pools so transparent that even at a depth of forty feet every water weed and sparkling red cray-fish can be seen. The enormous trout that live there 'seemingly slide through the air just by slapping their tails,' and all of them grow fat and to a ripe old age, for no fisherman or otter can hope to venture near in waters so clear.

So the stream is called the Daystar, for it is as clear and sparkling as the morning star.

And that is how preternaturally clear the dream came to Fallion, as clear as the waters of the Daystar.

He longed to continue dreaming forever, but for one thing: the air was so cold. He could feel frost beginning to rime his fingernails, and he shivered violently.

This frost will kill me, he thought. It will pierce my heart like an arrow.

And so he struggled to wake, and found himself . . . flying.

The wind rushed under him, cold and moist, and Fallion huddled in pain sharp and bitter.

He could feel a shard of steel lodged below his ribcage, like a dagger of ice. Drying blood matted his shirt.

He struggled to wake, and when his eye opened to a slit, it was bright below. The wan silvery light of early morning filled the sky. He could see the tops of pines below, limbs so close that if he had reached out he could almost have touched them.

Where am I? I'm flying above a forest.

In the distance he could descry a mountain – no, he decided, a strange castle as vast as a mountain. It was built into the sides of a black volcano whose inner fires limned the cone at its top and spewed smoke and ash.

All beneath, along the skirts of the volcano, a formidable fortress sprawled, with murderously high walls and thousands of dark holes that might have been windows or tunnels into the mountain.

There was no fresh lime upon the walls to make the castle gleam like silver in the dawn. Instead, the castle was black and foreboding. A few pale creatures bustled along the walls and upon the dark roads below, racing to flee the dawn, looking like an army of angry ants. Even a mile away, Fallion could tell that they were not entirely human.

Wyrmlings, he realized.

Fallion shivered violently, so cold and numb that he feared he would die. His thoughts clouded by pain, he struggled to figure out what was happening.

He was not flying under his own power. He was being borne by some great creature. Huge arms clutched him tightly. If a stone gargoyle had come to life, Fallion imagined that it would grip him so. He could hear powerful wings flapping: the wind from each downstroke assailed him.

Fallion could not see his captor, but he could smell the arm that clutched him. It smelled like . . . rotten meat, like something long dead.

Fear coursed through him.

I'm in the arms of a Knight Eternal, Fallion realized, one of the dead lords of the wyrmlings. And he began to remember . . .

The battle at Caer Luciare. The wyrmling warriors with their sickly pale skin and bone armor had attacked the mountain fortress, a fortress so different from the one he was going to. The limestone walls of the fortress had been glistening white, as clean as snow, and in the market flowers and fruit trees grew in a riot along the street, while leafy vines hung from the windows.

The wyrmlings had come with the night. The pounding of their thunder drums had cracked the castle walls. Poisoned war darts had pelted down in a black rain. Everywhere there had been cries of dismay as the brave warriors of Caer Luciare saw their plight.

Jaz! Fallion thought, almost crying aloud, as he recalled his brother falling. A black dart had been sprouting from Jaz's back as he knelt on hands and knees, blood running from his mouth.

After that, everything became confused. Fallion remembered running with Rhianna at his side, retreating up the city streets in a daze, people shouting while Fallion wondered, Is there anything I could have done to save him?

He recalled the Knights Eternal sweeping out of dark skies. Fallion held his sword at guard position, eager to engage one, heart hammering as the monster swept toward him like a falcon, its enormous black long sword stretched out before it – a knight charging toward him on a steed of wind.

Fallion twisted away from the attack at the last instant, his blade swiping back against the tip of the Knight Eternal's sword. Fallion had meant to let his blade cut cleanly into flesh, but the Knight Eternal must have veered at the last instant, and Fallion's blade struck the thick metal – and snapped.

As his tortured blade broke, Fallion had felt pain lance just below the ribcage. A remnant of his shattered blade lodged in his flesh. He fell to his knees, blood gushing hot over his tunic as he struggled to keep from swooning.

Rhianna had called 'Fallion! Fallion!' and all around him the noise of battle had sought to drown out her voice, so that it seemed to come from far away.

Struggling to remain awake, Fallion had knelt for a moment, dazed, while the world whirled viciously.

Everything went black.

And now I wake, Fallion thought.

He closed his eyes, tried to take stock of his situation.

His artificial wings were folded against his back. He did not know how to use them well, yet. He'd worn the magical things for less than a day. He could feel a sharp pain where they were bound tightly, lest he try to escape.

I dare not let the monster know that I am awake, Fallion realized.

Fallion's sword was gone, his scabbard empty, but he still had a dagger hidden in his boot.

If I could reach it, he thought, I could plunge it into the monster's neck.

Fallion was so cold, his teeth were chattering. He tried to still them, afraid to make any noise, afraid to alert the creature.

But if I attack, what then? The monster will fall, and I will fall with it – to my death.

His mind reeled away from the unpleasant prospect.

Moments later the Knight Eternal groaned and cursed, as if in pain. They had been flying in the shadow of a hill, and suddenly they were in open sunlight. Fallion's captor dropped lower, so that he was flying beneath the trees, well in their shadow.

There was a nimbus around them, a thick haze. It gathered a bit.

Of course, Fallion realized, the Knight Eternal is racing against the coming of day. He's gathering the light around him, trying to create a shadow.

He's struggling to get me back to the castle before dawn!

They had dropped lower now, and Fallion judged that he was not more than twenty feet above ground. On impulse,

Fallion reached for his boot dagger, and by straining managed to reach it, grasping it with two fingers. He tried to pull it free.

Just as suddenly, his captor tightened his grip, pulling Fallion's arms mercilessly tight. The boot knife fell, spinning away to land on the ground.

The Knight Eternal was crushing Fallion against his chest. It apparently had not even noticed what Fallion was doing. But the creature's grip was so fearsome that now Fallion had to struggle for a breath.

Fallion despaired. He had no other weapons.

Fallion wondered about Rhianna. If she was alive, she would have protected him to the last. He knew that about her at least. No woman was more faithful, more devoted to him, than she.

Which meant that like Jaz, she must be dead.

The very thought tore at Fallion's sanity.

My fault, he told himself. It is my fault that they're dead. I am the one who brought them here. I'm the one who bound the worlds together.

And as quickly as Fallion had fallen into despair, rage and determination welled up. Fallion was a wizard of unguessable power. In ages past, there had been one sun and one true world, bright and perfect, and all mankind had lived in harmony beneath the shade of the One True Tree. But the great Seal of Creation that governed that world had been broken, and as it broke, the world shattered, splintering into a million million parts, creating millions upon millions of shadow worlds, each a dull imitation of that one true world, each less virtuous, each spinning around its own sun so that now the heavens were filled with a sea of stars.

Now Fallion had demonstrated the skill necessary to bind those shadow worlds back into one. He had bound two worlds together. He had yet to bring to pass the realization of his dream: binding all worlds into one world, flawless and perfect.

But his enemies had feared what he could do, and had set

a trap. Fallion had bound his own world with another, as an experiment, and everything had gone terribly wrong.

Now Fallion's people had been thrust into a land of giants, where the cruel wyrmlings ruled, a ruthless people thoroughly enthralled by an evil so monstrous that it was beyond Fallion's power to imagine, much less comprehend.

I hoped to make a better world, to re-create the one true world of legend, and instead I brought my people to the brink of ruin.

The Knight Eternal that carried him suddenly rose toward a gate in the castle. Fallion could hear barks and snarls of alarm as wyrmling warriors announced their approach.

Where is the Knight Eternal taking me? Fallion wondered.

The knight swept through an enormous archway and landed with a jar, and then crept into a lightless corridor, carrying Fallion as easily as if he were a child.

Fallion's toes and fingers were numb. He felt so cold that he feared he had frostbite. He still could not think well. Every thought was a skirmish. Every memory was won only after a long battle.

He needed warmth, heat. There was none to be found. There had been no sunlight shining upon the castle. There were no torches sitting in sconces to brighten the way. Instead the Knight Eternal bore him down endless tunnels into a labyrinth where the only illumination came from worms that glittered along the wall and ceiling.

Sometimes he passed other wyrmlings, and whether they were mere servants or hardened warriors, they all backed away from his captor in terror.

Fallion could have used his powers to leach a little heat from a wyrmling, if one had come closer.

Maybe the stone is warm, Fallion thought. *Maybe it still recalls the sunlight that caressed it yesterday.*

Fallion could have reached out to quest for the sunlight. But there was a great danger. Fallion was a flameweaver, a wizard of fire. Yet he knew that at least one Knight Eternal had mastered such skills better than he: Vulgnash.

In earlier battles, each time that Fallion had tried to tap into some source of heat, Vulgnash had siphoned the energy away.

Of course, Fallion realized. That is why I am so cold now. The creature has drained me. I am in Vulgnash's arms.

I must not let him know that I am awake.

Vulgnash had no body heat that Fallion could use. Though the Knight Eternal mimicked life, the monster was dead, and it had no more heat in it than did a serpent.

So Fallion held still, struggled to slow his breathing, to feign sleep, as the Knight Eternal bore him down, down an endless winding stair.

We're going to the heart of the world.

I will have to attack quickly when the chance comes. A single torch is all that I'll need. I'll cause it to flash into light, to consume all of its fuel in an instant, and then draw it into myself. I'll use its heat to burn my enemies.

After long and long, the Knight Eternal reached a landing and walked out into an open room. The air was fetid, stifling, and smelled slightly of sulfur.

Fallion could hear children whimpering – along with the moan of some man, and the uncontrolled sobbing of a woman. These were not the deep-throated sounds of subhuman wyrm-lings. These were the whimpers and cries of his own people, beaten and wounded.

'Help! Someone please help us!' a boy cried in Fallion's own Rofehavanish tongue.

The cries of his people came from a knot at one side of the room.

The Knight Eternal spoke, its voice a growl deeper than a lion's, and around him came answering growls.

Fallion could see nothing through his half-slitted eyes.

So he closed them, and in a way that he had learned as a child, he looked upon the world with his inner eye, the eyes of his spirit, and he saw light.

He could descry the room. Each creature within it could be discerned not as flesh and bone but as a creature of light, with glowing tendrils arcing out in shades of blue and white – like the spines of a sea anemone. These were their spirits, easily discerned, while their flesh showed hardly at all. Bone and muscle seemed to have almost disappeared, becoming a cloudy nimbus. But still their shapes could be seen. Their skin was but a transparent sac, like the skin of jellyfish, and within that sac their spirits burned, giving light.

Fallion was surrounded by wyrmlings. The creatures were far larger than humans, though they were human in form. Each stood nearly eight feet tall, had broad shoulders, and could not have weighed less than four hundred pounds. Many were at least six hundred. The bony plates on their foreheads were topped with stubs that looked as if they would sprout horns, and their canines were overlarge. Their cruel faces seemed to be twisted into permanent sneers.

Wyrmling guards watched at every door, and three dignitaries stood at the foot of a throne. The light within these wyrmlings was very dim. Fallion could see black creatures, fluttering and indistinct, that fed upon their souls – the loci, parasitical beings of pure evil.

Fallion was not surprised by the loci's presence. His foster sister Talon had warned him that the wyrmlings had been raised to serve the loci. The wyrmlings vied for the parasites, believing that to be infected by a locus granted them immortality. They believed that their spirits were mortal, and could become immortal only once they were subsumed into immortal loci.

Upon the floor sprawled human prisoners, small folk like Fallion – people from his own world. Their innocent spirits shone as bright as stars. There was a mother, a father, and three children. They were roughly bound so that ankles and legs lay bleeding and, in the case of the father, twisted and broken.

Upon a dais sat a creature that horrified Fallion. It was not as large as a wyrmling, and not as deformed in the face. Thus, Fallion realized that it was one of the folk of Caer Luciare, who were giants by the standards of Fallion's world.

So, Fallion decided, it was a man, with long hair. Like the folk of Caer Luciare, who had been bred to war for countless centuries, he did not look entirely human. His face was narrower than a wyrmling's, and his skull was not as heavily armored. The bony plate on his forehead was not nearly so pronounced, and his canines were not so large.

His raven hair was tied at the back, and his haggard face shaven clean. His skin was rough and unhealthy, and his cheekbones were pronounced, as if he were half-starved. But he was not unpleasing to the eye. Almost, Fallion realized, he was handsome.

It was not his features that horrified Fallion: it was the creature that dwelt within this man. There was a locus feeding upon his bright spirit, a locus so dark and malevolent, Fallion could feel its influence from across the room. Indeed the evil seemed to be sprawling, and the locus was so massive that it could not fit within the fleshly shell of its host. Other loci were often not much larger than cats. But this one was vast and bloated, and it crouched, feeding upon its host's bright spirit, a spirit so luminous that Fallion could only imagine that the host had been a virtuous man, blameless and honorable – not some wyrmling horror.

The locus's sprawling gut filled more than half of the room. Indeed it seemed almost like the abdomen of a black widow spider, so huge that the belly dwarfed its head.

Fallion's captor dropped him to the floor.

In utter darkness, a voice spoke. 'Welcome to Rugassa, Fallion Orden.' The voice was deep, too deep to be human. It came from the lord who sat upon the dais. It came from the locus. The creature knew Fallion's name. 'I know that you are awake.'

'You speak my tongue?' Fallion asked.

'I speak all tongues,' the locus said, 'for I am the master of all worlds. I am Lord Despair. Serve me, and you shall be spared.'

Only then was Fallion sure where he stood. He was in the presence of the One True Master of Evil, who had tried to wrest control of the Rune of Creation from mankind, and who had shattered their perfect world into innumerable shards.

'I will not serve you,' Fallion said. 'I remember you, Yaleen. I remember when I served our people under the One True Tree. You could not sway me with your beauty then; you will not sway me with the horror that you have become.'

Fallion had fought a locus before. Using his flameweaving skills, he'd created a light so bright that it pierced a locus and burned it.

Quick as a thought, Fallion reached out with his senses and grasped for the warmth of the wyrmling guards. Their bodies were massive and held more heat than the human prisoners might have. Fallion planned to suck their warmth into himself.

Ghostly red lights fluoresced as heat streamed toward him.

But as quickly as he reached out, he felt a stab of ice lance through him, and his own inner fire raced away, along with the heat that he'd hoped to steal. Ice lanced through his guts.

'Aaaaagh,' Fallion cried as indescribable agony sought expression. He was suddenly swimming in pain, struggling to remain conscious.

Now he knew for certain: the Knight Eternal who stood over him was a flameweaver of consummate skill. It had to be Vulgnash.

Lord Despair said, 'If you will not serve me, you shall suffer. How great your suffering will be, you cannot guess. I have tasted such suffering in part, and even I could not bear it.'

Lord Despair clapped his hands. A guard brought a single thumb-light into the room, a tiny lantern that might have been carved from amber, with a wick that gave off no more flame than a candle. It allowed Fallion to see, though wyrmlings had to squint away.

The wyrmling guard wore armor carved from the bone of a world wyrm, armor as white and as milky as his warty skin. He strode among five human prisoners, letting the light shine above them so that Fallion could see. The first that he revealed was a child of four, a girl in a humble sacklike dress with golden hair whose face was a mask of purple bruises. Next to her lay a boy of twelve, some farm boy with two broken arms twisted and tied behind his back. Beyond was a woman who was obviously his mother, for they both had the same dark hair. She lay as if lifeless, though her chest rose and fell. Her bloody skirts suggested that the wyrmlings had put her through unspeakable torments.

Next to them was the father, a broken bone protruding through his leg. Last of all was a small boy of two, wrapped in a fetal position, his face a mask of terror.

They've captured a whole family, Fallion felt sure. They went into some farm cottage and ripped these poor folk from the lives that they had loved.

It's my fault, he thought. I'm the one who bound the worlds together.

Some of the prisoners now tried to struggle. The mother looked up around the room at her tormentors with eyes red and glazed from weeping.

'Pain can be a wondrous inducement,' Lord Despair said to Fallion in his deep voice. 'And you shall feel wondrous pain. Of all the worlds that you could have bound together, these two offer the greatest possibilities. The tormentors of Rugassa have been perfecting their art for five thousand years. Among all of my shadow worlds, there are no better. And now, because of you, they shall take their art to a higher level, to heights undreamed.'

He's going to kill the prisoners, Fallion thought. He'll torture them to death for his own amusement. Fallion had seen such tortures before, when the locus Asgaroth had taken men and threaded poles through them, leaving them skewered but somehow still alive as he raised their racked bodies up for the world to see.

But no torture was forthcoming. Instead, the Knight Eternal growled an order. Another guard came into the room bearing a red pillow.

Upon it were five small rods, each the length of Fallion's hand and as thick as a nail. Upon the head of each rod was a rune, bound within a circle.

These were forcibles, the branding irons that allowed a Runelord to draw attributes from his vassals so that he could garner their strength and speed, their beauty and wisdom.

Fallion had never tasted the kiss of a forcible. On his world the blood metal that they were forged from was so rare that only the wealthiest and most powerful lords ever owned it. And though Fallion's father had bequeathed him some forcibles, Fallion had refused to use them for a more important reason: he had not been able to stand the thought of drawing out the wit from a man in order to boost his own intelligence, for in doing so, he would turn that man into a drooling idiot. He could not even think of taking the beauty from some woman, leaving her a hag. He abhorred the thought of draining the strength from some burly peasant, consigning the man to such a state of frailty that his heart might fail at pumping his own life's blood.

So Fallion had refused to take endowments from his people.

What endowment is Lord Despair going to wrest from these poor folks? Fallion wondered.

But that question was dashed by a more significant realization. Since the binding of these two worlds, Fallion had hoped that the wyrmlings would not have discovered the rune lore that would allow the transfer of attributes, for it was only such lore that gave his own small folk the hope of beating the wyrmlings.

In the battle for Luciare he'd seen some wyrmlings running with seemingly superhuman speed, and had worried that they might have taken endowments.

Now, Fallion saw, the wyrmlings did indeed understand such lore, or at least, with the binding of the worlds, they had learned of it.

The guard brought the forcibles, the magical branding irons, to the Knight Eternal that loomed above Fallion. Vulgnash took one, studied it a moment, and then held it close so that Fallion could see. The rune engraved upon it was unknown to Fallion's people. But after a few seconds he realized that he recognized part of it – a rune of touch.

But there were other runes bound into the forcible, at least two or three others that Fallion had never seen, and suddenly Fallion realized that the wyrmlings not only understood rune lore, their knowledge far surpassed that of his own people.

'What? What is this?' Fallion asked, studying the forcible.

'You shall see,' Lord Despair said.

A wyrmling lord took the forcible and began to chant, a sound deep and soothing, mesmerizing. As he did, the tip of the forcible began to glow hot, like a branding iron that sits among coals, becoming brighter and brighter.

When it shone like a fallen star, he went to the farm woman in her bloody skirts, flipped her over so that Fallion could see her bruised face, and plunged the branding iron between her eyes.

The air filled with the reek of singed flesh and burning hair. When the wyrmling pulled the branding iron free, a white light stretched out from the woman's forehead, like a glowing worm. It elongated, following the forcible as the facilitator pulled it away and twirled the branding iron. The worm of light did not fade, but merely hung in the air, a ghostly presence.

'Wait!' Fallion cried, for the light revealed that the endowment ceremony was working, yet it did so despite the rules that Fallion understood. 'She must give her endowment willingly. You can't just rip it from her!'

In his own world endowments were most often given as an act of love, a gift to a worthy lord from a grateful vassal who hoped, by bestowing the gift, to protect his people. But it was also true that endowments might be coerced. Some lords bought endowments, granting great wealth to those who sold them. Vile lords sometimes devised torments so terrible that the vassal would relinquish an attribute in hope to escape the consequences.

But in all cases, the attribute had to be given by one who had a willing heart. It could not be stripped away like this.

Fallion reeled a bit, struggling to hold on to consciousness. The cold around him was so intense.

'I am taking their pain,' Lord Despair said. 'I am taking the whole of it: the pain of their wounds, the torment of their minds, all of their suffering and anguish. Who would not want to give that up? Even in their delirium, their fogged minds scream for release, and thus their endowments are taken willingly.'

Fallion peered up at Lord Despair and realized what he intended to do. He would give Fallion all of their torment.

Moments later, the wyrmling wizard bore the forcible to Fallion, and thrust its white-hot tip against Fallion's cheek.

The kiss of a forcible is said to be sweet, sweeter than any lover's lips. Perhaps in part, that was because the one who receives an endowment also receives strength or stamina or some other virtue that all humans long for.

Who has not looked upon a great sage and not wished for his wisdom? What woman has not gazed upon that rare beauty that is born with perfect skin and teeth, with shining hair and a glorious figure, and not longed that she had been so endowed from birth?

And it was true that Fallion felt a rush of euphoria that rocked him to the very core.

Yet, it was not as it was supposed to be.

It is said that he or she who grants an endowment does so at great cost. When a virtue is ripped from them, it causes indescribable agony, an agony so profound that only a woman who has endured a rough birthing can begin to comprehend it.

As the forcible lightly kissed Fallion's cheek, he felt the rush of euphoria, coupled with a pain so profound that it ripped a cry from his throat.

His muscles convulsed, and he was thrown to the floor. His back spasmed, as did his stomach, and he began to retch.

He felt the woman's pain. Not just the physical torment that came from being mauled and raped by wyrmling giants, being torn and bloodied. He felt the heartbreak that had come as her husband and children were forced to watch. He felt her humiliation and despair, a mother's maddening fear for her own children.

He'd never felt emotions quite so raw or profound. It was as if he were being sucked into a vortex, whirling down into perfect darkness, all of her sadness and torment suddenly blending together with Fallion's own remorse – Fallion's pain at losing his brother, of losing Rhianna, his shame at having bound these worlds together in such a way that the wyrmlings were suddenly loosed upon his innocent people.

The wyrmlings have perfected torture, Fallion realized as he lay on the floor, vomiting from guilt, wishing for death.

And then one by one, the wyrmlings stripped endowments of pain from each prisoner.

Fallion felt the father's helplessness and outrage and guilt for not having saved his wife, his regret that his children would never reach adulthood, even as the bone protruding from his shin festered and rotted, threatening to leach his life away.

Moments later, Fallion felt an infant's terror of the giant wyrmlings, her overwhelming sense of helplessness, and the pain where a wyrmling had bitten off her pinky finger.

So it went, each child in turn.

Fallion took upon himself each of their fears, their guilt, their loss and longing.

As endowments were stripped from the family, the children quit their whimpering and the woman left off her sobbing, each of them falling into silence as they went remarkably numb.

And with each endowment, Fallion felt as if he would be overwhelmed one more time.

I must not give in, he told himself. I must not let Lord Despair break me.

When has Despair tasted such torment? Fallion wondered.

And then his spiritual eyes opened, and he remembered . . .

Yaleen had tried to seize control of the world by bending the Great Seal of Creation to her will, and in the process, she had broken it. The Seal shattered, and suddenly the world splintered into a million million shadows.

Fallion had been there under the great tree, and as the deed was done, he had run out from under the tree and watched with overwhelming dread and awe: it was night, and Fallion watched entire shadow worlds, like phantoms – with their opalescent swirling clouds, and seas of endless blue, and their snow-clad mountains, their fiery sunrises – all exploding and fleeing away in every direction, a continuous succession of worlds, each sending a shock wave through his very bones as it streamed away.

He watched stars forming in the night sky – entire galaxies spawned in an instant, then scattering away as the shadow worlds formed.

The True Tree was uprooted. Mountains crumbled and crevasses opened, swallowing communities whole. Volcanoes roared to life, spewing ash while lightning shrieked at their crowns.

The destruction was magnificent.

Hundreds of thousands of people died, while others merely vanished, apparently cast off onto some shadow world.

Nothing like this had ever happened in Fallion's pure and perfect world. His people had never felt death, never suffered such devastating loss.

And when the deed was done, Yaleen fled.

Fallion was one of the Ael who was sent to find Yaleen and bring her back for judgment. After many days, he caught her.

She tried to use her feminine charms to persuade him to let her go. She begged him and berated him.

But he took her to the White Council.

There had never been need for a punishment like this. There had been no death, no murder in his world. There had been petty thefts by children, and unintended insults.

But no one had ever committed a crime so foul.

Fallion knew that Yaleen had not meant to cause such devastation. She had only thought it a childish prank, she insisted, though she was a person of terrible avarice.

But her act had such far-reaching consequences, it could not be treated lightly.

So a new punishment was devised.

The Bright Ones who were left alive after the fall were devastated – mourning for lost loves, for children that they would never see, for friends that were gone.

So many joined in Yaleen's torment — not all, for some could not bring themselves to exercise harsh judgment, but each person who desired revenge walked up to Yaleen, and with the tears from their own eyes, traced a rune upon her cheek.

In the past, the rune had been used by lovers, by those who wished to share their deepest and most sacred feelings for one another. It was a rune of Compassion.

It was the same rune that Fallion had seen upon the forcibles.

By granting it, the Bright Ones shared their own grief and loss with Yaleen, heaping it upon her.

Some told themselves that they were doing it for her own good, that they were only trying to teach her, lest she continue in her evil ways.

But Fallion knew that it was more than teaching.

And so each Bright One had taken vengeance upon Yaleen, until bitter tears streamed down her face and she fought to break away from those who had once been her friends. She clawed and wailed, while strong men held her.

Slowly Fallion saw a change take place. Where before there had been contrition and sadness in her face, Yaleen hardened and grew angry.

Yaleen quit weeping and fighting, and began to rage at her tormentors and rejoice in what she had done.

The runes upon her cheek were drawn with human tears, and as the tears dried, the sympathetic feelings that Yaleen was subjected to would fade and vanish.

Thousands stood in line to heap their pain upon her, but something in her broke long before her torment was ended. When the punishment was done, there was nothing but hatred left in Yaleen's eyes.

'I harmed your world by accident,' Yaleen said, 'and now you have made me glad of it. You gave me torment, and I will torment you in return. Down countless eons I will hunt you, and rule your world in blood and horror. From now on, you shall call me by my new name — Despair.'

An eternity past, Fallion had helped heap abuse upon Yaleen, and now the creature that she had become was returning the deed.

When all five prisoners had fallen silent, Lord Despair leaned forward eagerly.

Fallion tried to remain quiet, but his throat betrayed him, and sobs issued from him in rapid succession, each a part cough, part moan.

'Serve me,' Lord Despair whispered, 'and I will release you from your pain.'

Fallion knew of only two ways that he could be free of such pain. Lord Despair could force it onto another, leaving Fallion an empty husk, emotionless and numb. Or he could kill the Dedicates who had granted their pain, thus breaking the magical ties that bound Fallion to his people.

He'll murder this family, Fallion realized. He'll do it in front of me and make me watch.

He hopes that in time, I will be evil enough to crave such a thing. For when I consent to the shedding of innocent blood, a locus will be able to make its home in me.

No, Fallion realized, Lord Despair wishes more from me than even that. He doesn't just want to make me a worthy abode for a locus. He doesn't just want to punish me – Lord Despair hopes that I will *become* him.

But I will turn the tables. I can never succumb. I can never let him beat me.

'Thank you, Lord Despair,' Fallion said meekly.

'For what?' Despair demanded.

'For freeing these good people from their pain,' Fallion said. 'Thank you, for bestowing it upon me.'

The rage that flashed across Lord Despair's face was brief but undeniable.

Fallion nearly swooned. He felt on the verge of collapse, but knew that he could show no sign of weakness. He had Despair at a disadvantage. Despair could not kill this family without freeing Fallion from his torment, and so long as Fallion was willing to bear their pain, Despair would be thwarted.

And in a strange way, Fallion was indeed grateful that he could suffer instead of these innocents.

It is only right that I should suffer, he told himself.

Lord Despair rose from his throne. 'You have only begun to feel torment,' he said. 'This is but your first taste of the forcible. I have a mountain of blood metal at my disposal, and another shipment will arrive soon.

'You will not thank me, I think, when you have taken another ten thousand endowments. You will not mock me when a whole world's pain is thrust upon your shoulders. In time, pain will have its way with you, and you will grovel and beg for release, and you will tell me what I want to know.'

Only then did Fallion realize that Despair had not even bothered to ask a question.

'By having thrust upon me these people's pain,' Fallion said, 'you only strengthen my resolve. Your works wound the world. It is time that I do away with them.'

Despair scoffed, then turned and strode from the room.

Only then did Fallion give in to the need to succumb. He dropped to the floor, head reeling, barely clinging to consciousness.

1

DANGEROUS NOTIONS

To control a man fully, one must channel his thoughts. You will not have to concern yourself with issues of loyalty once your vassal is incapable of disloyal contemplation.

—The Emperor Zul-torac, on the importance of re-
inforcing the Wyrmling Catechism on the youth

Cullossax the tormentor strode through the dark warrens of Rugassa, shoving lesser wyrmlings aside. None dared to snarl or raise a hand to stop him. Instead, the pale creatures cowered back in fear. He was imposing in part because of his bulk. At nine feet, Cullossax towered over all but even the largest wyrmlings. The bony plate that ran along his forehead was abnormally thick, and the horny nubs on his head were larger than most. He was broad of chest, and his canines hung well below his lower lip. All of these were signs to other wyrmlings that he was potentially a violent man.

But it was not his brutal appearance alone that won him deference. His black robes of office struck fear in the hearts of others, as did his blood-soaked hands.

The labyrinth seemed alive with excitement. It coursed through Cullossax's veins, and thrummed through every taut muscle. He could see it in the faces of those that he passed, and hear it in their nervous voices.

Some had fear upon their faces, while others' fears deepened to dread. But some faces shone with wonder or hope, bloodlust or exultation.

It was a rare and heady combination. It was an exciting time to be alive.

Four days ago, a huge army had left Rugassa to destroy the last of the humans at Caer Luciare. The attack was to have begun that very night. Thus the hope upon the people's faces that, after a war that had raged for three thousand years, the last of their enemies would be gone.

But then two days past, everything had changed: a whole world had fallen from the sky, and when it struck, the worlds did not crash and break. Instead, they combined into one whole, a world that was new and different, a world that combined the magics and peoples of two worlds, sometimes in unexpected ways.

Mountains had fallen and rivers had flooded. Ancient forests suddenly sprouted outside the castle gate where none had stood before. There were reports of strange creatures in the land, and all was in chaos.

Now reports were coming from wyrmling outposts in every quarter: there was something new in the land – humans, smaller folk than those of Caer Luciare. If the reports could be believed, they lived by the millions in every direction. It was rumored that it was one of their own wizards who bound the world of the wyrmlings with their own.

Such power was cause enough for the wyrmling's nervousness. But there was also cause for celebration.

Within the past few hours, rumors had been screaming through the chain of command that the Great Wyrm itself had taken a new form and now walked the labyrinth, showing abilities that had never been dreamed, not even in wyrmling legend.

Strange times indeed.

The last battle against the human warrior clans had been fought. Caer Luciare had been taken. The human warriors had been slaughtered and routed.

The news was glorious. But the wyrmlings remained nervous, unsure what might happen next. They stood in small knots and gossiped when they should be working. Some were disobedient and needed to be brought back into line.

So Cullossax the tormentor was busy.

In dark corridors where only glow worms lit his way, he searched through the crèche, where the scent of children mingled with mineral smells of the warren, until at last he found a teaching chamber with three silver stars above the door.

He did not call out at the door, but instead shoved it open. There, a dogmatist stood against a wall with his pupils, wyrmling children fifteen or sixteen years of age. Few of the children had begun to grow the horny nubs at their temples yet, and so they looked small and effeminate.

At the center of the room, a single young girl was chained by the ankle to an iron rung in the floor. She had a desk – a few planks lying upon an iron frame. But instead of sitting at her desk, she crouched beneath it, moaning and peering away distantly, as if lost in some dream. She rocked back and forth as she moaned.

She was a pretty girl, by wyrmling standards. All wyrmlings had skin that was faintly bioluminescent, and children, with their excess energy, glowed strongly, while those who were ancient, with their leathery skin, faded altogether. This girl was a bright one, with silky white hair, innocent eyes, a full round face, and breasts that had already fully blossomed.

'She refuses to sit,' said the dogmatist, a stern old man of sixty years. 'She refuses to take part in class. When we recite the catechisms, she mouths the words. When we examine the policies, she will not answer questions.'

'How long has she been like this?' the tormentor asked.

'For two days now,' the dogmatist said. 'I have berated her and beaten her, but still she refuses to cooperate.'

'Yet she gave you no trouble before?'

'None,' the dogmatist admitted.

It was the tormentor's job to dole out punishment, to do it thoroughly and dispassionately. Whether that punishment be public strangulation, or dismemberment, or some other torture, it did not matter.

Surely, this could not go on.

Cullossax knelt beside the girl, studied the child. There had to be a punishment. But Cullossax did not have to dole out the ultimate penalty.

'You must submit,' Cullossax said softly, dangerously. 'Society has a right to protect itself from the individual. Surely you see the wisdom in this?'

The girl rolled her eyes and peered away, as if carried to some faraway place in her imagination. She scratched at her throat, near a pendant made from a mouse's skull.

Cullossax had seen too many like her in the past couple of days, people who chose to turn their faces to the wall and die. Beating her would not force her to submit. Nor would anything else. He would probably have to kill her, and that was a waste. This was a three-star school, the highest level. This girl had potential. So before the torments began, he decided to try reasoning with her.

'What are you thinking?' Cullossax demanded, his voice soft and deep. 'Are you remembering something? Are you remembering . . . another place?'

That caught the girl. She turned her head slowly, peered into Cullossax's eyes.

'Yes,' she whimpered, giving out a soft sob, then she began shaking in fear.

'What do you remember?' Cullossax demanded.

'My life before,' the child said. 'I remember walking under green fields in the starlight. I lived with my mother there, and two sisters, and we raised pigs and kept a garden. The place we lived in was called Inkarra.'

Just like so many others. This was the third today to name that place. Each of them had spoken of it the same, as if it were a place of longing. Each of them hated their life in Rugassa.

It was the binding, of course. Cullossax was only beginning to understand, but much had changed when the two worlds were bound into one.

Children like this girl claimed to recall another life on that other world, a world where children were not kept in cages, a world where harsh masters did not make demands of them. They all dreamed of returning.

'It is all a dream,' Cullossax said, hoping to convince her. 'It isn't real. There is no place where children play free of fear. There is only here and now. You must learn to be responsible, to give away your own selfish desires.

'If you continue to resist,' Cullossax threatened, 'you know what I must do. When you reject society, you remove yourself from it. This cannot be tolerated, for then you are destined to become a drain upon society, not a contributor.

'Society has the right, and the duty, to protect itself from the individual.'

Normally, at this time, Cullossax would afflict the subject. Sometimes the very threat of torment would strike enough fear into the heart of the reprobate that she would do anything to prove her obedience. But Cullossax had discovered over the past two days that these children were not likely to submit at all.

'What shall I do with you?' Cullossax asked.

The girl was shaking still, speechless with terror.

'Who is society?' she asked suddenly, as if she had come upon a plan to win some leniency.

'Society consists of all of the individuals that make up the whole,' Cullossax said, quoting from the catechisms that the child was to be studying.

'But which one of the people makes up the rules?' she asked. 'Which one of them says that I must die if I do not follow the rules?'

'All of them,' Cullossax answered reasonably. But he knew that that was not true.

The girl caught him in his lie. 'The catechisms say that "Right acts follow from right thinking." "But youth and stupidity are barriers to right thinking. Thus, we must submit to those who are wiser than we." "Ultimately the emperor, by virtue of the great immortal wyrm that lives within him, is wisest of all."'

Wyrmling education consisted of rote memorization of the catechisms, not upon learning the skills of reading and writing. The wyrmlings had found that forcing children to memorize the words verbatim trained their minds well, and in time led to an almost infallible memory. This girl had strung together some catechisms in order to form the core of an argument. Now she asked her question: 'So if the emperor is wisest, does not the emperor make the rules, rather than the collective group?'

'Some might say so,' Cullossax admitted.

'The catechisms say, "Men exist to serve the empire,"' the girl said. 'But it seems to me that the emperor's teachings lead us to serve only him.'

Cullossax knew blasphemy when he heard it. He answered in catechisms: '"Each serves society to the best of his ability, the emperor as well as the least serf,"' Cullossax reasoned. '"By serving the emperor, we serve the great wyrm that resides within him," and if we are worthy, we shall be rewarded. "Live worthily, and a wyrm may someday enter you, granting you a portion of its immortality."'

The child seemed to think for a long time.

Cullossax could not bother with her any longer. This was a busy time. There had been a great battle to the south, and the troops would begin to arrive any day. Once all of the reports had been made, Cullossax would be assigned to deal with those who had not distinguished themselves in battle. He would need to sharpen many of his skinning knives, so that he could remove portions of flesh from those who were not valiant. With the flesh, he would braid whips, and then lash the backs of those that he had skinned.

And then there were people like this girl – people who had somehow gained memories of another life, and who now sought to escape the horde. The tormentors had to make examples of them.

Cullossax reached under his collar, pulled out a talisman that showed his badge of office: a bloody red fist. The law required him to display it before administering torture.

'What do you think your torment should be?' Cullossax asked.

Trembling almost beyond control, the girl turned her head slowly, peered up at Cullossax. 'Doesn't a person have the right to protect himself from society?'

It was a question that Cullossax had never considered. It was a childish question, undeserving of consideration. 'No,' he answered.

Cullossax would normally have administered a beating then, perhaps broken a few bones. But he suspected that it would do no good. 'If I hurt you enough, will you listen to your dogmatist? Will you internalize his teachings?'

The girl looked down, the wyrmling gesture for *no*.

'Then you leave me no choice,' the tormentor said.

He should have strangled the child then. He should have done it in front of the others, so that they could see first-hand the penalty for disobedience.

But somehow he wanted to spare the girl that indignity. 'Come with me,' he said. 'Your flesh will become food for your fellows.'

Cullossax reached down, unlocked the manacle at the girl's foot, and pulled her free from the iron rung in the floor.

The girl did not fight. She did not pull away or strike back. She did not try to run. Instead, she gathered up her courage and followed, as Cullossax held firmly to her wrist.

I would rather die than live here, her actions seemed to say.

Cullossax was willing to oblige.

He escorted the girl from the room. Her fellows jeered as she left, heaping abuse upon her, as was proper.

And once the two were free of the classroom, the girl walked with a lighter step, as if glad that she would meet her demise.

'Where are we going?' the child asked.

Cullossax did not know the girl's name, did not want to know her name.

'To the harvesters.' In wyrmling society, the weak, the sickly, and the mentally deficient were often put to use this way. Certain glands would be harvested – the adrenals, the pineal,

and others – to make extracts that were used in battle. Then
the bodies were harvested for meat, bone, skin, and hair.
Nothing went to waste. True, Rugassa's hunters roved far and
wide to supply the horde with food, but their efforts were
never enough.

'Will it hurt?'

'I think,' Cullossax said honestly, 'that death is never kind.
Still, I will show you what leniency I can.'

It was not easy to make such promises. As a tormentor,
Cullossax was required to dole out the punishments required
by law without regard to compassion or compromise.

That seemed to answer all of her questions, and Cullossax
led the girl now effortlessly down the winding corridors,
through labyrinthine passages lit only by glow worms. Few of
the passages were marked, but Cullossax had memorized the
twists and turns long ago. Along the way, they passed through
crowded corridors in the merchant district where vendors
hawked trinkets carved from bones and vestments sewn from
wyrmling leather. And near the arena, which was empty at the
moment, they passed through lonely tunnels where the only
sound was their footsteps echoing from the stone walls. Fire
crickets leapt up near their feet, emitting red flashes of light,
like living sparks. Once, he spotted a young boy with a bag
of pale glow worms, affixing one to each wall, to keep the
labyrinth lighted.

Cullossax wondered at his own reasons for wanting to show
her compassion. It was high summer, and in a few weeks he
would go into musth. Already he felt the edginess, the arousal,
and the beginnings of the mad rage that assailed him at this
time of year. The girl was desirable enough, though she was
too young to go into heat.

The girl's face was blank as she walked toward her execution. Cullossax had seen that look so often before.

'What are you thinking about?' he asked, knowing that it
was easier if he kept them talking.

'There are so many worlds,' she said, her voice filled with
wonder. 'Two worlds have combined, and when they did, two

of my shadow selves became one. It's like having lived two lifetimes.' She fell silent for a second, then asked, 'Have you ever seen the stars?' Most wyrmlings in the labyrinth would never have been topside.

'Yes,' he answered, 'once.'

'My grandmother was the village wise woman at my home in Inkarra,' the girl said. 'She told me that every star is but a shadow of the One True Star, and each of them has a shadow world that spins around it, and that there are a million million shadow worlds.'

'Hah,' Cullossax said, intrigued. He had never heard of such a thing. The very strangeness of such a cosmology drew his interest.

'So think,' the girl said. 'Two worlds combined, and when they did, it is like two pieces of me came together, making a larger whole. I feel stronger than ever before, more alive and complete. Here in the wyrmling horde, I was driven and cunning. But on the other world, I was learning to be wise, to take joy in life.' She gave him a moment to think, then asked, 'What if there are other pieces of me out there? What if I have a million million shadow selves, and all of them combined into one person in a single breath? What would I be like? What things would I know? It would be like having lived a billion lifetimes all at once. Perhaps on a few thousand worlds, I might have learned perfect self-discipline, and on others I might have spent lifetimes studying how to make peace among warring nations. And if I were combined into one, imagine how *whole* all of those shadow selves would become.'

The thought was staggering. Cullossax could not imagine such a thing. 'They say a wizard combined the worlds,' Cullossax said. 'They say he is in the dungeon now.'

And I wish that I had the honor of being his tormentor, Cullossax thought.

'Perhaps we should be helping him,' the girl suggested. 'He has the power to bind all of the worlds into one.'

What good would that do me? Cullossax wondered. Perhaps I have no other selves on other worlds.

He was lost in thought when she struck. It happened so fast, she almost killed him. One instant she was walking blithely along, and the next moment she pulled a dagger from her sleeve and lunged – aiming for his eye.

But his great height worked against her. Cullossax dodged backward, and the dagger nicked him below the eye. Blood sprang from the wound, as if he cried tears of blood.

Fast as a mantis taking a cave cricket, she struck again, this time aiming for his throat. He raised an arm to block her swing. She twisted to the side and brought the dagger up to his kidney. It was a maneuver he'd learned as a youth, and he was ready for her. He reached down and caught her arm, then slammed her into a wall.

The vicious creature screamed and leapt at him, her thumbs aimed at his eyes. He brought up a knee that caught her in the rib cage, knocking the air out of her.

Even injured she growled and tried to fight. But now he had her by the scruff of the neck. He pinned her to the wall and strangled her into submission.

It was a good fight from such a small girl – well timed and ruthless. She was not just a victim waiting to go to her death. She'd planned this all along!

She'd lured him into the corridor, waited until they were in a lonely stretch of the warrens, and then done her best to leave him lying in a pool of blood.

Doubtless, she had some plan for escape.

Cullossax laughed. He admired her feistiness. When she was barely conscious, he reached into her tunic and felt for more weapons. All he felt was her soft flesh, but a thorough search turned up a second dagger in her boot.

He threw them down the corridor, and as the girl began to come to, he put her in a painful wristlock and walked her to her death, whimpering and pleading.

'I hate you,' she cried, weeping bitter tears. 'I hate the world you've created. I'm going to destroy it, and build a better one in its place.'

It was such a grandiose notion – one little wyrmling girl

planning to change the world – that he had to laugh. 'It is not I who made this world.'

'You support it,' she accused. 'You're as guilty as the rest!'

It happened that way sometimes. Those who were about to die would search for someone to accuse, rather than take responsibility for their own stupidity or weakness.

But it was not Cullossax who had created her world. It was the Great Wyrm, whom some said had finally taken a new form, and now walked the halls of Rugassa.

As they descended some stairs, a fellow tormentor who was climbing up from below called Cullossax to a halt. 'Have you heard the news?'

'What news?' Cullossax asked. He did not know the man well, but tormentors all belonged to a Shadow Order, a secret fraternity, and had sworn bloody oaths to protect one another and uphold one another and to promote one another's interests, even in murder. Thus, as a tormentor, this man was a brother to him.

'Despair has taken a new body, and now walks the labyrinth, displaying miraculous powers. As one of his first acts, he has devised a new form of torture, surpassing our finest arts. You should see!'

Cullossax stood for a moment, overwhelmed. The Great Wyrm walked among them? He still could not believe it. Obviously, with the binding of the worlds, Despair felt the need to confirm his supremacy.

The very thought filled Cullossax with awe. This was a great time to be alive.

'So,' Cullossax teased, 'Despair wants our jobs?'

The tormentor laughed at the jest, then seemed to get an idea. 'You are taking the girl to be slaughtered?'

'Yes,' Cullossax said.

'Take her to the dungeons instead, to the Black Cell. There you will find Vulgnash, the Knight Eternal. He has had a long flight and needs to feed. The girl's life should be sweet to him.'

The girl suddenly tried to rip free, for being consumed by a Knight Eternal was a fate worse than death.

Cullossax grabbed the girl's wrist, holding her tight. She bit him and clawed at him, but he paid her no mind.

Cullossax hesitated. A Knight Eternal had no life of his own. Monsters like him did not need to breathe or eat or drink. Vulgnash could not gain nourishment by digesting flesh. Instead, he drew life from others, consuming their spiritual essence – their hopes and longings.

Cullossax had provided the Knight Eternal with children before. Watching the monster feed was like watching an adder consume a rat.

In his mind's eye, Cullossax remembered a feeding from five years ago. Then Vulgnash, draped in his crimson robes, had taken a young boy.

Like this girl, the boy had screamed in terror and struggled with renewed fury as they neared Vulgnash's lair.

'Ah,' Vulgnash had whispered, his wings quivering slightly in anticipation, 'just in time.'

Then Vulgnash had turned and totally focused on his victim. He seemed unaware that Cullossax was watching.

The boy had cried and backed away into a corner, and every muscle of Vulgnash's body was taut, charged with power, lest the child try to run.

The boy did bolt, but Vulgnash lashed out and caught him, shoved him into the corner, and touched the child on the forehead – Vulgnash's middle finger resting between the child's eyes, his thumb and pinky on the boy's mandibles, and a finger in each eye.

Normally when a child was so touched, he ceased to fight. Like a mouse that is filled with scorpion's venom, he would go limp.

But this boy fought. The child grabbed Vulgnash's wrist and tried to shove him away. Vulgnash seized the boy by the throat with his left hand then, and maintained his grip with the right. The child bit at the Knight Eternal's wrist, fighting valiantly.

'Ah, a worthy one!' Vulgnash enthused.

The boy tried twisting away. He began to scream, almost

breaking Vulgnash's grasp. There was a world of panic in the child's eyes.

'Why?' the child screamed. 'Why does it have to be this way?'

'Because I hunger,' Vulgnash had said, shoving the boy into the corner, holding him fast. As the boy's essence began to drain, he shrieked in panic and shook his head, trying to break free of the monster's touch. All hope and light drained from his face, and was replaced by an endless well of despair. His cries of terror changed into a throaty wail. He kicked and fought for a long moment while Vulgnash merely held him up against the wall.

The Knight Eternal leaned close, his mouth inches from the boy's, and then began to inhale, making a hissing sound.

Cullossax had seen a thin light, like a mist, draining away from the child into Vulgnash's mouth.

Slowly, the child quit struggling, until at last his legs stopped kicking altogether. When the Knight Eternal was done, he'd dropped the child's limp body.

The boy lay in a heap, staring up into some private horror worse than any nightmare, barely breathing.

'Ah, that was refreshing,' Vulgnash said. 'Few souls are so strong.'

Cullossax had stood for a moment, unsure what to do. Vulgnash jutted a chin toward the boy. 'Get rid of the carcass.'

Cullossax then grabbed the limp form and began dragging it up the corridor. The boy still breathed, and he moaned a bit, as if in terror.

Grabbing the child's head, Cullossax had given it a quick twist up and to the right, ending the child's life, and his torment.

Thus, Cullossax knew how this feeding would turn out. The Knight Eternal would put a hand over this girl's pretty face, lean in close, almost as if to kiss, and with one indrawn hiss he would drain the life from her. He would take all of her hope and aspiration, all of her enjoyment and serenity.

Realizing her fate, the girl fought to break free. She jerked her hand again and again, trying to break Cullossax's grasp, but Cullossax seized the child's wrist, digging the joint of his thumb into the ganglia of the girl's wrist until her knees gave out from the pain.

He wanted to see this new form of torture, so he dragged her to the dungeon.

'Please,' she cried. 'Take me back to the crèche. I'll listen to the dogmatist! I'll do anything. I promise!'

But it was too late. The girl had chosen her fate. She let her knees buckle, refusing to walk any farther. Cullossax dragged the girl now, his fingernails biting into her flesh as she whimpered and pleaded and tried to grab the legs of passersby.

'We don't have to live like this!' the girl said. 'Inkarra does exist!'

That gave Cullossax pause. Could it be that there was a land without the Death Lords, without the empire? Could it be that people there lived pleasant lives without care?

For one person to tell of it was madness. For two to tell of it was a fluke. But this girl was the third in a single day. A pattern had emerged.

And then there was the matter of the small folk. Since the change, Cullossax had heard rumors that there might be millions of them in the world.

'Who is the emperor in this land of yours?' Cullossax asked.

'I did not serve an emperor there,' she said. 'But there was a great king, the Earth King, Gaborn Val Orden, who ruled with kindness and compassion. He told me when I was a child that "the time will come when the small folk of the world must stand against the large." He said that I would know when that time had come. Gaborn Val Orden served and protected his people. But our emperor only *feeds* on his people!'

The name Orden was known to Cullossax. It was a strange name, hard on the wyrmling tongue. As a tormentor, Cullossax was privy to many secrets. Just after dawn a prisoner had been delivered to the dungeon, a powerful wizard named Fallion Orden – a wizard who had been the son of a great king on another world, a wizard who had such vast powers that he had bound two worlds into one.

Now the great Vulgnash himself had been assigned to guard this dangerous wizard.

'Where is this realm of Inkarra?' Cullossax demanded.

'South,' the child said. 'Their warrens are to the south, beyond the mountains. Let me go, and I can show you. I'll take you there.'

It was a curious offer. But Cullossax had a job to do.

Down he led the child, past the guards who blocked his way, into the dungeons where light never reached.

The girl struggled, twisting and scratching at his hand, until he cuffed her hard enough so that she went limp, and her struggles ceased.

Her mouth fell open, revealing her oversized canines. Small rubies had been inset into each of them, rubies carved to look like serpents. It was a symbol of her status, as one of the intellectual elite.

How far you have fallen, little one, Cullossax thought.

At the outer gates to the dungeons, he took the necklace from around his neck and used the key to enter.

At last he reached the Black Cell, the most heavily guarded of all.

Cullossax drew near its iron door, and would have opened it, but a pair of guards blocked him.

Cullossax could see through a grate in the door. Inside, a bright light shone. Vulgnash stood in his red cowl and robes, his artificial red wings flapping slightly. He loomed above a small human, a man with dark black hair, and a pair of wings. The ground in the cell was rimed with frost, and Cullossax's breath came out as a fog when he peered in.

Within the cell stood a wyrmling lord, a captain dressed in black, a man with the papery hands of one who had almost given up the flesh, one who was almost ready to transition to Death Lord. He was holding up a thumb-lantern, examining the wizard Fallion Orden.

There was no sign of this wondrous new torture that the tormentor had told Cullossax about. Cullossax had expected to see some novel contraption – perhaps an advancement upon the crystal cage, the tormentor's most sophisticated device.

Now the Death Lord spoke softly, his voice almost a hiss.

Cullossax was not supposed to hear, he suspected, but wyrmlings have sharp ears, and his were sharper than most.

'We must take care,' the Death Lord whispered. 'Despair senses a coming danger. It is dim, but it haunts us nonetheless. He told me to bring warning.'

'A danger to whom?' Vulgnash asked.

'To our fortress guards,' the captain said. 'He suspects that humans are coming, a force small but powerful. They are coming here, to this cell. They hope to free Fallion Orden.'

'Then I will be ready for them,' Vulgnash said.

'We must be ready,' the captain said. 'The humans will send their greatest heroes. We must be sure that they are properly received. We have sent for forcibles. When they come, you will need further endowments.'

The Death Lord peered hard at Vulgnash. 'You look weak. Do you need a soul to feed upon?'

'I have sent for one.'

The Death Lord laughed softly, a mocking laugh, as if at some private joke. He was laughing at Vulgnash's victim.

Cullossax stepped back from the iron door, peered down at the girl at his feet. In that instant, he suddenly knew something beyond a shadow of a doubt.

They feed on us, Cullossax thought, just as the girl said. The Emperor Zul-torac, the Knights Eternal, the Death Lords – they care no more for us than the adder does for the rat. We are nothing to them.

In his mind, he heard the girl's question: Doesn't a person have a right to defend himself from society?

Cullossax had seldom allowed himself such dangerous notions.

It doesn't have to be this way. There is a place called Inkarra, somewhere far from here . . .

He tried to imagine a world worth dying for.

It is odd how the mind can snap. After a lifetime of service to the empire, Cullossax suddenly found himself smiling inanely.

What if I denied the Knight Eternal this meal? he wondered, gripping the girl's limp wrist. They would kill me if they caught me.

And with the thought, it seemed to Cullossax that he no longer had a choice.

He turned and began to drag the girl away.

'What are you doing?' a guard demanded. 'Bring her back.'

'She's dead,' Cullossax objected. 'I hit her too hard. I'll bring another.'

One of the guards snorted in disgust, a sound that said, I would not want to be you, when Vulgnash learns of your clumsiness, and Cullossax dragged the girl on, sweat streaming from his brow.

Sometime as he stalked through the corridors, the girl groaned in pain, then awoke with a snarl, clawing at him in her fury.

He dragged her on, toward the southernmost exit. Up he went, to the very surface, until he reached the gates that blocked the entrance.

Outside, the sun blazed in the sky, horrifying and malignant. It was midmorning.

'Open the gates,' Cullossax growled at the guards. 'I have business outside the fortress.'

'What business?' the guards snarled.

The girl whimpered and fought, trying to break free. She bit his wrist, sinking her canines in.

'This one wants to leave,' Cullossax said. 'It pleases me to let her go – and for me to hunt her. Her skin will hang inside the labyrinth's walls, as a warning to others.'

The guards laughed. With so many people trying to flee the city, it seemed a reasonable idea.

'You'll let her leave by daylight?' a guard asked.

'The better to burn her eyes out,' Cullossax said. 'Then I'll hunt her by night, while she staggers about, blinded by the sun.'

The guards roared in laughter.

So he let her go.

Gibbering in fear, the girl crawled a few steps, blind with terror and even more blinded by the sun. Then she suddenly found her courage, leapt to her feet, and went sprinting down the road, her hand over her face to shield her eyes as she headed for the forest.

Now Cullossax would wait, and as he waited, he vacillated. He wanted to see this girl's dream world. But he did not want to get caught. Perhaps it would be better to kill her after all. He could not be sure. With every passing minute, he worried that soldiers would be sent to apprehend him.

Cullossax stood with the guards for hours, gleaning the latest news from outside while the sun hit its zenith and then began to fall. Last night the battle had been won against the men of Caer Luciare, they all assured him, and rumor said that the warrior clans had been wiped off the face of the earth.

Such news contradicted Cullossax's own sources, and the guards had heard nothing about the Great Wyrm taking a new form, demonstrating marvelous powers.

They were only lowly guards, after all, and so knew little of import. But they talked of things that they did know. They spoke at length of how small folk had been discovered in every direction. They'd heard reports from the scouts themselves, and had seen small folk brought through their gate in chains.

Huge cities had been found only a hundred miles to the east, and over the past two nights, troops had been sent out to wreak havoc upon the small folk, with the aim of enslaving their men, while eating the women and children.

The small folks' rune lore was not helping them, the guards assured Cullossax. Already the emperor had mastered their lore and exceeded it, and was sending out his own wyrmling Runelords to do battle.

The fortress was emptying, so many warriors had left.

And in their wake, in the high keeps, strange new creatures were taking the wyrmling's place.

For a brief moment, Cullossax worried about this. The fortress was emptying?

He dared wonder how many people he might meet out in the wilds. There would be roving patrols of wyrmlings – and perhaps just as dangerously, there might be bands of angry humans, out for vengeance.

'It is a great time to be alive,' the guards all said. 'Surely this is history in the making.'

'Yes,' Cullossax exulted, voicing full agreement. Yet he wondered, why then does it feel like the end of the world?

Because I know that soon my masters will miss me, and learn what I've done. Probably, they already have. They will be searching the labyrinth, suspecting foul play. They will find the girl's knife with blood on it, and might even think me dead.

Up here is the last place they will look, he thought.

But they will look here all the same.

2

THE GATE

Put no trust in your fellow men no matter how fair their looks, for every man's face is a mask that hides terrible malice.

—From the Wyrmling Catechism

As Cullossax awaited his fate, far away upon the plains, the humans of the warrior clans fled their fortress at Caer Luciare, nearly forty thousand people racing through the morning light, heading east through fields of oats that had been burned white by the summer sun, past black-eyed Susans that towered above the straw, their golden petals circling their dark eyes, through thickets of thistles with wilted liver-colored leaves and heads of purple.

The people kept away from the alders and pines along the mountain's skirts, where wyrmlings might lurk in the shadows. Instead, they blazed a path through fields so dazzlingly bright that the wyrmlings could not follow.

The folk of Caer Luciare could not move swiftly, burdened as they were. Some women carried babes at their breasts or hoisted toddlers on their shoulders. Older children walked, struggling through the tall grass, while the oldest of the folks hobbled about with staffs to keep them upright.

Many warriors were wounded, and these had to be borne by their comrades, while everyone who could do so had brought something – food, water, a little clothing. The inhabitants of the castle had long known that they might have to flee, and so were prepared.

But where are we going? Talon wondered, as she stopped to shift a keg of ale that she carried upon her back. She walked beside her aged mother, at least the woman who had raised Talon among the warrior clans, a woman named Gatunyea. Talon's father had been much the same man in both worlds, a mighty protector of his people. Talon had known him as Sir Borenson among the small folk on one world and as Aaath Ulber among these warriors. And on each world, Borenson had taken a different woman to wife. Gatunyea of the warrior clan was nothing like Myrrima, the gentle wizardess. Gatunyea was a stern woman, heavy-boned and arthritic, with a blunt face and no tolerance for weakness. She had borne her husband two strong sons with features much like his own. They walked beside Talon now, her brothers, age nine and eleven.

But unlike Talon and Borenson, the rest of the family had not merged with their shadow selves when the worlds were bound.

That can mean only one thing, Talon reasoned: they had no shadow selves to merge with. Their counterparts somehow died or were killed before the worlds combined.

But how could that be? she wondered. How can I, the daughter of Borenson and Myrrima on one world, have different parents on another?

Only one answer sufficed. Gatunyea is not my birth mother, Talon realized.

She looked over at the woman. Gatunyea had wide cheekbones and a wrinkled brow. So did her sons. Talon had always felt grateful not to have inherited those features, for they would have made her appear more brutish.

'Gatunyea,' Talon asked, 'when were you going to tell me that you were not my birth mother?'

The aging woman faltered in her step and cast a sideways glance at Talon. She seemed to age three years in the space of a heartbeat.

'Never,' Gatunyea said. She fell silent a moment, and then explained. 'You are my daughter. I took you to my breast when your mother died. I nursed you as my own. That is all that matters.'

'What happened to my birth mother?'

Gatunyea shook her head sadly. 'She went to hunt for hazelnuts one morning when the clouds were lowering. A wyrmling harvester caught her in the forest. You were a month old. My own husband had been killed in a raid on the wyrmling supply lines months before, a raid that was led by Aaath Ulber. So your father felt . . . responsible for me. I was expecting a child, a son came two days after your mother disappeared, but his cord was wrapped three times around his neck. We managed to free him, but he did not last a day. So your father took me to wife. I am from good stock. He knew that I could bear him the strong sons that our people would need to fight, and I was happy for the chance. It seemed a prudent union.'

Talon's half-brothers peered up at their mother, their faces a study in surprise.

'Do you love my father?'

'More than life or breath,' Gatunyea said. 'That is the way of it. You cannot sleep with a good man for all those years and not grow into one. But I wonder,' she said, glancing off to the horizon, 'if he will still love me?'

Talon knew that her father faced a dilemma. His two shadow selves had merged, and on each world he'd had a different wife, a different family. Others in the city were facing similar problems. Which wife would he choose now?

Myrrima, Talon decided. Sir Borenson had more children with Myrrima than Aaath Ulber had with Gatunyea, and their bond was closer. They had fought side by side at war, and thus their relationship was probably deeper than the one that Aaath Ulber had with Gatunyea.

But now that his two selves had bound into one, what would Myrrima and their children think of him? He would be a giant in size, with a bony ridge upon his brow, and overlarge incisors. He would seem a monster.

'He will come to you,' Talon decided. 'Father will look more like one of the warrior clan than the small folk. He'll come to you.'

Talon's mother let out a small sob, a strange sound. Talon had never heard the stern woman cry. Talon hadn't known that Gatunyea was even capable of it.

Yet Talon feared that she had guessed wrong and thus given Gatunyea false hope.

Talon wondered if her two mothers might share her husband, as women in Indhopal did. But Talon doubted that they could manage it.

The company forged ahead. With each step full heads of grain scattered at Talon's feet, and the occasional grasshopper rose up on buzzing wings.

So how far can we run with all of these children? Talon wondered.

The wyrmlings had taken Caer Luciare, and they also held the fortress at Cantular. The River Dyll-Tandor had flooded after the change, and was all but impassable. And by destroying the bridge at Cantular during last night's battle, Warlord Madoc had been able to forestall some of the wyrmling invaders, but now it seemed that his heroic deed had also blocked his own people's escape.

I'm glad that Madoc's dead, Talon thought. I only wish that I could claim a part in his killing.

But now, by all accounts, Talon's people were on something of an island, with waters rushing all around, and only the mountains of the Great Spine to the south.

South, Talon thought, we will have to flee south.

But with women and wounded and old folks and children to slow them, the wyrmlings would harry their retreat.

Perhaps, she considered, there are some narrow mountain passes we can escape through. Certainly, the High King had plotted just such a retreat many times. He and his counselors had huddled over ancient maps for hours, considering what trails to use, where water and shelter might be found, and how best to defend themselves in just such an event. They'd spent months choosing the safest course, and planning for every contingency.

Just as surely, the wyrmlings had plotted how to defeat them.

But now everything was changed. Two 'shadow' worlds had combined. Mountains had shifted position. Some had risen and others fallen as the two worlds merged into one. The old maps, the old escape plans, were all but useless.

Still, we have to try, Talon considered.

Talon's mother and brothers carried food, bundled in blankets. But there were no spare clothes for winter, no food to last them even through a week. Still the refugees trudged through the fields, heading north.

But why? Talon wondered. There was no escape that way.

At midmorning, the Emir Tuul Ra called a halt in a huge meadow. A stream ran through it, and willows sprouted along its banks, so that some could stand in the shade.

Soldiers guarded the bank, lest any wyrmlings be hiding in the trees.

A young man of this world named Alun had been trudging beside Talon all day. Alun was the Master of the Hounds at Caer Luciare. He had but fourteen war dogs left to his credit, and on this morning he let them run. The dogs wagged their stubby tails and raced about in the fields, startling yellow butterflies and winged grasshoppers into flight, woofing at all of the excitement. In their lacquered armor and spiked collars, they looked fierce.

Now Alun sent some dogs east to scout for scents in the brushy thickets along the creek, and others to the west. If a wyrmling hid there, the dogs' barking would give ample warning.

After a brief halt, Talon spotted the Wizard Sisel, Daylan Hammer, and the Emir Tuul Ra off from the main body of the company. The emir's daughter, Siyaddah, a dark-skinned girl with a doe's soft eyes, was talking to her father.

Talon could not help but notice that Alun was gazing at her longingly.

Alun was not a huge man. He was a gangrel, thin in the ribs with a misshapen nose, spindly arms, and oversized hands.

Talon had hardly noticed him before. She had been born to the warrior caste, and so he, a mere slave, had not merited attention.

But now that the worlds had merged, a part of Talon suddenly recognized that he was another human being, a person who by birthright should have been treasured and treated with honor. She tried to imagine what his life was like.

Until recently, he had lived a life of hopelessness, never dreaming that he might be allowed to bear children. He had not even hoped that he would be free to buy a home, or to marry.

I was born with riches, Talon thought, but Alun had to work for what little he's got.

Only recently had he been accepted into the warrior clan, and rumor said that he had fought like a badger when the clans took the wyrmling fortress at Cantular.

I should give him his due, Talon decided.

'Why don't you go speak to her?' Talon asked.

'Oh,' he said, 'she wouldn't go for the likes of me.'

'Don't underestimate yourself,' Talon said. 'Siyaddah has a way of seeing through people, gauging their worth. You fought against wyrmlings yesterday, and you acquitted yourself well. Surely saying "hello" to her would require less courage.'

Alun just looked at Talon helplessly, as if she had asked too much of him.

Suddenly Daylan waved into the air, and Talon's foster sister Rhianna came swooping to the ground in front of him, her bright magical wings flashing like rubies in the morning sun. She landed with a jar. Rhianna spoke to Daylan and the emir.

She'd been scouting the trail from the sky, using the wings that she had won last night by defeating a Knight Eternal in single combat.

Rhianna was pretty in her way. She had cinnamon-colored hair and eyes more fiercely blue than any rain-washed sky.

Her red hair nearly matched the color of her wings. The tunic and pants that she wore were made of doeskin, the hue of summer fields. But right now her face looked wan and care-worn.

She did not have Talon's great size or blunt features.

Talon whispered to Alun, 'Come with me. Now's your chance.'

Talon went to hear Rhianna's report, while Alun followed in a nervous daze, but before Talon reached the spot, Rhianna rose up from the ground and flew east, flapping furiously.

Talon reached the party, and Alun stood beside Siyaddah shyly, as if wondering what to say. After a moment, he mumbled a greeting, and Siyaddah answered more boldly.

Talon left the two to their own conversation, and asked Daylan. 'Where is Rhianna going?'

'To warn the small folk of the world,' Daylan replied. 'If we can get them to unite against the wyrmlings, we might stand a chance.'

'She'll never reach help in time,' Talon said. 'The wyrmlings will be on our trail by nightfall.'

'There are trails that the wyrmlings cannot follow,' Daylan said mysteriously, and went trundling away.

The emir stood watching Rhianna fly off, and then turned to Talon and asked, 'Tholna, is it not – daughter of Aaath Ulber?'

'I go by the name Talon, now.'

The emir smiled at that, an odd smile full of concern. 'Why go by that name?'

Talon had to think before answering. The emir came near, standing just a bit above her. He was not tall. He did not tower above her. Yet his presence was imposing. He was a legend among her people, one of the great heroes of all time. Frequently he had led raids against the wyrmling harvesters that hunted her people, or had raided wyrmling supply trains or destroyed enemy outposts. In his youth, he had led the last of his people on a daring assault on Rugassa itself – and had returned wounded and beaten, the sole survivor.

Most important, Talon's own father, Aaath Ulber, credited the emir with saving his life in two separate raids.

So he was a legend, and Talon felt both honored and intimidated by his presence. By training, Talon's shadow self Tholna had been raised to hope to wed such a man, to bear him warrior sons. The hope had been drilled into her from the time she was born, and she found herself excited to be near him.

Or maybe, she thought, it is just his animal magnetism that excites me.

The emir was handsome. His dark hair was cropped short and brushed back. His eyes were a brown so deep that they were almost black, and they had a fire in them that smoldered.

So Talon found that she struggled for words as she tried to frame an answer to his question. 'I suppose that I wish to be called Talon because . . . I am not at all like the Tholna that my friends knew.'

The emir seemed intrigued. 'Interesting. And how have you changed, my little Talon?'

Talon had never spoken to the emir, not above a casual greeting when she had met him while in the company of her father.

'I . . . Tholna was a nothing. She was a breeder, meant only to bear sons to some warrior. Talon is a warrior.'

The emir smiled, obviously amused. 'There are women warriors among the small folk?'

'It is not common,' Talon admitted, 'but among the Runelords, a person's gender does not matter much. Forcibles tend to be great equalizers. Besides, my father was the king's personal bodyguard, and at times we were in great danger, so he taught me everything that he knew.'

The emir nodded appreciatively at that. 'The better to protect you. Very well, I shall call you Talon from now on. What does the name mean, in the tongue of the small folk?'

'It is a claw, like that found on a hawk,' Talon said.

'Interesting,' the emir said. 'Do you know what the name Tholna means?'

Tholna was a common name among girls. 'It is an ancient weapon, I've heard.'

'Not so ancient. It was often used in Dalharristan, when I was a lad. It had a handle that one could grasp in the hand, with two long hooks attached to it – hooks that protruded on either side of the middle finger. Thus, in ancient Dalharristan, the weapon was called a "talon."

'It is odd, don't you think,' the emir continued, 'that your father would give you the same name on both worlds? It makes me wonder how many other similarities there might be.'

The news was indeed intriguing. Talon had been trained in many weapons, but had never even seen a tholna. 'Why would I want to pull a foe in close, where he might strike within my kill zone?'

The emir seemed mildly surprised by the question, and appreciative of it. 'In the close combat of a large battle it was surprisingly effective. It was used only as an off-hand weapon, usually with a parry blade. The tholna could be hooked into the shoulder or leg of an opponent, to throw him off balance. Originally, it was developed by the wyrmlings – used to grasp fleeing humans.'

Talon considered. The parry blade was a short sword with a round guard so large that it was almost as big as a targe. In close combat, where hundreds of men might be fighting at once, the parry blade was an effective stabbing weapon, for it was difficult to avoid an expert blow.

'An interesting combination of weapons,' Talon said. 'But I do not think they would be of much use in our war against wyrmlings.'

'No,' the emir said, 'which is why they lost popularity.'

The company began to move out, and Talon prepared to march with it.

The emir asked, 'May I walk with you?'

'Me?' Talon asked. She could not understand why he would want to.

'I need to learn the tongue of the small folk,' the emir said. 'I was hoping that you could teach me?' Talon wondered why he did not just ask one of his warriors. Several men among the warrior clans had been bound into one, and thus knew how to speak Rofehavanish. As if divining her thoughts the emir added, 'I could ask one of my men, but to tell the truth, you are more pleasant to look upon.'

The compliment took Talon off guard and left her feeling weak in the knees.

She found the emir attractive. He was a widower, and therefore available. But she had never considered herself worthy of his attention.

Nevertheless, they were both of marriageable age, and among the warrior clans, men and women were taught to wed the strongest possible mate.

The Emir Tuul Ra was older than Talon, but he was blessed with a face and figure that were somehow timeless. He could have been any age between thirty and forty-five. Though he had a daughter just a few months older than Talon, she found him beguiling, and she imagined him to be young. She imagined that he had married as a young teen, as royals often did in his land.

Talon was eighteen years old – a free woman on her world, old enough to select her own husband – and she was considered to be of prime breeding age and stock.

The emir took her elbow gently, and walked beside her in a courtly manner.

She smiled shyly, and walked with him, pointing out things – grass, trees, sky, sun – and teaching him their Rofehavanish names.

The emir listened intently and experimented with each word, trying it on his tongue. He turned out to be a marvelously adept student, for in his youth he had been forced to master several languages. More important, he was from the ruling caste in his own land, and thus had been bred for intelligence. Thus, his forefathers had been selected not just to be great warriors, but to be men of sound character and deep wisdom.

They walked along for a pair of hours, Talon trying to match the emir's faster pace, until at last they reached the front of

the column, matching stride for stride. The emir learned with
surprising rapidity, and kept demanding to learn more, as if
he hoped to master the Rofehavanish tongue in a single day.

He feels an onus is upon him, she realized. His every muscle
is strung as tight as a bow. He has an entire nation to save,
and he thinks that knowing this language might be the key.

At Talon's back, Alun and Siyaddah were lost in their own
conversation, and time and again the war dogs came boiling
around them all in a pack.

But as they talked, Talon heard one man a few rows behind
question loudly, 'Where are we going? Ah, this is madness!
Who is in charge here?'

She realized that she had been hearing similar grumbles
farther off all morning long, and she herself had wondered
who was in charge, but the emir's lessons had captured her
attention and taken her mind from the problem.

The emir rounded and called, 'Halt! Halt! Everyone gather
around!' He leapt up on a fallen tree. The bark had stripped
away over the years, so that the bole was bleached whiter than
a skull. The Wizard Sisel came to stand at the emir's back on
the right, and Daylan Hammer to his left. Thus, with the emir
having some elevation, it felt almost as if they had formed a
natural amphitheater. The crowd began to gather around. There
was nervousness in the air. Talon found herself backing away,
farther into the crowd, hoping to assess its mood.

'There is grumbling among you,' the emir said – loudly, so
that he could be heard by all who were pleased to listen. 'You
are worried, as you should be. You ask, "Where are we going?"'
At that there were grunts of assent and wise nods. '"Who leads
us now, and by what right?" "Our king is dead. Warlord Madoc
is dead. Why are we traveling north, when the way is blocked?"'

They were good questions all, Talon knew.

'I will tell you,' the emir said. 'No one leads us now.' At
that the folks in the crowd glanced from side to side, and
some shook their heads. It was a problem that they had
never faced before. 'Here in our hour of greatest need, no
one leads us.'

'You should lead us!' one of the young warlords cried in a husky voice, and there were cheers from many. But almost instantly Warlord Madoc's sons shouted, 'No! No!,' and their supporters chimed in, while others hissed and jeered.

Talon was astonished by the ferocity of their response. The Emir Tuul Ra had always been a man of high station, well liked by the people. But many a peasant shook a fist in the air and adamantly rejected the notion that he should lead.

'Who are you to tell us what to do?' an old woman demanded at Talon's side. Others cried, 'Madoc! Clan Madoc!'

Old warlords raised their axes in the air and began to chant, 'Madoc! Madoc! Madoc!'

Talon felt bewildered, and had to wonder why so few would support the emir. In part, she suspected that it was because he was foreign-born and had lost his own war against the wyrmlings.

But the people didn't just seem to be rising up against him. There was genuine support for Clan Madoc.

Old Warlord Madoc had been a bold man, it was true, but his character had been flawed. He had gained popularity among the lesser lords by flattering them and offering bribes. If the Madocs took power, many a man would find himself given an office that he was not fit for, shoving aside men who were wiser and better qualified. The resulting upheaval, in this diffi-cult time, would be a disaster.

But it wasn't just secondary posts that Talon had to worry about. Madoc's sons were not their father's equal – not in courage, not in battle prowess, not in wisdom or intelligence or cunning.

But apparently some of the lords did not care. So long as the bribes continued and undeserved wealth and honors flowed into their hands . . .

'Emir Tuul Ra!' Talon cried. 'Emir Tuul Ra!' A few others raised the chant, and some old woman turned to Talon and raged, 'Shut your mouth, damn you. You don't know what you're saying!'

But Talon cried all the louder, and soon tempers were flaring.

In some knots, weapons were drawn. It almost looked as if it would turn to civil war.

A great good that will do, Talon thought. The wyrmlings will rejoice to see it.

Daylan Hammer whistled loudly, to capture folks' attention.

The emir held his hands up, begging for quiet, seemingly as baffled by the outcry and clamor as Talon was. He tried to dispel the rising tide of rage. 'I do not propose to be your leader,' he said. 'I led a nation once, a proud nation that was larger than all of your eastern realms combined. Where is it now? I will tell you: I led it to ruin. The wyrmlings destroyed it.'

Talon wanted to argue. It was not the emir's fault. Tuul Ra had been but a youth at the time when his father died in battle, and his people had been refugees fleeing the wyrmling horde. The war that destroyed them had been waged for centuries, and Tuul Ra had inherited his defeat. She remembered even as a tot how her father had said that the emir 'did a miraculous job of fighting an unwinnable war.'

Apparently, others knew the truth, too, for some cried, 'No! That is not how it was.'

The emir was a hero in Talon's mind. He had dealt savage blows to the wyrmlings against all odds. He'd captured the wyrmling princess, and thus forestalled last night's attack for more than a decade. He was such a hero Talon believed that his name would be remembered in the Halls of Eternity.

But the emir called the protesters to quiet. 'I will tell you who should lead you,' he shouted. 'Your prince – Areth Sul Urstone.'

There was silence for a moment. The naysayers had not expected that. Their prince had been taken captive by the wyrmlings years ago, and it was believed that he was still held in the dungeons of Rugassa.

'He can't lead us,' Connor Madoc shouted, striding from the crowd to confront the emir. 'If he's even alive, what's left of him – a gibbering shell of a man? The wyrmling torturers will have made a wreck of him.'

'I doubt it,' the emir said resolutely. 'All who knew Prince Urstone doubt it. The prince that I knew was the best man that I have ever met. If all men were such as he, there would be no need for prisons or judges or barristers, for there would be no crime. All men would dwell in peace and deal honorably and courteously with one another. All husbands would love their wives, and hold to their wives alone. All children would love and emulate their fathers, for their fathers would be worthy of their love. There would be no need for armies, for there would be no wars.

'Can you imagine what kind of world that would make? So much of our labor is only a waste. We wage an endless war against the evils among us, and it drains our every resource – our time, our wealth, and even our very hope.

'But that's the kind of man I knew – a good man, a just man. Perhaps he is just a memory. Perhaps you're right. Maybe he has been tormented beyond all reason, and his mind has gone to waste. He might now be nothing more than a maddened animal, craving his own death.

'But I hope for something better. There was a firmness in Areth Sul Urstone that put iron to shame. Never have I known a man of stronger resolve. I believe that he resisted his torturers through these years. I have been told that upon the shadow world, his shadow self was great indeed, and that he was a king beloved of his people more than any other. It is said that even the earth loved him, and granted to him great powers to protect his realm. Thus he was called an "Earth King."

'It is my hope that now that the worlds have combined, he may become such once again. I believe that he still lives, and it is my intent' – Emir Tuul Ra's voice suddenly turned to a snarl, as if terrible passions had long been building inside and only now fought their way free – 'to *bring him home!*'

At that some of the older men cheered and raised their battle-axes and danced in celebration. Some of the older women swiped tears from their eyes.

But Talon felt little. She had never known the prince. He'd

been captured when she was just a toddler. Most of the younger generation had never met him.

She had met his shadow self, of course – the Earth King Gaborn Val Orden. But how much like him could Areth Sul Urstone be? Areth Sul Urstone was from a world that had never heard of Earth Kings.

The Wizard Sisel hoped that with the binding of the worlds, the Earth Spirit would grant that title to Areth's shadow self. But Talon wasn't sure if that would happen.

'What would you have us do,' Drewish Madoc shouted at the emir, 'squat here in the field while you plot some mad rescue? We should get going. We should devise some fortification, prepare for battle. The wyrmlings will be upon us after dusk.'

'What fortification would you suggest?' the emir asked. 'Shall we dig a trench and build a nice little battle wall? How will that help us, when the wyrmlings took Caer Luciare – one of our greatest fortresses – only hours ago? It would be madness to fight them, and there is nowhere to run.' He jutted his chin toward Daylan. The immortal stood calmly. 'But Daylan Hammer has a plan for escape, one that is not without its own risks. I will let him tell you of it.'

Daylan stepped forward a few paces. 'As you know, our passage is blocked to the north. With the colliding of the worlds, a great sea is emptying and filling the River Dyll-Tandor. It has flooded to the north and the east, and it is filling the valleys to the west. We cannot escape in those directions. The mountains to the south might seem the only logical choice, but you all know the dangers. The weather there is likely to be harsh, even at this time of year. But there is another danger: with the great change that has been wrought, the mountains themselves will be unstable. Landslides are common enough in the wet season, they will be far more likely now. I do not think we should venture south.

'That leaves only one hope. You folk of Caer Luciare have no memory of how the worlds were formed. Among the wyrmlings it is taught that the Great Wyrm formed the world, and that is half-true.

'But a better world than this existed once, a world so pure and beautiful that your imaginations cannot do it justice. The Great Wyrm tried to seize control of it, and in the battle that ensued, the One True World splintered into millions and millions of lesser worlds.

'Your world is but a shadow of that perfect world, as many of you now know. And these shadows were wrought by Despair.

'But the One World, the netherworld, still remains. It is diminished from what it once was, but it exists. I can open a door into it, if you desire to enter.'

'And who will lead us,' Drewish Madoc demanded, 'you?'

'I have no desire to lead these people,' Daylan said.

'Damn you, I think you do!' Drewish growled.

'Please,' the emir said. 'Let us not quarrel – I beg you. Let us not choose a leader until after I bring my friend home.'

The Madocs could not easily mount an argument against that, not without seeming churlish. But their expressions showed that they wanted to.

Talon studied Connor Madoc, and inwardly she fumed. Her father had warned her of the danger posed by that man. Dozens of times he had tried to lure her father to his side with petty bribes and flattery.

Daylan said, 'I must warn you that even the One True World holds its risks. Still, it is much like your world, and you will not have to abide there long. There may be dangers ahead, but compared to the certain destruction that awaits us if we stay here, the risks are worth taking.

'I intend to open a door into that world, and over the next few days you can march at your leisure. In time, I will open another door to this world, and we can enter somewhere far away from here, beyond the knowledge of the wyrmling hordes.'

For an instant, the crowd was stone silent. But they could not remain silent for long. Daylan Hammer was offering hope where only minutes before there had been none, and now

Talon whooped in triumph. All of the rest of the people joined into the shout.

'Let us see this world first!' Connor Madoc clamored to be heard above the crowd.

Daylan Hammer shrugged in acquiescence, then begged use of a staff from the Wizard Sisel; the wizard complied.

Daylan touched the ground with the tip of the staff, and then swung it into a high arc, as if tracing the path of a rainbow.

When he brought the staff back to the ground, he stood for a moment, muttering an incantation. He raised his staff again and began drawing a rune in the air with its tip.

The air around the company suddenly seemed to *harden*: that was the only way that Talon could describe it. She could still breathe, but there was a heft to the air, as if it had grown heavy and torpid, like a pudding as it thickens.

The smell of a storm filled the field, and lightning sizzled and popped at the point of Daylan's staff.

Suddenly, it was as if an invisible wall fell away.

One instant, Talon was peering at Daylan and the others, and behind them she could see the white fields of summer, thick with dying thistles and black-eyed Susans. The next moment, it was as if a curtain had opened, revealing something Talon had never imagined.

There was a door in the air, shaped like a rainbow, high and arching, large enough so that several people could march through it abreast.

Beyond the door was a land different from her own. There was a vast glade with grass an emerald green. It was dawn there, or perhaps it only looked like dawn because of the huge trees that blocked the sunlight. A numinous opalescent haze filled the water-heavy air.

Not a mile ahead, at the edge of a small lake, a stand of pine trees rose up impossibly high, as if trees were mountains in that world.

Rich flowers filled the meadow. There were pink posies on the ground, each blossom the size of a child's fist, and bright yellow buttercups, and bluebells that grew so tall that one could look up into the hollow within their flowers.

Bees droned lazily as they trundled about in the morning air. A sweet scent blew from the netherworld, a perfume of flowers so rich that it threatened to overwhelm Talon, but it was mingled with an earthy scent of rich soil and sweet grass.

But even more than the serenity of the scene before her or the fragrance that blew from the netherworld, the call of morning birds beckoned Talon.

There were larks at the fringe of the meadow singing songs that were more intricate, more complex and variant in tone, than the loveliest song from a flute.

Almost by instinct, Talon longed to be there. She suddenly found herself shoved from the back as someone lunged toward the door. A shout rose from among Talon's people, and it seemed that they would stampede through the opening and bolt into the netherworld – not from fear but from desire.

Daylan Hammer shouted, 'Hold! Hold! All of you!' He held the staff at ready, barring the way, as if he would club the first person who tried to get past him.

A woman, a young mother holding her child, stopped in front of him, and a wordless cry of longing rose from her throat.

'Listen,' Daylan said. 'All is not as it seems. The world you see is beautiful, yes, but it can also be treacherous. There is perfect beauty there, and perfect horror, too.

'Some who walk through this door will die, I fear.

'Touch nothing until I tell you that it is safe. Keep quiet, lest you attract attention. Do not drink from any stream until I tell you that it is all right. Do not eat anything without asking me first.'

There were shouts of agreement to the terms, but still Daylan Hammer barred the way. He looked into the eyes of the women and children, as if to be certain that they understood, that they would heed his warning.

'One last thing,' he said. 'There are men on this world. Some of you have heard of them. You call them the "Bright Ones."

Their ways will be strange to you, and their magics may be frightening. You must not anger them. Neither should you quarrel with them, or lie to them, or steal from them.

'They have no desire to harm you, but their conduct to you may seem impossibly harsh.

'Most importantly, they will not welcome you. It is my hope that we will meet none on our journey. And if you happen upon them, and think them cruel, know only that their enemies are far crueler.

'If we are discovered, the Bright Ones will likely banish us back to your world. You will not be allowed to stay. I am opening a door to paradise, but only for a brief moment. You cannot stay forever. Understand this, and enter at your own peril.'

He tried to bar the way for an instant more, but the nether-world beckoned, and with a shout of triumph the woman went charging through the door in the air.

Daylan is wiser than I thought, Talon decided. He has just made himself our king, for no one will support the Madocs so long as they find themselves in a new and dangerous world.

While the crowd streamed through, nearly forty thousand strong, Talon suddenly felt a strange reticence.

This is more dangerous than we know, she thought. It may be more dangerous than it is possible for us to know.

3

RHIANNA'S WELCOME

It is only when you know that no one – not family, not friend, nor any force in the universe – cares for you, that you begin to learn the virtue of self-reliance. It is only yourself that you can trust, and only yourself that you must remain true to.

Thus, self-reliance is the Mother of All Virtues – the kind of fierceness, cunning, and unwavering resolve that one must master in order to succeed in life.

—From the Wyrmling Catechism

That afternoon, Rhianna rested on the wind as she soared toward the Courts of Tide, riding thermals of hot air that rose from the plains below.

The sun shone full upon her back, warming her wings. It had not been a full day since she had won them in battle, pulling the magical artifacts from the corpse of a Knight Eternal; she was not used to them yet. She was a fledgling still.

Learning to fly was every bit as hard for her as learning to walk is for a toddler. The journey of more than three hundred miles in a single day had been made only with frequent stops, where Rhianna had fallen in a heap, exhausted. She was dripping sweat from every pore – partly from her exertion, partly from the heat of the day.

But as the day warmed she had discovered currents of air rising along the sides of the hills, and if she held her wings rigid, she could ride those currents like a hawk.

From Rhianna's vantage point, she could see for miles in every direction.

She had passed this way only a week ago, walking through the pine forests and tramping through fen and field. She knew the landmarks.

But the land had changed. The trees and grass were dying, the edges of leaves were going brown. With the binding of the worlds, all of the world was falling under the wyrmlings' curse, a blight that killed wholesome plants and would leave only thorns and thistles and the most hardy of gorse.

Ancient ruins now rose from the ground everywhere – strange monolithic buildings, broken towers, thick stone walls.

These were ruins from the big folk, the warrior clans that had fled Caer Luciare. Rhianna had not imagined how marvelous their culture had once been.

The remains of great canals crisscrossed the land.

She did not have time to study the wonders. An urgent need was upon her. She had been charged to warn Fallion's people of the wyrmling threat and see if she could make allies of men who had once been his enemies.

More important, Fallion, the man she loved, had been taken captive to Rugassa. She would need help if she was going to free him.

She had little to bargain with – only a few forcibles, hidden in her pack. But a few, along with the promise of many more, might well be enough.

As she winged toward the Courts of Tide, she marveled at the changes that had taken place there.

For a thousand years, the Courts of Tide had been the richest city in all of Rofehavan. Built upon seven islands, the city was surrounded by the waters of the Carroll Sea, and great bridges spanned from island to island.

But now everything was amiss. The ground had risen, leaving fields of rotting kelp and sea urchins to the east of the city.

The odor of brine and decomposing fish assailed her. Carcasses from beached whales and a leviathan littered the plains.

Down below, islands had become hills. Ships in the harbor were stranded on dry ground, miles from any shore. Rhianna peered to the east, seeking for a glimpse of the ocean. She could not be certain, but she thought that she saw water far in the distance, twenty or more miles out. But it could have just been vapors rising from what was once the ocean floor.

Swooping into a dive, Rhianna headed for the old palace at the Courts of Tide. It still stood, tall and pristine. Its white towers gleamed in the morning sun. Atop its pinnacles, standards snapped in a sharp breeze – white flags with the red Orb of Internook at their center. Where once there had been alcoves open to the sea, where undines had risen on the waves to take council with ancient kings, Rhianna saw only rocks and ruin. All along the island's old shore, shanties and fishermen's huts and old inns leaned precariously, like so much driftwood washed up on the beach.

Children could be seen down below, where once there had been forty feet of water, searching through the remains of tide pools for crabs and urchins, while adults prowled about old shipwrecks, perhaps seeking for lost treasure.

Rhianna banked to her left and folded her wings, dropping toward the main road to the palace.

She was two hundred yards out when someone let a ballista bolt fly from the castle wall. She folded her wings, creating a smaller target, and hit the ground hard.

It was a terrible landing. She lost her footing and went tumbling, head over heels.

It might have been all that saved her. The marksmen upon the castle wall stopped firing, as one of the men shouted, 'I got it! I shot it clean through.'

Others cheered and celebrated.

Rhianna climbed to her knees and cried out, 'Parley. I come in peace. I come to speak with Warlord Bairn on an urgent matter, concerning the safety of his borders.'

Bairn was the current usurper squatting at the Courts of

Tide. He didn't really rule the place. The city was becoming a barren ghetto, where gangs fought for food and shelter. He was a mere vulture, picking at the remains of Mystarria.

Only when Rhianna looked up to the castle wall did she notice the bodies. There were three of them, hanging by their wrists in the shadows just below the battlements and just above the drawbridge. Human they were, but not like the small folk. They were the corpses of humans from the warrior clans at Caer Luciare. They had the bony head plates and the nubs of horns at their temples.

Two men and a woman hung dead on the castle wall.

Immediately Rhianna knew what had happened. When the worlds were bound, there were some people who lived on two worlds at once, people who had shadow selves. And when the worlds became one, those who lived on both worlds were bound into one person, retaining the memories and skills and abilities of both.

It had happened to her foster sister Talon, and to the Wizard Sisel.

But for reasons that Rhianna could not understand, when the two were bound into one, there seemed to be no pattern as to where they ended up. Talon's two 'selves' had merged at Castle Coorm, though one of her shadow selves had been hundreds of miles away, in Caer Luciare. And Rhianna knew from news at Caer Luciare that Sir Borenson's two halves must have merged on the far side of the world, for Talon's shadow father had gone missing from the fortress.

Perhaps one personality dominated the other, and the two halves merged with the dominant personality, Rhianna mused. Or maybe some other factor came into play. Perhaps it was all just dumb luck, random chance.

But these three unfortunate souls had merged here at the Courts of Tide. And because of their strange appearance, they had been killed.

The captain of the guard shouted, 'Hold! Don't move!'

He was a big man, with golden-red hair and leather armor made of seal-skin. He didn't bother wearing a helm.

He eyed Rhianna, curious. He demanded, 'What are you?'

'A woman,' Rhianna said. 'I come as a friend, bearing a message.'

The captain studied her suspiciously. By some instinct, Rhianna flapped her wings slowly, trying to cool herself. This amused the captain, and he leaned over the castle wall, peering down at her, as if to peek down Rhianna's blouse.

'Never have I seen a dove with bigger wings or finer breasts,' the captain said. Behind him the pikemen and marksmen upon the wall chortled at the jest. 'If you are really a woman, prove it.'

Anything I say will just be a joke to him, Rhianna realized. She refused to rise to the bait, and just stood glaring at him.

He was dying to find out how she had gotten her wings, and Rhianna was just as determined never to tell him.

'So,' the captain of the guard said at last, 'you hope to speak to Warlord Bairn. On what business?'

She decided to command his interest.

'A mountain of blood metal has risen within the borders of Mystarria,' Rhianna told him. 'I thought that I should warn Bairn to get it, before his enemies do.'

The captain of the guard suddenly straightened and took interest. 'Where is this mountain?'

'That is information I will sell – to Warlord Bairn alone.'

The captain's brown eyes glittered with malice. He raised his hand. 'Archers!' he commanded, and suddenly dozens of bowmen rose up from behind the merlons of the castle wall. 'Ready arrows.'

The archers bent their bows to the full.

The captain studied Rhianna, to see if she'd squirm.

'Kill me,' Rhianna promised, 'and Bairn will have you hanging from the city gates before sundown.'

The captain considered her threat. He warned the archers, 'Don't let her leave,' then turned and raced from the castle gate.

Rhianna sat down and waited, folding her wings about her. The artificial wings draped over her shoulder suddenly, so that the folds of skin looked like a crimson dress.

The archers held their bows at the ready for long minutes, until their arms grew tired and they went to rest.

Bairn did not summon her to his great hall. Perhaps he feared this woman with wings. So he came to the top of the gate himself, like a king negotiating a siege.

He was a tough-looking man, with dark hair and sharp widow's peak. He had a broad, cruel face and thin lips. His eyes seemed colorless and looked glazed, as if he had been drinking.

'Name yourself,' he demanded. He was wearing a cloak of black, and as he casually leapt up and sat upon a merlon, he suddenly reminded Rhianna of a huge black vulture worrying over a corpse.

'Rhianna,' she said, 'Rhianna Borenson.' She did not want to use her real name, and so she used the name of her foster father.

'Borenson . . .' he said. 'That name is known to me.'

'My father was once guardsman to the Earth King,' she said. 'He held forth at this very castle.'

'You have his red hair,' Bairn mused. That was true enough, though she was not blood kin to Borenson. Still, it was a name that commanded respect.

'I've come to give you warning,' Rhianna said. 'There is a new danger in the land – a type of giant, called wyrmlings.'

'We have found some,' Bairn said, nodding toward the dead folk on his walls. 'They are responsible for this . . . mess.' His eyes roved across the armor, taking in the fields of rotting kelp below them.

Rhianna didn't know if she should argue. Warlord Bairn was known to be a brawler, and took offense when none was intended.

More important, she needed Bairn to help save Fallion – the man who was truly responsible for the mess.

'The wyrmlings are larger than these,' she said, jutting her chin toward the dead. 'These poor folks are humans, or what passed for human upon the shadow world.

'But wyrmlings stand a head taller, and are broader at the

shoulders. Their skin is whiter than bone, and their eyes are like pits of ice. They cannot abide the daylight. They eat only flesh. They think that human flesh is as good as any other.'

'So,' Bairn said, 'these humans were their enemies? Or were they seen merely as food?'

'Sworn enemies,' Rhianna said.

'What are the wyrmlings' numbers?' Bairn asked, like any good commander.

'Millions,' Rhianna said. 'They command strange magics. Their lords and emperors are wights, and no common weapon can kill one. My mother, the Lady Myrrima, is a water wizard, and had blessed my own weapons, and so by luck I slew one of their Knights Eternal, a creature more dead than alive. I took my wings from it.'

With that, she unfolded her wings, and raised them in the morning light. Until that instant, she suspected that Bairn had not been willing to believe her. But he could not deny the evidence of his own eyes.

'You say that they have blood metal?' he asked.

'A mountain of it,' she affirmed. 'When the two worlds were bound, the mountain rose from the plains. Upon that other world, the folk had little use for it. Now it is a treasure untold.'

Warlord Bairn got a cunning look. 'Why would you tell me all this – you the daughter of the vaunted Sir Borenson?'

Rhianna considered a lie, but settled on a half-truth. Somehow, she could tell that this was not going well. 'He loved this land, these people. He would not want to see them harmed. You could be a powerful ally in the coming wars.'

Bairn seemed to think a moment. 'You would have us go to war against giants – giants at war with the men of their own world? Why should we unite with the smaller humans? Perhaps there is some way that we could make the wyrmlings our allies?'

'Haven't you heard me? They eat human flesh. They have a mountain of blood metal. They . . . at best they would make you their slaves, though I think they'd prefer to make you a meal.'

That seemed to satisfy Bairn. He stood straighter, looking less like a vulture.

'And where is this mountain? My captain said that you planned to name your own price for it.'

'First, we must see if you will meet my price,' she said.

Bairn snorted, as if this was but a formality. He would give anything for a mountain of blood metal. 'What is it that you want?'

Rhianna did not like the look of him. He glanced away to the north and south. He acted as if he were too busy to waste his time with her, but she suspected that he feared to look her in the eye.

'There are two men held captive in the wyrmling stronghold. When you get the blood metal, I want you to take endowments, break into the wyrmling stronghold, and set my friends free.'

'Let me get enough endowments,' Bairn said, 'and I'll slaughter the lot of these giants for you. Then you can walk into the wyrmling dungeons and set your friends free yourself.'

'Agreed,' Rhianna said, but she still felt uneasy.

'Now,' Bairn asked, 'where is this mountain of blood metal?'

Rhianna feared to tell him the truth. She wanted to see what he would do once he got the information. So she devised a ruse.

If he is an honorable man, she decided, I can tell him the truth later.

'It is hidden beneath a wyrmling stronghold, on the slopes of a volcano, eighty miles northwest of the city of Ravenspell.' She had just given him directions to Rugassa. If he followed them, he'd lead his men to battle against the entire wyrmling horde.

He smiled warmly, and then glanced to the captain of his guard. 'Kill her,' he said dismissively.

Bairn turned to leave just as the captain of the guard raised and dropped his hand, signaling the archers to fire.

Rhianna was ready for them. She whirled to the right and leapt over the bridge as arrows and ballista bolts plinked onto the paving stones beside her.

She plummeted fifty feet before she opened her wings, catching the wind. She veered beneath the bridge and skimmed above rocks that had been submerged just three days ago, and now were covered with white barnacles and colorful starfish.

She flapped her wings and went soaring away, using the bridge above her as a shield. Arrows plunked above her, raining down on the stone bridge, snapping on impact. The archers had done their best, but had not been able to get a clean shot.

Now their chance was gone, and Rhianna flew beyond their range.

She felt saddened by the warlord's betrayal. She had hoped to make an ally, and instead had found only an enemy. He would take his men to war against the wyrmlings, of that she felt sure. He couldn't afford to ignore the risk.

But who will help me now? she wondered.

Rhianna consulted a mental map. There was nothing left of Mystarria to save. The warlords of Internook had taken the coast. Beldinook had taken the west, while South Crowthen claimed the middle of the country. Gaborn's realm was no more. There was little to save, little worth fighting for.

So where else should I go? Rhianna wondered. Beldinook was now the most powerful nation in all of Rofehavan, with its fine armor, strong lancers, and heavy warhorses. The castles and fortresses of Beldinook had been spared in the past war. But Beldinook was a sworn enemy of Mystarria and its ruler, Allonia Lowicker, would not be willing to help rescue Fallion Sylvarresta Orden, a scion of Mystarria.

Rhianna considered flying to Heredon.

It had once been the queen's home, and it too was rich with steel and people, but it had fallen under the shadow of South Crowthen.

Where else can I look for help? she wondered.

Fleeds, the land of the horse clans.

The land of my youth, she thought. Her mother had been born in Fleeds. Rhianna's grandmother had been queen. For a short time, Rhianna had been raised there. Her time in Fleeds had been the happiest time of her life.

Fleeds was not rich in steel, but a powerful Runelord had little need for such defenses. Fleeds did not have great fortifications, but the women of Fleeds had great hearts. And they had loved and honored the Earth King. They would respect his son.

Home, she told herself. I'm going home.

With that, she flapped her wings, banked to her left, and soared up from under the bridge, into the open sky. Eagerly she flew to the west, into a setting sun that gleamed like a white pearl as it settled into an opalescent haze.

4

THE STRANGER WITHIN

*When lions feast, the timid get what they deserve —
nothing.*

—*From the Wyrmling Catechism*

*In the wyrmling keep at Rugassa, Areth Sul Urstone was a stranger
in his own body. He walked and talked, but it was another's will
that moved him, and it was another person's words that were
spoken, another's emotions that he felt. The Great Wyrm, Lord
Despair, had taken control. Areth Sul Urstone felt like a mouse,
trapped and cornered in some king's great hall, watching as the
ponderous affairs of state rolled by.*

Lord Despair stood in the uppermost bell tower while the stars
drifted on a warm wind above. The day had passed, and it
was nearly midnight.

Gazing up at the stars, Despair saw not piercing lights that
smote his heart with their beauty – but only the scattered bits
of his longed-for empire.

Despair reached up as if to gather the stars in his hand. For
so long they had remained outside his grasp. But now, now
he could almost touch them.

Areth watched the gesture, felt Despair's longing, but Areth could not quite comprehend Despair's turbulent thoughts, his undying hatred, his far-flung plans.

Now Despair peered down at his minions toiling in his fortress, hundreds of yards below, admiring their greatness.

Enormous rookeries had been built high upon the sides of the volcano to house his otherworldly graaks. Wranglers were trying to get one of the enormous creatures into its new home, but it spread its massive black wings and reared back, pulling one of its handlers to its death.

Already doors to half a dozen shadow worlds had been opened, and soon reinforcements would arrive from all over, creatures that the wyrmlings had never dreamed of.

First I must consolidate my hold upon this world, Despair knew, and then I can take the others.

Yet he did not exult in his power.

All day Despair had felt uneasy, experiencing a strange and growing sense of alarm.

Danger is coming to the fortress, the Earth warned. Yet the warning did not come in coherent words. Rather it was an emotion, an instinct that nudged him to action and niggled his mind. Danger is coming. Send your people to safety.

Lord Despair had used Areth's awakening Earth Powers to 'choose' certain wyrmling lords, creating a bond with them, allowing him to sense when they were in danger and warn them. Not only did Despair sense danger to some of his lords now, he knew what they had to do.

'Flee,' the Earth whispered. 'Tell them to flee.'

But Areth Sul Urstone, overwhelmed by another's will, could do nothing. He could not warn the doomed lords, for Despair now dominated him completely, and Despair refused to send the lords to safety.

I will act when the time is ripe, Despair whispered his own reassurance to the Earth. None that I have chosen shall be lost.

Lord Despair had devised a different way to save his people. He had won the battle for Caer Luciare. Already,

Despair's servants were digging blood metal from a hill near the fortress, and by dawn the first shipment would be rushing to Rugassa. Once it arrived, he would grant massive endowments to his men, and prepare a trap for those who attacked.

I will so arm my people that they will be undefeatable, Despair told himself.

But he could not be certain of that. Despair could not sense the source of the danger. He imagined that Runelords were coming, most likely some powerful lords that had been routed from Caer Luciare. Such men would pose a great danger. They would come in a few hours perhaps, or a day. He could not be sure when they would arrive. He only sensed the danger the way that one can feel the coming of a storm even when no clouds darken the horizon.

Lord Despair spun, and orders leapt from his mouth: 'Send word to the emperor,' he told the captain of the guard. 'I want a giant graak dispatched to Caer Luciare to retrieve our first shipment of blood metal ore. I want that ore at first dusk tomorrow.'

'Yes, O Great Wyrm,' the guard said.

Despair considered next how he would get his Dedicates. It did not make sense to take endowments from wyrmlings. He would need them to fight his war.

No, he thought, I must garner endowments from my would-be enemies.

Almost as an afterthought he said, 'There shall be no more harvesting of the small folk for a time. The horde has enough meat for now.'

The captain seemed surprised. 'You'll spare them, show them mercy? Don't they present a danger?'

'Letting them live is not the same as showing mercy,' Despair explained patiently. 'I'll want prisoners, lithe women to give endowments of grace, cunning men to lend me their wit. I'll need folk with strong vision and hearing. But most of all, I'll want those with great beauty and those with fine voices.'

'My lord?' the captain asked, for he was as yet untrained in the art of stripping endowments from his enemies.

'There are tens of millions of small folk scattered across the earth,' Despair explained. 'They outnumber us, and so, as you say, they present a danger.

'But I will force them to love me. I will command their devotion.'

The captain of the guard nodded. He'd do Despair's bidding, but there was still no understanding in his eyes.

That did not matter. In time, the dull creature would comprehend what Despair was plotting. The captain turned away, to carry the message.

'Ah, one last thing,' Despair said. 'Tell them to set apart the strongest of the small folk alive, along with the smiths and jewelers. We can use them to work the mines by daylight and make our forcibles. Thus our slaves shall forge their own collars.'

'Yes, Great One,' the captain said, and he rushed from the parapet.

Despair stood beneath the stars a moment longer, wishing for them, his heart still heavy with alarm. He could not tell when the attack would take place. Tomorrow, the day after?

It had been almost a full day since the Knight Eternal Vulgnash had brought Fallion Orden to the keep. The young wizard should have had time to heal.

Despair told his guards, 'Take me to the dungeons, to the Black Cell.'

And they began the journey down the winding stairs and into the labyrinth.

The *labyrinth* had not gotten its name by chance. Most of the wyrmlings in Rugassa had only a cursory knowledge of their surroundings. They had sleeping quarters, a place to work, and perhaps a nearby arena or alehouse to furnish some diversions. That is all that a person really needs in life, Lord Despair believed. The wyrmlings were functional, productive. They did not need to know what existed beyond their cramped lives.

So few of them knew what existed upon the surface. They were told horror stories of a bright sun that would burn out their eyes, or of fierce creatures that could swallow wyrmlings whole. Of all these enemies, mankind was always held to be the greatest threat.

Thus, the wyrmling lords were not seen as slave masters, but as saviors.

Now with the great change there was unrest in the warrens. Some wyrmlings had bound with their shadow selves from Fallion's world. They knew not to trust the wyrmling catechisms, and many of them were trying to escape.

But how could they leave the labyrinth if they could not find a door out?

Even now, Despair's servants were spreading misinformation so that the 'bound' wyrmlings would fall into traps. Those who were caught – well, the battles in the arenas for the next few weeks promised to be quite entertaining. There is something especially exhilarating in watching a comrade fight for his life.

Yet some of the bound wyrmlings escaped.

After half an hour, Despair reached the Black Cell. Vulgnash sat on the floor next to the young wizard. The room was cold as death.

When Vulgnash heard his master coming, he leapt to attention, fanning his red wings out wide. The jailors hurried to open the door, letting Despair into the cell.

'How is our young friend?' Despair asked.

'Not well,' Vulgnash replied. 'His wound became infected. I burned away the pus, and had to use a tong to pull a shard of metal, a broken sword, from his torso. It would be well if our wizard slept, but with the endowments of pain that he has taken, he cries out and writhes in his sleep. There is no escape from his torment.

'So I have taken to keeping him cold, so close to death that he knows nothing. I'm giving him time to heal.'

'Warm him,' Despair said. 'Let him feel his torment for a while. Bring him to a stupor.'

'Great Wyrm,' Vulgnash said, bowing a bit and cringing, 'he is too close to death.'

'He is young and strong. I have known him through many lifetimes. This one can resist death well. Revive him, just a little.'

Vulgnash stood above Fallion for a moment, with his left hand raised, palm downward, and unleashed a wave of warmth. It hit Lord Despair like a blast of hot wind from the desert.

The heat's effect upon Fallion was instantaneous. The young wizard gasped in pain as he neared consciousness, then lay groaning, huddled in a fetal position.

Despair stepped forward, used the toe of his boot to roll Fallion onto his back.

Lord Despair had lived through millions of lifetimes upon millions of worlds, and deep was his lore. The fleeting folk of this world had no idea who they were dealing with.

He spat upon Fallion's dirty forehead, anointing him with his own inner water. Then he leaned forward and peered into a drop of spittle, using it as a lens, and let his focus go deep, through flesh and bone, into Fallion's mind, and from there into his dreams.

Fallion imagined himself to be in his bedroom, far across the sea. The room was small and cluttered, with a pair of cots against each wall. It was dark in the room, blackest night. A chest of drawers leaned against the far wall, covered in sand-colored rangit furs. A collection of animal skulls adorned the top of the bureau – weasels and burrow bears, a dire wolf and a fossilized toth. These were all lit by the thinnest rays of starlight.

Fallion shouted to his brother Jaz, 'You left the window open again! It's freezing.'

Sure enough, as if conjured by Fallion's outburst, bits of snow began to swirl through an open window above the chest of drawers; tiny flakes of ice sifted into the bedroom, blanketing the skulls and furs.

Fallion was suffering various pains in his arms and legs, the pains he had taken upon him in his endowment ceremony. He was in so much pain, he could not understand why. His mind was muddy, his thoughts unclear. He wondered if he had been hurt.

'Jaz, come close the window,' Fallion begged, nearly weeping tears of frustration.

With a mental push, Despair entered the dream.

He darkened the room, so that it was pitch black, even the thin starlight fading into gray.

He chose a form, the form of someone that Fallion loved: a girl, he saw in Fallion's mind – his foster sister Rhianna.

She entered the room shyly, as if coming to a tryst.

'Fallion,' she asked. 'Are you awake?' She tiptoed across the room and closed the window.

'Rhianna?' Fallion asked. 'What happened? I'm hurt. I'm hurting everywhere.'

'Don't you remember?' Despair asked in Rhianna's soft voice. 'You fell. You slipped down a rocky slope and hit your head.' In a pitying tone she asked, 'Wake up, sweet one. We have much to do today.'

'Wha—?' Fallion begged. 'Wha?'

'The binding of worlds,' Rhianna begged. 'Remember? You promised to tell me how it was done. You said that it was so hard. You asked for my help.'

Fallion moaned and tried to look around. But the thin light and his own pain defeated him. He peered at Rhianna for all of half a second before his eyes rolled up, showing only the whites, and he turned his head away in defeat.

'The binding of worlds,' Rhianna begged. 'You promised. You said that you would show me how? So much depends on us!'

'Wha?' Fallion cried out in real life, not in his dreams. He made a gagging sound. His voice was thick from disuse, or perhaps from lack of water.

'Would you like a drink?' Rhianna asked in Fallion's dream. 'I have some sweet wine.'

'Please,' Fallion begged.

Rhianna reached out, and in the way of dreams, a purple flask appeared in her hands. She took it to Fallion, sat on the bed beside him, and let him sip. He peered into her eyes longingly, and Despair ratcheted up Rhianna's scent, so that the sweet smell of her hair mingled with the sweet wine, each lending the other potency. She leaned close to Fallion, forcing him to become aware of her curves, her desire.

Lord Despair leaned back, his focus drifting between Fallion's dream and the real world.

He wanted Fallion's thoughts to clear, and needed to free him from some of the pain. He reached out and placed a finger upon each side of Fallion's back, just below the first vertebra, placing pressure in a way that had been learned on many worlds. By pinching the nerve he dulled Fallion's pain.

Nor did he want Fallion to think too clearly, so with his left hand he placed a thumb upon Fallion's carotid artery, just enough to slow the flow of blood to Fallion's brain. The lack of oxygen would soon leave Fallion's head spinning.

In his dream, Rhianna poured her sweet wine down Fallion's throat. Fallion opened his mouth like a robin's chick, hoping for a worm. Rhianna fulfilled the lad's needs.

When the flask was empty, Fallion lay moaning from ghost pains. He had taken endowments of compassion, and now his Dedicates were in the torture chambers, receiving torments on Fallion's behalf. Some had been put into crystal cages. Others had been dismembered, losing hands or toes or worse.

Despair gloated.

The boy had the nerve to thank me for giving those

endowments, Despair thought. I wonder how he enjoyed feeling bits of flesh ripped from his body.

Despair knew that those who suffered such acts of mayhem agonized most of all. It was not the physical pain that tormented them so much as the mental anguish, a sense of being un-whole for the rest of their lives.

The tormentors had been ordered to strip certain prisoners of various body parts, until Fallion imagined himself to be only a stump of a person.

Let him thank me then, Despair thought, a small smile forming on his lips.

'Why are you smiling?' Fallion asked Rhianna in his dream. The stupefied boy's head had begun to reel, and he imagined that the wine was dulling his pain.

'I smile because I love you so,' Rhianna said softly. 'Now, my love,' she whispered, 'about the binding of worlds. You promised, remember? You promised to tell me how it was done?'

Of course no such promise had been tendered, but the unconscious mind does not track such things well. Besides, Fallion's head was reeling, and Lord Despair was counting upon Fallion's stupor to aid in the deception.

'What?' Fallion cried, still wincing and shaking from unseen ailments.

'The binding of worlds? How did you do it?'

'It's . . . it's easy,' Fallion said. 'So easy, once you see it.'

That shocked Despair right out of the dream.

It was *easy* to bind the worlds?

Despair had always imagined that it was complex, that it would require great cunning, followed by lengthy preparation and exhaustive steps – major magical routines that were broken into dozens of subroutines. He had tried every easy solution, but the truth was that the Seals of Creation baffled him in their complexity.

He dove back into the dream.

*   *   *

'Yes, yes,' Rhianna said. 'I know that it's easy for you. You've said that before. But you're wiser than you give yourself credit for – much wiser.

'Come,' Rhianna begged, 'to the Seal. Come show me how it is done.'

And in the way of dreams, she took his hand in the darkness and led him outside the front door of his father's cabin.

There in the yard, in the clear spot where the chickens scratched in the grass by day, beneath a white gum tree, the Seal of the Inferno lay upon the ground, a great circle of ghostly green flames dancing upon the lawn.

Blinking in surprise, Fallion stared at it.

Fallion swallowed, opened his mouth, and started to speak.

Despair leaned forward, straining to hear, lest he miss a single syllable.

'I . . . something's wrong. There's something wrong here.' He peered at the Seal as if studying it.

Despair had made the Seal the way that he remembered it. But in his dream, Fallion stumbled around the thing, peering at flames, listening to the hiss and roar that they created, as if baffled.

'Things are out of place,' he said, confused.

'Perhaps a few,' Rhianna said. 'Show me how to bind the world.'

Fallion stammered, 'You just – you . . .'

He wetted his tongue, then frowned in concentration for an instant – an instant too long. He whirled and peered at Rhianna, the light of dancing fires shining in his eyes, and peered not at the girl, but into her soul.

So powerful was Fallion's gift that Lord Despair was laid naked.

Suddenly Fallion's eyes flew open and he peered at Despair, his glazed eyes focusing on him, and shouted, 'No!'

I almost had him, Despair realized. For a moment, I had him. But the opportunity had passed.

Despair turned and nodded to Vulgnash; the Knight Eternal

stretched forth his hand, drawing the heat from the room until Fallion curled up again in a fetal position, his teeth chattering and every muscle trembling from cold, as he plummeted into a deep, deep slumber.

Somewhere in the recesses of his mind, Areth Sul Urstone watched the whole scene unfold, sickened and horrified at what Despair was plotting.

5

THE HUNTERS

Every soul, from the greatest warrior to the smallest child, has immense worth in the sight of the Great Wyrm. The Great Wyrm has made us stewards over each other, and that is why we must never let our fellows escape.

—From the Wyrmling Catechism

Cullossax had felt anxious throughout the evening. He'd known that he would be missed, and that eventually his fellow tormentors would come looking for him.

Often he had to fight the impulse during the day to flee out into the light.

At last, when the shadows grew long enough to indicate that the day was almost gone, Cullossax bade farewell to the lowly guards, took an iron javelin, and ran after the girl, giving chase.

Her path was easy to follow.

The girl had headed into the forest, witless with terror and blinded by light. With every step her heels had gouged into the thick humus that lay like a blanket under the pines.

Cullossax had seldom been outside the fortress, but he had been taught a bit about tracking, for it was a skill that tormentors were called upon to use even within the labyrinth.

The air was fresh, and soon the forest filled with night sounds – the scurrying of mice among the remains of leaves, the buzz of insects, the querulous peeps of birds, the songs of crickets and cicadas.

The air smelled sweet. Cullossax could not recall the last time he'd tasted fresh air.

The stars came out, blinding points of light so silver-bright that they left an afterimage when he squinted up at them.

Soon, he knew, he would have hunters on his trail, but Cullossax felt resigned to his fate, happy. He was no stranger to death. He'd dealt it out time and time again, and had always known that his turn would come.

With a light heart, Cullossax ran, chasing after a girl, heading for a land that might be no more than a child's dream. . . .

After long hours, Cullossax still plunged through the pine forest, lost in the chase. His heart pounded a steady rhythm as his legs stretched wide. Greasy sweat streamed down his forehead and face, and stained his tunic with a V down his back. His thirst made him wish for pools of water.

But his mind barely registered these things, for his eyes followed the torn sod in the starlight where his quarry had run.

Unthinking, he leapt over a fallen fir tree, and ducked beneath the boughs of another. In the brush to his right, he heard the snort of a stag. He stood for a moment, heart racing, as he wondered what the sound might portend. He had been outside the fortress only twice in his life, and then not for more than a night. He knew little about wild creatures. Then the stag went bounding away, and he saw it between the trees.

His stomach growled at the thought of fresh flesh.

He could not let himself be distracted. With every long stride, he knew that he drew closer to the girl. She was young and small, and would not be able to keep up this pace forever.

But in the back of his mind, Cullossax worried. He was hunting, but by now he would also be hunted. He should have checked in with his master hours ago. He would be missed, and eventually the story of what had happened would unravel.

The best of his own kind would hound him. No one could exact vengeance like a tormentor of the Bloody Fist. The punishment exercised upon one of their own kind, one who had shamed them and brought their reputation into question, would be harsh indeed.

In Rugassa, torture was not just a science, it was an art. Cullossax pondered long and hard, but was certain that he could not imagine what they would do to him.

They would torture him in public, of course, and the tormentors would vie for the honor of inflicting the most horrific insults upon his body.

In time they would let him die. That at least was certain. It was not a question of how long Cullossax would live, but a question of how long he would suffer before they let him die.

He wondered which of the torturers would come after him, and that gave him pause. There were stories of a new kind of magic in Rugassa. The emperor's elite troops had been drawing attributes from the lowest of the slaves – strength, speed, blood-lust. These new warriors could run faster than a common man, and longer.

Cullossax wondered what he would do if he had to face such a warrior.

And then there was Vulgnash himself. Cullossax had taken food from a Knight Eternal.

That kind of insult was unheard of.

Cullossax only hoped that Vulgnash could not be spared to lead the chase.

For most of the night Cullossax ran through hills, through a land of seemingly endless forests. Sometimes he had scrambled up hills where aspen trees spread their white branches in the moonlight, gleaming like bones, and other times he descended into vales filled with oak and ash.

But always there was the forest, and Cullossax hoped that if Vulgnash gave chase, the trees might hide him from above.

The midsummer's air hardly cooled during the night, and as Cullossax neared a stream, he finally found the girl.

She was lying in the ferns and moss beside the water's edge, curled in a fetal position. When she heard Cullossax draw near, she yelped in panic, then began crawling toward the brook, shaking so badly from fear that she could not stand.

Cullossax ran to her. The iron javelin was heavy in his hand, and he could have pierced her if that had been his intent.

'No, please!' she whimpered. 'Let me go.'

Cullossax laughed, not because he enjoyed her fear but because there was something so odd about her. She had a softness that was pure and innocent and completely unlike anything he had seen. No wyrmling had such a soft heart.

As he laughed, the girl struck. She suddenly leapt up and lunged, aiming a sharp stick at his heart.

Cullossax grabbed her arm and wrestled the weapon away. It was not hard. She was young, and the long chase coupled with her own fear had weakened her. A simple head butt made her swoon.

'I have not come to kill you,' Cullossax said. 'I've come to help you.'

'I – don't understand.'

'I could have fed you to Vulgnash,' he said. 'I should have. And for my audacity, I may yet die. But I chose to let you live.' He nodded south. 'How far to this Inkarra?'

'Beyond the Great Spine,' she said.

Cullossax bit his lower lip. Three hundred miles at least, maybe four. A warrior, running, might make it in three nights. But Cullossax was a tormentor, and was not used to such exertion. Neither was the girl.

'Can you run?' he demanded.

The girl dropped her head. No.

Some primal instinct warned him to hurry. He grunted, grabbed the girl, and threw her over a shoulder. 'Then rest.'

He jumped into the brook and splashed downstream. His wyrmling brothers had strong noses, he knew, and he hoped to throw them off of his track. After a few hundred yards, he turned back the way that he had come, and then began a zigzag path heading east.

The land in that direction was dropping away, and as it neared dawn the sound of morning birdsong began to fill the air. Larks twittered and jays ratcheted.

He found himself on a small hill, peering down into a meadow. Miles away, he could see a line of alders. The stars had all faded from the sky, and the sun would be up soon. Bits of cloud on the horizon were bloody red.

The girl stared toward the sky, a curious look on her face.

'What do you see?' Cullossax asked, worried that she had spotted a sign of their enemies.

'The sunrise, it's beautiful this morning,' she said. 'There are colors in the clouds – faintest blue along the edges, and palest gold in the sky.'

Blue and *gold* were words that he had never heard before. She had to use Inkarran words to describe these colors.

'You see colors,' he asked, 'like the humans do?'

'Yes,' she admitted, 'ever since the joining of the worlds. That is how I know that this is not all just some simple madness.'

By now, his shoulder ached and his legs were failing. 'Can you run yet?' he asked the girl.

'Yes,' she said.

He set her down and pointed east. 'We must reach those trees before sunrise. It will be a race. Can you make it?'

She grunted, the wyrmling sound for yes, and they were off. They sprinted through the tall grass. Rabbits bounded away from their trail and finches flew up out of the thistles.

The sun began to crest the horizon, a cruel red light looming upon the edge of the world. The sight of it brought tears of pain to Cullossax's eyes.

But the tree line was just ahead, promising shade and protection from the sun.

Cullossax ran until he felt as if his heart would burst, and the girl began to fall behind. He grabbed her wrist and pulled, urging her to greater speed.

The sun was a blinding orb ahead of them, and Cullossax averted his eyes, threw an arm across his face, and tried to ignore the pain.

At last he staggered into the cool shadows of the woods. The girl threw herself to the ground well inside the tree line, and Cullossax stood for a moment, grabbing his knees, as he hunched in pain, gasping for breath.

He glanced back along the trail that they'd taken, saw how the bent blades of summer wheat betrayed their path. In the distance, two miles back, three wyrmling warriors gave chase, loping down out of the hills.

Cullossax halted for an instant, studied them. They were running with incredible swiftness.

Speed, he realized. They've taken attributes of speed. He did some mental calculations. It would have taken an hour or two for anyone to notice that he'd gone missing, another hour to figure out where he'd gone.

I should have had a great lead on them.

But these men moved faster than normal wyrmlings, twice as fast, perhaps three times. They'd taken endowments of speed, and probably of strength and stamina as well.

I cannot outrun them, Cullossax realized. And I cannot hope to slay all three of them.

Yet as they raced down from the hills and reached the edge of the distant field, the rising sun smote them. They peered along the trail. They could not see him here, hidden in the shadows. They threw their hands up, trying to shelter their eyes.

At last, in defeat, they turned away and trudged back up into the hills, into the trees, to find some shadows deep enough where they could hide from the sun for the day.

It was with just such a hope that Cullossax had run to the east. No wyrmling could withstand such burning light.

He hid there in the shelter of the woods, and sat for a long moment, thinking. The girl lay gasping for breath.

'Do you have a name?' he asked. It was not an idle question. Many young wyrmlings of the lower castes were not permitted names. They had to be earned.

'Ki-rissa,' she said. 'Kirissa Mentarn.'

'That is not your wyrmling name. It is an Inkarran name?'

She nodded. Cullossax frowned at the odd gesture, and she grunted yes, to appease him.

'Kirissa,' he said. 'There are soldiers on our trail. They've been granted strength and speed by the new magic. Have you heard of it?'

'The rune magic? I know of it. It came from the other world.'

This admission made Cullossax wonder what other helpful things she might recall.

'The soldiers trailing us are fast. We won't be able to outrun them. So we must outsmart them.'

'All right,' she said. She put on a studious face.

'They know which way we're running,' he said. 'So we must change directions. Instead of going south, we should go east or west. And we must take time to cover our trail, and hide our scent. We must hide it perfectly. To do less, is to die.'

'All right,' Kirissa agreed.

Nearby a squirrel began to give a warning chatter. Cullossax halted for a moment, listening, but realized that the squirrel was warning others away from *him*.

'One last thing,' he said. 'We must leave now. We can't afford to rest through the day. Those who hunt us are moving too fast. But the days are long, and the nights are short. It may be that if we can get far enough ahead of the Bloody Fist, they will lose our trail in the dark, and we will be safe.'

'We will go sunblind,' Kirissa argued, her face paling from fear.

'Close your eyes and hold on to my hand, if you must,' Cullossax said. 'I will watch for the both of us.'

He did not say it, but if he tried to walk in the open sun for long, he was the one who would go sunblind. At that point, she would have to leave him.

Kirissa stared for a long moment and finally asked, 'Why are you doing this? You were supposed to be my tormentor.'

Cullossax wanted to answer, but when he opened his mouth, he could think of nothing to say.

He had no dreams. It wasn't as if he'd secretly longed for escape his whole life.

Nor did it have to do with her. Kirissa was not quite old enough to mate. He had no lust for her, no desire to possess her. Even now, he imagined that he could strangle her if he wanted.

Yet he admired those who fought against their own executions. How had her Earth King put it, 'The time will come when the small folk of the world must stand against the large'?

Certainly, in attacking him, Kirissa had fulfilled her Earth King's prophecy.

Cullossax wondered if he had spared her through idle curiosity. He wondered if he had spared her only because he had spent his whole life in the labyrinth, and secretly he yearned to see what life was like outside.

As a child he had played a game. The world was a harsh place, and instinct told him that he also had to be cruel in order to survive. But he had once heard a lord say that such instincts were bred into the wyrmlings. A man's chances to breed were tied to his ranking, and a man's ranking rose in proportion to his capacity for cruelty.

If that was true, he had considered, then would it not be possible to engineer a different kind of world, one that was less cruel?

He had not been able to imagine such a world. But Kirissa claimed to come from one. And so he was curious.

But that was not it, either. He'd never been a man of great curiosity.

No, Cullossax felt inside himself, and knew only that something was broken, something more vital than bone – his very soul. He had grown sick of his life in the labyrinth. Life there seemed like no life at all, as if it was a walking death, and he had only been waiting for the day when he no longer breathed.

At last he answered, 'I came with you because I am weary of living. I thought maybe that in another world, my life would have been better.'

'You can't be weary of life,' Kirissa said. She reached up and stroked Cullossax's face, a gesture that he found to be odd and discomfiting; it felt as if a bug were crawling on him. 'Among the wyrmlings,' she said, 'no one is really alive.'

6

TASTES OF THE NETHERWORLD

Despair created the earth, the moon, and the stars. Despair owns them all – every world that spins about even the dimmest sun.

That is why, when you look into the heavens at night, you feel so small and desolate. It is your heart bearing witness to your own insignificance, and to the overwhelming power of Despair.

—From the Wyrmling Catechism

The first full taste of a meadow in the netherworld was something that Talon would never forget.

The aroma staggered her senses: sweet grass, rich loam, and the perfume of tens of thousands of flowers – from deep beds of clover to vines of honeysuckle and stalks of wild mint. There were wood roses in the meadow, and flowers for which Talon had no name.

And all around, birdsong rose from the thickets, curiously complex in its music, as if by nature birds were meant to compose arias and had only somehow forgotten this upon Talon's world.

When the company was all gathered upon the netherworld, Daylan Hammer returned to the Door of Air, and with the Wizard Sisel's staff, drew another rune. In an instant there was a thundering boom, like lightning striking, and the door collapsed.

Daylan turned to the company.

'Remember my warnings. Touch nothing. Drink from no stream. We will head east, but must find shelter before nightfall.'

'Why is that?' someone called.

'Because *things* come out at night,' Daylan answered.

And he was off, striding across the glade. A trail ran through it, a winding trail like a rabbit run.

Daylan walked along it carefully, as if treading across a fallen log.

'Stay on the trail,' he called. 'We walk single-file.'

The folks began forming a line, and soon they were winding down the hill, looking like a great serpent slowly slithering through the grass.

Talon strode along behind the emir. They gave up on their language lessons, and walked silently. No one talked. As well as they could, the forty thousand complied with Daylan's wishes. Babes cried, and occasionally someone yelped as they tripped, but overall, the journey was a remarkably sober one.

They had not gone for half an hour before a child screamed, not a dozen paces ahead of Talon. She peered around the emir and saw a girl, perhaps six or seven, drop a huge posy, its pink flower falling to the ground.

She screamed and held up her hand. 'Help!' she cried. 'A bee stung me!'

'Help yourself,' her mother whispered impatiently. 'You've been stung by bees before. Pull the stinger out – or let me do it.'

But the child held her hand up and studied it in shock, then let out a bloodcurdling cry. 'I'm on fire! Help. I'm burning!'

To Talon it did indeed seem that the child was burning. Her hand was turning a vivid red, a color that Talon had never seen in a human limb, and near the sting it had begun to swell terribly. The girl screamed and fell to the ground, writhing in pain.

Suddenly Talon could hear the angry sound of bees swarming,

and she looked up to see a cloud of them, rising from the glen in every direction, hurtling toward the girl.

Folks shouted in warning, and some stepped away from the child, frightened by the massive swarm that had begun to form.

'Stay on the trail!' Daylan Hammer cried out up ahead, but folks shouted for help. In moments Daylan was racing back down the line, until he reached the fallen child.

The bees had formed an angry golden-gray mass, and merely hovered in the air above the wounded girl, like sentries waiting to do battle.

Daylan cried out in warning, speaking in a tongue that Talon had never heard before. Yet Daylan's words smote her like a mallet. They seemed to pierce Talon, to speak to her very bones.

'Hold!' Daylan called to the bees. 'The child meant no harm. Spare her. She is still ignorant of the law.'

The bees buzzed angrily, their pitch rising and falling, and Talon suspected that they were speaking to Daylan in return, answering in their own tongue.

Daylan reached the fallen child and stood between her and the bees, using his body as a shield.

The girl wept furiously, and soon began to wheeze.

'It's nothing,' the girl's mother said as if to reassure Daylan. 'It's only a bee sting. She's had plenty before.'

'On this world,' Daylan said, 'a single honeybee has more than enough venom to kill a man. Let us hope that she was not stung too deeply.'

He stood between the girl and the swarm, and called out again. 'Please, she did not know that these were your fields,' Daylan apologized. 'She meant only to enjoy a flower. She did not mean to steal pollen from your hive.'

He spoke slowly, as if hoping somehow to break through to the dumb insects.

For a long tense moment the swarm buzzed angrily, and the bees began to circle Daylan, creating a vortex, so that he seemed to be at the center of an angry tornado. He turned to follow their leaders with his eyes, keeping himself between them and the girl.

For her part, the wounded child stopped whimpering, and lay now only wheezing. Talon caught a good glimpse of her – pale blue eyes staring emptily into the air as she struggled. Her face was blanched, and her whole body trembled.

The swarm stayed at bay, and their buzzing eased.

At last Daylan reached out his palm toward the swarm. 'Show me the way to your hive,' he begged. 'Let me speak to your queen. I have not violated the law. You cannot deny me.'

After a thoughtful moment, a single bee flew out of the mass and landed upon Daylan. It walked around in circles on his palm, stopping to waggle from time to time.

'That way!' Daylan said, pointing to the southwest. 'About a league.'

He called out to the Wizard Sisel. 'Come here.' To the crowd he warned, 'The rest of you, stay where you are.'

He glanced down at the failing child. Her breathing was slowing from moment to moment. Daylan told the wizard, 'Cut open the sting. Suck the poison out. Keep her alive, if you can.' He gave the company a warning look. 'And don't move. Don't take so much as a step from the trail or touch a flower, lest the bees attack. There are enough of them to wipe out our whole company!'

Then Daylan was off, racing through the grass.

The Wizard Sisel hunched over the girl and did as Daylan had said, sucking out the poison. He was a master at healing, and Talon had great confidence in his abilities. But Sisel fretted as he muttered incantations and gently rubbed a balm into the child's fist. 'So hot. I've never felt a sting so hot.'

Talon peered around at the folks nearby. Most of them had been born serfs, and so were dressed in drab attire. They had never had an education, and did not know much about the world at large. But even the dullest of them knew that this was all wrong. One did not negotiate with honeybees, or make truces with them. One did not die for picking flowers.

Talon felt foolish and vulnerable. The netherworld held dangers that she could not have anticipated.

The emir stayed where he was supposed to, until he could endure no more. Slowly he edged to the child, and at last stood above the Wizard Sisel. 'Is there anything I can do to help?'

The wizard shook his head no.

The emir sat down in the grass and held the girl's head in his lap, then smoothed back the child's tawny hair and stroked her cheek, making soothing noises.

The child's mother stood nearby, watching. Perhaps she would have comforted the child, but she was cradling one toddler in her arms while she clung to a bag that held everything that the family owned.

'Don't be afraid,' the emir whispered.

Talon felt curiously jealous of the emir's touch. She longed for him to stroke her that way.

The emir bent over the girl and brushed her forehead with a kiss. The girl kept wheezing, but closed her eyes, relishing the attention.

The cloud of bees continued to hover over the spot unnaturally, like an army at war.

It made Talon nervous. She had to pee, but dared not step off of the trail, lest the bees attack. So she held it in, and just stood, her heart pounding in fear.

'Wonder what happens if you run into wasps,' one of the folks down the line said nervously, then broke out laughing at his own inanity.

The little girl appeared to be sleeping peacefully now, and the emir just sat in the grass, singing softly to her for a long time.

It was almost an hour before Daylan returned, a few bees following at his back. The bees entered the angry swarm, and in moments it dispersed, with honeybees scattering in every direction, flying back into the clover and honeysuckle.

'Good news!' Daylan shouted as he drew near. 'All is forgiven. Just keep to the trail. Move along!'

Up ahead, the group began to walk again, and as he drew near, Daylan knelt next to the emir.

'Is the child sleeping well?' he asked.

The little girl appeared to be sleeping peacefully now. The emir had kept up his singing the whole time.

'Sleeping?' he asked. 'No. She died not half an hour ago.'

The girl's mother cried out, and Talon choked back a sob. Some angry farmer demanded of Daylan, 'Why didn't you warn us about the bees?'

Daylan looked up at him, his thoughts seemingly far away. 'Warn you? I did not think to warn you. I guess that I have known of bees all my long life. And of all the dangers here, this one seemed so small as to be almost insignificant.'

After a long march, thunder roared on the horizon at sunset, a continuous snarl with barks and growls like a pack of dogs fighting to the death. Towering clouds lumbered over the hills, threatening a storm that would unleash a fury unlike any that Talon had ever imagined.

Lightning flashed at the crowns of the thunderheads, strobing in a dozen places at once, and the hair on the back of Talon's arm and neck bridled with every flash. The clouds swore to unleash a torrent.

At Talon's side, Alun's war dogs whimpered at the sight of it, and backed off in alarm, peering ahead while their thighs quivered and their tails went fearfully still.

For a long hour the company had been marching toward some massive pine trees that towered above them like a mountain.

'Quickly,' Daylan Hammer cried. 'We must get beneath that largest tree. Those clouds may be hiding more than rain!'

Talon had only a vague idea what Daylan feared. She suspected that Darkling Glories might be riding in those clouds. She dared not ask him, but the worry in the immortal's brow was warning enough. Daylan urged the people forward, nearly forty thousand refugees from Caer Luciare. They were a hungry, tired lot, worn to a frazzle. Many were wounded from battle and so they limped along in bloodied bandages. Those who were healthy still bore what treasures they could – weapons or blood-metal ore from the mines at Luciare, food and household goods. For many a mother, the only treasures that she could bear were her babes.

The refugees began a slow jog, but Daylan urged them on. 'Run, blast you!' he shouted. 'Now is not the time to dawdle. Run for your lives.'

He pointed to a rocky crag three miles ahead, covered in pine trees larger than any that Talon had ever imagined in her own world. Indeed, he singled out one vast pine, larger than the rest. Here upon this new world, the trees were great and venerable. A day here had not been time enough to let Talon grow accustomed to the change in scale. The great pines ahead rose high in the air, their tops hidden in clouds. Each tree's myriad branches splayed wide, so that each tree was half a mile at the base, creating a canopy that one could not see through. Talon could not guess how thick the boles of the trees might be, for they were hidden in utter darkness.

Since coming to this world, Daylan had been urging the refugees forward all day long, and from the early afternoon he had been rushing them toward this outcrop. There were other trees in the hills, but this site alone seemed to call to him.

Daylan shouted, 'Hurry now! Death is upon us!'

Talon ran, with the emir just ahead and Alun behind. With Alun came his war dogs – fourteen large mastiffs, boiling around his legs. He did not have them leashed, and so they swarmed around him as if he were the leader of the pack.

The warriors ahead of Talon ran through tall golden grass that smelled of honey. Wildflowers nodded in the breeze, great red poppies that grew over one's head. Birds flew up from the grass at the people's approach, larks as bright as sparks from a forge.

Talon had never felt so invigorated, so alive. Her people had camped beside a stream at noon, where Daylan Hammer had begged the stream first for water, and surmised by something in its waves that the stream approved, or at least would relinquish a drink. The blistering cold water had tasted as sweet as nectar. The children had hunted for berries beside the stream, and found salmonberries on the shore that somehow were more filling, more wholesome than any she'd ever known.

This world, this One True World, was more perfect than hers in every way.

But even it had its dangers. Ahead lay a perfect storm.

For half an hour they ran, while the storm rolled toward them. The boom of thunder grew louder, so that the earth began to shake with every peal.

Talon watched the outcropping of rock draw closer, saw the tops of the vast pines sway in the wind.

They had almost reached the trees when the storm began to unleash its fury. The wind rushed this way and that, lurching like a drunken man, and suddenly the storm front hit and the wind drove straight into the ground. Hail began to slash through the skies, huge balls as big as a child's fist. Women screamed and old men cried out in pain.

Ahead, the emir took the war shield from his back and raced to a young mother who ran in a crouch, trying to shelter her infant son from the hail. The emir held up his shield and ran beside her, protecting them the best that he could, while hail pummeled down.

Talon raced to the mother's other side, and walked with her between, all of them huddling beneath one shield, protecting the mother and child.

All around, every warrior in the clan did the same.

Beside Talon, an old man took a hail ball to the back of the head and then dropped like a stone, a streak of blood running through his silver hair. 'Do you need help?' Talon cried, but the old man did not answer. Hail balls slashed from the sky like iron shot from a trebuchet, and Talon realized that in moments the man might be dead, if left here alone.

The emir gave his shield to Talon, and cried, 'Get the babe to shelter!'

Then, mindless of the danger to himself, he stopped and began to drag the old man as best he could. War dogs swarmed around the emir curiously, sniffing at blood, looking fierce with their blood-red leather masks and spiked collars. The dogs sniffed at the old man, but a few hailstones convinced them to abandon him and race for shelter in the trees.

'Hurry!' the emir cried to the refugees who scurried past him, but the refugees were already running as fast as they could.

Talon jogged forward with the shield held high, sheltering the mother.

Up ahead, the first of the warriors reached the tree line and raced under the branches, leading in the women and children, then sprinted back with shields held high to gather other refugees.

Lightning boomed and the earth shook. Rain began to fall among the hail, slashing like knives.

Balls of frozen ice struck Talon in the back, and one shattered against her shoulder. She cursed at the pain and ushered her charge under the trees, panting and wet.

Under the pines, it was as dark as night and as still as a tomb. The smell of leaf mold was overwhelming, and huge yellow mushrooms, like misshapen heads, dotted the forest floor.

Talon turned to see if anyone else needed her help, and saw hundreds of men of the war clan bringing people in, including ten dozen folk that had to be dragged or carried.

The emir carried the old man under the pine and laid him down on a soft bed of pine needles. Then he grabbed the shield from Talon and raced back out into the storm.

The Wizard Sisel had the poor folks laid just beneath the great pine, and there he bent over the injured, treating them as best he could.

In green robes that looked more like roots that had grown together than any cloth spun by human hands, the wizard looked like some strange fungus.

Racing out into the storm, the emir found a child, a young

boy crying and bloodied from hail, and raised his shield above the lad and brought him in.

By the time he returned, nearly everyone was under the shelter of the tree. Dozens lay on beds of fir needles, dead.

Talon stood with her mouth agape, amazed to see that even a couple of minutes in a summer storm here could be so devastating.

She knelt beside the emir and studied the young boy. He was still breathing fine, but the child stared at the dead in shock. The emir spoke to him, gently calling out, until the boy was able to focus once again. But still the boy sat in a daze.

'Where is your mother, boy?' the emir asked. The child looked to be no more than six or seven years old. He had curly blond hair, and deep brown eyes. He had the strong features of one of the warrior caste.

'Gone,' the child said, eyes growing wide.

'Gone where?'

'I don't know. She's been gone for two days. My da went off to fight the wyrmlings, and he didn't come back either.'

Talon considered. The child's mother must have disappeared when the worlds were bound. If she had merged with her shadow self, there was no telling how many hundreds or thousands of miles away she might be. At this very moment, she was probably teary-eyed and desperate to get home.

Like my own father, she told herself. Sir Borenson would be desperate to reach her.

As for the boy's father? Well, there were plenty of corpses along the outer walls of Caer Luciare.

'Tell you what,' the emir offered. 'I'll be your big brother for a while. I can take care of you. Are you hungry?'

The child knew better than to talk to strangers. He hesitated for a long moment, then admitted that he was hungry. The emir offered him some cheese from his pack.

The Wizard Sisel came to their aid, stood over the child for a moment, then reached into the pocket of his robe and pulled

out a handful of moss, which he used as a compress to stop
the boy's bleeding.

In the gloom under the trees, Daylan raced ahead, calling,
'Quickly now! Quickly – everyone into the cave!'

Talon could see nothing ahead but blackness, no sign of a
cave. Still, she got up and followed the sound of moving feet,
until suddenly a brilliant light shone out up ahead.

Up on the hill, between the boles of two vast pine trees,
Daylan stood holding a star in his hand. Its brilliant light cut
through the shadows, revealing a sanctum here among the
woods.

He stood beside the boles of twin pines that seemed almost
to grow out of the same root. Each bole was hundreds of feet
in diameter. Carved into each tree was the face of a man, with
solemn eyes and a serene expression. Leaves of oak stood in
place of his hair and beard.

It was an ancient symbol, and feared among the folk of
Luciare. But on Talon's world it was a welcome sign. It was
the face of the Wode King.

The carved faces on each bole seemed to peer inward, and
each hovered above Daylan, dwarfing him, for each of the
images was sixty feet tall.

But the Wode King did not seem frightening on this world.
Instead, Talon felt comforted by the images, as if they exuded
an aura of tranquility.

Daylan pushed on an outcropping of jagged gray stone, and
suddenly a hidden door swung in, revealing a large round
hole, like a burrow, tall enough for a man to walk through.

Daylan stood at the door, shouting, 'Quickly! Get inside. It
is safe in here, for the time being. And you don't want to be
caught out in the dark.'

Talon did not know what might be found in the night.
Strengi-saats, Darkling Glories. Those creatures she had heard
of. But Daylan spoke in terror, as if worse things might prowl
the edges of these meadows.

But no one moved forward, for the tunnel ahead was dark.

'What is this place?' the Emir Tuul Ra asked.

He peered into the hole cautiously, his daughter Siyaddah at his back.

'It's a sanctuary,' Daylan said, 'long abandoned. Once it housed many folk, and was a joyous place. It should be large enough to shelter the whole company. There is fresh water below, fed by underground streams. You may bathe there, and drink. You will find it quite pleasant. Make yourselves comfortable—

'But first, send some warriors down if you must. I suppose that it would be wise to make sure that nothing . . . *unpleasant* has found its way in.'

At that, bark suddenly stripped from the trees and three men appeared from the shadows at Daylan's back, striding into view. Their skin and faces were bark for a second, but smoothed in the space of a heartbeat, as if they were trees turning into people.

Each of them was perfect in his way. One man had hair of yellow as gold as sunlight, and another had hair of red, while the third had long tresses of hair like spun silver. They were of different heights and builds, yet each was handsome beyond words, and each stood boldly, eyes shining as with inner wisdom. Each of the men bore a staff of golden wood, and they stood, barring the entrance.

Bright Ones, Talon realized. These were perfect men.

One of them spoke in a strange tongue, and the words smote Talon, for they seemed to penetrate her mind, and she understood him as if he spoke her own tongue.

'Daylan Hammer,' the tallest of the three said, a man with long silvery locks who wore a doublet in colors hard to define – gray as charcoal, it seemed, but it flashed green when he moved. 'What have you done?'

Daylan turned to the three. 'So, the sanctuary is not as empty as I had hoped.'

A Bright One said, 'Daylan, you were banished from our world. It is only out of respect for what you once were that I do not destroy you now!'

Daylan said, 'My life is mine to keep or spend. You cannot take it from me, Lord Erringale.'

Erringale, the leader, was a man of stern features. He looked to be elderly, but in an indefinable way. His body seemed young and strong, as if he were only in his mid-forties, but his face was lined with care and creased with worried wrinkles, so that he looked as if he might be sixty or even seventy. But it was his eyes that revealed his true age. There was a wisdom in them that was vast and indeterminable, and there was the sadness in them that can only come from someone who has seen far, far too much death.

He isn't forty or fifty or even sixty, Talon thought. He is millions of years old.

Daylan had warned them that there were folk in the netherworld of vast powers, strange and dangerous powers.

She somehow knew that Erringale was one of these. There was too much light in his eyes, just as there was too much light in Fallion's eyes. And he seemed to shimmer when he walked. Bright Ones. Truly he was a Bright One.

Erringale strode forward, peered down at Daylan. 'You defy us! It is forbidden to bring even one shadow soul to our world, yet you bring a host?'

'I bring allies,' Daylan said, 'in the fight against our common foe.'

'You bring women and children,' Erringale said, 'who will cry for protection. You bring men so imperfect that they cannot even withstand a summer storm.'

'They are good people,' Daylan argued. 'And though they may appear weak and imperfect to you, they are strong and brave. More importantly, they are in need. Have you no compassion? Our ancient enemy has taken their world, and they need a place to hide – not for long, a few days at most. Should you deny them that privilege our enemies would rejoice.'

'The stink of evil is upon them,' Lord Erringale said. 'We cannot hide them from the enemy. Despair will sense their presence.'

'They are young,' Daylan said. 'They are not truly evil, but only suffer the flaws of youth. The oldest of them has not lived a hundred years. It takes time to ripen in virtue, to purge one's self of all selfish thoughts and desires. Ten thousand years is hardly enough. How can such . . . children be expected to perfect themselves?'

The Bright Ones peered down at Daylan Hammer doubting his arguments. 'There is great darkness among them,' Erringale said. 'I feel it. You must sense it, too. Take them home.'

Daylan stood his ground. 'I will not. There is much at stake here, more than you know. You by your traditions say that this is the One True World – that all others are but shadows, cast off from it when the Great Seals were broken. You say that these folk are shadow souls. But I tell you that they are not. All worlds contain bits of truth to them, some bits that you have lost. In ways, some worlds are truer than this. . . .'

'You have made this argument before,' Lord Erringale said, 'to no avail.'

'I make this argument because I have proof. Our enemy knows that it is true also, and that is why she has made her home upon these people's world.'

Erringale's pale green eyes flickered to his companions, as if they spoke with a look, faster than thought. The three seemed inclined to listen a moment longer.

'There is more,' Daylan said. 'The Torch-bearer knows that it is true, for he too has been reborn upon their world *and I have news of great significance*. At long last, the Torch-bearer has bound two worlds together.'

There were gasps from the Bright Ones. Erringale took a step backward in shock.

'Yes,' Daylan said. 'You always thought that he would be here when he did it, that he would bind our world to some lesser shadow. But he has bound two worlds together, two worlds rife with power. The binding was flawed, it is true. People died. But he bound two worlds nonetheless. Great magics are at work in these lands, and the enemy has mastered them.

'To our woe, the Torch-bearer has been captured and is now in Despair's hands. He has not had time to fully awaken to his past lives, and so he may not know how to defend himself.

He does not know the vast resources of his enemy. Thus Despair hopes to twist him to its purposes.'

'He bound two worlds together,' Erringale asked, 'without the aid of the True Tree? This cannot be.'

Talon called out, for she had been present with Fallion Orden when he bound the worlds. 'He stood beneath the True Tree when he bound the worlds.'

Even Daylan Hammer seemed astonished by this news.

'How can you be sure that it was the Tree?' Erringale asked.

'It was like an oak,' Talon replied, 'but one of unspeakable beauty. It had bark of gold, and an earthy scent, and it spoke peace to our minds and urged us to be strong, to be gentle and compassionate and perfect in all things!

'I have a leaf from it here in my pack,' she recalled. She had picked it up from the ground as a souvenir.

Talon unloaded her pack, then rummaged through it a moment before pulling out a single golden leaf. She rushed up to the three Bright Ones, held it up to their view.

Of all that had been said, this impressed the Bright Ones most. Talon saw their lips trembling and eyes glistening with tears. With great tenderness and respect, the eldest of the bunch took the leaf from her and held it gingerly in his palm, as if it were a treasure beyond words to tell.

'The True Tree has sprung forth,' Erringale said, 'upon a *shadow* world?'

The Wizard Sisel cried out, 'That is a thing I would like to see!'

Daylan exulted. 'There was an Earth King there not long ago. How long has it been since one has walked upon this world? There is rune lore at work there, and the True Tree. The Torch-bearer practices his magics there, and Lord Despair has resorted thither. For countless ages we have waited for the days foretold by the Bright Ones when the True Tree would grow again. Surely the Restoration is upon us! Surely the days long foretold are coming to pass.

'We have brought gifts of blood metal, and with them we can create an army of Ael, as in times of old. We must join

forces with our brethren from the shadow worlds and fight –
not for *your* world or *their* world, but for all worlds!'

Lord Erringale was obviously moved by Daylan's words. He
seemed cautious, as if he feared to believe in the long-hoped-
for news. He cast a gaze off into the distance, as if listening
to a far-off voice. 'We must call a council, and your tale will
be heard. Enter,' Erringale said. 'Enter as friends. We have little
in way of food and supplies, and so cannot hope to entertain
you as we should. But what we have, we will share.'

Suddenly the hallway behind him began to glow with a
silvery light, beckoning the people to sanctuary.

7

SISTERS

A great leader commands through fear, but at times you may find that it is best to cooperate with others as equals. It is the job of the statesman to inspire greed in others, so that two parties share a common hope for reward.

—From the Wyrmling Catechism

An arrow whisked past Rhianna's neck with a stinging sound. From the horse-sisters' camp down below came cries of alarm, followed by the bleat of a war horn. The horse-sisters' silken pavilions glowed like gems in the early evening, each lit from inside by bright lanterns, each a different hue – ruby, emerald, sapphire, diamond, and tourmaline.

Warriors boiled from the pavilions, pointing up at Rhianna in the air, and many grabbed their steel war bows, short and broad of wing, and began to let arrows fly.

Some raced to the campfires, lighting arrows and then sending them aloft so that the archers might better see their target. One went soaring just beneath Rhianna.

I'd hoped for a warm welcome, she thought, but not *that* warm.

Other women ran to care for the horses, which were tied outside of camp.

Rhianna flapped madly, rising in the air, to get out of archery range. It seemed the horse-sisters loved her as little as the warlords of Internook had.

The journey from the Courts of Tide had taken nearly all of the evening and part of the night, but it turned out to be easier than Rhianna had imagined. During the day, she had been fighting a slight headwind. But tonight she had a strong following wind, and warm thermals had flowed up from the ground, keeping her aloft. More important, though, she had been driven by great need, and so had denied herself any rest. Thus she had made four hundred miles in only eight hours.

'Sisters,' Rhianna cried. 'I come in the name of Clan Connal, and I come in peace!'

Perhaps she was too high above them. Perhaps none heard. They certainly could not see her well in the darkness, and the din of war horns and the cries of alarm only grew louder.

Rhianna wheeled above the horses the sisters had, and noticed something strange – hundreds of red blood mounts, a strain of horse bred for its powerful night vision. They were common in Inkarra, but when Rhianna had lived here as a child, they'd been so rare that they were almost a myth.

Added to that was another mystery – these horse-sisters were far from home, hundreds of miles east of where they should have been.

Reaching into a pouch at her belt, she grabbed a single forcible, and flapped higher into the air, well out of bow range.

When Rhianna was soaring just above their campfires, she let the forcible drop.

The magical branding iron was not a heavy thing – less than an ounce in weight – and it would probably not hurt someone if it hit them. Her greatest concern was that they would not see it.

The forcible landed in the dirt, and in the darkness Rhianna could not see where it had fallen, but one of the horse-sisters must have heard, for a bow-woman reached down, picked it up, and began to shout excitedly, 'Hold your fire! Hold!'

It took a moment for the sisters to calm themselves, and Rhianna merely circled patiently as the camp quieted. 'I come in the name of Clan Connal,' she cried. 'I come in peace. I have forcibles to trade, if you want them.'

The women raised a cheer, and dozens of them backed away from the fire, giving her a clear landing site.

Rhianna plummeted from the sky, and then beat her wings hastily as she neared ground. She felt thankful that in the end, her landing was not as clumsy as most.

The horse-sisters peered at her in wonder. 'I was born to Clan Connal,' Rhianna said. 'I am Rhianna Connal, daughter of Erin.'

The leader of the horse-sisters stepped forward, a woman in lacquered leather mail, with a small round ornate helm, crusted with precious stones along the brim. Her long red hair flowed loose at the back, and she bore a red lance – the symbol of her ascendancy in the clan.

'I knew a Rhianna Connal as a child,' she said suspiciously. 'But she did not have wings.'

Rhianna wondered how to explain her wings. If the horse-sisters knew that they were a magical artifact, that they could be removed only after Rhianna's death, it might invite someone to hasten her demise. But these were horse-sisters, not some brutish warlords from Internook.

'Much has changed with the binding of the worlds,' Rhianna said, offering the first evasion that came to mind.

There were grunts of assent from the women. 'Yes,' their leader said. 'Our lands were once vast plains fit only for horses. Now shaggy elephants range here in great herds, and the grass is going bad. There is a blight upon the land. There are mountains and canyons where there should be none, and there are giants in the land. Do you know the cause of these things?'

Rhianna nodded. 'The Earth King's son, Fallion Orden, is a flameweaver of great power. He tried to bind the worlds into one, to create a better one. But you see the results.

'I've come to bring you warning. The world has changed. There is a great evil to the east, wyrmling warriors, giants with pale white skin. They pose a threat unlike any that the world has known.'

The women muttered, and many of them looked as if they would run to their horses, prepare for battle.

'We have already met their like,' one of the horse-sisters said.

'But not all of my news is ill,' Rhianna said. 'There is blood metal in this new land, enough to make the horse-sisters of Fleeds the mightiest nation on Earth!'

The horse-sisters cheered, and Rhianna saw toddlers at the edge of the tents leaping for joy, though they did not understand the cause of the celebration. She knew from that alone that she had them.

The generosity of the horse-sisters exceeded anything that Rhianna could have imagined.

She had hoped for a decent meal. Instead they brought her a feast of sweet lamb, delicately spiced and cooked on skewers, followed by summer melons, hearty brown bread, and a pudding made from horse milk, sweetened with honey and cumin.

She had hoped for a trough to wash in. The horse-sisters brought her warmed rose water, and young women made a game of bathing her.

She had hoped for a piece of safe ground to lie on. They offered her silken pillows in their tent.

Well had Thull-turock spoken when he had told Rhianna that though Fallion Orden had no friends in the world, 'You should be able to buy the friends you want with those forcibles.'

It was nearly dawn when the feasting was done and the festivities finished. Many of the clan had gone to bed, but others lingered beside the campfire as Rhianna told her tale – beginning with her birth, her mother's flight from the dungeons of Crowthen, and Rhianna's betrayal and capture by her father. She told of her flight beyond the Ends of the Earth in order to escape the assassins that hounded Fallion, and she told of his return to Mystarria, the binding of the worlds, and his battle with the wyrmlings and his capture by the Knights Eternal.

To Rhianna her own tale sounded like something from an ancient fable, not the life that she had lived. But she had her proofs – the wings that she wore, the scar from the forcible when she was forced to give an endowment of wit to a sea ape.

Clan Connal was well known here. Erin's grandmother had been a queen, and though the horse-sisters formed a matriarchal society, their royal station was not inherited. Instead a leader was chosen every generation based upon merit alone. So though Erin had no special rights as an heir, her lineage was held in high esteem.

The current leader, Sister Daughtry, listened to Rhianna's wild tale, ending at last with her quest to raise aid from the warlords of Internook, beastly and ravenous men who would not stir themselves to save the Earth King's heir. So Rhianna had come home, seeking aid.

'You chose wisely,' Sister Daughtry said at last. 'The warlords of Internook have the hearts of swine – more than most men. They are not to be trusted.' She glanced patronizingly toward her own lover, a tall man in fine livery who stood guard just outside the fire.

'Some men can be trusted,' Rhianna countered. 'The Earth King could be trusted, as can his son Fallion.'

'The Earth King was more than a man,' Sister Daughtry said. 'He was a force of nature – as steady and reliable as the sun, rounding in its course.' She looked penetratingly at Rhianna. 'You love this Fallion Orden, don't you?'

'More than I can say. More than you will ever know.'

'Love him then,' Sister Daughtry warned, 'but do not trust him completely. He is a man, like all others, subject to an inborn urge for conquest and domination, but with too little in the way of wisdom or compassion.'

'Men are not alone in having a grasping nature,' Rhianna argued gently.

'Still,' Sister Daughtry countered, 'your Fallion may have good intentions, but look at the harm he has wrought.'

Rhianna could not help but notice how she referred to

Fallion as *your Fallion*, as if Rhianna had already put a bridle on him, claiming him as her own.

If only life were so easy, she thought. But Fallion was not from the horse clans. He would not have accepted such a gesture on her part, and she doubted that she would ever share his love. He was a noble, and thus would save himself for a royal match with a woman of similar birth. He had made that clear to her before. No matter what his feelings for her, too much was at stake.

Sister Daughtry reached down to the fire where a pot of warm water was brewing, and poured some into a clay mug. A serving man stepped forward and dropped in a twisted brown vanilla bean and a couple of leaves rolled into a pearl. Sister Daughtry gave the goblet to Rhianna, and she held it for a moment, letting the flavors mix. It seemed a lifetime ago since she had tasted plains tea.

Overhead was a sea of stars drifting among gauzy clouds. The moon was in full retreat tonight, and did not favor them with even the smallest sickle. Out on the prairie, a hunting cat roared, and out at the pickets, some horses nickered in fear.

'You have blood mounts in your herd,' Rhianna said, still surprised at this strange turn.

'The Earth King warned us to bring them into our herds a decade ago, even as he died. He warned the folk of Carris to flee, too, and for a decade we have wondered why. Now, with the great change, the reavers have emerged from the Underworld again. Our scouts say that a host of them is heading north.'

'Reavers?' Rhianna said. It was a word that struck dread in her heart. She reasoned, 'With the earthquakes and shifts in landscape, it only makes sense that the reavers would be riled.'

'Take a hornets' nest, shake it up, and beat it with a stick – and you will get some idea of how our reavers feel. My scouts say that not a stone of the city is left standing – not that there is any harm. The whole region has become infested with strengi-saats, and is as bare of meat as a well-chewed bone. Now the reavers are stirred up, and may be coming this way.'

Rhianna consulted a mental map. If the reavers were heading from the southeast to the northwest, they could easily miss the camp by miles. 'With any luck, they'll bypass you and march right into the wyrmlings' fortress at Rugassa.'

'One can only hope,' Sister Daughtry said. 'It wouldn't hurt if these reavers were to club a few wyrmlings for us.'

Rhianna wondered. Could Gaborn have been preparing the horse-sisters to battle the wyrmlings by having them buy mounts? Could he have really sensed the danger to Carris so many years ago?

She couldn't imagine that.

And yet . . . it made perfect sense. The horse-sisters were renowned for their ability to fight on horseback, with either the lance or the bow. They would need blood mounts with perfect night vision if they were to defeat the wyrmling horde.

Of course, one could not discount Carris and Gaborn's warning to evacuate.

I was so wrong about Gaborn, Rhianna thought. He died years ago, but he has not left us.

The very thought gave Rhianna a thrill of hope.

I was right to come here, she thought. The Earth King is still with us, and watching over us as best he can. He trusts the horse-sisters, and so can I.

'You are far out of your own territories,' Rhianna said. 'Aren't these Lowicker's lands?'

'There was a prairie fire this summer,' Sister Daughtry explained. 'It burned much of our lands. Beldinook sold us grazing rights for the fall – at the cost of much gold.'

Rhianna wondered at this. Relations had not been so friendly between the two countries a decade ago. But perhaps they were not friendly now, either. There was an edge to Sister Daughtry's voice, a tone of anger or outrage.

Rhianna felt sure that there was more to the story, but Sister Daughtry changed the subject. 'These giants that you warned us of, the wyrmlings. Should we kill them on sight, or can we reason with them?'

'Not all wyrmlings are evil,' Rhianna suggested. 'I saw defectors at Caer Luciare – spies that worked for High King Urstone. But I do not know if you will be able to speak to them, for their tongue is strange, a combination of grunts and barks and growls.'

There was a long moment of silence as Sister Daughtry thought.

'So, will you help Fallion, then?' Rhianna pressed.

'You spoke of a trade,' Sister Daughtry said. 'Is this the coin you want in return for forcibles – the rescue of your mate?'

'It is in part,' Rhianna said. 'I offer you a great treasure, but in making the offer, I ask that you act responsibly. The whole world will have need of forcibles – not just the horse-sisters, but all of the world, including the kingdoms of men.

'The horse-sisters have not been treated well in the past. Your people were once the poorest of all, at least when wealth is measured in forcibles. But soon you may be the richest. I know where a vast treasure lies, and I will lead the way to it, but I do so in fear and trembling at the thought of what may follow. I would ask that you not take vengeance for ancient wrongs, but share your power with what decent men you can find.'

'Spoken like a true leader,' Daughtry said. 'You never met your grandmother, but I think that she would have been proud.' She sighed deeply. 'I will honor your wishes. Lead us to this mountain of blood metal, and we will free your lover. And we will share this treasure with the good men of the world.'

Rhianna smiled wryly, and tested her. 'Do you think there are any good men left in the world?'

Sister Daughtry reached down and picked up a stick, poked the stump of a burning log, moved it deeper into the embers.

'The Knights Equitable are all gone,' Daughtry said. 'They were good men, for the most part. But the Brotherhood of the Wolf remains. Though the warlords of Internook may hold our world by the throat, it is rumored that good men still fight them in secret, as best they can. Scoundrels among the warlords, the worst of them, often end up murdered, their throats slit as they lie in drunken stupors, or they find themselves ambushed while off on one of their little jaunts a-whoring. It is only because of the Brotherhood that the thugs from Internook show any restraint at all. I suppose that it is time for the horse-sisters to join their cause.'

Rhianna considered her words. The Brotherhood of the Wolf had been formed under Gaborn's patronage, and had been a powerful force for good ten years back. It seemed that once again the Earth King was watching over them.

Good omens all.

So she reached across the fire to shake, clasping hands at the wrist, and thus sealed the bargain.

'A force of heroes is gathering,' Rhianna said, 'preparing to breach the wyrmling stronghold in order to free Fallion Orden, along with Prince Areth Sul Urstone. They may need your help. They may need Dedicates.'

'We can find Dedicates,' Sister Daughtry said. 'But I ask one thing in return – parity. If we are to empower men, we must also empower our women to the same extent. I demand that a horse-sister be allowed to join this company of heroes. She should be granted great power.'

Rhianna bit her lip. It was obvious what Daughtry wanted – her own set of endowments.

'I trust that the horse-sisters have chosen wisely,' Rhianna said. 'Your skills in battle along with your wisdom have earned your people's trust – and mine. Go with the rescue party. Lead it if you like. I would give you my own endowment, if I could.'

But of course, Rhianna had granted an endowment when she was young, and thus could never do so again. Even the most talented facilitator could not draw a second attribute from a Dedicate.

The knowledge saddened Rhianna, for she desperately wanted to help.

Sister Daughtry smiled. 'Oh, I was not asking for me. I'm

thinking that *you* should be the horse-sister to go. Don't you agree?'

Rhianna was stunned. She had imagined that if she made this bargain, the forcibles would be granted to some powerful lord, skilled in war, hungry for power. She never imagined that she would be granted so much as a single endowment. 'I, uh, why me?'

'Because your motives are pure,' Daughtry said. 'You want the power only to save the man you love, and to fight our common enemy. You yourself fear that these forcibles will fall into the wrong hands. Having lived a lifetime of pain and torment, you have become acquainted with unwarranted suffering. You know how much evil this power brings, and you will guard your heart against it.'

Rhianna suspected that Daughtry was right, but Rhianna also doubted her own heart.

'You fear to take them?' Sister Daughtry asked.

'With power comes pride, and with pride comes a sense of entitlement,' Rhianna said, recalling something that her mother said. 'And from a sense of entitlement, many evils are born.'

Sister Daughtry smiled, peered both at Rhianna and through her. 'Yes, I think I have chosen well.'

She changed the subject. 'And now, about this mountain of wyrmling treasure . . .'

To the best of her ability, Rhianna sketched a rough map on the ground. She knew that the fortress of Rugassa was three hundred miles north of Caer Luciare, and suspected that the fortress was close to a hundred miles from where they now stood.

'It will be a long ride to that mountain of yours,' Sister Daughtry said. 'If the wyrmlings are mining the metal, they will have begun taking endowments.'

'Perhaps not,' Rhianna said. 'The wyrmling lords are still in Rugassa. I suspect that they will want it first. Being voracious creatures, they will not want to share with their underlings. That means that the wyrmling soldiers will have to send the blood metal north. They will pull it in large handcarts. They are powerful men, and tend to march a hundred miles per night.'

'It has been only a night since your battle at Caer Luciare,' Sister Daughtry said. 'That means . . .'

'The wyrmlings should be delivering their first shipment in two days at dawn.'

'The wyrmlings must never see a single forcible,' Sister Daughtry said, her face hardening. 'We should head south, try to cut them off near Caer Luciare, where they will be far from help. But two hundred miles is a far ride. The horse-sisters will never be able to reach the wyrmlings in two nights.'

Now Rhianna brought out the rest of her treasure, opening her pouch and spilling two hundred blank forcibles onto it. 'You can make it if you have force horses to ride.'

8

EARTH'S SPIRIT RISING

Time is a thief that steals our memories. With each passing day they recede from us, and more has been forgotten than shall ever be known.

There is no lock that can hold against Time.

It is only when a great wyrm seizes us that we find ourselves with a worthy guardian, one that can withstand the onslaught of Time.

—From the Wyrmling Catechism

The Sanctum had long been used for worship among the wyrmling hordes. A small oval dais of gray agate lay on the floor, with golden filigree forming the three-pointed star upon the ground, where orators could address the lords of the wyrmling horde. Seats made of polished cedar climbed in rows above the dais.

Behind the dais, against the back wall stood an onyx statue of a woman – not a wyrmling woman with a bony ridge on her brow and oversized canines – but a Bright One, a woman flawless and perfect, who stood with her back straight and her angry face glaring down at the ground, as if wrenching away from the audience in disgust.

Her hands stretched down, her fingers pointed to the earth, every finger rigid.

Many a lord had wondered at the statue. It was supposed

to represent the Great Wyrm, and so they imagined that it should be a world wyrm that stood carved there. But Despair had inspired the artist. It was a statue of Yaleen – at the moment that she turned away from the world in horror and bitterness.

Now, in the theater, Lord Despair awaited the chance to take endowments. Humans had been brought into the amphitheater – small folk captured from a nearby castle. Dozens of them huddled in groups, fathers giving comfort to their wives. Young girls weeping. Children with eyes round from fright.

Some had been wounded in the battle. One boy had blood running down his neck where an ear had been ripped off.

But most were whole and healthy, ready to be harvested.

Despair gauged the worth of each.

His eyes fastened upon a boy of five, one with piercing blue eyes. He had a wholesome look to him, and soulful.

He pointed to a guard. 'Bring me that child.'

The guard waded in among the small folk and plucked the boy from the crowd. His mother shrieked and tried to hang on to the boy, but the guard shoved her back. The men called out for mercy, and some looked as if they would fight. Their shouts became a riot of noise in the background.

The guard brought the child to Lord Despair and sat him on Despair's lap. The boy trembled and struggled to leave.

'Sit,' Despair said in a voice that brooked no argument.

The boy sat, shaking in terror.

'Look at me,' Despair said. 'Do not look away.' The boy complied, and Despair reached up with one finger and ran it along the ridge of the boy's cheek. He had a strong cheek, a strong nose, and curly blond hair that fell to his shoulders.

'You are a handsome lad,' Despair said. 'Did you know that?'

The boy bit his lower lip, nodded.

'I'm sure that you do,' Despair said. 'Your mother tells you this all of the time, doesn't she? She tells you every day?'

The boy nodded again.

'You love your mother, don't you?'

Fear shone in the boy's face.

Despair nodded toward the nearest wyrmling soldiers, who made up a wall of flesh that stood between him and the crowd. 'You see those wyrmlings, those monsters? They want to hurt your mother. They want to take her away from you.'

'No!' the boy pleaded.

'No, I don't want them to do that either,' Despair said. 'It would be frightening for you I think, and it would break your mother's heart.'

Despair peered into the child, using his newfound gift of Earth Sight. He could see the child's hopes and fears, his deepest longings.

He was a good child, smart and honest. He would grow to be the kind of man that others trusted someday, a leader. He would be the kind of man who could win people's hearts.

A mayor, perhaps, Lord Despair thought, or maybe he'd become the master of some guild.

As he peered into the child's heart, Despair felt a soft mental nudge.

'Choose the seeds of mankind,' the Earth Spirit whispered. 'You must save some through the dark times to come.'

The nudge was soft, insistent.

But Despair had a better use for the child. 'You love your mother,' he whispered, 'I can see that. I can speak to the wyrmling guards for her. I can make it so that you can stay with your mother. I can make sure that no one hurts her. But if I am to help you, you must give me something in return.'

Despair did not need Earth Powers to see how much the child wanted that. The boy grasped Despair's sleeve in the attitude of a beggar. 'What do you want? I'll give you anything.' The boy fished in the pocket of his tunic, and brought out a boar's tusk – obviously a prized possession.

'No,' Despair said, pushing it away. 'I need something else. I want your beauty. I want to be every bit as handsome as you.'

The boy thought for a moment, unsure what was being asked of him. Then he nodded.

The boy didn't need to know how his glamour was to be taken. He didn't need to know how much it would hurt, or how he might regret it in coming years. All that the boy needed to do was give it with a willing heart.

'All right, then,' he said, gathering his courage.

'Fine,' Lord Despair said. 'Let's go in the other room for a moment, so that you can give it to me, and then I'll take you back to your mother.'

That night Lord Despair, Master of all Rugassa, slept on the stone floor in his chamber, eschewing the tiny cot that made up his bed. Perhaps it was only habit that made him long for the floor. Lord Despair had not yet completely subdued Areth's soul, and found himself reacting at times as Areth might. After long years in the dungeon, Areth felt more at ease upon the stone floor than on a bed. Somehow, the closeness of the stone also succored him. Its earthy scent filled his nostrils as he lay so close.

And so the two, enjoined at the spirit, slept on the floor.

It had been a good night's work. Despair had managed to take several endowments – nine of glamour, four of voice, two of brawn, three of grace, two of wit, one of sight, one of stamina, two of hearing, and two of metabolism.

In doing so, he had become more than human, and when further forcibles arrived, he would become the greatest of all. So he slept peacefully.

In his sleep, Lord Despair dreamed. . . .

A storm was coming. The skies had grown dark on the horizon as clouds rushed in, the sickly greenish blue that portended a hurricane. Lightning flickered at the crown of the storm, sending booms that faintly rattled the bones, and the wind suddenly gusted and screamed in far places. The acrid tang of dust, blown in the wind, permeated everything, and beneath that lay the heavy scent of water.

He was standing on the parapet outside his bedroom, open to the sky, gripping the rails to the parapet. Enormous stone gargoyles flanked each side of him, long-toothed hunting cats of the plains, sculpted from yellow jasper. The wind blustered through his hair, and his cape billowed behind him.

He peered down into the walls of his keep and saw tens of thousands of people of all kinds, wyrmling and small folk, and even humans from Caer Luciare – he espied children with sticks doing mock combat in the streets under the stars, women hanging washing out to dry, men singing as they split logs for beams to fortify the tunnels – all of them innocently going about their affairs.

A boom sounded, startling him, and shook the stone floor of the parapet. The whole tower rocked from it, and he saw bits of stone dust flake away from the gargoyles and go drifting down, down, hundreds of feet.

The people below did not react to the thunder. They continued to go about their affairs, unaware that a storm was brewing – nay, not a storm, Despair decided, a hurricane, the kind of monster that comes only once in ten thousand years.

Lord Despair could feel the threat of it. The wind would lift children from their feet and hurl them about like leaves. The rain would fall in a deluge, and those caught within it would be swept away in floods.

In his dream, the voice of the Earth whispered, the voice of a young woman, as his eyes were held riveted upon the wyrmling horde. 'The End of Time is coming. Behold your brothers and sisters, eating and breeding and toiling. You have been granted the power to save them, as was done with your fore-bearers. There are so many to choose from. Look upon them, and choose.'

Lord Despair could not turn away. He peered down at a small boy sweeping a wagon that the teamsters had unloaded, and he felt such compassion for the child that his heart nearly broke. He wanted to shout a warning, but he was too far away to do so.

'Choose,' the Earth whispered, and Despair recognized the woman's voice. Lord Despair whirled, and saw a young woman, graceful and beautiful to look upon. Her name was Yaleen. She was made of pebbles and stones and soil and crushed leaves, as if the humus from a garden had taken human form. Yet she was as beautiful as if she had been freshly sculpted from flesh.

In all of the millennia of existence, Despair had never felt such awesome power as this woman exuded. There was such profound love in her voice, such compassion. She was trying to bend Despair to her will.

'Who are you,' Despair demanded. 'What are you?'

Upon many worlds, of course, Despair had seen the tribes of men worship the Earth. Some thought it was only nature, some called it a god or an impersonal force. And upon all of the millions of millions of shadow worlds, no one really knew what it was that they worshipped.

Personally, Despair suspected that it was the spirit of some great wizard – a wizard whose powers had split when the One True World shattered. But it might also have been some innate force within that One True World itself, a force that was constantly seeking to heal the broken worlds, to bind them back into one.

Few were the mortals who had ever seen the Earth Spirit. But now, the creature showed itself to Despair.

'How can you have lived so long,' the Earth whispered, 'and still not know me? I have not hidden myself from you. I make myself manifest in every breath of wind, and in every cool sip of water. I am the dark between the stars, and rocks beneath your feet. I am love and war and all righteous longing. I am the grass on the hillside and the lion in its den.'

'You seek to bend me to your will,' Lord Despair accused.

'As you seek to bend me to yours,' Earth replied, 'even though you swore to be my ally.'

Lord Despair was about to object, but he could feel a small presence in his skull, tiptoeing around. It was the consciousness of Areth Sul Urstone, the remnants of what he had been, still struggling desperately to regain dominance. Lord Despair had been aware of him. It was not uncommon. Despair was a parasite, vast and bloated. He had seized the young man's body, and in time the soul would weaken and die, and that feeling of being watched would leave.

It was Areth, of course, who had sworn vows to protect the Earth. And now, the Earth peered at Lord Despair, and she did not focus her eyes upon him, but past him, as if speaking directly to Areth.

'You swore to save the seeds of mankind through the dark time to come. Remember your vows, little one.'

Yaleen stepped forward, reached down to the ground, and picked up a pinch of soil, then stood and threw it. Lord Despair tried to duck away, but some soil struck him between the eyes. 'The Earth hide you,' she whispered, 'the Earth heal you. The Earth make you its own.'

Suddenly, in his mind, Areth reared up and tried to seize control.

Areth tried to raise his left hand to the square.

'Choose some of those people,' the Earth urged. 'Certainly some are worthy of life? Look into their hearts. Search their dreams, and sift through hidden ambitions that even they do not know of. Peer into their pasts, and learn their loves and fears. Choose who shall survive the coming storm. Choose who will build the new world.'

Areth wrenched his neck and peered down over the parapet. There were so many people. They were so far away. They were like ants. He couldn't see their faces.

With a scream of anguish, Lord Despair roared and brought his hands down, clutching the edge of the parapet.

He woke and lay for a moment, beads of sweat upon his brow. Lord Despair gasped, the earthy dust of the floor filling his lungs.

Sweat stood out on his brow and on his upper lip, and his heart beat irregularly. In his dream, he had loved his people so much.

But Lord Despair loved no one. He fought back, tried to push the memory of it from his mind.

'My spirit shall not always strive with you,' Yaleen's voice seemed to whisper deep inside. 'You have not chosen wisely. Use the power I have given you, or it shall be bestowed upon another.'

For eons Despair had wished to possess the body of an Earth King, and at last had found the opportunity.

But now he saw that with the power came a deep compulsion. It was time to begin saving the seeds of mankind.

Despair considered.

Dare I risk losing this power? No. The Earth demands a partnership, and its demands are light. It does not tell me who to choose, or why. Only that I must use my gift to ensure that some survive.

But whom shall I choose?

He had selected a few already in the moment when he'd taken this body. He'd done it not for love, nor because he desired their better welfare. He'd merely selected wyrmling lords, men that he could use as . . . alarms. When danger threatened them, he would know that an enemy was about to attack.

That is all that they were. He did not care for these creatures any more than if they were roaches.

But now Despair was being warned to begin the process in earnest.

I will not let Earth bend me to its will, he told himself.

9

THE STRANGE RIDERS

Covet all good things. It is only by letting our lusts shape our actions that we can lay hold of every good thing.

—From the Wyrmling Catechism

Cullossax and Kirissa spent the morning hours in the depths of the forest shadows, walking in a large circle, crossing the same ground over and over to hide their trail. Their scent would be strong here. Twice they set up false trails, leading from their little circle, only to return, walking backward, step by step, into their own tracks. Then they carefully broke from the circle one last time and treaded along firm ground, beneath the alders.

It is not an easy thing for a five-hundred-pound wyrmling to hide his tracks. Cullossax and Kirissa did the best that they could, raking leaves over their trail, taking an hour to cross less than a mile. They found a small lake and waded across its length to a rocky beach, then climbed into some dense woods.

Even with the tree cover, the sun was blinding to a wyrmling, and often Cullossax had to hold Kirissa's hand as she blinked back tears of pain, unable to see.

Cullossax did his best to ignore his own discomfort. But as morning wore on, the sunlight striking down through the trees burned his pale skin until it turned red and began to welt; he winced at the slightest touch. His salty sweat only heightened the pain.

The two refugees were forced to strike north and west, their backs to the blinding sun, heading almost the exact opposite direction from where they wanted to go. At length they discovered a road. It was not a wyrmling road, broad enough for the massive handcarts that were used to haul meat and supplies. It was a dainty road, almost a trail, the kind used by small humans.

In the great binding, the road had been superimposed upon a trackless waste. Thus the human highway had a few thistles growing up through it, and places where it was broken by outcroppings of rock. But it was serviceable enough.

It wound down out of the hills.

Cullossax ran now through the heat of the day, ignoring the welts that the sun raised on his burned skin, warily following the old road.

Soon they reached a village, a hamlet for the small folk. Cullossax stopped at the edge of the trees and peered out at it, bemused.

Quaint huts with chimneys of stone rose among serene gardens. The walls of the cottages were made of mud and wattle, painted in blinding shades of white, with windows framed in oak. A couple of cottages still had their straw roofs attached, though most had been broken into.

Wyrmlings had already been here.

'Come,' Cullossax said. 'Let's see if we can find food.'

He did not know what the village might hold. There was no sign of living animals – no cattle or pigs, though a few corrals showed that such animals had been here recently. The wyrmlings had taken the livestock as well as the villagers.

Cullossax hoped that perhaps one of the small folk might be hiding in the village still.

Flesh is flesh.

They ransacked the hamlet, tearing the roofs off of cottages, searching through barns. Kirissa found a few human weapons

– carving knives and a small half-sword. Cullossax would have preferred some heavy war darts, or a great axe.

Some type of fowl scampered about the village green. 'Chickens,' Kirissa called them, but they darted away from Cullossax's grasp.

At last, he realized that there was nothing to eat, at least nothing in easy range.

'I will show you a secret,' Cullossax said at last, and he took Kirissa to a garden. There he found a wide variety of plants. He sniffed at a round leafy thing, then hurled it away. But he picked some pods and pulled up a few red tubers.

'Eat these,' Cullossax said. 'Some will deny this, but a wyrmling can survive on plants, at least for a short time.'

'I know,' Kirissa said, surprising him. 'On the old world, I ate plants all of the time. These green things are called beans. The tubers are beets. I like to boil them with a little olive, but they can be eaten raw.'

So they squatted in a darkened stable, and Cullossax bit into his first beet, and laughed. 'Look!' he said. 'It bleeds! I have gutted fat soldiers that bled less.'

The vegetables tasted terrible, of course. They tasted of dirt.

But they filled his belly, and the two rested in the barn, slathering themselves with water from a trough in order to cool their blistering skin.

An hour later Cullossax felt sick and bloated, until he emptied his bowels. The strange food did not suit him well. Afterward the barn stank so badly, he decided to leave. The two of them found human blankets and threw them over their heads and backs, to keep the sun at bay.

The rest of the day, they continued their run. The sun was a blinding demon, and as it began to settle to the west, once again Cullossax had to turn from his track. He headed south for a bit, then due east. They passed more towns and villages. In each one, the humans and livestock had all disappeared. Obviously, Rugassa's hunters were in a frenzy. Game had been scarce the past few years. Suddenly it was plentiful again.

Kirissa dogged along at his side, growing ever slower with each step.

This pace is killing her, Cullossax realized.

Worse, she is slowing me down. If I left her, the hunters on our trail would find her, and perhaps they would stop for a bit to amuse themselves with her.

That slight diversion might mean the difference between my death and escape.

He decided to leave her behind. Yet he did not act upon that impulse, not yet at any rate.

Kirissa grew light-headed and at last she swooned. He picked her up and carried her for an hour while she slept.

I am going to need a miracle, he thought.

And at last he found it. He entered a town that rested upon the banks of a clear, cold river. To the due east he could see a human castle with pennants waving in the breeze, not four miles off. Sentries of the small folk were marching upon the ramparts.

Off to the west, Cullossax heard a bark, the sound a wyrmling guard makes to let others know that he is awake.

Apparently, Cullossax's kin had not been able to take the castle yet. But an army was near, hiding in the shade of the woods.

I will need to keep away from the trees, he thought.

Cullossax spotted a large skiff on the banks of the river, large enough to hold a wyrmling tormentor and a girl. He checked the boat quickly, laid Kirissa inside, and then shoved the craft out into the cool water.

The current was not the rampaging torrent that he might have wished. The river was almost too shallow for such a heavily laden boat. The crystal stream rolled over mossy rocks, and glinted in the afternoon sun. Water striders danced on its surface, and trout rose to take the mosquitoes that dared rest on the surface. A few swallows darted along the river, taking drinks.

But otherwise the lush willows growing along the bank provided a screen from any prying eyes.

The boat carried them along, making sure that Cullossax left no scent, letting him and the girl escape even as they took their rest.

Cullossax startled awake well past dark.

Kirissa had risen, and now she worked the oars, streaming along. The boat scudded against some submerged rocks, which scraped the hull. That was what had wakened him. The river was growing shallow.

The landscape had changed dramatically. They were away from the lush hills and the pleasant towns, with their groves of trees.

Now, along both banks, a thin screen of grass gave way to sandstone rocks, almost white under the starlight. There were no shade trees, no hills.

'I've heard of this desert,' Cullossax said. 'It is called Oblivion. There is nothing to eat here but lizards, along with a few rabbits. This must be the Sometimes River. It winds through the wastes for many leagues in the wet season, but the water sinks into the sand out in the wastes, and only rises again occasionally. To the east of here is the hunting grounds – the land of the shaggy elephants.'

He thought for a long moment. The hunters on his trail would find it hard to survive in this waste. So would he and Kirissa.

The blazing sun shining off the rocks would blind them by day, and the few lizards would offer no food. The lizards would hide under rocks during the night, when the wyrmlings were accustomed to hunt.

Away from the river, water might be scarce – or even impossible to find.

'Give me the oars,' Cullossax said.

He steered the boat toward shore. When he found a place where rock met water, he landed the boat and had Kirissa step out.

He considered setting the boat adrift, but knew that it might only travel a hundred yards before it beached. He didn't want it to be found, and did not know what attributes his pursuers might possess. Would they have noses strong enough to track a man by scent?

Many scouts had that skill, and the Bloody Fist recruited only from among the best.

But he knew that the rocky slopes would not hold his scent for long. If he was to escape, this was the place to do it.

So he took his iron javelin and punctured the hull of the boat. He threw in a few heavy stones, then waded out into the deepest part of the river, and made sure that the boat sank.

Then he climbed up out of the water, and the two set off once again, racing over the sandstone.

The valley here had once been a land of great dunes ages ago. The sand had compacted into stone, leaving a gentle slope that looked sculpted, as if waves of water had lapped away at it. It was an easy trail to climb, and even a heavy wyrmling left no tracks.

They ran through the night, heading south. The rocks still carried the heat of the day, and it radiated up from the ground, keeping the temperature warm.

It was a comfortable run.

Dawn found them staring down into a great canyon where sandstone towers rose up, strange and twisted hoodoos, creating the illusion of mystical castles along the canyon walls, while other pillars seemed to be grotesque wyrmlings, standing guard.

In the valley below, amid the tall grass alongside a great lake, a herd of shaggy elephants could be seen grazing – creatures twenty-five feet tall at the back, their pale fur hanging in locks, their enormous white tusks sweeping over the grass like great scythes.

Nearby, herds of hunting cats lazed in the shade of twisted oak trees, waiting to take the young and unwary from the herd of shaggy elephants.

'Will those cats attack?' Kirissa asked.

'We'd make an easier meal than an elephant,' Cullossax replied. 'But I'd worry more about the elephants. They fear us, fear our hunters, and the bulls will attack if they see us two alone.'

Cullossax felt nearly dead. The sun had burned his pale skin, causing boils and chills; the lack of meat combined with their monumental run had left him famished and weak.

He could not go on.

Wearily, he spotted a crack in some rocks ahead – and led Kirissa to safety. The crack was formed when a cliff face had broken away from a great rock. It left a narrow trail, perhaps two hundred feet long, through the rock. On the far side, he could see starlight.

It was not as good as a cave, but the shelter would have to do. He wedged himself into the rocks, and then pulled his blanket over his head to hide from the rising sun.

'Rest,' Kirissa said. 'You kept guard over me yesterday, I'll keep guard today.'

Cullossax closed his eyes, and soon fell away into an exhausted sleep.

'Help!' Kirissa shouted, seemingly only seconds later. 'We've been found.'

Cullossax woke with a start. He tried climbing to his feet. Ahead of him, Kirissa stood with his javelin. A wyrmling scout was just in front of her, lying on the ground, snarling in rage, dragging himself toward her.

Cullossax found his feet, tried to shove his way past Kirissa, but the crevasse was too narrow.

'Damn you, woman!' the wyrmling scout snarled. He bore a wickedly curved knife for cutting throats, its blade a jet black, and he was dragging himself heavily across the ground, leaving a slimy trail of blood.

He could not gain his feet. It took a moment for Cullossax to realize why: one of his legs had snapped in two. Adding further to his wounds, a couple of small human knives were lodged in his belly.

A depression in the ground nearby showed where Kirissa had dug a hole, creating a mantrap for him to step into, and then had buried a pair of daggers in the hard ground for him to fall upon.

Yet the wounded tormentor fought on. He had crawled a dozen yards, moving as quickly as a snake, and still he tried to make his way to Kirissa.

She held him at bay with the javelin, but just barely. The wyrmling lunged back and forth. Two endowments of speed, three he might have had. Cullossax could not be certain. But if the scout had had room to maneuver, he'd have easily lunged past her slow parries.

Cullossax pulled his own dagger from its sheath behind his neck, and hurled with all of his might. The wounded scout tried to dodge, but the blade took him full in the face.

Kirissa lunged for the killing blow, impaling the tormentor through the ribs, and then leaned into her javelin with all her weight, pinning him down. The scout struggled fiercely, and it was not until Cullossax himself leaned into the spear that the scout began to slow. Soon it was only his legs that jerked and twitched.

'We've got to get out of here,' Cullossax hissed. 'This was their leader, the fastest of them. But the other two cannot be far behind.'

Cullossax dared not go back out the way that they had come. The other tormentors were probably rushing toward the entry now.

So he grabbed Kirissa's hand and pulled her through the crevasse, out the back side of the rock.

The sun was just setting behind them. A bat squeaked overhead and flitted away.

On the far side of the crevasse, a steep cliff led down into the wastes of the shaggy elephant.

There was only one way to go: down the slope, past the sandstone hoodoos, and into the vale, filled with hunting cats and elephants.

Cullossax leapt down the cliff and tried to keep his feet as he descended in a cloud of dust and scree.

At the bottom of the cliff, Kirissa stopped for an instant. A long, piercing howl sounded from the rocks above.

They turned and glanced up to see two wyrmlings in the shadows, not three hundred yards behind, both wyrmlings dressed in black tunics.

'Run!' Cullossax shouted.

The chase began in earnest.

Cullossax sprinted until he thought that his heart would burst, and then he ran some more. Through the thick grass he and Kirissa charged, grass so tall that it reached Cullossax's chest, and he worried whether the grass might harbor hunting cats.

Thin clouds had drifted overhead during the day, creating a bloody sunset that died and darkened into full night within an hour.

At the end of that hour, the hunters had still not taken them. He could see them pacing behind, yet they did not press forward.

He wondered if they were wounded. Perhaps in tracking him across the open desert of the day, they had gone sunblind and still could not see well.

It might be that they're afraid of you, he told himself. But probably not.

No, he decided, this is the first part of the torment.

A wyrmling torment was not just a punishment – it was a rite, sacred and profound. It was society meting out justice.

My hunters have endowments of speed and strength, and I do not. They could rush in and take me at any moment. But now they hold back, and laugh. They plan to run us into the ground.

He passed a large herd of shaggy elephants to his right, and worried that the bulls would attack. But they only formed a living wall, standing tusk-to-tusk, to bar Cullossax's way to their calves.

After two hours, Kirissa was reeling from weariness. Even her good wyrmling breeding would not let her go on forever. Her steps became clumsy and she staggered almost blindly.

Still they ran.

A hill loomed ahead, a small hill on the rolling plains, and Cullossax told himself, I will climb that hill, and I can go no farther.

But Cullossax had one last hope. As a tormentor, he was allowed to carry a harvester spike to use in an emergency. It was in a pouch, hidden inside his belt.

In a battle, he would have jabbed the spike into his carotid artery so that the precious secretions on it could be carried quickly to his brain. Now he elected to use it more cautiously. He pulled the tiny bag from his belt and rammed the spike into his palm.

In seconds he felt his heart began to pound as adrenaline surged into him, granting him a second wind. His eyes misted, and a killing haze settled over them.

So he pounded through the deep grass, blazing a trail for Kirissa, until he neared the hill.

The hunters came for him then, howling and laughing in sport, rushing up behind.

They were almost on him now. He could practically feel their hot breath on the back of his neck. He was almost at the top of the hill. There was just one steep rise between him and the far side.

'Run!' he shouted to Kirissa. 'It is me that they want.'

He whirled to meet the tormentors, pitting the old magic of the harvester spike against the new magic of the Runelords.

Kirissa ran like the wind, and Cullossax wheeled on his foes. The wyrmlings that raced toward him hardly looked like men. Their faces were pocked and reddened from sunburn. Their eyes were glazed from physical abuse.

The men raced toward him at three times the normal speed, but the harvester spike had worked its magic. Time seemed to have slowed for Cullossax, dilating as it will when the passions run high.

He raised his javelin and feinted a thrust to one man's face, but instead hurled it low, catching the harvester in the hip. The man snarled in pain.

The fellow lunged at Cullossax, hurtling through the air like a panther.

The harvester spike was no match for endowments. Cullossax tried to dodge, but the man plowed into him anyway.

Cullossax was a big man, larger by far than most wyrmlings.

I do not have to kill him, Cullossax thought, only wound him.

He grappled with his attacker, pulling him in close, grabbing him in a bear hug and then crushing with all his might.

He heard ribs snapping, smelled the tormentor's sweaty clothes, saw the wyrmling's eyes widen in fear.

Then the attacker wrenched his arm down with surprising strength, and drew the black knife from its scabbard. Cullossax knew what the man was trying to do, and tried to stop him by hugging him tightly, holding his arms against his chest, but the attacker was too strong, too quick.

Cullossax felt three hot jabs in quick succession as a knife snicked up into his rib cage. Hot blood boiled from his wounds.

I do not have to kill him, Cullossax thought, only wound him.

With all of his might, Cullossax jerked his arms tight, snapping his attacker's back.

The knife came up, slashed Cullossax across the face, and then Cullossax hurled the tormentor away.

He stood for a moment, blinded by his own blood. The man that he'd wounded with the javelin had pulled it free, and now was limping toward him.

Blood bubbled in the cavern of Cullossax's lungs, and he grew dazed. His head spun.

The wounded tormentor hurled his javelin, catching Cullossax in the sternum, just below the heart. The power of the blow, combined with his own dizziness, knocked Cullossax backward.

Cullossax lay on the ground, gripping the javelin.

He missed my heart, Cullossax thought. He threw too low. But it did not matter. His lungs had been punctured, and his life would be over in a matter of seconds.

His heart was pounding, and his tormentor laughed at him in derision, when suddenly Cullossax realized that he heard the thunder of hooves rising through the ground.

He heard Kirissa shout something strange, 'Gaborn Val Orden!' The name of her Earth King.

And suddenly he realized that they had reached human habitations.

Kirissa must have dashed over the hilltop just as a phalanx of horses crested from the other side.

Cullossax wrenched his neck and peered up the hill. He'd never seen horses before, not like this.

These were blood-red in color. They wore steel barding on their heads and chests, and the metal masks made their faces look hideous and otherworldly.

Their riders were just as terrifying – wild human women with frightening masks and long white lances. Some of the women bore torches, and the horses' red eyes seemed to blaze in the fierce firelight.

Their captain saw the three wyrmlings and shouted in some strange tongue. The riders charged toward the lone scout who was still standing, lances lowered.

Cullossax's eyes went unfocused then, as the wyrmling assassin met his fate. His death cries rent the air, a wailing sound like a dog dying.

Grinning in satisfaction, Cullossax faded toward unconsciousness.

Run, Kirissa, he thought. Perhaps when all the worlds are bound as one, we will meet again.

10

ONE TRUE WORLD

*Wyrmlings are such needy creatures. Food, water, air
– the Great Wyrm has provided for all of our needs.
She even offers us immortality, so long as we obey her
every demand. Blessed be the name of the Great Wyrm.*

—From the Wyrmling Catechism

Talon walked into the Bright Ones' sanctuary down a long,
winding tunnel, where the curved walls were as smooth as
eggshell, a soft cream in color. The floor was formed from
slabs of stone, with strange and beautiful knots and whorls
chiseled into them. At the landing, the entryway fanned out
into a great hall. It was unlike anything that Talon had ever
imagined.

The room was large enough to hold ten thousand refugees
and more. The walls off to her right seemed to be natural
stone, as pale as cloud, and several waterfalls cascaded down
over some rocks into a broad pool, raising a gentle mist. Lights
like stars blazed above. They hung motionless in the air, only
a dozen yards overhead, bright enough that they held the room
in an enchanted twilight, as if just before the crack of dawn.
Up near the top of the waterfalls, the stars gave just enough
light that they nurtured some strange creepers that hung like
tapestries from the rock, the pale leaves dotted with brilliant
red flowers. White cave crickets sang in the wan light, creating

a gentle music that merged with the tumble and tinkle of falling water.

Hallways and corridors yawned ahead, and many in the company forged deeper into the cavern, into antechambers where they might find some privacy and collapse for the night.

Few of the Bright Ones seemed to be here in camp. Talon saw no more than two dozen of their men and women in the cavern. Several of them moved off with Daylan Hammer into a small vestibule to hold their council.

She saw bright flashing lights a few moments later, and she went near the vestibule on the pretext of calming one of Alun's mastiffs that was trotting around, woofing in excitement.

Talon halted beside the stream, called to the dog, and scratched at its neck, beneath its fearsome collar. A white cricket fell from the roof and landed in the water. The stream boiled as a fish lunged up to take it.

Talon glanced into the side tunnel.

The Bright Ones stood with Daylan Hammer in a circle, each of them gazing down at a round stone table as if deep in thought. Above them, creatures circled, like birds made not of flesh but of light, each about the length of a man, with ethereal wings that did not move. They were the source of the flashing lights that had drawn Talon.

Glories, Talon realized. According to legend, the Glories were the spirits of just men who had forsaken their own flesh – much like the Death Lords, Talon mused, though she suspected that she had it backward. Legend said that the Glories had existed long ago, back in the dim recesses of time, but the Death Lords had to be more recent, for legend said that they had been created by Despair.

The Glories seemed to exude life and light, but the Death Lords of Rugassa had no life or light in them; they survived only by draining life from others.

The Death Lords are but a vile mockery of the Glories, Talon realized.

As Talon's eyes adjusted to the light, she studied the room. The vestibule was circular in shape, with a table made from a single piece of jasper. Fine chairs carved from cherrywood lined the outer wall. Tapestries of red embroidered with threads of gold carpeted the floor.

Erringale was speaking in the council chamber, but his liquid voice mingled with the sounds of running water, the chatter of people, and the chirp of cave crickets. Talon could not make out what he said, and even when she could make out the liquid tones of his voice, she could not understand him. It was as if she could understand his words only when he willed her to.

In the great hall, people fanned out. Some went to the lake and began to drink. Others unpacked bedrolls to sleep on, for they had not slept in nearly two days. Some just threw themselves to the ground in exhaustion.

Alun came to retrieve his mastiff, and as he stood beside Talon patting its muzzle, he too peered into the council chamber.

Alun was an ill-formed man, with big ears, a crooked nose, and spindly arms.

A voice spoke at Talon's back. 'So, what you thinking?' It was Drewish, one of the sons of the dead Warlord Madoc. Drewish and his brother Connor stood leering over Alun.

'Thinking?' Alun asked. 'Nothing.' Somehow, it seemed that he did not want to be accused of thinking. Talon imagined that he didn't want to have to reveal his thoughts to the likes of Drewish.

The Madocs seemed not to even notice Talon. She was, after all, only a young woman, and so, like Alun, was beneath them.

'A smart man would be thinking about how to better his lot in life,' Drewish said. 'A smart man would be thinking about how to get himself some forcibles. That's the way of the future. All of our breeding, it won't count for a turd – not when a man like you could take the strength of five men, the wisdom of ten, and the speed of three.'

'What are you talking about?' Alun asked.

Talon knew that Alun had heard about this new rune lore,

of course, but apparently he hadn't entertained the notion that he might actually be granted endowments.

'Forcibles, you know,' Drewish said. He reached into his tunic, pulled out a long purse, and let it sway like a bell. Talon could hear forcibles clanging together, like dry pieces of wood.

'Where did you get those?' Alun asked. He reached up to grab the bag.

But Drewish pulled them just out of his grasp. 'The blood metal is everywhere. No big trick to having someone make a few forcibles for you, if you know who to talk to. The big trick now will be finding someone who is willing to give you an endowment. Take your pick – wit, stamina, grace? Who will give you theirs? What coin can you offer to get it?'

'I don't know,' Alun said, mystified.

Certainly, Talon thought, no one would give *Alun* an endowment.

He must have thought the same. 'What are you offering?' Alun asked. 'Do you want my endowment?'

'Not yours,' Drewish laughed. 'Your dogs'. A dog can give up an endowment as easily as a man. You want strength? Those mastiffs of yours have it. You want stamina, speed? There's a dog for that. Scent and hearing too. But we need the dogs to give up those endowments. We need their master to coax the gifts from them. That's where you come in. The dogs love you. You're their feeder, their handler. They're completely devoted to you, not to us.'

Drewish took out a pair of forcibles. 'One forcible for every six dogs,' Connor said, 'that's what I'm offering. You'll be a Runelord if you take me up on it.'

Alun considered.

Talon knew that it was tempting. Alun had fourteen dogs. If he sold Connor and Drewish a dozen endowments, he'd have a pair of forcibles and could take two endowments himself.

He'd be a Runelord. Perhaps with some strength and stamina, he could become more of a warrior, raise his own lot in life.

But Connor and Drewish would both still be far more

powerful than he. Right now, they loomed over him, subtly threatening.

And where would Alun go to get endowments from humans once his dogs had all been used up? No one would give them to someone like him.

It wasn't much of an offer, Talon decided.

Petty bribes and threats, that's how the Madocs led.

She wondered if she might buy the endowments from Alun herself, but she had little coin to offer. There were a few treasures in her dowry box, but she'd been forced to leave that back in Cantular. Doubtlessly, her pair of fine gold rings would end up decorating some wyrmling lord's nostrils.

From the council chamber, she heard Daylan cry out in anguish, 'There is no law against compassion. It is true that I broke your laws, but I did it only to obey a higher law. How can we serve society if we do not serve the individual first?'

There was a brief moment of silence, and Daylan cried out again. 'If you would resist evil, you cannot just stand idly by and watch its dominion spread. You must thwart Despair's every design!'

Both Connor and Drewish turned to glance into the council chamber.

Talon realized that Daylan was in the other room searching for a way to save the world, while she, Connor, and Drewish were plotting how to overthrow it.

I don't want to be like them, she told herself.

And suddenly she knew that she could not let the likes of Connor and Drewish get control of those dogs – or take endowments from any other man or woman.

He is a fool who empowers his enemies, Talon thought. It was something that her father used to say.

Connor and Drewish were rotten to the core. Their father, despite all of his talk of serving the people, had been no better than his sons, and in the end, when Talon had watched him fall to his death from the parapet at Caer Luciare, she had felt no more loss than if she had ground a cockroach under her heel.

'How can we do this?' Alun asked the Madocs. 'How can we grant you these endowments? People will see what we're up to. Some will object.'

'We will do it with their permission,' Connor said. 'The jewelers and smiths are already at work making the forcibles, putting the runes in them. Daylan Hammer and the emir plan to lead a team to Rugassa to free Areth Sul Urstone and that runt of a wizard Fallion. I want to go with them. I want to be among the heroes that helps free them.' He hesitated for a moment, as if Alun might object, but Alun held his tongue. 'So when the time comes, I want you to offer your dogs as Dedicates, and suggest that we be granted those endowments. It will sound better coming from you.'

Talon wondered. She could think of no good reason why the Madocs would make such a grandiose gesture as to join the rescue.

Connor was rumored to be an outstanding swordsman, but in raids against the wyrmlings, neither he nor Drewish bloodied their weapons. They consistently failed to prove themselves in battle.

They preferred to stand back from the front and observe the engagements, as if they were superb strategists who were studying wyrmling tactics so that they might use their knowledge to great advantage to win some future war.

Meanwhile, Talon thought, Alun has risked his neck and cut down the wyrmlings in a haze of rage.

Even that runt Alun is better than them, Talon thought. They might have the breeding for war, but they don't have the heart for battle.

No, she did not trust the Madoc clan.

Talon began to suspect the Madocs of darker motives. Neither of the Madocs would want to see Prince Areth Sul Urstone take the throne.

It would be far better for them if he died, along with Fallion, the emir, and anyone else who took that journey.

Talon suspected that she understood precisely why Connor and Drewish hoped to join the rescue party.

But Alun could not deny them, not without incurring their wrath – and risking retribution.

'I'll do it,' Alun said. Connor reached out a hand to shake. Alun shook at the wrist, as was the custom with warriors. Moments later, the Madocs stalked away.

'You can't help them,' Talon whispered when they were out of earshot. 'Those men are up to no good. You can't empower your enemies.'

'What else can I do?' Alun asked.

'Offer the dogs to the emir,' Talon said.

'What? And wind up with my throat cut in my sleep? No thank you.'

'I'll protect you,' Talon said. She meant it.

'What, a girl – protect me? I'd rather you let me die.'

Talon suddenly realized that he had never seen her fight. In fact, on his world, he'd never seen a woman warrior.

It was hours later when the council finally broke up.

Erringale led the way from the darkened council chamber, with the emir, Daylan Hammer, the Wizard Sisel, and the rest of the Bright Ones behind. The Glories had departed.

Talon could see from the smile upon Daylan's face that the council had gone well. Inside the great hall, Erringale climbed a short landing beside the river, and began to speak in his strange tongue, the words filling Talon's mind.

'The White Council has spoken,' Erringale said. 'The Bright Ones and Glories of our world have all been consulted, and a consensus has been reached.'

Talon wondered at those words. Certainly these few Bright Ones in the sanctuary couldn't be 'all' of the Bright Ones in the world.

So Talon could only imagine that Erringale had spoken to their minds, as he spoke to Talon now.

'The people of Luciare are free to remain here for three days, to rest yourselves, recover from your injuries, and refresh your spirits. But at the end of those three days, you must return to your world.'

At that, the people around Talon gave a cheer. Erringale raised his hands for silence and in a few moments, the people quieted. 'Daylan Hammer has petitioned our help. He hopes to free your prince, Areth Sul Urstone, from the wyrmling horde, along with our Torch-bearer.

'We also wish to see them freed.

'But our people cannot lightly interfere in the affairs of the shadow worlds. Therefore, we offer aid in the form of council: we urge you to do harm to no man, be he human or wyrmling. To do violence to another is to injure your own soul.

'Still, we recognize that it is not always possible to remain free from another's blood.'

New thoughts struck Talon as Erringale spoke, strange notions that she had never considered. It was as if a great argument had been raging for eons among the Bright Ones, and now a thousand thoughts came swirling into her head.

The war between the Bright Ones and Despair was an endless one, and was not a war between creatures of flesh. Rather, Talon recognized that the life of the spirit was more important to Erringale and his people than the life of the flesh. And certain acts did not just *injure* the spirit, they could wound it to death.

A man who steals from another, Erringale warned, *a man who does injury to the truth, or who does violence to another, wounds his own soul in the process, and weakens his spirit. We warn you against such things. It is only as you remain true to your conscience that your spirit can grow and mature.*

Talon was baffled by that. She considered Erringale's argument, and then just as quickly set it aside, neither wholly rejecting it nor accepting it.

She had been trained to fight wyrmlings from birth. They had murdered millions of her people over the past few centuries.

Of course she would kill them in battle. She could see no dishonor in that.

'Though we cannot offer our service in battle,' Erringale said softly, 'we wish to send emissaries to your world. I wish to come. I would commune with the True Tree, if you will let me.'

Talon understood more than the words that were spoken. She realized that Erringale would not visit her world unless he had an invitation from its people.

As one, the folk of Luciare said, 'Come.'

At that, the emir of Dalharristan got up to speak. 'For far too long, my friend Areth Sul Urstone has languished in the dungeons of Rugassa. He was once like a brother to me, and already I have told you of his character. I pray that he is still alive, though long have I feared for him. Now it is time to set him free. I ask for help as a friend, not as your leader. High King Urstone was your leader, and Areth is his heir. There is none worthier to lead us, none braver or wiser, none more compassionate or just.

'Few of you here knew him as I did. Few of you can call him friend. But I need you to look into your hearts and see if you can serve him now.

'I have sworn to the Glories that I will free Areth Sul Urstone and Fallion Orden, and that I will do it with as little violence as I can.

'But I am only one man. I need the strength and speed of many if I am to accomplish this task. I would take endowments from the others if I could – from the small folk of the world, who will soon be caught up in our war. But we stand in desperate need *now*. I cannot go searching afar.

'Among the Bright Ones there was once a race of lawmen called the Ael. They were given endowments by their people, strengthened by them. The Bright Ones have agreed to grant endowments once again, the first in many long years.

'Who among you can find the daring within yourselves to come with me? Who among you can offer up an endowment, that you might free your king?'

There was dead silence in the great hall. All that could be heard was the tinkling of water, the call of cave crickets. As a whole, the people of Luciare did not understand much about the endowment system yet. But Talon knew it well.

If you gave up your wit, you gave it up so long as both you and your lord should live. The chances were good that you would die an idiot, unable to feed yourself, unable to recognize your best friend or child or even the woman that you loved.

If you gave up strength, no matter how mighty you were, you became so enfeebled that you might not be able to hobble across a room or draw enough breath to speak. Many were the men who died after giving strength, for their hearts soon wore out. To give an endowment was a curse.

Talon was standing beside Alun. Suddenly Connor whispered 'Now!' and gave Alun a shove, so that he went lurching forward.

Alun cleared his throat. He did not have to feign nervousness, for it came to his tongue naturally. 'I – I,' he stammered. 'I would like to offer my dogs . . .'

And he then fumbled, as if he could say no more.

Smart boy, Talon realized. He could not refuse to offer the dogs to the Madocs. But by feigning nervousness, he'd made half an offer.

Let the emir have the dogs' strength and speed. Let the emir be empowered. And Alun could only hope that Connor and Drewish did not exact too much revenge.

A brief silence followed as the emir considered the offer. Seeing that Alun had fumbled his words, Connor stepped forward.

'I would join you in this quest,' Connor said. 'And it is with heartfelt thanks that I accept Alun's generous offer.'

The emir gave Connor a piercing look. Certainly he suspected Connor's motives. 'I believe,' he said dryly, 'that Alun offered his dogs to me.'

At that moment, a man stepped forward, a wealthy merchant of forty years whose finery was perhaps unsurpassed in all of the warrior clans. His name was Thull-turock. In Caer Luciare he had been a wealthy merchant, but Talon recognized him as a man who had lived a double life. Upon Fallion's world, he had been a powerful facilitator, a man who made his living by crafting forcibles, choosing potential Dedicates for his lords and then transferring endowments.

In a matter of two days, Thull-turock had risen to become one of the most influential men among the clans.

He strode forward, with glittering eyes like a snake's, and shouted into the emir's face. 'And how do you propose to regain this prince of yours without taking endowments? For surely you will not receive them from my hand.'

'I . . .' The emir stood, confused. Thull-turock had long been a friend, and had dined with the emir at the lords' table many a night, reveling in the emir's presence, jesting with him. Now Thull-turock had turned against him.

'I will not grant you endowments,' Thull-turock repeated. 'Once I called you friend, but I know you too well!'

Talon was stunned. She thought, The Madocs seem to have corrupted more men than I thought possible.

'What?' Tuul Ra demanded of Thull-turock. 'Which of my good deeds do you decry?'

'It is not your good deeds upon this world that I decry,' Thull-turock shouted. 'It was what you did upon the shadow world. It is what I suspect that you are destined to become that I decry.'

From an old woman at Talon's back came a shout, 'Murderer!' From around the camp arose cries of 'Fiend!' 'Warmonger!' 'Monster!'

From the rage on various faces, Talon realized that hundreds of folks had evil memories of the emir, and a full third of the camp had heard rumors of what he'd done on Fallion's world.

Talon had lived on both worlds. She felt that she should know what was wrong, but right now, she was baffled.

The emir only gaped in astonishment. His dark-skinned daughter, Siyaddah, came to his side defensively; tears sprang to her eyes, and she stood peering about like a wounded dove, shaken.

'Wait!' Daylan Hammer cried, calling for quiet. He spoke to Thull-turock in a soft and reasonable tone. 'Does your law allow you to condemn a man for a crime that he has not committed? The emir is innocent. You know that! Look in your heart, and you must find him innocent.'

'Until now Tuul Ra has shown no desire to take endowments,' Thull-turock explained, 'and so I have kept my silence. But you must know, I will not grant endowments to him. He must never taste the kiss of the forcible!'

Daylan said in a soft tone, reasonably, 'You think that a taste of the forcible will corrupt him?'

'It has corrupted other men. It corrupted his shadow self. As a facilitator, I swore an oath never to grant endowments to a man that I mistrust.'

'The emir is made of better stuff than other men, I think,' Daylan argued. 'Surely you would agree?'

Thull-turock growled, 'You know what he did in Indhopal.'

Suddenly Talon understood – the Fiend of Indhopal, Raj Ahten. She had never met the man. Her father, Borenson, had helped kill him before she was born. Could the emir be the Raj's shadow self?

It seemed impossible. Raj had been an old man when he'd marched against the nations of Rofehavan.

But had he been old, Talon suddenly wondered, or had his forcibles aged him?

He'd taken thousands of endowments of brawn, wit, and stamina, of course. And he'd taken many endowments of metabolism.

Like any man, he would have aged quickly afterward. If he'd taken eight or ten endowments of metabolism, he might have grown old and died within a decade.

Yet the emir seemed young to her – younger than Sir Borenson.

Then, she realized, her father had taken endowments of metabolism, too. Both men had aged preternaturally.

The emir stared at Thull-turock in blank horror. 'What did I do on that other world?' he begged. 'Tell me. Accuse me.'

'That was not the emir,' Daylan argued, forestalling the inevitable revelation with a wave of the hand. 'It was but a shadow, a creature that this emir could have become.'

'And yet,' Thull-turock countered, 'it seems that there is a pattern to things. In Indhopal, Raj Ahten was the most powerful lord of his time. In this world, the emir is much the same – a man with an unnatural talent for war.'

'And so you fear that he will become another Raj Ahten?'

'I cannot help but see the potential,' Thull-turock said.

'Don't be afraid to give him endowments,' Daylan said. 'It is true that the kiss of the forcible corrupts many, but it will not sway the emir.'

'So say you,' Thull-turock argued. 'But Raj Ahten loved the forcible, and craved it like nothing else.'

The emir stepped between the men, and raised his hands in surrender. 'Thull-turock, if you do not trust me to take endowments, then I will not. But I cannot go back on my oath. I must free Areth Sul Urstone.'

'And if you were to try to break into Rugassa without endowments my friend,' Daylan said gently, 'it would be suicide. Even with your talent, I fear that you could not stand against a Runelord.'

Daylan looked to Thull-turock pleadingly. 'The emir is unlike his shadow. He is mature, and wise. But Raj Ahten was only a child when first he felt the ecstasy of the forcible.' Daylan turned to Thull-turock and asked, 'How many children have you heard of who can resist the forcible, once having been subjected to it? It is a heady wine.'

Thull-turock mused, 'A man who will become a sot will do so no matter how old he is when he begins to drink.'

'Perhaps,' Daylan said. 'But we are not talking about wine here – we are talking about greed, and vanity, and lust for power. That is what destroyed Raj Ahten. But who has seen such vices in the emir?' Daylan reached into his tunic and pulled out a small book with a doeskin binding. 'I found this among Fallion's effects. It is the Earth King's own journal. It reveals much about Raj Ahten and how he fell.' Daylan raised the book overhead and spoke to the crowd. 'Raj Ahten was a young man of fourteen, lusting for power, when he first tasted the fruits of the forcible. He had seen reaver attacks in his own land, reavers slaughtering his friends and father; ancient guardians revealed to him that the reavers were going to rise from the earth in force and that he was among the few who had the means, the strength, and the will to stop them—'

'Much as our emir hopes to save the world from the wyrmling horde,' Thull-turock put in.

'But with one difference,' Daylan countered, 'The Raj was but a child, filled with a child's daydreams. And he was surrounded by sorcerers, flameweavers that pandered to him and aroused his lusts.

'The emir is no child,' Daylan continued. 'He has held power – held it and lost it again, so that its allure has faded. Now he rejects your honors. He does not ask to be your king. He asks only for the boon of saving the best man among you.

'He has learned the price of leadership. He does not ask to direct these people, rather only that he be able to restore the rightful leader to power.

'How can you argue against that?'

Thull-turock inclined his head, thinking. He took a step away from Daylan Hammer, and peered off into the dim recesses of the cavern while he considered. 'Both Raj and the emir were convinced that they were doing what was right when they started down this path. And Fire whispers to them, seeks to claim them. Surely you cannot ask me to grant endowments to someone that you *know* to be a flameweaver.'

'Is he a flameweaver?' Daylan asked. He turned to the emir. 'I have never heard such.'

The emir could have lied, Talon thought. But he admitted softly, 'I have some small skill. I can keep smoke from following me at the fire, and I can twist flames if I want. But I have never sought that power, and in fact I shy away from it. It fills you with a hunger that can never be fulfilled, and so it must be shunned.'

That satisfied some, but others remained unconvinced.

'Raj Ahten became the greatest flameweaver his world had ever known,' Thull-turock said. 'In the end, he lost his humanity.'

'But our emir has not gone down that path,' Daylan countered. 'If I were you, I would rejoice that our Emir Tuul Ra has this gift. If we are to rescue Fallion Orden and Prince Areth Sul Urstone, we will have need of a flameweaver. Vulgnash has consummate skill in the art, and he has endowments to boot. Thus Fallion has proven helpless against him. But perhaps Fallion and the Emir Tuul Ra together . . .'

Daylan let the thought hang in the air. 'But we cannot rely upon their skill alone. We have no way of knowing how many endowments Vulgnash has garnered; we must suspect that he will be one of the wyrmlings' greatest champions.

'Thus, the emir may be our only hope. And he will need to have more than just endowments – he must begin to develop Raj Ahten's mastery of Fire.'

Talon had been inclined to give the emir a chance, to judge him on his own merits. But suddenly she found her heart thrilling from fear.

'This is madness!' Thull-turock exclaimed. 'You would create a new Raj Ahten?'

'Not all flameweavers are evil,' Daylan said. 'There are men who have mastered their passions to such a degree that Fire could not control them. In ancient times, some of these men were more than monsters. They became vessels of light, pure and radiant, filled with wisdom and intelligence and compassion. They were great healers. Fire revealed the future to them, and hidden dangers, and thus they were a boon to their people.

'Hence, they were called the "Bright Ones," and even today, the ignorant people of Fallion's world call all men of the netherworld such, not realizing that thereby they are bestowing false honors upon many.' Daylan jutted his chin toward Lord Erringale, and Talon knew that he, too, must be a skilled flameweaver. 'Of all Bright Ones, the man you call Fallion Orden was perhaps the greatest.'

'My little Fallion?' Thull-turock asked in astonishment.

'Has been born time and again,' Daylan said, 'a thousand times over. For eons he has sought a way to bind the worlds, and finally he has succeeded.

'If the Bright Ones' prophecies prove true, great things are at hand: a war that will rage across the universe, and that, if all goes well, could end with all of the worlds reuniting into one perfect whole, where death will be but a memory, and all pains and wants vanquished.

'That world is what Fallion seeks to create. That is what our enemy hopes to thwart – or to sieze.'

The emir had been listening carefully, and now he seemed lost in thought. Talon knew what Daylan was asking of him. He would have to sacrifice much. By taking endowments, he would be giving up his life in service for his fellow men. By studying the lore of flameweavers, he would be giving up his life in service to Fire.

It was a slippery tightrope to try to walk. No man can serve two masters. Raj Ahten had failed miserably.

How could the emir hope to do more?

'Daylan,' Thull-turock said, 'if you think there is nothing to fear from the emir, then you are mad!'

'No,' Daylan said. 'I am not mad. But I am desperate, and one might reason that desperation is its own kind of madness. Certainly, too often it leads to folly. But only in taking this desperate course can we hope to win a nearly impossible reward.

'But I must tell you, Thull-turock, that I believe that your fears are not justified. It was neither the love of the forcible nor of flames that Raj Ahten succumbed to in the end. At the very last, Raj Ahten demanded that others call him by a new name – Scathain, Lord of the Ashes. Have you heard this?'

'I have heard that he went by that name,' Thull-turock said. 'What of it?'

'That name is well known here in the netherworld,' Lord Erringale said loudly, his voice cutting through the room. He gazed down, held his hands reflectively. 'It is the name of a powerful locus, a wyrm if you will. Among the loci, Scathain was second-in-command to Despair herself. Many worlds has that one destroyed.'

This news seemed to discomfit the emir more than anything

that had been said. He was at a disadvantage in the argument, for he could not have known what had happened with Raj Ahten. But he understood the lore of wyrms.

'If this is true,' the emir reasoned, 'then when your Raj Ahten was killed, his wyrm did not die with him! How do we know that this Scathain will not seize me? How do we know that I am not already host to a wyrm?'

Around the circle, there were cries of agreement. Talon glanced at Drewish Madoc and saw the young man's eyes glimmering insanely. He loved this. He loved watching a good man be destroyed.

'Consider this,' Daylan called to the crowd, 'the emir is a generous man, a giving man, and a courageous one. He has always spoken the truth in my presence, so long as it is polite to do so and not too hard for his hearer to bear. His word has ever been his bond. He is faithful to his people, and has no lust for honor, no craving for wealth.

'A man who is infected with a wyrm doesn't retain such virtues. And Scathain is one of the most sinister of all wyrms. Even if Scathain had entered the emir and tried to hide his lusts and deceit, he would not be able to do so for long.

'The emir is pure. No wyrm has taken him. And so long as he remains pure of heart, none can, not even one so powerful as Scathain.'

At that there were also cries of agreement. Daylan Hammer had assuaged nearly all of Thull-turock's concerns, and Talon could feel that the crowd was swaying toward Daylan's cause.

'It may be,' Daylan said loudly, addressing the crowd, 'that the only reason that the raj succumbed to a wyrm had more to do with the raj's ignorance than his weaknesses. The lore of the loci had been all but lost upon his world.'

'They knew nothing of the loci?' Lord Erringale asked, astonished.

'The knowledge of loci was purposely hidden from the populace thousands of years ago. There was a time on Fallion's world when those suspected of harboring a locus were executed summarily, and many innocent men and women died; much evil was done in the name of self-preservation.

'The folk of Luciare have had similar purges, though never to the same extent.

'And so that knowledge was concealed.

'Thus a man who might have been a great ally on Fallion's world succumbed to a wyrm, never suspecting that such a creature even existed. The raj took one misstep at a time, heedlessly bumbling down the path of destruction, until at the very last he became so filled with rage and lust for power that he could not withstand the wyrm when it seized him.'

There were looks of astonishment on people's faces. From birth, Talon's mother Gatunyea had instilled a fear of evil in her. Talon had been trained to fear nothing so much as the thought that she might someday be seized by a wyrm.

Daylan said at last, 'So, it will not happen to the emir. He has known of the existence of wyrms since childhood, and he has ranged far to avoid the danger.'

The facilitator clasped his hands behind his back, and peered down at the ground. 'I don't like this,' Thull-turock said. 'I don't like the way we're rushing into this. The emir needs to be tested in so many ways. Yet you urge me to hasten to make forcibles.'

'We have no choice,' Daylan said. 'Our enemies have set the timetable. Already the wyrmlings are digging up a mountain of blood metal and have sent their first shipment to Rugassa. The journey there will take them three nights – perhaps less, since they will be in a hurry to please their lord.

'Think what will happen once the emperor gets those shipments: he'll begin creating his own champions in earnest. And who will he grant the endowments to?'

'The Knights Eternal,' Thull-turock said, as if chilled by the thought.

'The emperor has millions of people that he can use as Dedicates. What's more, Rugassa lies close to the borders of Beldinook. By now, the emperor is already getting acquainted with his new neighbors. What do you think he will do with the small folk?'

In the old days, Talon knew, the wyrmlings would have just butchered them, harvesting their glands for their fearsome elixirs or simply using their bodies for meat. They would not even have considered taking slaves. But in this new world, the wyrmlings would put the small folk to better uses: they could put them to the forcible, take their attributes.

'I see,' Thull-turock said.

'We cannot let that happen. We cannot let any forcibles reach Rugassa. We must act swiftly. We must have a war party take endowments and be ready to leave tomorrow – at the latest. And *we cannot fail*! My heart warns me that we may get only one chance at this, one chance to save ourselves before the wyrmlings take their mountain of blood metal and seize control of the world for all time.'

'A single day is not much time to grant endowments.'

Daylan said, 'Our champions won't need a full complement. They won't need to be battle-ready. We only need them to get started. We can pass more endowments to them as they travel, vectoring them through Dedicates. Erringale's people will help you make the forcibles.'

'How many shall we send into battle?' Thull-turock asked.

'We will need some men to help carry those that we rescue. We'll need others to act as point and rear guards. At a minimum, we need four champions, probably five. I would like more, but it would stretch our resources to try to endow so many. I would invite the Cormar twins,' Daylan suggested. 'They already have some endowments and they proved themselves at the battle for Caer Luciare. I would like to go, too, for I have a few endowments to my credit. That leaves only two openings. The emir is the best man for the job . . .'

Instantly, Talon knew that she had to be among that war party. Fallion was more than just a friend to her. He'd been raised as her brother, and she loved him dearly. It was only right that she go with the rescue party.

Thull-turock said, 'You sent Fallion's woman, Rhianna, to

seek for Dedicates among the small folk. Can we afford to wait for her to return?'

'I sent her mainly to forewarn the small folk,' Daylan countered, 'so that they can protect themselves from the wyrmling troops. We must hinder the wyrmlings any way that we can. It may be that the small folk will offer us some support, but we cannot rely upon them, and we dare not wait.'

Talon wished that she had known where Rhianna was going earlier. She would have hugged her and bade her farewell. It would not be easy trying to find allies for Fallion. But no one in the world loved Fallion as much as Rhianna did. No one would try as hard as she.

'You propose taking a great risk,' Thull-turock said.

'Take the risk with me,' Daylan begged. 'We need to stand together on this. We need the emir, and he will need your people to grant him endowments.'

'And what if we fail? What if this great wrym takes the emir? What if we breathe life into a monster?'

'There is a fiend in each of us,' Daylan said, 'in every man, woman, and child. The emir wrestled his into submission long ago.' Daylan said this with finality, as if he was sure of his argument.

'And if it escapes?'

'Then I will kill the emir myself,' Daylan replied.

The emir shook his head in dismay. 'I would take my own life, rather than allow a wyrm to have it.'

All of them were quiet for a moment. The facilitator seemed unsure. 'Help us,' Daylan begged Thull-turock. 'Help us all create a better world. This is not just about me and you. It is not just a war confined to these few thousand people. Worlds are at stake here. Eternities are at stake. We fight for things beyond your ability to even dream . . .'

'Is not every war such a war?' Thull-turock asked. 'At least, we tell ourselves so.'

The men stood a moment, poised in thought.

Talon wondered at the consequences of this public argument. In order to grant endowments to another, it had to be done willingly. But who would give endowments to the Emir Tuul Ra now, knowing what all of them knew? Even if their minds wanted to give up the endowment, the heart would balk.

Daylan Hammer seemed to have won his argument, but he had done so only in appearance.

The emir held his daughter, Siyaddah, trying to comfort her. But it seemed to Talon that the emir was the one who would need comforting. Thull-turock had poisoned the crowd against him.

After a lifetime of proving himself to Talon's people, the emir needed to do so once again.

Siyaddah peered up at the emir and declared loudly. 'I want to be first to offer an endowment to my father. I grant you my speed, that you might hurry into battle, if you will take it?'

No daughter had ever broken her father's heart so cruelly. The emir needed endowments. He needed his people to step forward, and by offering her speed, Siyaddah was urging others to follow her example.

At the same time, she was placing herself forever beyond his reach. For once she gave an endowment of metabolism, she would fall into an enchanted slumber, never to waken until he died, or else to die in her sleep.

More than that, she was placing herself beyond the heart of any man. The emir had long hoped that she would marry his closest friend, Areth Sul Urstone. She herself was more interested in Fallion. Now, neither of the men would ever win her heart.

It was a cruel gift to offer, for the emir could not refuse it. He had sworn to save his friend.

'Very well,' Erringale said. 'It is in the finest tradition of the Ael that those who know the candidate best be first to offer up an endowment. Who else among you will grant this greatest of gifts?'

There was a moment of utter silence as each of the emir's supporters waited for someone else to offer an endowment.

This isn't right, Talon thought. The emir is one of the best swordsmen in the clans, and he is by far the finest strategist. He knows the enemy better than does any other man.

And suddenly, Talon realized how the emir might prove himself to his people once again.

She strode to the emir and slapped his face, hard.

'Emir Tuul Ra,' she said, 'I challenge you to a duel. I'll fight you for the right to win a place in this rescue party.'

11

BEAUTY

Power is beautiful, and the Great Wyrm is the most beautiful of us all.

—From the Wyrmling Catechism

Rhianna saw that the horse-sisters' preparation for the raid on the wyrmlings took precedence over all else that night. They immediately went to work setting all in motion for battle. Because Caer Luciare was far away, the first order of business among the sisters was to feed their horses miln, a rich mixture of grain and molasses, to ready them for the long run.

Then the sisters began to pack, taking only light weapons and armor. That decision alone astonished Rhianna. To fight a wyrmling was an act of courage. To fight one in nothing but a horse-sister's leather jerkin was heroic.

Meanwhile, facilitators, smiths, and jewelers began making forcibles – recasting each metal rod with the proper rune at its tip, and then filing and hammering the soft blood metal into shape.

Once each forcible was deemed usable, the facilitators could transfer endowments from one horse to another – giving each horse two endowments of metabolism, one of brawn, and one of stamina.

The smiths worked fast, far faster than the men of Caer Luciare had been able to. In part they sped along because they knew *how* to make forcibles. It was an ancient art here. In part they worked quickly because the women's small hands and nimble fingers found it easier to do the work. In part they flew through the work because the master craftsmen each first took endowments of metabolism. Thus, they hoped to accomplish in one day what might otherwise have taken weeks.

The making of force horses would prove to be their greatest problem, Rhianna knew. It was a time-consuming process.

With horses, an endowment could only be transferred to the leader of a herd, whether it be a stallion or a mare.

Thus, creating a force horse sounded as if it should be easy. You could just cut the leader from the herd, and then draw endowments from the colts above one year of age.

But it wasn't so easy as all of that. You didn't want to take endowments from just any colt. For brawn, you might want a heavy war horse, perhaps one of the imperial breed. For speed, a racehorse from the desert. For stamina, a simple workhorse might do, though mules were sometimes used. For wit, there was a breed called the Carther Mountain ponies.

And so before the facilitators could endow a horse, they had to take the strongest adults, horses two years or a bit above of age, and corral them with five or six others, creating a small herd, and then give the animals a day to fight.

Once a herd leader emerged, the endowments could be stripped from the others.

By dusk, Rhianna hoped, the first forty force horses would be ready to go.

But humans were not so finicky when it came to granting endowments, and before dawn a facilitator came to Rhianna's tent. She was a small woman with dark hair, in costly attire.

'We are ready for the ceremony,' she said. 'Which endowment would you like first?'

Rhianna hadn't given it much thought. Brawn, she wondered. Or speed.

In that moment's hesitation, the facilitator made up Rhianna's mind for her. 'Glamour,' she said. 'When creating a powerful Runelord, the first few should always be glamour – and then

voice. It makes it easier for others to give their endowments
to those that they love, and you will be stronger for it in the
long run.'

Rhianna's heart skipped a beat at the thought. Glamour. Raj
Ahten had been rich with it, so rich that women who should
have hated him were filled with lust, and would spread their
legs for him. Men who saw him imagined that there could be
no maliciousness in him.

'When you see the face of pure evil,' an old saying went,
'it will be beautiful.'

Rhianna wanted to be beautiful, as fair as a summer morn,
as powerful as a tempest. She had heard of Raj Ahten's wife
Saffira, with hundreds of endowments of glamour. No man
could resist her. To look upon her made men weak with desire.

Fallion will love me, Rhianna thought. I can make him love
me more than he could ever imagine.

And as quickly as the thought came, she repented of it,
trying to force the selfish desire away.

'Glamour,' she confirmed.

The endowment ceremony took place in Sister Daughtry's
pavilion, with Rhianna and her new Dedicate resting among
plush cushions.

Her first Dedicate was a young girl, perhaps no more than
sixteen. In the blush of youth, her eyes were bright and her
skin as white as cream.

'In giving this gift,' she said, looking noble and tragic, 'I
honor you, and I give myself for my land. Use my gift well,
milady.'

The girl's courtly mannerisms were overstated. She tried to
look brave, but she was trembling in fear.

'Be of comfort,' Rhianna said. 'Your gift does you honor. I
promise to engage it in the service of our people, and I will
remember always this covenant between us.'

But even as Rhianna said the words, she wondered how she
could keep such a promise. She wanted the girl's beauty so
badly, she ached for it.

The facilitator took a forcible and inspected it, then began her harking song as she sought to ease the mind of the Dedicate. All too quickly, the forcible began to glow white-hot. The facilitator touched it to the back of the girl's neck, and then pulled away a snake of light. It seemed to extend from the girl, growing longer and longer, as the facilitator examined it.

Rhianna was lost in her imaginings all through the ceremony, wondering how well Fallion might love her. And in a moment, the facilitator touched the forcible to Rhianna's breast, and her mind seemed to explode. The feeling of health that entered her, of well-being and ecstasy, was something she could never have imagined. It struck through her like lightning, and for an instant the pleasure was so intense that she blacked out.

When she came to, a facilitator's aide put a robe over the new Dedicate, and pulled down a deep brown hood, so that Rhianna could not see the girl's face.

Rhianna knew what the girl would look like, though. Those fine bright eyes would be dull and lusterless, their whites having gone to sickly yellow. Her smooth skin would be dry and papery. Her gleaming hair would have turned limp and dull. Her face would be a wreck.

The facilitator studied Rhianna for an instant, the way that a sculptor might look at his own work, searching it for defects. 'Beautiful,' she said. 'You look so beautiful.'

It was near dawn, and the campfires sputtered and raged in a contrary wind outside the tent. War horns blew in the distance, and there was some commotion as riders came into camp, announcing that they had caught a wyrmling woman. Rhianna went outside to see the cause of the commotion, and saw only a young girl, giant though she was. Her hands were tied together, and she had been forced to run for miles while horse-sisters drove her from behind at lance-point.

'What is this?' Sister Daughtry called to the sisters as they brought their charge toward camp.

'One of the white giants,' the horse-sisters said. 'We found her to the north, with three men on her tail. She speaks Inkarran.'

Sister Daughtry studied the girl, impressed at her size. 'So this is one of your wyrmlings,' she whispered under her breath to Rhianna. 'This is what we must fight?'

Sister Daughtry called out to the girl, 'Kwi et choulon zah?'

'Kirissa Mentarn,' the girl answered. Then she began to speak rapidly. Sister Daughtry inclined her head and frowned.

'Was there a man with her, a huge wyrmling?'

'There was,' one rider answered.

'She asks what happened to him.'

'He's dead. He fought two other wyrmlings, and wounded both before they killed him. We avenged him,' the rider said.

Sister Daughtry broke the news to the girl in halting words. The wyrmling girl did not seem surprised, and though there was sadness in her face, she was not overwrought with grief.

Instead, she kept peering at Rhianna, at her wings, as if Rhianna were some icon of great power. Indeed, though she faced the others, her eyes stayed riveted upon Rhianna, as if she believed that Rhianna led the clans.

Kirissa kept talking, spewing out words in flawless Inkarran so quickly that Sister Daughtry seemed incapable of following. 'She says that when the worlds were tied together, two halves of herself became one,' Daughtry explained. 'At least that is what I think she is saying. She found herself among the wyrmling horde, and tried to escape. She wants to go home, to Inkarra.'

Rhianna said, 'Ask her if she has seen a wizard, a young man with wings like mine.'

Daughtry asked the question, and the girl nodded violently and began pointing to the ground, as if to explain where she had seen him. She demonstrated how the man had wings like Rhianna's.

Fallion, Rhianna realized. This woman had seen Fallion. Everything in Rhianna made her want to grab the wyrmling girl and force the information out of her, but Rhianna knew only a few words of Inkarran.

Sister Daughtry grew thoughtful. 'We must find a translator. The girl knows of your man. She has not seen him personally, but knows where to find him. I do not speak enough Inkarran to trust myself to the task of translating.'

One horse-sister offered, 'Sister Gadron speaks the tongue well. She is riding in the Winters' Camp, last I heard.'

'Go and beg her to join us,' Sister Daughtry said. Then she told the riders, 'Feed and water this girl. Untie her. Treat her as a guest. Though she is a giant, she is not much more than a child. When Sister Gadron arrives, we'll learn what we can learn.'

Rhianna studied the girl, who squatted on the ground timidly while children from the camp circled her, gaping. For her part, the girl peered up at Rhianna in frank wonder and jutted her chin toward Rhianna's wings once again, as if to remark upon them. Then the girl lowered her head in a token of respect.

She knows what I had to kill to win these wings, Rhianna realized. What she doesn't know is how many more of the Knights Eternal I plan to kill.

Rhianna went back into the tent, and left the wyrmling girl out on the plains, the wind blustering through her hair while smoke from the campfires roiled across the ground.

By noon Rhianna had taken eighty endowments, including enough brawn, grace, stamina, and metabolism from the clan's strongest men that she could fight any wyrmling warrior.

But more than that, she had three endowments of voice from the horse-sisters' finest singers. Hearing and scent were taken from camp dogs. Endowments of wit came from three of the horse-sisters' brightest young students.

Rhianna had never imagined what it would be like to be a powerful Runelord.

With three endowments of wit, she was able to recall nearly everything that she saw and heard flawlessly.

Her endowments of hearing and scent seemed to open whole new worlds of perception, for with endowments of scent from dogs, the world seemed to expand, and her mind came alive to nuances of smell and taste that had always been beyond mere mortals. She could taste the scent of blood on the wind from miles away, and suddenly she realized how this keen new sense might warn her of future dangers.

With three endowments of hearing, she became aware of women whispering in their tents a hundred yards off. With endowments of sight, finches and sparrows in the far fields seemed to stand out with crystalline clarity.

She had gone nearly two days without sleep, but with her endowments of stamina, she did not feel weary.

I need never sleep again, Rhianna realized.

Late that morning, the translator arrived to question Kirissa. Sister Gadron was a small mousy woman who rode a blood mount. She smelled of sheep and children, and had marvelously white skin – almost as pale as a wyrmling's. Her long silver hair hung neatly down her back, and dark tattoos snaked along her leg and circled her wrist like bangles. She was obviously a full-blooded Inkarran.

Rhianna followed her into a tent, where Kirissa hid from the daylight beneath a sheepskin.

The sun beating through the red silken walls of the tent burned Kirissa's eyes so that she kept her head turned aside and down, and closed them as much as possible as she spoke with the Inkarran.

The presence of one of the winged ones in the room made Kirissa nervous. Among wyrmlings only the Death Lords wore wings, as did the royals. Kirissa could not be sure whom the woman had killed for the wings.

At first, the questions were easy: What is your name? Where are you from? Why are you here in the desert?

For two long hours the translator asked questions, and Kirissa answered them all. Only a few times did the questions stump her. The first was of her lineage. It was important in Inkarra, and Kirissa was able to tell Sister Gadron about her family there, but among the wyrmlings family was nothing – unless one was of royal blood.

Then it was queries about ancient history. Where did the wyrmlings hail from?

It was a question that Kirissa had never heard an answer to. The study of history was not important to wyrmlings. Time wiped away all clues to the past.

The horse-sisters grilled her about leadership. Sister Gadron asked what the emperor planned to do with the small folk? What would he do if he was attacked?

Kirissa told her, 'I can only guess at the emperor's plans, but what does that matter? The Great Wyrm now walks the labyrinth. Despair himself is in charge. The emperor is now just another Death Lord, a shade.'

'Who is this Great Wyrm?' Sister Gadron asked.

'Despair, the creator of heaven and earth, the great lord of all wyrms. It takes human form from time to time, and two nights ago, the Great Wyrm seized the body of a new host.'

At last Sister Gadron was satisfied with Kirissa's story, unsettling though it might be. Now the questions turned to Cullossax.

'What did Cullossax do in Rugassa?' Sister Gadron asked.

Kirissa answered, 'He was a tormentor. It was his job to torture and punish those who broke wyrmling laws, whether their offense consisted of actively doing wrong, or failing to do well. By killing the weak and unruly, he culled the horde.'

'Why did he run? Was he your lover? Your father?'

Kirissa hesitated. 'I think he wanted to destroy the horde, to help·create a better society.'

'So you converted him?'

Kirissa shrugged. 'It appeared so.'

'Can many wyrmlings be converted, do you think?'

Kirissa had never considered that question. 'No,' she said. 'Most of them would be too afraid to run. They have heard of the terrors of life outside the keep – the burning sun, the merciless humans. I ran only because I knew that there was a better life.'

Sister Gadron's next query was foolish. 'Did he love you?'

'Humans love,' Kirissa answered. 'Wyrmlings merely spawn. It is not the same.'

'Why do you have nubs on your head?' Sister Gadron asked.

'Because I am old enough to grow them.'

'Do you have a wyrm feeding upon your soul?'

'How would I know?'

'Why do you want to give your soul to a wyrm?'

Again, Kirissa hesitated. 'I never wanted that. Not all wyrm-lings do. Only the most devout have such hopes. I was always afraid that the wyrms wished only to feed upon us.'

'How many of your own wyrmling people have you killed?'

'Two,' Kirissa said. 'I killed another girl when I was four, and one when I was eight.'

'Why did you kill them?'

'They angered me. Among the wyrmling horde, what I did was not considered wrong. I fought them with knives, and won the respect of others.'

'Do you know right from wrong?'

'I know wyrmling law,' Kirissa said, 'and I know Inkarran law. I have a feeling that matters of right and wrong go deeper than either law.'

'You said earlier that when Cullossax took you from your school, he was supposed to lead you to slaughter. Have you eaten the flesh of your own people?'

'I ate what was put before me,' Kirissa said. 'Among the wyrmlings there is a saying, "Flesh is flesh." It does not matter whether it is human or animal, but some prefer wyrmling flesh.'

'Why is that?'

'It is said that wyrmling flesh tastes better than that of other animals. The meat of a child is sweetest of all.'

'When you killed other children, did you eat them after-ward?'

'That is an honor that I won,' Kirissa said.

Sister Gadron rephrased some of her questions. The small woman asked again about wyrms. Do you have a wyrm in you? Do you take orders from a wyrm? Are you infested with a wyrm?

At last when she was satisfied, the woman with wings asked a question, and Sister Gadron translated. 'Can you draw a map of Rugassa?'

Kirissa hesitated. For two hours she had been burning with curiosity about the winged woman. Now she dared ask the question that haunted her. 'First, may I have the honor of asking some questions?'

The translator said, 'I suppose.'

'Who did you kill to get those wings?'

The translator spoke to the winged woman, and she answered, 'I slew a Knight Eternal, at the battle of Caer Luciare.'

The news made Kirissa's heart swell with relief. She began to weep tears.

'Why are you crying?' the winged woman asked.

'Because the Knights Eternal can be killed,' Kirissa said. At her hosts' expression of bafflement, Kirissa continued, 'From the moment that I decided to run, one question has burned in my mind: will the wyrmlings kill us all, or will we be able to fight and destroy them. When the Earth King died, he warned me that "the time will come when the small ones of the world must stand against the large." But having seen the wyrmling horde, I am terrified. My fear is that they will overwhelm us. I have heard rumors of strange things happening – beasts being brought from shadow worlds, and the coming of Despair. The wyrmlings are more dangerous than you know.'

Kirissa continued, 'But if you can kill a Knight Eternal, if you can strike down their leaders, then there is some hope.'

Kirissa studied the winged woman, her pale red hair and strong cheeks. There was an air of dangerousness about her. She had the taut posture of one who has practiced with the sword for long hours, and the thickness of her thighs, calves, and biceps all bore witness to such labors.

'Do you have a name?' Kirissa asked.

'Rhianna,' the woman said, and Kirissa repeated the name in her mind, over and over.

Rhianna, she thought, my savior.

Rhianna asked her question again, this time speaking in Inkarran. 'Can you draw a map of Rugassa?'

'That would be impossible,' Kirissa said. 'It is said that no one knows the labyrinth in whole – at least not among the common folk. The labyrinth is vast, and there are many passages with many twists and turns. The corridors rise and fall, so that you never know what level you are on. I knew only a small part of it. I could try to make you a map, but I know some passages by their look. If I were to miscount the doors you had to pass to get somewhere, you would be forever lost.'

'Do you know where the wizard Fallion Orden is kept?' Rhianna asked through the interpreter, and there was a depth of longing in her voice.

'He is in the dungeon, in the human wing,' Kirissa said. 'I saw him.'

'Was he alive?'

'Yes,' Kirissa said, 'last that I saw.'

'Do you know where Areth Sul Urstone is kept?'

'I do not know what cell he is kept in.'

'Is he alive?'

'I do not know.'

'Could you lead me to them? Do you know the labyrinth well enough?'

Kirissa pondered. 'No. I was there once, but only once. My tormentor cuffed me unconscious along the way. I don't remember how to reach the dungeons. I'm sorry.'

Suddenly Rhianna fell silent, became thoughtful.

Kirissa asked, 'Are you going to free me?'

'If you were free, what would you do?' Rhianna asked.

'Go home,' Kirissa said.

'How could you go,' Rhianna asked, 'knowing what the wyrmling horde is going to do? Would it not be better to fight? You could be a great help to me.'

Kirissa bit her lower lip, and considered. Somehow, in the back of her mind, she'd known when she left the keep that it would come to this. The Earth King himself had warned her that this time would come.

'I'll help you,' Kirissa said. 'What will you ask of me?'

Through her interpreter, Rhianna said, 'We are going to rescue Fallion Orden and Areth Sul Urstone.'

Kirissa recalled the guard that she had heard about in

Fallion Orden's cell. 'That will be difficult. Vulgnash guards him, and it is rumored that he has taken many endowments.'

'Of course,' Rhianna said, undeterred. 'We anticipate that the wyrmlings will do all within their power to thwart us. But we must try anyway. Will you help us?' she asked. 'You have said that you want to make a better world. This would be a fine place to start.'

'If I go back with you,' Kirissa said, 'my life is over. My only hope for survival is if you grant me endowments.'

Rhianna studied her, eyes narrowing, showing the smallest worry lines. 'Who would grant endowments to a wyrmling?' she asked. 'Perhaps we can find another way . . .'

In the early afternoon, Rhianna paced through the camp. She felt so strong, so full of energy that she could not hold still. That was part of her problem. But more than anything else, she worried.

Sister Daughtry came and walked beside her. 'You've heard troubling news?'

Certainly Sister Daughtry had heard everything that Rhianna had. Still, it helped to have someone to talk with.

'If Kirissa is right, there is a new enemy leading the wyrmling horde, one that has gone by many names – the Great Wyrm, Despair, the One True Master of Evil.

'Daylan Hammer and the others need to know this. But there is no way that I can reach them.'

Sister Daughtry's face was an unreadable mask. Rhianna suspected that she was trying hard to hide her own alarm.

'Your friends said that they would make their attack on Rugassa within three days, is that correct?'

'Yes,' Rhianna said. 'But I'm worried that they will take too long. Rugassa's new master will need forcibles, thousands and thousands of them.'

'And of course,' Sister Daughtry said, 'the wyrmlings will be out to impress their new master. You said that the wyrmlings can be expected to travel a hundred miles in a night. But your little Kirissa has shown us that a wyrmling can travel by daylight, if the need is strong enough.'

'Exactly,' Rhianna said. 'Daylan Hammer, I'm sure, imagined that the wyrmlings would travel only by night. He may be right. The blood metal is so precious, they'll want to have Death Lords and Knights Eternal to guard their caravan, and the Death Lords cannot abide the day.

'But for the sake of haste, the wyrmlings might elect to move the blood metal by air, using their giant graaks. Even a Knight Eternal might carry a few.'

'If you're right,' Sister Daughtry said, 'it might well be that the wyrmlings have already moved some ore, flown it from Caer Luciare to Rugassa.'

'I doubt it,' Rhianna said. 'The wyrmlings took the city at dawn two days ago. I saw no sign of them mining by daylight when we left. That means that they waited until sunset to begin. They would have started digging last night. But the refining process is easy, and it won't take long.

'Blood metal boils at a low heat. You must heat it, stir, let the impurities settle and cool a bit, then pour off the clean metal from the top. Several times, if I recall.'

'Twenty times is best,' Sister Daughtry said. 'Though it can be done fewer.'

'So refining it will still take more than a single night,' Rhianna thought aloud.

Sister Daughtry said, 'They would have taken the ore into the fortress and worked on it throughout the day.'

'That means that their caravan probably did not get on the road until last night, at sunset, at the earliest.'

'If the blood metal was sent by graak,' Sister Daughtry said, 'then it may have already reached Rugassa.'

Rhianna fought back the urge to pace.

'You will not rest until you know where that shipment is,' Sister Daughtry said, giving her a knowing look.

Rhianna did not hesitate. She leapt in the air and took off in a rush of wings, flying toward Rugassa. She was determined to go there first, then trace the route south as she searched for the wyrmling convoy.

With so many endowments of metabolism and brawn, she

sped through the air like a bolt. In less than an hour she neared Rugassa. With her endowments of sight, she could see the roads well enough to recognize that there were no convoys traveling in the afternoon sun.

Her only hope was that the convoy was still farther south.

She veered, hurtling along. Her four endowments of metabolism made her swifter than a falcon.

Rhianna skirted above the trees and brush, staying nearly half a mile in the air. Much of the country was lush fields that had gone brown with the summer sun. The intermittent oaks were a dark green.

She found the convoy none too soon. The sun was falling in a red haze.

A giant black graak could be seen ahead, sleeping beside a rocky crag, in the shadows on the northern exposure of a wooded hill. It raised its snake-like neck and peered up into the trees. She could see perhaps a dozen wyrmling guards breaking their camp, some of them hauling chests to load onto the graak while others puttered around.

Rhianna was loath to do battle with so many wyrmlings, but she had no choice. If she left them to their own affairs, their load of forcibles would reach Rugassa tonight.

And if she did not attack now, she would lose the advantage of daylight.

She climbed high in the air, flying toward the sun, then folded her wings and dove toward the guards.

They never saw her coming. At the last instant she folded her wings, molding them to her body, and went hurtling just overhead of the huge graak – a sharpened sword snicking the neck of the graak, then taking the heads off of two guards.

The graak roared in panic and tried to lift into the air, but a great leather rope bound it to a tree, so that it flapped and roared and lurched about angrily as it died.

The wyrmlings were thrown into a panic. Their reaction surprised her. Six of the guards scattered, rushing blindly into the shadows of the trees, trying to escape. Two others threw down their weapons, hoping for mercy.

Only two of them prepared for battle.

Rhianna suddenly realized that she was moving so blindingly fast that the wyrmlings hadn't got a good look at her. They saw only the wings, and most of them seemed to believe that she was one of their own Knights Eternal. Perhaps they feared that they had displeased their masters somehow.

With a rush of insight, Rhianna realized that she would not need allies for this raid.

I am an army, she thought.

With that she dove into the wyrmlings, to take vengeance for the man she loved.

She swept into two defenders who had kept their wits. One of them hurled an iron war dart, but she easily dipped a wing, dodging the missile.

He raised his axe high, and Rhianna folded her wings at the last instant, letting her weight carry her under his guard. She cut him down at the knee, hurtled past him; then in a thunder of wings she slowed her course, flipped in the air, landed, and faced the next challenge.

The second guard roared and spun to meet her with such speed that Rhianna realized that he must have taken a few endowments himself, but she was endowed like one of the great Runelords of old, and he was no match for her. She plunged her blade into him three times before he could raise a shield to defend himself, and while he began to stagger from his death blow, she whirled and went after the surrendering guards, cutting them down even as they realized their error.

Then she flew into the woods, giving chase to those that had fled.

Two minutes later, not a wyrmling was left.

The giant graak lay on its belly, bleeding its life away, panting from exertion.

There were half a dozen chests on the ground. Rhianna lifted one, heard the clank of forcibles. By its heft, she figured that it weighed a hundred pounds, and held a thousand forcibles.

One by one, Rhianna lugged each chest into the sky, and

then flew them to an abandoned well near an old farmhouse some twenty miles off.

There was no way to erase the signs of her battle. The enormous graak lay in a ruined heap, and Rhianna could not afford to waste time by trying to hide the body.

As a trophy of war, she carried a chest with a thousand forcibles back to the horse clans.

12

ORACLES

The appearance of weakness invites attack. Therefore, show weakness only when you want to lure others into battle.

—Lord Despair

The sun had just begun to fall beyond the horizon when Lord Despair sensed the attack.

He was at the summoning fields, hidden within the bowl of the volcano that was Mount Rugassa. Here Zul-torac had opened the gate to a shadow world called Thiss, and even now emissaries from that brutal world awaited him – the Chaos Oracles.

They stood in the gloom of the evening. The first star shone overhead, and bats flitted about in the sky above. But the Chaos Oracles could not be seen, not clearly at least. Vague forms could be sensed, monstrous creatures with spurs of bone that rose up from their backs and heads like cruel thorns, but a storm seemed to swirl about them – ragged bits of cloud and striations of darkness screaming in a whirl, hiding their forms, so that all that could be seen from time to time was the odd horn or glowing eye.

There were four of them in the field, or perhaps five. Even Lord Despair could not be certain, and the folks in his retinue reacted to the strangers with a mixture of fear and revulsion.

Strange thoughts passed through Despair's mind – wisps of memories of torture, half-forgotten dreams, the voices of people who had died long ago, the faces of strangers seen in childhood. There was no order or coherence. Random images and sounds flashed through his mind. It was a sensation unique to those who met Thissians.

At Despair's side was his trusted servant Emperor Zul-torac, a sorcerer who had forsaken his flesh, and now only hovered, draped in a wispy black cowl to lend him some form. At their backs was a retinue of a dozen wyrmling dignitaries – a pair of Death Lords, a pair of Knights Eternal, and the High Council from the Temple of the Wyrm. Last of all came the emperor's own daughter, Kan-hazur, who had just escaped two nights ago from Caer Luciare. The girl limped along slowly, her visage gray and weary.

Her years in prison have made her weak, Despair thought. We should put her to work in the mines, toughen her up.

Despair's fearsome servants did not seem to know how to react to the Thissians. The strange visions and distorted sounds had frightened his men.

Despair stood, studying the Thissians warily.

'Why do they not speak?' one council member whispered.

'It is a custom on Thiss,' Despair answered. 'When strangers meet, they announce their benevolent intent by standing silently for several minutes, regarding one another. The Thissians are searching your minds, sifting through your dreams and ambitions, reliving the memories that have shaped you. They are getting to know you better than most of you will ever know yourselves.'

The wyrmlings seemed to accept the statement, but after a long moment Emperor Zul-torac asked, 'Why can we not see them?' His voice whispered like the wind among dead grasses.

'They can bend light to their command, just as do my Darkling Glories or the strengi-saats,' Despair explained. 'Night hunters on dozens of worlds have developed this skill – but few of them so powerfully as the Chaos Oracles.'

He said no more, but one of the High Council members

whispered, 'Ah, I see: that is why you are bringing us all together.'

Dull creature, Despair thought. He should have seen it much sooner.

Despair marked the man for death.

'But darkness has nearly fallen,' Emperor Zul-torac noted. 'Surely these ones can let their mists dissipate.'

'No,' Despair whispered, 'they will never let the mists of darkness down. Among the shadow worlds, the Thissians are unique. Their forms are hideous even to themselves, and to others of their own kind. Thus they have learned to clothe themselves in mists and wisps of darkness, to hide themselves from themselves. They do not look upon one another, even to copulate.'

A Knight Eternal, Kryssidia, said boldly, 'I want to see them anyway.'

'And if you saw one,' Despair said, 'you would regret it for as long as you live. The image would haunt you, torment you, and drive you mad. Be thankful that they hide themselves.'

The world of Thiss was unknown to Despair's ancient enemies, the Bright Ones of the netherworld. There were so many worlds to monitor, to map, that the Bright Ones had given up long ago. Despair, of course, had made certain that they were too occupied to turn their eyes to these far places.

Thiss was but one of tens of thousands of worlds that had fallen into Despair's grasp. While the Bright Ones remained woefully ignorant of such worlds, Despair comprehended them all.

At that moment, Earth's warning struck, and Despair gasped. 'Something is wrong,' he said. 'Something in the world has changed. Our enemy has raised his hand against us.'

The emperor shifted at Despair's side. 'Are you certain?'

'The Earth Spirit has been whispering to me for days that an enemy is coming,' Despair answered, 'telling me that my servants should flee Rugassa. I have ignored the warnings. My shipment of blood metal should be here soon, and our allies are coming – things that should tip the scales in our favor. But something has happened . . .'

'Perhaps your enemies have begun taking endowments,' the emperor said, his robes fluttering just above the ground.

'We need not guess at our enemy's plans,' Despair said. 'We have the Chaos Oracles to guide us. Listen . . .'

He had waited a full five minutes to address his guests, time enough for them to get acquainted.

'Have my servants told you why I summoned you?' Despair called out.

From within the vortex of swirling mists and tatters of night, a voice answered. 'No one has told, but we know.' The accent was strange, soft and crackly, and the voice was filled with hisses and pops, like the sound of meat sizzling above a flame. It carried the hint of the Thissian tongue, but the Thissians had sifted through the wyrmlings' memories and learned their language well.

'Tell me, why I have sent for you then,' Despair said, 'so that my friends may begin to understand your worth.'

'You seek to create an alliance so powerful that you will overwhelm the inhabitants of the universe. You seek to dominate them for all time. You need us to translate your desires to creatures from a thousand worlds.'

'And can my plans succeed?' Despair asked. This was a question in his mind. He had pondered the plans for eons, and he wished to know if all was in order. Despair planned to create alliances among the cruelest races in the shadow worlds.

'Your plans will succeed, O Great Darkness,' a Thissian answered. 'Worlds shall grovel at your command.'

One of Despair's men whispered, 'How can they know?' His voice was so soft that the question should not have been over-heard, but a Thissian answered.

'Can you not see it? Time is like a river, flowing down-stream, but not all of the water moves one way. There are eddies and whorls and backflows, if you look closely. Time is this way. Not all can be seen, but glimpses can. I behold countless worlds, groaning beneath Despair's burden. I behold seas of blood. I witness darkness falling across the heavens, smothering out all light.'

Despair felt pleased, and he looked to see his wyrmlings' reaction. Some seemed doubtful, others eager.

'What do I offer for your aid?' Despair asked, not because he doubted that they knew, but so that the Thissians could prove their powers to the others.

In answer, a hand rose above the swirling mists of darkness – a hand with but two enormous fingers, both of them twisted and covered with bony thorns. It pointed toward the first star of the night. 'Worlds without end,' the Chaos Oracle intoned, 'all under our sway.'

'And do you accept the offer?'

There was hesitation. 'Your people are strong in the ways of war, and races from among the stars shall flock to your call. But none are like us. None are like the people of Thiss. You are unperceptive, hardly more sentient than stones.'

'That cannot be helped,' Despair said.

'We are so alone,' the Thissians mourned.

'Nor can I offer any comfort to you,' Despair said. 'In the whole universe there are no others like you. You will remain alone, yet I will cherish you above all other allies.' Despair paused. 'Will you share my fate?'

The Thissians hissed and crackled for a moment as they spoke in their own tongue; after a bit one answered, 'We shall.'

Despair smiled in satisfaction.

'Now,' he said, 'the Earth warns that my fortress will soon be under attack. From what quarter comes the danger?'

The Thissians hesitated a moment. 'There is a treasure that you seek – rods of blood metal. They have fallen into enemy hands . . .' After a bit longer, 'They will use them . . . they come . . . to free the Worldbinder.'

'Can we thwart their plan?'

'Yes, O Great Wyrm, easily. Send your Knights Eternal . . .'

Despair stood facing one of his Knights Eternal, Kryssidia. 'Take your companion and fly to Caer Luciare in all haste.'

The Death Lord in command of Caer Luciare had been slain. Despair did not even know the name of the wyrmling now in charge. 'Tell the commander of the fortress that I need a shipment now – enough blood metal for two thousand forcibles, no less.'

Despair felt in his heart. Giving this command would make a difference, the Earth agreed. The danger diminished, but did not dissipate completely. Despair did not understand why. Perhaps two thousand forcibles was not enough. Or perhaps they would not arrive in time.

He considered ordering a larger shipment, but that did not ease his mind. No, he needed them quickly – just as the Thissians had warned.

It was a long way to Caer Luciare. The Knights Eternal would not be able to fly there and back in a single night. They would be forced to land short of their mark, wait out the day tomorrow. So he added, 'Let nothing delay you. Fly there and return without rest. It would be better for you to break your necks in your haste than to let me down.'

Kryssidia glanced uncomfortably upward to where the thin evening light streamed above the rocks along the bowl of the volcano's cone, but he did not hesitate. He dropped to one knee, put a hand upon the hilt of his sword, and said, 'Your every desire commands my deeds.'

Then he nodded to his companion and the Knights Eternal leapt into the sky.

Despair wished that he had more knights like these. His Death Lords, with their ability to communicate from spirit to spirit across the leagues, had certain advantages, but they could not take endowments.

He made a mental note to have some warriors go down among the wyrmling horde to find some pregnant females. Knights Eternal could only be recruited from stillborn babes. The rites necessary to create the proper conditions were long and arduous, and as part of the ceremony, his priest needed to strangle a fetus while it was still in the womb, and then rip it from its mother. As the child lay dying, it would crave air, crave life, and if the child was cunning enough, the Death Lords had a brief window of opportunity to teach it the spells necessary to tear the life force from those around it.

If it survived the first five minutes out of the womb, its training would begin in earnest. Only one in thousands survived those first five minutes.

Yet even the diligence of the Knights Eternal did not lessen the coming danger.

Despair stood for a moment in the cone of the volcano and peered upward, gazing at the stars for a long moment before he headed into the fortress.

There is much to do, he thought. There are worlds to conquer.

Held captive in his own body, Areth Sul Urstone was witness to the evil imaginings of Despair's heart. Despair looked up at the stars and could not admire their beauty. Instead, they were only a reminder of his failure. He wanted only to seize them, bind them, and rule over a world perfect but for one flaw – himself.

Areth considered what to do. It was said that a man could resist a wyrm. Do good, legend said, and they will flee from you. Do evil, and they will bind you and make you theirs.

Already, Areth wondered if he had the will any longer to resist Lord Despair.

For his part, Despair heard the stirring of Areth within his skull, and mocked. 'Plot as you will, your soul is mine. You gave it to me freely, to save your people. And I shall keep my word: your people shall live – under my rule.'

13

THE DUEL

Every creature must struggle for that which it needs.
Do not waste sympathy on the vanquished. The weak
get what they deserve.

—From the Wyrmling Catechism

'Emir Tuul Ra of Dalharristan, I challenge you to a duel!' Talon
intoned. 'I fight for honor, and for the right to take endowments to battle the wyrmling horde and save my brother.'

The emir's face was still turned to the side. He worked his
lips, and spat blood and spittle onto the ground. Then he
looked up at Talon and smiled wolfishly.

The emir knew what she was after. The Cormar brothers,
Tun and Errant, could gather endowments easily. Their skill
was legendary, and those who were capable of sacrificing their
own brawn or grace would gladly make a gift to such worthy
warriors. But Talon was no one, a girl, and among the warrior
clans no woman challenged a man, unless she sought only to
humiliate him.

'Are you of an age where you can even make such a challenge?' the emir asked.

He studied Talon's demeanor. She was a handsome girl, and
strong. He admired her spirit.

But he could not let her make a fool of him, not if he hoped
to win the endowments that he'd need to free Areth Sul Urstone.

His question seemed to have caught Talon off guard.

'On your world,' she said, 'I am eighteen years. But on the other I was seventeen. It is not that I was born at different times, but that the years on this world are shorter than on the other.'

She stopped her rambling, focused on the question. 'In both worlds, I am old enough to make my own decisions in life.'

'Then I hope you know what you're doing,' the emir whispered. 'This is dangerous. I won't hold back. For my people's sake, I can't hold back.' It was not an idle threat. The Emir Tuul Ra knew that he was the finest warrior of his generation.

Talon gave him a wolfish smile of her own. 'I can take the best that you've got – and more.'

The emir sighed. He didn't want to fight her, but neither could he refuse the challenge.

In part he did not want to fight her because Talon was the daughter of a friend. And she was young, too young to know what she was doing.

But more important, he had just been in a council meeting attended by Glories. There had been a sweetness in the room, a feeling of inner cleanliness, so profound that it had made him want to weep.

It made him want to be like them. He wanted to feel holy, to carry his own inner peace with him.

How could I bear it, he wondered, if I were to take the life of this girl?

Yet he knew that he was the best warrior for the job. The life of a friend and comrade hung in the balance. He could not spare the girl, for to do so would put his friend, and the future of his people, in jeopardy.

'I have no choice but to accept your challenge,' Tuul Ra said.

It was raining when they exited the cave. The thunder that had shaken the sky earlier was gone, but the emir could hear it growling on the horizon. The skies were so leaden gray that it seemed that it was night, and rain was falling in sheets out on the grasslands.

But the magnificent pine of the netherworld held the storm at bay. A few great dirty drops splashed from the limbs of the tree, but it shed most of the water well beyond where they stood. The storm's only effect was to make a rushing sound as the wind tore through the pine boughs, and the treetops swayed under its onslaught.

Talon followed the emir onto their battleground, out at the far edges of the tree, where the light would be better. Pine needles and twigs lay thick all around, creating a soft carpet that crackled underfoot. The emir reached down with a toe and dug a large circle in the ground, roughly forty feet in diameter.

'To cross this line is to admit defeat,' he said.

Talon nodded in understanding. As the challenger in this duel, she was forced to ask, 'Choose your weapon!'

Choose the sword, he thought. It would be the gentlemanly thing to do. A bastard sword would be perfect for her, both in weight and size. He wanted to give her that much advantage. But a skilled warrior would recognize what he'd done.

'Wyrmling battle-axe,' he said. It was a heavy weapon – almost too heavy for a human to use. But it was a favorite of wyrmling warriors, and no doubt, if the girl hoped to enter the wyrmling keep, she'd have to show that she could deflect a blow.

The weapons were brought forward, and Talon regarded them in silence.

The wyrmling axe was not a weapon to be trifled with, nor was it easily controlled. If the emir took a swing, he realized, he could not pull back.

Talon would either have to block it or dodge it – or get sliced in two.

They took their axes, heavy things with double blades. Each weighed roughly thirty pounds. They were made for lopping off heads and arms.

The emir felt the edge of his blade. It was filled with nicks and had grown dull. There was blood on it. This was not a weapon human-made. Someone had taken it as a trophy of war, won it at the battle at Cantular.

If Talon got hit, her death would not be pretty.

If he got hit, his death would not be easy.

I cannot win this battle by slaughter, he suddenly realized. If the girl defeated him, no one would grant him endowments. And if he killed her, the horror of the spectacle would turn the people against him.

The only way to win, he realized, is to throw her from the arena.

One of the warlords stepped forward and drew a line at the center of the circle. The warriors faced each other, one on each side of the line.

The warlord held a coin in the air. When he let it drop, the battle would begin.

The emir studied Talon for a moment, eyeing the way that she held her axe. There were numerous fighting styles with the axe. Some men might hold it near the end of the handle, and take large, sweeping strokes, relying upon the weight of the weapon to do its damage. Such men were dangerous on the attack, but left themselves vulnerable.

Other men sought to balance the axe. They might block a blow with their axehead, hoping to ruin an attacker's weapon in the act. Or they could reverse the axe and use its handle to stab quickly.

A man who was quick with his hands could adjust his grip from one second to the next, using a number of tactics.

Talon held her axe with both hands, keeping it firmly balanced, unwilling to give away her battle tactics.

The emir spun his axe in one hand, limbering his muscles.

'Talon,' the emir said. 'I don't want your blood on my hands. There is still time to withdraw – with honor. I beg you to do so.'

'If I'm willing to risk my life against wyrmlings,' Talon said, 'I'll risk it against you. It makes little difference where I die.'

The emir nodded his agreement, and Talon added for good

measure, 'If it is any consolation, I don't want your blood on my hands, either. I urge you to withdraw. If you don't . . . well, one of us won't be going home for dinner.'

The warlord looked each of them in the eye in preparation for the battle.

The Emir Tuul Ra thought, There is no room for error with these weapons. I can't just look good, I must *be* good.

The warlord dropped his coin, and both combatants instantly sprang back a step, giving the warlord time to break clear of the battlefield.

Talon stood perfectly still, conserving her energy, sizing up the emir. She did not want to reveal her tactics, or her repertoire of skills, too early in the battle.

The emir took his battle-axe and began stalking around the circle, twirling it in one hand, ready to lunge in and swing.

After an instant, he paused, stood with his axe lowered at his side, and offered, 'Ladies first.'

Talon couldn't resist.

She twirled her own axe, not as a demonstration of her prowess, but in the 'Circle of Steel' style – which lent itself to defense but could swiftly turn into an attack.

Then she exploded for the kill. She raced in, her eyes pinned to the emir's, watching in order to anticipate his next move. She raised her own axe slightly, as if she would go for the throat, then dropped beneath his guard, rolling as she swept past his feet.

The crowd erupted into shouts of astonishment at her speed, and she nearly took his leg off with her first swing, but her axe met only empty air.

The emir leapt so high that he nearly seemed to take flight.

Many in the crowd gasped in astonishment, for though they had heard rumors of his prowess in battle, they had not all seen him in action.

He came down, his own axe slamming toward her.

His heart was filled with regret, for he knew that it was a killing blow.

Talon waited until he was committed to the attack, and the

last instant planted the handle of her own axe firmly into the ground with the head of the axe up high.

She caught the head of his axe on her own.

His blade shattered; sparks and shards of steel flew out. One hit Talon in the throat, and instantly blood coursed down her neck.

But he didn't give her time to recover; the emir reversed his axehead so that he came at her with a fresh blade, and struck again.

Talon leaned away, and the emir's blade narrowly missed her foot.

With one axe blade broken, the emir's weapon would no longer be balanced. It meant that his swings would require more energy to control, but were also more likely to go awry. It was a dubious advantage.

Talon swung at his unprotected back.

The emir tried to dodge, but she grazed his flank, then danced out of range.

'Getting slow in your old age?' Talon asked. 'There's still time to withdraw.'

The emir grinned. 'What, and miss sparring with such a lovely opponent?'

Talon glanced back, grinning at him, her eyes flashing dangerously. He had never fought a woman before, and suddenly her beauty and her vulnerability smote him.

He stepped back a pace, wishing that he were not here, feeling like a cornered animal. I'm not just fighting her, he realized, I'm fighting all of my protective instincts.

The emir circled wide, then rushed at her again. He was used to ranging the fields and woodlands, doing a hard day's work, and he knew that he could put up a good, long, sustained fight. But what he couldn't know was how hard *she* had trained, in those days when with every moment, she had to watch her back for assassins.

For the next five minutes, the two of them raced around the ring, putting on a demonstration of skills that both of them had purchased with a lifetime. Many were the cheers and the *oohs* and *ahs* of the crowd. Many times he feared that he would kill her with the next swing, and many times she survived, until he began to realize that he might well have met his match.

Sweat began to glaze his brow, and it made Talon's long red hair cling to the sides of her face. Both of them began to pant from exertion, but she seemed to be able to go on all day.

The axes whirled and sang. The two of them danced away from blows and took them head-on.

Some old graybeards began to murmur in astonishment, 'In seventy years, never have I seen two such worthy opponents!'

Within moments, the entire crowd began to take up chants, some cheering for the emir, some calling, 'Talon, Talon, Talon!'

The emir felt grateful. He suddenly realized what Talon had done. Whoever won this battle would truly gain the support of the people, enough support to take endowments.

But he could not let her win.

This is Aaath Ulber's daughter, he thought. We fought side by side. Dare I betray a friend so? Dare I kill his child?

Suddenly he realized that he had been holding back, making a show of it. He hadn't truly committed to a killing blow.

If she lives through this next one, he decided, she will have earned a victory. If she can beat me, she truly deserves the honor of saving her brother.

He swung mightily, giving it all that he had.

It was dangerous for her to try to block such a blow, for her axe handle could easily break. But among the warrior clans, a warrior needed to demonstrate the strength to take a blow in order to win her people's approval. Talon lunged in, forcing the emir to try to shorten his lop in midswing.

She brought up her axe handle and braced herself for a crushing blow. It landed with such a jolt that the emir's joints ached and his bones seemed to shiver.

The audience cheered.

To the emir's astonishment, she not only managed to block the blow, she smiled through it.

Then Talon pushed her weight back and leapt in the air,

doing a complete somersault. Two more leaps and she was at the edge of the circle.

The emir charged, his axe spinning, though with one blade shattered it was a bit wobbly. He tried to swing with his own version of the 'Circle of Steel,' but had never had to practice with such an unwieldy blade.

Talon committed to a lop, a downward stroke that could split a man in two. He halted a hairsbreadth before the blow landed and had brought his own axe handle up to block.

It will be a simple matter to kick her from the ring, he thought.

Her blow landed, and immediately the emir prepared to kick her in the chest, pushing her from the ring, but quicker than thought Talon grabbed his axe and somersaulted over his head. She held on to the handle as she flew, so that it rose in the air.

Instantly she was over his head, and she jerked the handle tightly, so that she and the emir were standing back-to-back, with her gripping the handle while it rested against his throat.

Her momentum gave her the advantage, and when she hit the ground she merely arched her back, tipping the emir up onto her shoulders, so that she had him in a stranglehold.

The emir's back was upon hers, and though he kicked, he could find no place to land his feet. She had the axe handle to his throat, and he could not break her grip. She was strangling him. He kicked and twisted, struggling to break free.

Where did she learn this move? he wondered.

Not on this world, he realized. I've seen hundreds of axe fights. This tactic is not from this world.

The crowd gasped and broke into applause for Talon.

The emir struggled, strangling, as she balanced him on her back. It would have been a small matter for her to jerk the handle forward while shrugging at the same moment, and thus break his neck, or at the very least, crush his esophagus.

The crowd was wild with anticipation, watching their finest warrior struggle, at the mercy of a mere woman.

She has them, the emir thought. She has won.

Talon turned a half-circle and lifted up a bit. The emir gasped, and then got a fresh grasp on the handle of his axe. He planned to renew the fight, just as Talon dropped her shoulder and threw him – out of the ring!

Amid the cheers and the applause, the emir sat among the pine needles for a moment, gasping.

Talon picked up her axe, then offered him a hand up.

The emir waved her away; he was still struggling for air. When he was able, he climbed to his feet and stood beside her, raising her hand in sign of victory. There was no anger in his heart, only well-earned respect.

'Aaath Ulber has trained his daughter well,' the emir said, as the people cheered. 'For my part, I believe that she has won the right to fight in Rugassa to free her foster brother, Fallion Orden. If anyone here would like to argue the point – well, then you try fighting her.'

There was a good deal of clapping from the crowd. No one challenged her.

The emir added, 'And if there are any who are willing to grant her their endowments before she goes into battle, I encourage you to do so.'

The applause faded, and one woman shouted, 'Speed, I can give her my speed.' 'Grace,' a second woman said. And others called out their offers – all women, offering to gift their champion. A young man, a boy of perhaps seventeen, called out soberly, 'She'll need a man's strength. I'll give mine.'

Then the offers began in earnest.

The emir patted her shoulder, and headed back under the base of the tree. He felt like a failure, like a whipped dog slinking away from a fight. He'd felt this way far too often before – but only after battling wyrmlings.

'Where are you going, Tuul Ra?' one old warlord called. It was grandfather Mallock, a scarred old graybeard who had survived many campaigns but was so crippled by arthritis that he had been forced into retirement.

The emir wasn't certain where he was going. 'I want a drink, something strong, though I doubt that much can be found in camp.'

Old warlord Mallock laughed and reached down under his breastplate and pulled out a glass flask with honey-colored liquid. 'Will whiskey do?'

The emir took the proffered bottle, downed a swig.

He thought his old friend would offer condolences. Instead Mallock was studying the emir's face with reverence. 'I saw Bannur Crell fight with a wyrmling's axe back in my youth. He was a legend in his own lifetime, but you could have bested him easily.'

A couple of other graybeards stood at Mallock's back, and they grunted agreement.

'I haven't got much time left on this earth,' Mallock said. 'The wyrmlings took my home, my family, my country. But I've got my wits still. Will you carry them into battle one last time for me? Perhaps they'll do you some good.'

The Emir Tuul Ra merely stood for a moment, too surprised and too overcome with emotion to answer. 'Wit!' Mallock shouted. 'I offer my wit to the Emir Tuul Ra!'

'Brawn!' another graybeard called. 'I'm still as strong as any man in this camp. I offer my brawn.'

The emir saw what they were doing. These were old men, venerable. They were showing him more support than he had dared dream.

A young woman called out, 'Grace. I'll give you my grace. You both fought as if you had harvester spikes in your necks. I'd like to see the wyrmlings try to stand against the pair of you.'

So the folk stood out in the gloom for fifteen minutes, while night fell upon the meadows around them and a facilitator registered the offers of endowments.

When the offers were done, the emir had been promised nine to Talon's ninety. He would not be her equal in combat, far from it, but then, he told himself, I was a fool to think that I ever was her equal.

The crowd filed off, back down into the cavern beneath

the pine. For some reason, the emir did not want to go back. The battle fury was still upon him, making his hands tremble. Apparently Talon felt the same. She too lingered outside and leaned with her back against the tree. Behind her was one of the huge carven faces of the Wode King. It was taller than she, so that her back arched against its chin.

Daylan Hammer hesitated before heading for cover, and warned, 'Do not stay out long, and do not leave the shelter of the tree. Night is coming, and with it the Darkling Glories begin their hunt.' He cast a glance out into the gloom, 'Though I daresay with this rain, not many will be about.' Daylan rushed down the hole, beneath the tree.

The emir smiled at Talon. 'Congratulations,' he said. 'You won your endowments. And you gave me mine. Was that your plan? Are you really such a clever girl?'

The two of them still stood in the gloom while out beyond the shelter of the tree the rain sizzled amid the open fields, and overhead the great pines creaked and sighed softly in the wind.

She grinned. 'I had hoped that they would give you more. Is it enough, do you think – nine endowments?'

'I've fought the wyrmlings all of my life with only the strength of my own two arms. So I will go. I had hoped to lead this expedition, but now I'll be satisfied if I can only keep up with you.'

He came and stood close to her, only an arm's breadth away, and smiled in satisfaction. He had never been in the presence of a woman as powerful as Talon, a woman that he respected so much. He found himself attracted to her.

A lovely girl, he thought. It is a shame that she is not older.

In his native Dalharristan, it was the custom of old lords to marry young women, in hopes of siring one last extraordinary child. But it was not a custom that he ever hoped to engage in. The very thought sickened him. For him, marriage was a lifelong commitment. He believed that men and women should be of equal age when they married, so that they might mature, grow old, and die together. In an ideal world, the two might stand together at the last, holding hands, and die in one another's arms.

But men who married young girls in the hope of siring children upon them were selfish. He could not imagine feeling any kind of peace as he died in old age, knowing that he had left his children only half-grown.

So he held back from Talon, as a gentleman should, determined to conceal his attraction.

But there is a closeness that two people share when they have faced death together – even when they have faced death at each other's hands.

The passion that the battle had aroused in Talon came swiftly.

She grasped him by the shoulder, then pulled him close. As if reading his mind, she said, 'I'm old enough to know what I want.'

She kissed him then, and he was surprised at the ferocity of it – and at his own passion.

They stood for a long moment thus, holding one another, hearts beating as lips met. It felt good to be in her arms. It felt like coming home after a hard day's labor. He had never felt so . . . honored to have the love of a woman. He had known love before, but in his society, a wife was rarely considered a man's equal.

'What would your father say of this?' the emir asked softly.

'Which father? Aaath Ulber loves you like no other. He would leap for joy to have such a match. You've saved his hide more than once.

'But Sir Borenson, I fear, would be incensed to find that I love the shadow of Raj Ahten. He killed you once. And if he knew that you kissed me, he'd try to kill you again.'

'Well then,' the emir said, 'let us break the news gently.'

He held her, and suddenly became worried that in the coming battle he might lose her.

After long minutes, Tuul Ra pulled out of her embrace and prepared to go back down into the cavern.

'One question,' he asked last of all. 'On that shadow world, how was I, the mightiest of all flameweavers, killed?'

'Raj Ahten's limbs were lopped off with axes,' Talon said. 'Then he was wrapped in chains and thrown in a lake to drown. My father had as much to do with it as anyone.'

'So I was killed by good men?'

'Yes.'

The emir absorbed the news. 'It was an act worthy of a hero. I must thank him, when next we meet.'

It was with a heavy heart that the emir ducked beneath the hanging roots of the great pine, shoved the door securely closed behind him, then descended the stone stairs with Talon at his side.

At the foot of the stairs the great room opened up; once again the emir was struck by the magical atmosphere of the place.

Crowds of folk were settling in for the night against the walls, having laid their bedrolls upon rafts of dry moss. No cooking fires burned. Crickets chirped merrily, while out among the crowd a trio of musicians played softly on woodwinds. The air was thick with the scent of water and clean soil. Stars seemed to hang in the air above them, and it seemed lighter now than before. But that had to be an illusion, he decided. When first he had entered the shelter, he'd come in from the harsh light of day, and all had seemed dim. Now he had come in from the gloom of dusk and storm, and the same room seemed bright.

In a far chamber, the emir could hear the facilitator Thull-turock chanting. He was already preparing to start the endowment ceremony.

'How soon shall we leave?' Talon asked the emir.

'A couple of hours at most,' he said.

'That is not much time to say good-bye.' Talon had probably been thinking of her own mother, Gatunyea, but the emir drew a sharp breath of pain. His daughter, Siyaddah, had offered her own endowment to him, and once the endowment was transferred, he would never be able to speak with her again. It was a terrible sacrifice, and the emir spotted

Siyaddah down in the crowd, waiting near the foot of the stairs for him.

Alun stood at her side, and as the emir approached his daughter, Talon withdrew a few paces to offer some privacy. Siyaddah strode forward, her eyes glistening from tears in the light of the false stars.

'Father' was all that she managed to say.

He stood before her, admiring her, but could not speak.

'Tell her not to do it,' Alun suggested. 'I will give you one of my dogs. You won't need her.'

'And if I back out,' Siyaddah said, 'won't the others who have offered their endowments feel deceived? They made their gestures in part because of my sacrifice.'

The emir did not answer. She was right. He just held her eyes, admiring her.

Such strength, such goodness, he thought.

He admired her more than words could tell. But he spoke as well as he could: 'Why are there not more men with such great hearts as yours?'

'You can have all of my dogs,' Alun offered. 'I don't care about them.'

But no one was listening. To steal endowments from a dog would be a churlish thing, the emir decided. To take advantage of a dumb animal because of its faithfulness – it was beyond his power. He did not have that kind of cruelty in him.

'Take my endowment!' Alun offered.

The emir smiled at the young man. Alun was a mongrel, an ill-bred man, but it was obvious that he loved Siyaddah. It was just as obvious that her affection for him was as a friend, not a lover.

My daughter seems intent to break many hearts today, he thought.

'I thank you for the offer, Alun,' the emir said. 'But I fear that I would be taking it under false pretenses, and that would be dishonorable.'

'I love your daughter,' Alun said. 'There is nothing false in that. And because I love her, because I wish to honor her desires,

I offer my endowment. She made her offer because she believes in you, believes that you are the best hope for this rescue. I think she is right.'

The emir needed endowments, that much was true. Another one, offered honorably, would be greatly valued. But he did not want to give Alun false hopes that he might win his daughter's hand. Nor did he wish to take an endowment from someone whose motives were not entirely pure.

Alun was hoping to buy Siyaddah's love, and the emir knew that it could not be purchased.

Had Alun begged to give his endowment in order to free his king, or to save his people, the emir would have taken it gladly.

But the Emir Tuul Ra had recently been in a council meeting attended by Glories, and he wanted to be like them. Something inside him whispered that taking Alun's endowment would be wrong.

It is not a gift that he offers freely, he realized. It is a bribe, one that carries an onus.

'I thank you for your offer,' the emir said, 'but I must decline. You hope to win my daughter's heart, and it may be that you shall. But you will have to find another way.'

14

FORWARD INTO BATTLE

*Battles are seldom won with an axe and shield upon
the field. More often, they are won by cunning before
a blade is ever swung.*

—*From the Wyrmling Catechism*

Things moved quickly for Talon after her match with the emir.
The endowment ceremonies took only an hour. The facilitators
had put the finishing touches on a few forcibles during the
march, carefully filing the runes upon the heads of each. Thus
Talon and the Emir Tuul Ra were ready to garner their first
attributes – one endowment each of brawn, grace, metabolism,
stamina, sight, smell, and hearing.

The ceremony took place in a small chamber away from
the public, where only a few potential Dedicates and their
families could sit at once. The air smelled fresh here, for a
crack in the high stone roof let Talon see up a natural chimney
to where the stars shone. The stream that had fallen into
limpid pools in the great room earlier now flowed into this
room, becoming a burbling brook. There was no furniture
here, only rocks to sit upon and some rafts of moss to lie
upon.

Daylan Hammer presided over the ceremony, with Lord
Erringale standing tall at his side in raiment that shimmered like
sunlight upon green leaves. Each of them inspected the forcibles

before the rite proceeded, Erringale frowning at the forcibles for a long moment.

'You taught the shadow folk well,' he said to Daylan, with an undertone of subdued anger, 'though you were sworn to secrecy.'

'The Runelords·of that world discovered most of the lore themselves,' Daylan said. 'I gave them a little help, mainly to stop the horrifying experiments that they were performing.'

Talon wondered at this news. The discovery of rune lore was lost in history. She had not suspected that the technology was first a product of the netherworld, or that it was meant to be hidden from them.

'It was not well done,' Erringale said. 'There are no more true Ael anymore, not since the shattering. The power to grant proper endowments has been lost. There can be no more Ael.'

'It is true that the rune lore does not work as it once did,' Daylan said, 'and the Runelords are seldom as honorable as our Ael once were. But overall, the good that has been done has outweighed the bad.'

Erringale said no more.

The Cormar twins were first to take attributes. They had already been granted dozens of endowments before the fall of Caer Luciare, but now they asked an honor that Daylan Hammer was loath to give.

'We wish to twin our mind,' one of them said. Errant, Talon thought it was, though she could never be certain, for the two looked so much alike. 'Thull-turock has said that among the ancient Runelords, this was sometimes done.'

'Sometimes it works,' Daylan said, 'but more often it leads to grief. I would advise you against it.'

'But you will not stop us?' Tun asked. Or at least she thought it was Tun. Her father once said that Tun was a hair taller, and a bit more reckless. Talon could not tell them apart, either by voice or by appearance.

'I don't have the authority to stop you,' Daylan said. 'I am not your king, nor your lord. As I see it, no man is. I suggest that instead of asking me, you put it to your comrades, as representatives of all your people. They are the ones who will be most affected, if this fails.'

So the Cormars stood before Talon and the emir and offered their argument.

'By twinning our minds, Errant and I will be able to read one another's thoughts, to fight as a perfect team – two men, four arms, but only one heart. And if it works,' Tun said, 'it will be a great benefit. I will always know what my brother is thinking, what he sees and hears.'

'Yes, and if it doesn't work,' Daylan said, 'it will lead to madness and a loss of self-control.'

The emir studied the men, looked to Talon for her thoughts. 'You're the one with experience in such matters,' he said. 'I know nothing of Runelords and their strategies.'

'I know a little about it,' Talon offered. 'In ancient times, it was sometimes done. There were some great fighters, the Sons of Wonder, who did this. Most often, it was done with men who were raised as twins, who often sparred with one another, and so were already intimately familiar with each other.'

'And what factors lead to madness?' the emir asked.

'Selfishness,' Talon said. 'Twinning works best with those who love one another truly, who share no secrets from each other.'

The emir thought for a long moment. Errant Cormar urged, 'We are going up against the combined might of the wyrm-ling horde. We are going to fight wyrmling lords and Knights Eternal with endowments of their own – how many we cannot know. And the Death Lords will be there, led by their emperor. We need every advantage.'

Obviously, the Cormars were concerned. The emperor's troops loomed large in their imaginations. In their world the wyrmlings were seen as unbeatable. But Talon had lived in both worlds. As a Runelord she knew what kind of damage a single highly endowed assassin might do. History could show dozens of instances where entire kingdoms fell within moments as Dedicates were brought low.

After a long moment the emir sighed. 'I would advise against it. This is a new art to me, and by nature I mistrust it. Yet so much depends upon us. The world depends upon us to succeed, to bring Areth Sul Urstone and the Wizard Fallion home. I cannot advise you yea or nay.'

'I think it is well worth the gamble,' Thull-turock said.

But of course you would say so, Talon thought. You're a facilitator, and if you succeed in this, it will greatly add to your reputation.

She didn't dare voice her thoughts. Talon worried that they were too small-minded.

And so, leaning upon their own counsel, the Cormar twins granted one another an endowment of wit. It was a ceremony that offered little in the way of danger. For one moment after surrendering his wit, Errant Cormar became a gibbering idiot. But then his brother granted an endowment in return, and then both men looked normal.

They did not begin twitching and shrieking, as it was said sometimes happened when two men fought for control of their joint mind.

Yet it was obvious to Talon that they were in turmoil, for they stood for a long moment, both of them gazing off reflectively as their eyes darted this way and that.

They're sifting through one another's memories, Talon realized, learning the things that they thought no one would ever know about them – their most secret memories, their hopes and fears.

Daylan saw it, too, and said, 'Gentlemen, come with me for a moment. We need to talk of supplies, and strategies. I would like your ideas on how to proceed. . . .' And he led them from the chamber.

He's trying to distract them, and focus them, Talon realized. And suddenly it was her turn to take endowments.

There were few surprises for Talon in the ceremony. As a child, she had seen the white scars left by the branding irons upon her mother and father, and with wide eyes had asked about the rites. 'What does this one stand for, Mother?' she had asked, looking down at the squiggly lines inscribed within a circle.

It was no design that could be easily described. All runes seemed to have a look of rightness to them, as if in form alone they held some power, but you couldn't tell what that power was just by looking at the rune.

'That one stands for hearing,' Myrrima had answered.

'Who gave you their hearing?'

'I got one from a dog,' Myrrima had answered, 'a special little yellow dog, bred to give hearing to Runelords.'

'Did it hurt?'

And Myrrima had told her, 'It's a terrible thing to take an endowment. It didn't hurt me at all – or if it did hurt, it hurt because it felt so good. There is a point where pleasure can be so great, it feels almost as if it will take your life. I've seen Runelords swoon from the pleasure when they take an endowment.'

'I wish I felt that good,' Talon had said.

'Ah, but it hurts the giver. The dog that gave me his endowment, he yelped and yelped in pain and would not stop for half an hour. Tears came to his eyes, and he ran away from his master who had been holding him during the endowment ceremony. The dog felt bewildered and betrayed.'

'But did you hear better afterward?'

'I heard surprisingly well,' her mother had answered. 'I could hear the high-pitched squeaks of bats at night so loudly that sometimes it would keep me awake if I tried to sleep. If I lay down on the ground, I could hear mice burrowing beneath the grass, and the baby mice squeaking as they cried for their mother's teats. Then of course, there was always your father. I could hear his stomach gurgling and churning from his evening meal, and if he began to snore – well, I could forget all about sleep!'

Her parents had seemed almost . . . disfigured to her. Masses of white scars covered her father's chest and arms. Sir Borenson had always pretended that he could not remember where most of them came from. He'd been only sixteen when he took his first endowments, and over the years he claimed that his memories had faded.

When questioned, he would act befuddled, and then find some excuse to walk off.

Talon had thought that he was hiding something until her mother explained, 'Your father took endowments of wit when he was young, so that he could learn to fight more quickly. But when his Dedicates were slain, the men from whom he had taken wit had died, and your father forgot a great deal. Imagine for a moment that you took four endowments of wit, and studied hard for several years; then one day someone stole four-fifths of all that you had learned. That's the way it is with your father.

'It's not that he is embarrassed to talk about it, I think. But it hurts him to admit how much he has lost, for you see, each Dedicate who died, your father took as a sign of his own failure.

'It is a Runelord's duty to protect his Dedicates. It's not important to do it just to make sure that you keep your endowments. It's a matter of honor. The people who give you your endowments, they're people just like you – with homes, and families, and hearts that break. You get to borrow their strength, or their vigor, or their beauty. And while you rejoice, they suffer terribly.'

Talon's curiosity about her parents' scars had never really waned. She'd heard stories about them so often that in time the tales of the ceremonies seemed more like memories than history.

So she knew what to expect – the harking chants of the facilitators, the smell of charred hair and burning flesh, the glowing worms of light that came from the forcible as it was pulled away from the Dedicate's skin, the rush of ecstasy that came at the touch of the forcible to her own skin.

Talon took her endowments before the emir did. Many of those who had offered attributes were girls who had been friends when she was small. They had played games together, chasing blue-bellied lizards among the rocks along the hillside of Caer Luciare, planting flowers amid the vegetables in the garden, and studying at the crèche school as toddlers.

Before the ceremony ever began, the facilitator Thull-turock took the potential Dedicates aside and asked if they understood what they were doing, if anyone had tried to coerce them into this agreement, and if they understood what they would be giving up.

He was pleased to see that so many of her friends came forward of their own volition, offering their attributes because they believed that it was right to do so.

And so for each endowment, one of her closest friends offered up an attribute.

It broke Talon's heart to see a young warrior give up his strength. His name was Crel-shek, and as a youth he had hoped to marry her, but Talon's father had forbidden it, claiming that he was of inferior breeding.

As she garnered attributes Talon grew stronger and suppler, inhumanly quick and filled with vigor. Alun brought his dogs, and she took endowments of scent and hearing from them, while an old man with uncommonly keen night vision gave his sight, and thus Talon sharpened her senses.

But all of my virtues are bought with blood, she realized, and suddenly she began to understand why her father had never wanted to speak of his past as a Runelord.

When she had taken her endowments, the emir finally was granted his. First came his daughter, Siyaddah, and he went to a corner and talked to her softly, saying his good-byes. Talon could not help but overhear. With her sharpened senses, even her own breathing seemed loud.

He spoke the words that any father might speak at such a moment, telling her of his love for her, his pride in her, his hopes for her future, for a life well lived and well loved.

But it was his final words that caught Talon's attention, for before he left, he whispered, 'Sleep peacefully, my child. I borrow your speed for but a while. It shall not be long before you wake.'

That's when Talon knew.

He plans to return his endowments to the givers, Talon realized.

But the only way that he could do that would be to give up his life.

He can't do it before the battle is won, Talon thought. He must make certain that the wyrmlings are defeated.

So he will die at his own hand thereafter.

It was a noble thing to do. Few were the Runelords in history that had undertaken such a feat.

But Talon knew of the emir's courage and determination. He was just the kind of man to do it.

The thought both thrilled and horrified her. It thrilled her to think that he was so noble of heart. It horrified her because it made her desire him more.

The emir's face was stoic as he began taking his endowments, and then it was time for Talon to go.

She went first to her mother, Gatunyea, and to her little brothers, and said her farewells. Then she gave her thanks to her Dedicates, and to those who would yet grant endowments to her through those Dedicates.

Talon went to get her pack, and sat quietly examining her clothes and her small stores of food, deciding which to take. Nearby sat Alun, who was quiet and sullen. He hunched over his dogs, caring for them from long habit. Now a young girl knelt beside him, his new apprentice.

I should go and thank him, too, Talon decided. He loves his dogs as if they were his own children.

The camp was settled for the night, and in a far room someone was singing, filling the chamber with sweet sound. Nearby, the water lapped on the shore of the underground pool.

Two of Alun's dogs cowered close. These were the ones that had given hearing and scent. They peered up at him with sad eyes, as if stricken and betrayed. After all of their love and service, he had done this.

Other dogs – Wanderlust and some of the old ones – hovered nearby.

Alun sat there petting the dogs. He hadn't liked taking their endowments. Each time an attribute had passed into Talon, the dog that gave it had yelped in pain, then floundered to the ground or crawled off, alternately yelping and whining. They could not understand how deeply Talon needed their gifts, or how grateful she felt. But now Alun sat petting them, and the dogs licked his hands, as if to tell him that all was forgiven between them.

There was movement nearby. Talon ignored it, thinking that someone must just be going to relieve themselves in the night.

'Back with the mutts?' Connor Madoc asked, slipping up behind Alun.

Talon turned to see Connor and Drewish hovering above Alun, leering down.

'Just putting them to sleep,' Alun said, 'for the night.'

'Those should have been mine,' Connor said, nodding at the dogs. 'We had an agreement.' He leaned close, threateningly. Talon could not help but notice that Drewish had his hand on the pommel of his dagger.

'I, I'm sorry,' Alun said. 'I, I got so nervous!'

Talon did not hesitate.

She leapt up, rushed five paces, grabbed Connor by the collar of his shirt with one hand, by the belt with the other, and then hurled Connor as far as she could out into the pond.

He only went ten feet, but she was gratified to see how far Connor flew.

Drewish did not have time to react. Talon's endowment of metabolism saw to it that before Drewish could draw his dagger, he went hurtling, as if intent on catching his brother in midair.

Both of them landed with a splash, and from a few yards off came heavy clapping.

'I'm glad to see you putting those endowments to good use,' Daylan Hammer said. 'I daresay that those two can use the bath.'

'Aye,' Talon agreed. 'But there is a kind of filth in them that water cannot remove.'

The Madocs peered up at Talon, then at Daylan Hammer, and went slogging off without another word.

Daylan came close to the dogs, knelt next to Alun, and

patted Wanderlust, smoothing out the grizzled hairs on her snout. 'Do not use this dog for endowments,' he said. 'She's too old. I fear that she would die from the transfer.'

'I wasn't thinking about that,' Alun said. 'She's earned her retirement. I just want her to live to a ripe old age.'

Daylan smiled. 'Let us hope that that is a very long time indeed.'

That dog might live longer than me, Talon thought, for I am going into the wyrmlings' lair.

Even if she survived, Talon would be taking six endowments of metabolism from men and dogs, so that she might move swiftly. But in doing so, it was like taking poison. Her life would pass away as if it were a dream. A day to her would seem like seven, and if she should ever have a daughter, Talon would age and die before the girl ever grew old enough to bear her own children.

I will wither before my parents do, Talon realized.

Daylan said absently to Alun, 'Our facilitators are taking a rest now, but when they have recovered, they will prepare more forcibles, and grant us more endowments.'

'But, aren't you leaving sooner than that?' Alun asked.

'Yes, we're leaving, but our Dedicates are staying. They can take endowments for us now.'

'How can they do that?' Alun asked.

'Imagine that a man gives you his strength. When he gives that endowment, his strength flows to you, like a stream of water flowing into a lake.

'Now, imagine that another man gives more strength to your Dedicate through another endowment. His stream of water flows into that man's flow, just as happens when the winter showers create new streams. What happens then?'

Alun's face crinkled up as he tried to envision it. 'There is more water in the first stream?'

'Exactly. The strength does not pool in your Dedicate. Instead, the strength of both men flows to you.

'Thus, as Talon's Dedicates take endowments, and vector those attributes to her, she will gain their powers as the day progresses. From time to time, she may feel a surge of strength, or a rush of wholesomeness when stamina is added.'

He turned to Talon. 'Are you ready to go?' Daylan asked. 'Have you said your good-byes?' His voice was sober. He knew that they might be going to their deaths.

'I've spoken my farewells,' Talon said. 'Is the emir ready? The Cormar twins?'

'Give them a few minutes more,' Daylan suggested.

Talon glanced across the chamber and saw the emir talking to some old battle companions. The Wizard Sisel and Lord Erringale stood at his side, waiting for him to finish. At his back were the Cormar twins.

One of the twins was gazing off, deep in thought, when suddenly he burst out laughing. The emir turned to see what had caused the outburst, and the young man said, 'Sorry, just thought of a joke.'

Talon turned back to Daylan.

'Daylan,' she asked softly. 'I heard Lord Erringale say that you had been banished from this world. Why was that?'

Daylan smiled, considered how to answer. 'Ages ago, there was a great danger on your world, the world of the Runelords. It was thousands of years ago. A young king had arisen, and his people were set upon by reavers. He begged for my help. His people were already studying rune lore, and they knew how to give one another "blessings," by drawing runes upon their friends with their fingers. But it was a crude craft, barely understood, and those who gave the blessings failed far more often than not. Besides, such blessings fade quickly.

'So they begged for my help.

'I had only begun to suspect something back then. The Bright Ones call this world the "One True World," and for countless ages the Bright Ones and Glories alike have thought that when the binding came, it would be upon this world, that it would be bound to some lesser world.

'You see, not all worlds are equal. Many of them are deeply flawed, and of all the worlds, this one reminds us most of what the world should be.

'But I had begun to suspect that looks can be deceiving. For rune magic worked on Fallion's world. In some cases, it worked better there than it does here. It was as if this "True World" of ours was only partly true, as if it had some fundamental flaws.

'Each of our worlds is like a puzzle with missing pieces, but no two worlds are missing the *same* pieces. This world, Fallion's world, the wyrmlings' world – each seemed to contain something that the others had lost.'

Talon asked 'What powers were on the wyrmlings' world that the others lacked?'

Daylan hesitated, as if he did not want to answer. 'The dead were more alive there than upon other worlds. The barrier between the physical world and spirit world was thinner there. That is why they had the Death Lords and the Knights Eternal.'

'So you were banished for teaching rune lore?'

Daylan nodded. 'I brought my friends before the White Council, and I pleaded their cause.

'But the Bright Ones did not want to interfere. They knew the dangers of teaching such lore. They were afraid that evil men would take the rune lore and use it for selfish reasons. And they were right. Many evil men have been empowered by it. But the Bright Ones were afraid of something more: they were afraid that the lore might be spread from one shadow world to the next, a thousand times over, becoming a plague that runs through the universe.'

'And has it?' Alun asked.

'No,' Daylan said. 'Men do not long to conquer worlds that they have not seen, or that they have never dreamed of.'

Talon realized that Daylan was right. She'd never seen any worlds but her own, had never imagined that there could be other fine worlds.

'Are there worlds that are not in peril?' Talon asked. 'Fine places, I mean. Worlds where you might go just to rest from your cares?'

Daylan laughed, as if it were a naïve question. 'As I said the other night, there are more worlds than you can count, more than you can imagine. Some have life on them, and others are void. Some have people on them, not too different from you.

'But the worlds mirror each other. Somehow, even on worlds where one type of mold is struggling to dominate another, the great drama unfolds.

'No,' Daylan laughed, 'there is no fine place where you can really rest – unless, of course, we manage to bring peace to *your* world.'

'And if we do, won't peace come to all of the worlds?'

'I suppose it will.'

The emir, the Cormar twins, the Wizard Sisel, and Erringale were still saying their good-byes. Daylan glanced at them, got a sly look on his face, and whispered to Talon, 'Come here.'

He went to the back wall, and embedded in it were tiny stones like diamonds no larger than an infant's thumbnail. They glowed softly, so that from a distance they had looked like stars. It was these stones that lit all of the rooms, Talon realized.

Daylan said, 'The folk of this world call these "sunstones," for when left in the sun, they store its light. The beams then leach from the stones at night when darkness falls.'

'They're pretty,' Talon said. 'A stone like that would be worth a man's weight in gold on our world.'

Daylan pried a sunstone from the wall, cupped it in his hand so that the light would be hidden, then pinched it hard. The light flashed brightly.

'The harder you pinch, the brighter it flashes. Try it. The stone gets quite warm when you do. The sun's heat is stored in them, too.'

He held the stone out for her, and Talon's fingers wrapped around it. She held it in her fist so that no one would see. She squeezed it briefly, felt it flare. It was like a tiny fire in her hand, leaking light so brightly that it glowed red through her fingers. She had to drop it.

Suddenly, understanding spread across her face.

'A flameweaver could make good use of these,' Talon said.

'They are quite common here,' Daylan whispered. 'The Bright Ones mastered the craft of making them ages ago. I cannot explain the process fully, for it would take hours, but it requires only coal from the fire and sand, along with bits of shaved metals – zinc, silver, and others that your peoples have no names for. Then the ingredients are blended and crushed under great weight until the pieces fuse.

'Now, Erringale will not allow weapons from this world to be taken to yours. But if a few sunstones were to fall from the wall, he would not miss them . . .'

Talon saw the possibilities. 'How would the wyrmlings have fared against us,' Talon wondered aloud, 'if we had borne sunstones into battle? Our whole world might have been saved.'

'It might yet be saved,' Daylan suggested.

'And Fallion will be able to make use of these. If I but pinch one . . .'

'The stones are everywhere here in the sanctuary,' Daylan said. 'Look around, while I go speak to Erringale.'

So he left Talon alone for a moment. She was not a thief. She would not have taken a man's purse no matter how much gold it held.

But she knew what Daylan wanted. Perhaps he feared that Erringale would have him searched before they left. Or perhaps taking the stones would violate one of his oaths. She knew full well that he was a man of high ideals – too high, sometimes.

Yet he had given knowledge to her people in times past, and now he was asking her to steal light and fire from the Bright Ones in this hour of need.

In a few moments, Talon had five sunstones hidden in her leather purse.

Then she heard Daylan call 'Talon?' and it was time to go.

Erringale's people provided packs filled with food and flasks of warm beer, and then they were off.

The good folk of Luciare cheered them on their way as they raced up the steps of the tunnel, and exited out of the great tree, then stood there in its shadow.

Full night was upon them, and the storm had passed. Broken clouds sailed through the sky like the wreckage of ships upon a dusky sea. A moon larger and fuller than that on Talon's world gave copious light, but they did not set off through the fields, which were still wet with rain-slicked grass.

Instead Erringale raised a small stick and traced a pattern in the air, until suddenly a gust of wind blasted them all in the face, and they stood peering back into a duller world – a world of stunted grasses and twisted trees and air that somehow smelled fouler and more acrid than the air of the netherworld.

No wonder Erringale's people think so little of us, Talon realized. We are like poor cousins to them.

The Cormar twins rushed through, followed by Daylan, Talon, the emir, and finally the Wizard Sisel and Lord Erringale himself.

They found themselves standing on a nasty plain thick with grass, tangled with weeds. The bitter scent of wild carrots filled the air, and the white tops of their flowers grew an arm's length away, rising almost to her chest.

Talon thought at first that the air smelled so badly because of her new endowments. But she noticed that the grass nearby looked more sere and dry than it had before, and the leaves on the trees were going brown.

The curse, she recalled – the wyrmling curse. Before the binding of the worlds, the wyrmling world had been all but free of plant life. Only the nastiest and most unwholesome still survived. But with the binding, entire forests had appeared, a blessing from Fallion's world.

Now those trees were dying, blasted by the wyrmling curse.

That is the cause of the smell, Talon thought. The good plants are dying, while the evil ones thrive and choke them out.

Though it had been full night in the netherworld, the sun here was nearly up, just breaking free of some golden clouds on the horizon. Yellow moths dipped and glided all around, and the air was filled with morning birdsong.

Good, Talon thought. The wyrmlings will be looking for places to hide for the day.

The company halted, peering around, trying to get their bearings.

'Over there,' Sisel said, pointing just to the south. A low hill rose in that quarter, with stately elms spreading their branches wide. Just beyond them, Talon could see the gray stone tops of the fortress at Cantular.

'But our road lies that way,' Daylan said, pointing east.

Talon had traveled this same highway only two days before, with Rhianna, Jaz, and Fallion, after High King Urstone had rescued them from the wyrmlings. So much had changed.

I'm a different person altogether, she thought. She had taken endowments from men and dogs, and felt so much power coursing through her, so much health and energy yearning to break free, she almost imagined that she was like a young robin in its nest, yearning to escape and take flight.

The scents of dry grass and bitter weeds came so strongly it was as if she had never smelled before. The cheeping of birds, the bark of a distant squirrel, sounded so loud that it felt as if she'd gone through her entire life straining to hear anything at all.

But she had taken endowments from more than dogs. She'd taken them from half a dozen good men and women from the warrior clans.

She felt eager to run to Rugassa. But the Wizard Sisel and Lord Erringale would never be able to match the grueling pace that the others would set.

'It is time to part,' Sisel said, as if reading her thoughts. 'Erringale and I will go west, to commune with the One True Tree. But you must go north to rescue your friends. Any last words?'

'Be well,' Daylan said. 'May you find joy beneath the True Tree.'

'There is little advice that I can give,' Erringale told them. 'I have fought enemies much like your wyrmlings for far too long. I have only one final word of advice. Free your friends, but do as little harm as possible. It is better that you die than that you put a stain upon your soul.'

'I would gladly give my soul if in so doing I might free my friend,' the emir said.

Erringale gave him a harsh look, as if to rebuke him, but thought better of it. 'Our enemy is devious,' he said. 'Never trust such a trade. Let your conscience guide you.'

Talon grunted as if in agreement, though she could hardly imagine how they would break free of Rugassa without letting flow a river of blood.

Erringale bade them farewell, placing his right hand upon Daylan Hammer's shoulder and then squeezing. He whispered, 'You have ever been faithful to your vows as an Ael. By keeping them, you have kept your soul. Yet I fear for you now. The path before you is dark, and not even a sunstone can light your way.'

Talon's heart fell, for she felt certain as she looked into Erringale's wise eyes that he knew that she and Daylan had conspired to steal the sunstones.

Then Erringale grasped the emir upon the shoulder and squeezed, and Erringale's eyes filled with light. For just a brief instant, there in the Bright One's eyes she beheld a vision; Talon saw the emir wrapped in flames. Erringale backed off in surprise. 'Often upon your hunts for the wyrmlings have you walked crooked roads,' he said softly, 'but the road before you is glorious.'

He grabbed the Cormar twins by the shoulder, holding each for a long second and peering into their eyes. At last he said, 'Be well, my friends. Be well.'

Last of all he took Talon by the shoulder and peered deep into her eyes for a moment, probing, as if to peer into her very heart. She saw only kindness in his eyes, and wisdom deep and profound. Erringale looked worn, as if he had been endlessly longing for peace.

He didn't see us steal the stones, Talon decided. He wasn't watching. It's just that now he sees through us.

'You go in search of a brother,' Erringale whispered, 'yet your heart is torn, for you fear for a father and mother, too. I see them. I see them. A white ship is setting sail from a distant shore.'

The words were totally unexpected, and they brought tears to Talon's eyes. She leapt forward and hugged Lord Erringale out of pure joy, then pulled back, embarrassed, for she did not know whether it was appropriate to treat a lord of his world so.

Then she hugged the Wizard Sisel, and the two lords said, 'Farewell,' and took off to the west, the Wizard Sisel striding through the bitter grasses with his staff swinging in long arcs while Lord Erringale marched grimly at his side, as if the entire world before him was repugnant.

Daylan Hammer, invigorated by endowments of his own, said, 'Let us be off!'

He leapt away, and soon a race was on, with the Cormar twins taking the lead while Talon, the emir, and Daylan Hammer followed close on their trail.

Talon loped along easily. She was bred to the warrior clans, and as such, it was expected that she be able to run eight miles in an hour, a hundred miles in a day.

Now, with her endowment of metabolism, she could run twice that pace with ease. And with endowments of strength and stamina, even while running she did not weary.

The landscape was much as it had been two days before. This was a desolate land. Farmsteads huddled here and there, spread out across the wilds – places where the small folk had lived before the binding of the worlds. But the cottages had been knocked down by wyrmling troops, their roofs thrown off and the inhabitants taken.

The sight saddened Talon.

After five miles, they stopped to kneel at a stream and drink, for even a Runelord needs food and water.

'Milords,' the emir asked, 'does anyone here have a plan for how we might break into the fortress at Rugassa without taking a few thousand lives?' Away from the prying ears of the Bright Ones, he apparently felt free to broach the dilemma for the first time.

Daylan suggested, 'We will enter by stealth, if we can. The wyrmling stronghold was not made to defend against Runelords.

I suspect that we can find a way in, either by climbing walls or leaping over them. By day the wyrmlings sleep, and if we go in the middle of the day we may get far without being noticed.'

'There is no night and day in Rugassa,' the emir argued. 'In its depths there is only endless darkness. I have trod those roads before. Wyrmlings will be about.'

'Then,' Daylan said, 'we will do as little harm as we can.'

There had been little in the way of planning so far, and this worried Talon. 'When we get to Rugassa, how are we going to find the prisoners?'

'We'll learn when we get there,' Daylan said. 'I have no plan. I don't think any of us does. I have never been to the depths of Rugassa. None of us have. All that we can do is search for our friends until we find them, and that may take a very long time.'

Talon scratched her cheek and sat there wondering and worrying.

'Have no fear,' Daylan said, smiling at her befuddlement. 'Our chances are better than you might think. Rugassa's forces have been drawn thin. Tens of thousands of wyrmlings were required to take Caer Luciare. And if these broken cottages along the road are any indication, Rugassa must have sent troops scattering in every direction to probe their borders and welcome their new neighbors.' Daylan smiled at his own jest. 'Thus, the military might of the fortress is less now than it has been in two dozen years.'

'And not all wyrmlings are warriors,' the emir added. 'Most of them have more humble professions – miners and craftsmen. Of course, most of them are but women and children. I cannot imagine that there will ever be a better time to break into Rugassa and free our friends than there is now.'

They're right, Talon thought. There won't be a better time to probe the wyrmlings' defenses. Yet she could not feel at ease.

She peered up at the sky. 'How do you think Rhianna has fared?'

Daylan cupped a hand and drew water from the stream; he

spattered it on his face and wiped his brow. 'She should have found some help by now. When you're giving away forcibles, it isn't hard to find hands willing to take them.'

'I worry about that,' the emir said. 'What kinds of friends will she find in this world?'

'People not much different from your own,' Daylan said. 'I asked Rhianna to watch this road if she can. We may meet up with her soon.'

Talon worried. She knew what small folk around here were like. The whole of Mystarria had been carved up by its enemies. Fallion Orden was the rightful king of this land, but his rivals had hunted him since childhood and driven him to the ends of the earth. On his return, he should have had a kingly welcome. Instead he had found his lands beleaguered, his country embattled and torn, lorded over by brutish men.

Where would Rhianna go for help?

If she did offer these lords forcibles, surely they would take them. But like a rabid dog, they would then turn and rend her.

Rhianna's treasure might lead to her own demise.

'Let's go,' Talon said, eager to have some of her questions answered.

Soon, Talon received more endowments. She felt a distinct slowing of time as her Dedicate was given an endowment of metabolism. The emir must have gotten similar endowments, for in a few minutes the race began to grow more furious.

They charged over the broken road at thirty or forty miles an hour, going airborne when they topped a small rise. Around them, the world was revealed as never before. Though a slight wind was blowing, as evidenced by a bending of the grass, Talon could not feel it.

Bumblebees that rose from the stubble seemed to hang in the air, and she could see their wings clacking together where there should have been only a blur. The sun seemed to hang as motionless as a shield upon the wall of some keep, and when a cottontail tried to race from the path ahead, Talon could easily have reached down and snatched it by the ears.

The road itself was an odd thing, broken up in the great binding. Rough grasses, weeds, and the occasional gorse bush had sprung up during the change. So it was easy to see where travelers had passed recently.

Wyrmling sign was heavy. Several handcarts had left their marks upon the trail.

Talon shivered. She had been down this road before.

All too quickly, the company reached an abandoned inn among some trees, where the folk of Caer Luciare had fought the wyrmlings only days before, when Talon and her friends had been rescued. The roof had been blown off of the building. The cloying scent of blood filled the glen. It had been a fierce struggle, but the forest showed little sign of violence. The squirrels still barked in the trees, and the mother robins still flew to their nests in the bushes. The sunlight was slanting brightly into the little clearing. It was as if already the forest was erasing all evidence of the battle, eager to forget.

But flies lay thick upon the corpses of the few wyrmlings lying there by the inn, warriors whose fingers had gone black and whose bodies had bloated. The human men who had died so bravely here had been laid to rest in nearby graves.

How much easier this battle would have gone, Talon realized, if even a few of my people had taken a handful of endowments.

Talon and the men hurried on for several miles, racing over a long, low hill. They had not gone far when Daylan called for a halt. 'It's time to eat,' he said. 'Listen to your stomach. A Runelord cannot choose to eat with the rising and the setting of the sun. It takes as much energy to run a dozen miles for a Runelord as it does for a common man. But with your endowments of stamina, it becomes easy to ignore your basic wants, such as hunger.

'Your body needs sustenance, and you will need to eat often. The battles ahead are hard enough, without battling hunger at the same time.'

Talon stopped, and the company got food from their packs. There was venison with onions and mushrooms cooked into pastries, and some sort of sweet roll with elderberries. The fare was hearty but light. For drink, Talon sampled from her skin. What came out was a remarkable beer, dark in color and hearty in taste. It seemed to renew her and take away small aches of the journey at the same time.

The company wolfed down their fare and soon was off again.

Endowments were being added quickly now, one every few minutes. At times Talon would feel renewed vigor, or her thoughts would feel more cogent or her senses would sharpen as various attributes were passed on through her vectors.

Talon wondered at Daylan's warning about the battle ahead. Right now, she felt so powerful that she could not imagine a skirmish that would be hard. She suspected that she could cut down wyrmlings all day, felling them like cordwood, without breaking a sweat.

But the wyrmlings had begun to take endowments, too.

And among them were fell sorcerers whose powers might dismay even a Runelord.

For thirty miles they ran, following hard on the wyrmling trail. Twice they saw villages in the distance where the small folk had lived. But the roofs had been torn off of houses and the animals were gone, proof that the wyrmlings had already taken their toll.

Still, after a bit, Daylan called another halt, and the company set a quick camp in such a village. They gathered chickens for lunch, raided vegetables from a garden, and made a quick stew in order to supplement their rations.

Talon searched for any sign of survivors, but the wyrmlings had left none. She found evidence of children snatched from their rooms, babes robbed from their cradles. She found blood-smeared walls, and the bodies of a pair of young lovers whose heads had been taken so that the wyrmling harvesters could remove their glands to make foul elixirs.

Anger seemed to harden in her stomach, and Talon longed for retribution.

Erringale warned me not to strike in anger, she thought.

But how can I not hate the wyrmlings who have robbed so
many of so much?

The party finished their meal and sprinted forward again,
traveling a dozen more miles. They neared a small, heavily
forested hill when suddenly Talon caught a familiar scent in
the wind.

'Halt!' she cried, and drew her blade. She stood warily at
guard, and the Cormar twins drew their own weapons.

'What's wrong?' they asked.

'I smell death,' Talon said. The endowment of scent that
she'd taken from Alun's dog was serving her well. 'I smell fear,
too. A battle happened here not long ago.'

Talon cautiously led the others to the top of the hill, and
in the morning sun began to find wyrmling corpses littering
the woods. On the far side of the hill was a giant dead graak,
still tied to an enormous pine.

'There has been a battle here,' one of the Cormar twins said,
stating the obvious. 'But who fought, over what, I cannot tell.'

There were no horse tracks. The wyrmlings were large, and
some of them weighed as much as five hundred pounds. With
such weight, their feet had left deep gouges in the dry forest
floor as they skirmished. But their foes seemed to leave little
sign. There were no heavy tracks from a warhorse, no tracks
from men.

In the depths of the trees they found a cave near the crest
of the hill, its opening obscured by brush. A cooking fire had
burned there recently. The ashes were still warm.

'The wyrmlings camped here,' Daylan said. 'But they were
attacked last night. But by whom, I wonder?'

'Perhaps the wyrmlings killed each other,' the emir hazarded.
'The only sign that I see is from wyrmlings. See there?' He
pointed to two bodies that had fallen near one another, as if
they had slain each other in a duel. 'It looks as if this was a
robbery of some kind.'

'Wyrmlings often fight one another,' Daylan confirmed. 'But
usually not on such a scale.'

As they neared the giant graak, Talon caught a familiar scent.

'Rhianna was here,' she said, astonished.

'Are you certain?' the emir asked.

'Yes,' Talon said, rejoicing to know that her foster sister was still alive. 'I smell the jasmine perfume that she often wears. It is all through her clothes.'

She studied the scene with new eyes. The wyrmlings lay scattered about in every direction. Rhianna had taken them on the wing. She would not have had to land in order to fight, and even if she did land for a moment, her smaller weight hadn't left much in the way of tracks on the ground.

The wyrmlings had not been dead long. Their stomachs had not grown distended; the blood on them was congealed but not crusted.

'They fought only a few hours ago, it would seem,' Talon said.

Talon detected something else – a coppery scent very much like blood, but subtly different. 'There were forcibles here.'

Like a bolt, understanding hit her.

'Yes,' Daylan said. 'The wyrmlings were shipping them to Rugassa on their foul graak. Rhianna must have wiped out the guards and stolen their treasure. Good girl, to keep it from Zul-torac's troops!'

'Rhianna must have taken a few endowments of her own,' Tun Cormar suggested. 'She was not such a warrior when last we met.'

Talon bit her lip, peered around. 'If Rhianna won the wyrmlings' forcibles, where did she take them? She could not have flown far with so much weight.'

The emir suggested, 'Ah, but if she had endowments, there is no telling how far she traveled. We could spend all day searching for them in these hills. I suggest that we ask her when she comes.'

He peered up along the horizon, as if searching for Rhianna, and suddenly his face went pale and stricken. 'Hide!' he shouted, and he grabbed Talon's sleeve and pulled her back behind the dead flier.

She looked up to the south, saw what he had feared. In the

distance several miles away was a cloud, a gray haze hurtling toward them just above the tree line. Within the haze she could see wings flapping, and the crimson robes of Knights Eternal.

The five of them scattered, racing to the giant black graak, crouching beneath an outstretched wing. Blades were drawn, and the five lay quietly.

'Knights Eternal flying in daylight?' the emir whispered.

'From Caer Luciare,' one of the Cormars added.

'Their business must be urgent,' the other said.

Talon's heart was beating. She had not fared well against the creatures when last they had met.

They might have seen us already, she thought. She hoped not. The sunlight was anathema to wyrmlings. It blinded them.

But even if they haven't spotted us, Talon realized, they'll see the dead wyrmlings below them, the dead graak. They may come to investigate.

The others were all breathing heavily, each of them filled with dread.

'If it comes down to a fight,' Daylan Hammer whispered, 'don't hesitate to attack. The sunlight makes them more vulnerable. Take off their heads if you can.'

No one spoke for a long minute. The only sound that Talon could hear was the beating of her heart, the rush of her breath as it filled her lungs.

Then came the pounding of wings overhead, the labored flapping. Darkness blotted out the sun. They've spotted us by now! she thought.

One of the Knights Eternal called out, howling like a wounded wolf.

Talon knew that howl. She had heard it from her father. It wasn't a cry of warning or distress. It was a wyrmling call, a salute to fallen comrades.

They aren't stopping, she realized. They don't need to investigate. They already know what was done here.

The Knights Eternal flew off into the distance, wings flapping thunderously.

The Cormar twins both stuck their heads out from under their gruesome shelter at the same instant, peered up at the passing enemy.

Why can't just one of them look? Talon wondered.

When the Knights Eternal were well gone, the Cormars whispered in unison, 'They were carrying something – clutching bags.'

What could they be carrying that is so important? Talon wondered.

But the answer was obvious. The fliers were coming from Caer Luciare, heading toward Rugassa.

'Forcibles,' Daylan Hammer whispered.

The emir looked Daylan in the eye. 'We must attack before the enemy can put them to use.'

Daylan clasped him on the shoulder. 'We shall.'

15

THE BRAT

Greed is how a man motivates himself from inside. It is our lust that drives us to work long hours, to train hard for battle, to succeed.

But it is fear that motivates man from the outside. It is through terror and intimidation that a lord forces his servants to conform to his desires.

Do not be deceived. The humans sometimes try to motivate through other means, but they almost always fail.

—From the Wyrmling Catechism

It was well past midnight when Rhianna reached the horse-sisters with her treasure of forcibles. The sisters had broken camp and set off to the east, astride their blood mounts, riding swiftly.

It had been a generation since such a cavalry rode. Though they were but forty women with lances, bows, and blades, they were all Runelords, for each warrior had an endowment of brawn, one of grace, one of metabolism, and one of stamina. And each rode upon a warhorse that was both well trained and endowed. In but a few short hours, they had traveled nearly a hundred miles in the night.

The sight of it made Rhianna giddy with hope. It was a small contingent in number, but great in power, and it brought to mind the glory of ages past.

Aside from the horses, there was little in the way of supplies.

A wagon carried some food; another carriage of sorts followed bearing the wyrmling girl Kirissa.

Rhianna called out a greeting from the sky as she neared the troops, then swooped and landed in a flurry of wings.

She dropped the cask of forcibles onto the ground, produced a key still smeared with wyrmling gore, and pulled the chest open to reveal its contents. She was breathing hard.

Sister Daughtry climbed down from her mount, pulled off her war mask, and looked narrowly at the forcibles. 'We can't use that many. We have people willing to become Dedicates back at camp, but we don't have the resources to care for them. For every Dedicate, we need at least a dozen people to till the soil, weave cloth, act as guards, and otherwise nurse them.'

She was right, Rhianna realized. The horse-sisters were fierce warriors, but they never had been large in number. Beyond that, they were spread out over thousands of square miles. It would take weeks just for them to assemble.

'The time will come when we have to look elsewhere for Dedicates,' Rhianna suggested. 'You're already traveling through Beldinook. We can take endowments here.'

Beldinook was a large country and wealthy. But Beldinook had long been an enemy to the horse-sisters, to Mystarria – and to the rest of its neighbors for that matter.

Old King Lowicker of Beldinook had once belittled the Earth King, Gaborn Val Orden, demanding a display of his powers.

Gaborn had proved his powers by summoning an earthquake, one which startled Lowicker's horse, causing him to fall. Lowicker died from the injury, and his daughter Rialla had nursed her hatred for House Orden. Because of her frequent tantrums, people had called her 'the Brat.' She died only a week into her short reign, and a younger sister, Allonia, took the throne in her place. But Allonia's foul temper exceeded Rialla's. So when the kingdom fell to her, the title 'the Brat' came with it.

Allonia was her father's daughter in every way. Once the Earth King had passed away, she struck quickly and in concert with Gaborn's enemies. She managed to carve out a fine chunk of Mystarria in that manner.

Rhianna suspected that Sister Daughtry would be pleased at the idea of taking Beldinook. But Daughtry only frowned. 'You would have me become another Raj Ahten, strengthen myself by taking other kingdoms?'

'No,' Rhianna said. But the more she thought of it, the more she realized that they would be forced to deal with Beldinook. 'Beldinook has long been a torment to all of its neighbors. It boasts the finest steel and the largest cavalry in the world. And with the fall of Mystarria, it also boasts the strongest castles. You will need those castles to protect your Dedicates. That is the one great weakness of the horse-sisters: you love the open plains and your pavilions, but you have few strongholds stalwart enough to house Dedicates.

'More importantly, the Brat of Beldinook will live up to her name. She has always been eager for conquest. If she gets her hands on some blood metal, you know that she would not spare you. It is only by overwhelming this enemy that we can hope to retain power.

'So we must strike first. Your horse-sisters could drain endowments from the strongest lords in her realm, turning their strengths into your strength. *Her* serfs will take care of your Dedicates. *Her* steel must become your steel. Her fortifications must become yours.

'Taking them does not make you into another Raj Ahten. He took endowments to gratify his own lusts. We will take them to save the world.'

'And what kind of world will it be?' Sister Daughtry asked. 'It was perilous enough when forcibles were rare. What will become of it if blood metal proves so common that any man with a pair of dogs can make himself into a Runelord?'

'I can't say,' Rhianna replied. 'But you and I know what kind of world it will become if the Brat and her allies take control.

'And the danger is real. I've seen a mountain of blood metal near Caer Luciare. Who knows how many more there might be? Who knows what new veins of ore might lie exposed within Beldinook's borders – or those of her allies in Internook? Right now, the brutish warlords of Internook may be digging up their own hills of blood metal and dreaming of conquest. Or perhaps in Indhopal some band of cutthroats has already seized a nation and is eyeing a million potential Dedicates in its own realm.

'My heart tells me to move slowly, to be generous and optimistic, to take only as many endowments as we need. But who knows how many endowments we need? The safest course – the only wise and sane course – is to seize the world by the throat while we can.'

Sister Daughtry looked dully at the forcibles. Reluctantly, she conceded. 'We go to fight an army of wyrmlings. My warriors are strong, but, they will need to be stronger still. I see no flaw in your argument. I only wish that such arguments did not need to be made. I fear that children in Beldinook will see what we do, and think us evil. Beldinook is a giant of a nation, a sleeping giant. We wake it at our own peril.'

The journey to Castle Lowicker did not take long. Two hours past dawn, the horse-sisters had crossed the leagues, and all too soon the riders found themselves outside a great fortress, sitting on their tired mounts, peering up at the massive walls.

As fortresses go, there was none larger in a thousand miles – at least nothing of human make. Castle Lowicker had been growing for two thousand years, and now it sprawled atop a great long hill in tiers. The imposing outer walls stood a hundred and twenty feet high and were topped with crenellations. At the foot of the outer wall stood a lake.

This was no ordinary castle. It had been erected to withstand the onslaught of powerful Runelords, and thus the outer walls were well plastered, so that even the most powerful lord could not get a fingerhold between the stones. The lake provided safety from siege towers.

Atop the walls, ballista towers had been erected every eighty feet, and the ballista bows were made of fine Sylvarresta steel. The ballistae were made in the style of Toom: a cranking winch would let a man tighten them, and then the whole ballista was mounted upon a seat that pivoted so that the marksman could quickly adjust his aim to the right or left, while the bow itself was perfectly weighted and could be raised and lowered. Thus a well-trained marksman could swivel quickly to take aim on any attacker and send a bolt flying.

Within the outer walls, the city rose in sections, seven walls in all, climbing more than a thousand feet above the plains. At the very crown of the hill stood the lord's tower, where in days of old dozens of far-seers had watched from the highest ramparts, and within the lord's tower was the Dedicates' keep; nearby stood a broader, squatter tower – the graakerie, where the castle's messengers were housed alongside their giant flying reptiles.

The walls atop this majestic fortress were alive with soldiers – archers and marksmen by the thousands. Rhianna had never seen so many warriors gathered in one place.

'It looks like an ant mound,' Sister Daughtry said. 'The troops must have discovered that they have wyrmlings on their border. They're on high alert.'

'We'll never breach those walls,' one of the horse-sisters said. 'It doesn't matter that we're Runelords.'

'It looks like a good place to take endowments to me,' Rhianna countered.

Sister Daughtry shook her head. 'How do you propose that we take it? Those archers will make pincushions of us. I feel very small, squatting out here.'

Rhianna studied the walls. Forty Runelords would find it hard to take the place. But the castle had its weakness. It had not been made to defend against an aerial attack. Until now, there had never been a need for such defenses.

'Give me a moment,' Rhianna said. She steeled her nerve. Then she flapped and rose into the air, lazily, like a graak gaining altitude. She climbed in a spiral, winging above the outer walls, high above all of the walls, until she was fifteen hundred feet in the air.

She found currents to her liking up there, warm thermals

just beginning to rise from the plains, and she rode them like a graak, her great leather wings held taut as she glided above the uppermost tower.

And then she dove, plummeting at eighty miles an hour.

There were no defenses to stop her from above. The archers on the outer wall had steel bows and the marksmen had their ballistae, but there were no defenders atop the lord's tower – only a pair of far-seers keeping watch.

As she neared the tower, she poured on speed. Five flaps of her wings sent her hurtling through the air at over a hundred miles per hour, faster than a falcon. She banked and rolled, dodging the pair of paltry arrows that assailed her from one of the battlements far below, then stretched her wings to break her fall.

Atop the lord's tower, the pair of old men who apparently still had endowments of sight backed away in terror; one of them grew so frightened that he tumbled over the railing.

Rhianna leapt past the last man, unlatched the portal from above, and leapt down into the tower, dropping forty feet, ignoring the ladder and breaking her fall with her wings.

She hit the floor running.

There were no guards to stop her. They were all down at the lower levels. She unlatched doors and raced through unopposed, and with her endowments of metabolism it took her twenty seconds to reach the queen's apartment.

They're lucky that I'm not a Knight Eternal, Rhianna realized. Castle Lowicker is indefensible from the air. Which means that I must hunt the Knights Eternal down and slay them one by one, as quickly as possible, lest they come and kill my Dedicates.

A pair of guards stood at the queen's door. To Rhianna's surprise, in these days when so few men had any endowments, this pair was still strong.

But the battle was brief. The men had endowments, but had not seen a forcible in years. Most of those who had given them grace, brawn, and stamina seemed to have died long ago, so that they had mainly speed to their credit. A well-balanced Runelord needed strength and grace as well as speed. But these men were 'warriors of unfortunate proportion.'

She took pity on them, and did not slay them. She broke one man's arm when he tried to block a blow from her sword. She kicked the other savagely, smashing ribs, and left them both in a heap on the ground.

Better to leave them alive, she thought. They can vector their endowments to others, and make my people strong.

Inside the royal apartment, Allonia Lowicker was still asleep at this late hour, lying on a great four-post bed that could have slept a harem. Sheer curtains of lavender gauze hung like a net over above the bed, while its sheets and numerous pillows were all covered in whitest silk with lavender trim. The room was overly perfumed.

Queen Lowicker had never married. Rhianna discovered that she had a fondness for young maidens. Half a dozen of the naked creatures graced her bed.

They screamed like children and raced to cover themselves at the sight of Rhianna bursting through their door, with a bare blade in hand.

Allonia Lowicker stirred herself, looked up at Rhianna with puffy eyes. She was a young thing, not yet twenty-two years of age, and she was prettier than Rhianna had expected. Rumors of her older sister's unfortunate appearance had prepared Rhianna for the worst.

'My,' Allonia Lowicker said, 'aren't you a lovely thing. Are they wasting forcibles on glamour nowadays?'

Rhianna had almost forgotten that she had taken endowments of glamour. She had always had a certain sterile beauty, but now it was much enhanced.

'Queen Lowicker,' Rhianna said, 'surrender your realm.'

'To whom?' Allonia said.

'The horse-sisters of Fleeds.'

'Monsters to the east of me and Runelords to the west,' Allonia said. 'What ever shall I do? Oh, I know. You want my kingdom? Well you can *have* it.'

Those who called her the Brat had spoken truly, Rhianna

decided. There was a jarring petulant quality to this woman that Rhianna found disquieting. Almost, Rhianna wished that she could send the queen flying over the nearest parapet.

But the bravado was false. Rhianna could see that Allonia's face was pale, and her heart was beating in her chest like a caged bird. Her eyes were puffy. Obviously she had not slept well. Perhaps she had been up worrying about her kingdom through the night.

'I'll want your endowment as proof of surrender,' Rhianna said. 'And you must also convince your troops to lay down their arms. Those monsters at your door, they're called wyrmlings, and they're worse than anything you might have dreamed. I can save you from them. I can save your people. But I can't do it if I have to watch out for you over my shoulder.'

The two endowments of voice that Rhianna had taken must have done their trick, for tears sprang to Allonia Lowicker's eyes, hot tears that went leaping down her cheeks in a stream.

'I know,' she said, as if relieved to be rid of her kingdom. 'I'll give it to you, whatever you want. Please, save my people.'

Wit, Rhianna decided. She had to take Allonia's wit. A person who had given grace or stamina might be weakened, but they could still plot against you, still whisper into the ears of would-be conspirators. But a lord robbed of wit was nothing but a burden to those who cared for her – a creature that needed to be diapered and fed and sung to like a child.

'Wit,' Rhianna said at last. 'I want your wit.'

Rhianna tried to demand the endowment stoically, but inside she felt that she was breaking.

I am becoming Raj Ahten, she thought. I am thinking as he thought, acting as he acted.

She knew the danger. She had shed blood before, and been seized by a locus. Fallion had burned the creature up, and said that she no longer had a stain on her soul.

But Rhianna was walking a thin line. She was acting like a wolf lord.

'You can have it,' Allonia said. 'With what I've heard about the feeding habits of our new neighbors, I don't want to know what happens.'

By midmorning, the Brat had a rune branded on her forehead, and Rhianna had her wit.

Queen Lowicker had several facilitators on staff, and they were quick to press local jewelers and silversmiths into service, preparing forcibles. Rhianna herself took a dozen more endowments each of glamour and voice.

Some women gazed upon her now and grew sick with envy. They looked upon her lustrous skin, her radiant eyes, and they despaired of ever being loved, while men gaped at her and seemed almost beyond restraint, like men who are dying of thirst and are suddenly confronted with water.

Rhianna took a few more endowments from Lowicker's nobles – sight, hearing, and touch, so that she would better find her way around when she breached the defenses of Rugassa, along with more brawn, grace, wit, and stamina.

Near noon, she went to where the wyrmling Kirissa was hiding from the sun. The wyrmling girl was forced to sit in an enclosed wagon, a crude carriage with windows that could be shuttered against the light.

Inside the wagon, Kirissa applied a salve to her sunburned skin. One of the horse-sisters had given it to her. She had not asked for it, and it seemed a great boon. In Rugassa, a wyrmling was expected to bear her pains stoically, as a sign of strength. No balm like this existed.

If the wyrmlings knew of such medicines, Kirissa thought, they would kill their masters and storm out of Rugassa, never to return.

So she rubbed it on the bridge of her nose and on her ears and cheeks and hands, the places where she'd burned the most. The burn was a raging fire, but the touch of the balm soothed it instantly.

She prepared to hide the balm under her seat, in the wyrmling manner, to save for later.

Yet something about the salve intrigued her. It was a symbol. She had not asked for it. The horse-sister who had given it to her had done so for no other reason than that she saw that Kirissa was in pain, and the girl desired to help. She asked for no coin in return.

These people bear one another's burdens, Kirissa realized. They do not use others as tools, or seek solely to profit from them.

Kirissa was having a hard time divorcing herself from the wyrmling catechisms. Before the binding, part of herself had lived among the Inkarrans, but that shadow self had never been philosophically inclined.

In Kirissa's mind the whole notion of a society built not upon greed and fear, but upon love and compassion, seemed revolutionary.

Her thoughts began to explode. She could see how simple acts of kindness, multiplied over and over as tens of thousands of people per day made small gifts, might be the foundation for a new world.

In Inkarra, her people had prided themselves on fairness. Yes, elements of fear and greed were used to motivate people, but primarily her society was founded upon fairness.

Perhaps things were different here.

She had heard of the horse-sisters, but Kirissa had lived so far away that the horse-sisters were no more than fables. Legends said that these women had the bodies of horses and the heads and breasts of women, because long ago they bred with horses.

So when the winged woman, Rhianna, came early that afternoon with Sister Gadron to the wagon to speak, Kirissa was eager to get to know Rhianna better. Earlier, Kirissa had been able to ask only a few questions.

Rhianna began speaking through the translator and began to query Kirissa in detail. 'When we reach Rugassa, how can we enter without being seen?' she asked.

'You can't,' Kirissa said. 'The wyrmlings watch by day and night. Many eyes will be following you as you approach.'

'How many guards are at each entrance?'

'I don't know,' Kirissa said. 'I saw a dozen when I left the fortress, but that was the only time I've ever been through an outer gate.'

'What defenses do the guards employ?'

'There are kill holes above each entrance,' Kirissa said, 'and hidden tunnels behind the walls. Once you enter the labyrinth, you must fear getting lost. There are other defenses. Some of the main tunnels can be flooded with magma if the need is pressing.'

Rhianna went on like this for an hour, grilling Kirissa about troop strengths, about the quarters where the Knights Eternal slept, about the habits of Death Lords – asking questions that Kirissa really could not answer. Rhianna asked about other threats – the emperor himself, the Great Wyrm, and the kezziard pens. She asked about other creatures within the pens – giant graaks and things that were stranger still – but while Kirissa had heard tales of creatures from the shadow worlds, she had never seen such things herself.

At the end of that hour, Rhianna began speaking to Kirissa in Inkarran. Rhianna's vocabulary was limited, childishly so, and in some instances she confused the order of words, but the words were precisely formed and Kirissa could understand her intent.

More interestingly, though Rhianna was human, she spoke to Kirissa in her own voice, in the deep voice of a wyrmling.

She learns faster than any wyrmling, Kirissa realized. She has memorized every word that I have spoken in the past hour.

Kirissa stared at her in awe. Rhianna was of the small folk, and her size was unimpressive. But it had been hundreds of years since a human had slain a Knight Eternal.

This is a mighty lord, Kirissa realized, as dangerous as Emperor Zul-torac himself.

But she had little time to ponder the implications of this observation, for Rhianna immediately began to delve into new topics, having the translator ask, 'How do you tell a wyrmling to surrender? How do you say, "Throw down your weapons"?'

'I think that it is unwise to ask them to surrender,' Kirissa said. 'They will only arm themselves again later, and come after you in greater numbers.'

Then Rhianna asked her one final question. 'If you were to return to Rugassa, what would be done to you?'

Kirissa thought long about that. 'They would kill me,' she said. 'But they would torture me first, in order to punish me.'

'Will they take you to the dungeons where Fallion is kept?'

'Yes,' Kirissa said, growing worried at her line of questioning.

'If I asked you to do this for me, would you do it? Would you let yourself be captured?'

Kirissa recognized what Rhianna needed. Kirissa would not be able to find her way down to the dungeons. Even if she had known the way, she would slow down a pack of force soldiers intent upon a quick strike.

'How would you know where they take me?' Kirissa asked.

'I'm a Runelord,' she said. 'I have a small tincture of perfume, sandalwood oil. I would place it on you and then follow the scent. No matter where they took you, I would be able to find you.'

Kirissa was afraid to volunteer for such a ruse. The Earth King had warned her long ago that the time would come when the small folk of the world would need to stand against the large, but she had always thought that she would meet her enemy with a good blade in hand – an axe or scimitar.

It was only the Earth King's words that gave her the courage to say, 'Yes, I will go down with you. But we may need Cullossax's key if we are to breach the dungeons.'

Rhianna gave a meaningful look to Sister Gadron.

'I'll get right on it,' Sister Gadron said.

As it turned out she did not have to go far to get the key. A wyrmling's necklace with an ornate key carved from bone had seemed a fine trophy to one of the horse-sisters.

The summer sun shone down with the intensity of a blast furnace as Rhianna came winging to Caer Luciare, its white granite walls gleaming.

She flew over the market streets, with their cobbled stones and quaint shops. The folk of Caer Luciare had favored vivid colors – bold peach, avocado, and plum – but now the gay shops clashed with the macabre decor of the new inhabitants. The wyrmlings had already begun marking everything with their crude glyphs – images of Lord Despair as a world wyrm, rising up. Other glyphs showed the image of the Stealer of Souls, a spidery creature, or of various clan markings that she was just beginning to recognize – the dog's head of the Fang Guards, or the three black skulls of the Piled Skulls clan.

Every cottage and market was somehow defiled. Either windows were shattered or doors caved in, or vile drawings covered the walls.

Like dogs, Rhianna realized. The wyrmlings are like dogs peeing on trees and bushes. There is some inner dictum that forces them to mar or destroy the lands that they take.

But it was more than just the paintings that adorned the places. The carnage looked worse than she remembered. It wasn't just the new damage to structures or the sickening graffiti. The wyrmlings had not yet begun to reclaim their dead after the battle, so now their white corpses lay strewn about, stomachs bloating and festering, oozing foul smells that rose up on the thermals. With her endowments of scent, the odors seemed overwhelming.

The dead were not just part of the decor, she realized, they were the centerpiece.

Rhianna dropped to the ledge of a lower wall, near where Jaz had died. She saw bloodstains on the cobblestones that might have been his. His body lay hacked and ruined.

My brother, she thought, look what they've done to him.

She did not care if the wyrmlings saw her there. She suspected that some were watching from Caer Luciare, from the dark corridors. Certainly there were enough spy holes in the place. But none would dare issue forth in this blazing sun to test her prowess in battle. And if they did, she would be happy to show them a thing or two.

So she stood for a long moment, weeping above Jaz's corpse.

'The wyrmlings have a lot to answer for,' she said to him. 'And I shall make them pay.'

But first, she thought, I need a weapon that will kill a Death Lord.

That was what she had come for. She had lost her staff while fighting against Vulgnash, the staff that the Wizard Binnesman had inscribed with runes and magic stones for the Earth King Gaborn Val Orden.

Vulgnash's endowments of metabolism had been too much for Rhianna to overcome. She hadn't been able to even come close to hitting him. And after the folk of Caer Luciare had fled, she'd been afraid to return for the staff.

But now she was ready to meet Vulgnash once again.

She turned and flew to the upper wall, where Fallion had taken his wound, and where she had slain a Knight Eternal. She found the mummified corpse still lying on the ground, its crimson robes draped about it. Rhianna kicked the corpse over. Carrion beetles crawled about underneath it, went blindly scattering this way and that, seeking to escape the sunlight.

Rhianna separated the robe from the corpse.

Odd, she thought, that the wyrmlings haven't scavenged from their own dead.

But then she began to wonder. Perhaps that was the point. Perhaps it wasn't out of laziness that the wyrmlings had left their dead on the battlefield untouched – but more out of respect.

These wyrmlings had died on the field of honor, and now it appeared that they would remain – in some sort of macabre memorial.

Rhianna had heard of people in Indhopal who would not touch their dead for three days, as a token of respect.

It might only be something like that, she thought.

She threw off her own robe and draped herself in the cowled bloody red robes of a Knight Eternal.

Flying fast, she wouldn't be distinguishable from one of them.

She flew to the base of the mountain, beneath the parapet where Warlord Madoc had fallen.

The Earth King's staff should be near here, she thought. But she could not find it. Warlord Madoc lay dead and broken upon a rock, his back arched painfully, arms spread wide, his dead eyes gazing up into the sun.

But Rhianna couldn't see the staff.

She hoped that wyrmlings had not defiled the weapon, as they had the buildings. She knew that the Death Lords had tried to curse the weapon, destroy it that way.

But after several seconds, she could not see it.

There were a number of large rocks here, scree from the tunneling in the mountain up above.

Perhaps, she thought, it has fallen under the rubble where I cannot see it. She began to peer around, peeking down under the shadows.

Just then, she heard a noise above. She glanced up to see a large boulder bouncing down from a parapet. She leapt aside as it slammed into the ground, then went bouncing away.

Perhaps the sun is not as great a deterrent as I'd imagined, Rhianna thought.

She heard the gruff laugh of a wyrmling coming from somewhere far up the mountain, drifting down. He called out a taunt.

She did not need a translator. The tone said it all: I know what you're looking for. Come and get it if you dare.

Suddenly, she realized how dangerous that just might be.

The wyrmlings have had a night to dig up ore from the mountain, and two full days to refine it and take endowments. Surely they have done so by now.

Their taunts are not idle threats.

Rhianna leapt up and flew away.

I will have to go to Rugassa without my staff, she realized.

16

ILL MET BY DAYLIGHT

Trust not in your own arms, but in the Great Wyrm. No chick falls from its nest without the Wyrm's knowledge. How much more then does the Great Wyrm know your needs? It alone knows all, and has all power.

—*From the Wyrmling Catechism*

Lord Despair was impatiently touring his armory when his Knights Eternal returned that morning, three hours after sunrise.

He was studying the wyrmling weapons mounted on the walls – axes for chopping, hooks for grabbing one's prey, battle darts in various weights and sizes, war bows and spears. All of them were overlarge for a human.

But Despair wasn't interested in weapons for humans. The Emperor Zul-torac had opened a door to the netherworld, and now the Thissians were negotiating with a murder of Darkling Glories. The Darkling Glories normally hunted with only teeth and talons, but Despair felt that they might benefit from wyrmling technology.

All day, his unease had been building, like the static that builds before a storm, waiting to be unleashed. He wanted to know what was happening at Caer Luciare. He wanted his shipment of forcibles. Three days ago, it would have been no small thing to look into the mind of his Death Lord and learn what was going on in Luciare. But now his Death Lord there was gone, and Lord Despair had no idea which of his warlords now ruled in Caer Luciare.

The Knights Eternal stopped outside the armory, and both of them hesitated at the door.

They looked haggard, bleary-eyed.

'Yes,' Despair demanded. 'What word do you have of my forcibles?'

The Knights Eternal cringed, a rare thing. Their kind were usually fearless. Lord Despair knew instantly that the news would not be just bad, it would be horrific.

'We have returned from Caer Luciare, and the news is not favorable,' Kryssidia said. 'But we have brought a gift of blood metal, in hopes of turning aside your wrath.'

The Knights Eternal each dropped a heavy black sack at their feet, and pushed it forward. By the size, it had to represent a hundred pounds of blood metal, perhaps enough to make a thousand forcibles.

I shall have to send it to my facilitators immediately, Lord Despair thought. A thousand endowments will give me the strength I need to resist the coming attack.

Inside, something eased. The Earth's warning was not as persistent. But it was still there.

'Your gift is appreciated,' he said, turning away from the wall of weapons and drawing closer. 'Now, tell me of the ill news.'

Kryssidia knelt. 'Master, your warriors at Caer Luciare have discovered the pleasures afforded by the forcibles. The Fang Guard have taken over the fortress, and they are taking endowments from many warriors. The place is filled with carnage, with fallen warriors strewn about by the thousands. They have not been felled by axes – but with forcibles.

'The Fang Guards imagine that they are a great nation, and that Caer Luciare now rivals Rugassa in power. We demanded forcibles, but their leader, Chulspeth, brandished a weapon from the small folk at us – a powerful staff filled with runes – and said, "Tell your emperor that I have sent him all of the forcibles he will get. We have taken many endowments, and we have a weapon now that will kill the Death Lords. Tell him to surrender. If he wants to live, he will do so under my rule. Tell him to come himself – and grovel before me. Perhaps I will let him lick my boots."' Kryssidia added. 'Since they would not give us forcibles, we dug some blood metal ourselves.'

Despair's blood rushed from his face, and he stood for a moment fighting back a cold fury. He had not received a single forcible from Chulspeth.

The fool.

He considered how to fight, what warriors to send. It had to be someone he trusted, and it had to be someone who could battle a Runelord with hundreds of endowments.

Lord Despair had no warriors with endowments to match, but he had servants with other powers.

Vulgnash. He felt inside himself, and felt peace. He had used his Earth Powers to choose Vulgnash, put him under protection. And so he could send the Knight Eternal into battle. The Earth did not warn against it. Vulgnash's skills as a flameweaver would do nicely. And with his endowments of metabolism, he could fly to Caer Luciare and back in only a few hours.

Yes, he would do nicely. It would give him a chance to atone. This mess, after all, was his fault. He had gifted the Fang Guards with endowments of bloodlust, and had left them untamed.

But Despair could not spare his pet at the moment. The human attack was imminent, and Vulgnash would be needed here.

'I will send Vulgnash tonight. Tell him what you've seen. You will go with him to punish the Fang Guards. Tell him to burn Chulspeth. There is to be a new lord at Caer Luciare, one who will do my bidding . . .' Despair considered. He needed someone he could trust, but someone whose presence he could spare. Kryssidia had been gifted with a dozen endowments in the past two days. Over the last few millennia, Lord Despair had elevated his Death Lords to the highest positions because he could commune with them from afar. But having a physical body, it seemed, now offered more substantial benefits. 'You, Kryssidia, shall keep the order at Luciare. You shall take endowments there, no less than two hundred, and you shall hold the title of emperor of Luciare.'

'I am honored,' Kryssidia said, bowing low.

Despair had taken some endowments already – brawn, stamina, metabolism, and grace. He would need more for the coming battle. 'Take the blood metal to my facilitators quickly, and have them begin making forcibles and extorting endowments. I want a thousand endowments in the next five hours.'

The demand was outrageous, impossible. There weren't enough facilitators to do the work. But the need was upon him.

Despair felt inside himself, listening to the Earth's warnings.

Yes, the danger was still there, but it had grown less. The humans were coming soon, but not with sufficient force.

Deep inside, he heard the voice whispering. 'Now is the time. Choose to save the seeds of mankind.'

But Despair had no desire to choose further. He'd tried to use the new-found protective powers to choose his Death Lords, but they were so far gone toward death that he was powerless to save them.

All right then, he thought, I will choose.

The Knights Eternal had picked up the blood metal and were racing to take it to the facilitators.

He turned to the fleeing Knights Eternal. 'I choose you,' Despair whispered.

He felt a connection made, weak and tenuous. With one foot in the grave, and one foot out, the Knights Eternal were almost beyond his powers to reach. He wondered if, when he sent them word of danger, they would even be able to hear his call.

That is the Earth Spirit's problem, he thought, and laughed.

Human flesh. That was what the Earth wanted him to choose.

Lord Despair opened a latch to the nearest door and found one of his guards. 'O Great Wyrm,' the guard said, 'we have brought more small folk to give you endowments, as you requested. They await you in the Sanctum.'

'Well done,' Despair said. 'I shall be there shortly.'

The small folk. They could be both a cursing and a blessing. He considered the Wizard Fallion. There was a slight chance that the small folk would succeed in rescuing him.

But there was a way that Despair could keep track of him.

The Earth Spirit wishes me to choose, Despair thought, and so I will choose.

He immediately called his guards to escort him to the dungeons – to the cell of Fallion Orden.

Vulgnash sat over the wizard, a forcible in hand, filing a rune at its head. The room was as cold as an ice field with the north winds lashing across it. Vulgnash leapt up as Despair neared; he raised his wings to full span, as if in salute.

'What would please my master?' Vulgnash asked.

Despair peered down at Fallion Orden, who lay sprawled unconscious upon his belly. Frost rimed his collar, and he was barely breathing. Using his Earth Powers, Despair looked into Fallion's heart.

Here was a man who dreamed simple dreams. Fallion did not want to rule the world. Lord Despair had never wondered what the young wizard might desire most of all, yet Despair knew that he would need to know.

There it was in his imagination – a small fishing boat, a coracle that he could row out onto the sea at dawn, and there cast his nets and hopefully be done with work for the day by noon. He wanted a cottage at the edge of the sea with a fine thatch roof to keep out the winter rain. He wanted children sitting on his knee as he told them bedtime stories. He wanted a wife to hold at night, and to cherish.

Such simple things. So repulsively wholesome.

'Yes,' the Earth's voice whispered deep inside him. 'This one is worthy to inhabit the world to come.'

Despair raised his left arm to the square and said, 'The Earth hide you. The Earth heal you. The Earth make you its own. I choose you through the dark times to come.'

When it was done, Despair stared down at the wounded boy.

Now you are truly mine, he thought. Wherever you might go, I will be able to find you.

'Vulgnash,' he said. 'It is time to begin the tortures in earnest. Give another hundred endowments of compassion to Fallion Orden today. It is time to force Fallion to tell us what we need to know.'

17

FLAMES

Despair is the greatest of all teachers. Others may instruct you in some matters, but Despair can teach you all that you need to know.

—From the Wyrmling Catechism

The Emir Tuul Ra felt taut with anticipation. The five heroes had spent the better part of the morning racing toward Rugassa, and he knew that they were near. He felt so overwhelmed with emotion that he wanted to shout.

There was hope, yes. Finally the people of Caer Luciare were going to strike back against Rugassa. But there was fear in his heart, also, and mourning. His people had been driven from their homes, from the very world of their native birth, and now squatted beyond its borders, plotting revenge.

But revenge would be hard to come by. The wyrmlings had a mountain of blood metal, and they knew how to bend it to their will. In a matter of days, the wyrmlings would have it in their power to take so many endowments that the folk of Caer Luciare might never be able to break the wyrmlings' stranglehold on the world.

So there was a moment, a brief time that they might be able to strike. Today is the day, he thought.

Preparations were being made. All morning he had felt endowments being vectored to him, some from men.

Metabolism, that was most of what he got. Seven endowments of speed. He was not the strongest in the group, far from it. But he would be the quickest, and he had learned long ago that great speed is enough in battle.

But now his quiver was full. The endowments had stopped coming an hour ago, though he could still see Talon growing in power from moment to moment.

They raced now along a broken road. In the binding of the worlds, the old human highway had crossed through the wyrmling wastes. The road was here, and it was serviceable for the most part. But in many places rocks had risen, creating a nasty path, and thorns and thistles burst up through the ground everywhere. Still, it had been beaten down some. It was rife with wyrmling sign. Troops had marched over it recently.

So the company raced through open fields in the lowlands, and over wooded hills, each of them running with superhuman speed.

The Cormar twins took the lead, sprinting side by side. They moved like dancers, each stepping forward with the left leg at precisely the same time, each swinging the right forward the same.

Yet their movements were too choreographed. They weren't dancers. They were marionettes, moving to a single will. The sight of it was somehow profoundly disturbing. The strangeness of it only seemed to grow.

The group stopped for a brief meal just after noon. There was little in the way of formal plans. They hoped to meet up with Rhianna, find out what news she might have to tell. But if they did not, so be it. Their assault would continue today, as soon as Talon and the Cormar twins finished getting endowments vectored to them.

So the five stopped at midday and set a small fire, a gleaming gem of heat and light that beckoned to the emir as always, and they prepared to cook some meat. It had been easy enough to come by. As they had run through the woods, a pair of grouse had fluttered up at their sides.

With his endowments of speed, time seemed to have nearly stopped, and the emir watched them – fat and ponderous and tempting – as they sought to escape.

He altered his course in midstride, leaping into the air, and harvested the pair of them, and now after pulling off the skin and putting them on a skewer, he went down to wash his hands in a nearby brook.

Talon squatted beside the stream among some willows and splashed water under her arms, then ran it over her face and neck as best she could.

The emir was downstream from her a pace. He washed off his own hands quickly, scrubbing them with coarse sand from the bottom of the stream, then let the dirty water glide away for a moment. He then cupped his hands and took a long draught, unconcerned that the water might be mingled with Talon's dirt and sweat.

It wasn't that he didn't notice her muddying his water. But he was used to fighting in skirmishes with small bands of men. He was used to tight quarters and a lack of privacy.

The emir leaned back on his heels, and sighed. 'I thank the Powers that be that I have lived to see this day,' he said, glancing over to Talon. 'Finally, I hope to free my brother, Areth Sul Urstone.'

Areth Sul Urstone was not his brother by blood, of course, only a brother-in-arms. They were as close as two men can be.

'It is a great day,' Talon replied.

'Hmmm . . .' The emir signaled his agreement, then peered at Talon inquisitively. 'It is said that you knew Areth's shadow self?'

'I did,' Talon agreed. 'We called him Gaborn Val Orden, the Earth King.'

'I have never known another man like Areth Sul Urstone,' the emir said. 'Never could there be a better friend. He was not just generous. Some men can share what they have. But Areth was the kind who would give you all that he had and regret that he did not have more to give.

'It was not that he was courageous. Many men can go into

battle with little fear. But Areth had a kind of courage that
went deeper than that. He had the courage to stick to his
principles, regardless of the consequences.

'It was not that he was honest, it was that he was unwavering
in his faithfulness. Areth Sul Urstone's word was stronger than
flint.

'Tell me,' the emir asked, 'is that the kind of man that he
was on your world, too?'

Talon thought for a moment, as if trying to decide how to
frame her answer. 'He was all of that and more. He was a man
of such deep compassion that it became a vice. He loved others
too much for his own good.'

'Aaaah,' the emir said. 'I have always believed that of Areth,
too. He suffers when others are hurt. Many times I have thought,
"I should gather a band of men, break into Rugassa, and set
him free." Yet I knew what it would cost. Even if we managed
to free him, the backlash would have been unbearable. The
wyrmlings would have struck so hard, Caer Luciare would
have been destroyed – and Areth would never have been able
to be at peace with that. Indeed, I think that he would rather
have rotted in his cell for an eternity, knowing that others lived
with some degree of peace and prosperity, than to be set free.

'That is why I captured the wyrmling princess. I hoped that
by taking her, I could buy his life.'

'And do you think he is even still alive?' Talon asked. 'I
mean today – now that the wyrmlings have got their princess
back?'

'I hope so.'

'And if he is alive, is he still the man that you knew fourteen
years ago?'

The Emir Tuul Ra did not answer quickly. He lowered his
head in thought. Talon knew that men could be broken. With
enough pain and deprivation, even the strongest men turned
into craven animals. And the tormentors of Rugassa had turned
the breaking of men into an art form.

'I can only hope that my brother is alive, and that there is
something left of what he once was. I intend to set him free,

and if the people will accept him, I hope to see him sit upon the throne. No man is more deserving.'

'He is fortunate to have you as a friend, and an ally,' Talon said.

The emir did not like compliments. He never quite knew what to say.

'Now,' the emir said, 'I must ask you of this Fallion Orden – the son of his shadow self, the son that, in my world, at least, he never had. What kind of man is he?'

'He is a young man,' Talon said. 'I have followed at his back since I could crawl, and so I know him well, perhaps as well as anyone alive . . .'

'So I have heard,' the emir said.

'Everything that you have said about the father, is doubly true of Fallion . . .' Here she hesitated.

'But?'

'Everything but the compassion,' she admitted at last. 'The Earth King's compassion was the stuff of legend. He loved his people so much that in the end he gave his life for them, and went traveling the world, seeking out good and humble folk, and bestowing his blessings upon them. Even long after the threat was over, he kept traveling the world, never able to rest.'

'Perhaps,' the emir said, 'he could not rest because he knew that the war was not over. My father said that sometimes when a war is coming, you can smell it far off, years or decades in the brewing. Other times it is thrust upon you at a moment's notice.'

'Yes,' Talon said. 'I suppose that could be. Anyway, Fallion is not like his father. He loves, but not indiscriminately. He is a man of . . . tremendous discipline.'

Talon seemed not to want to say more, but the emir said, 'He is a flameweaver, is he not? It would take tremendous discipline for one like him to lead a normal life, to take on the responsibilities of a home and family, wouldn't it?'

'Yes,' Talon said. 'Yet you manage it, don't you?'

'I have never given myself to the flames,' he said after a

long moment. Then he glanced back toward his pair of roasting grouse.

The fire licked their flesh, and their fat dripped into the flames and sizzled, sending up a sweet-smelling smoke.

'It's time,' he said. 'I'll be facing Vulgnash, a Knight Eternal, a flameweaver of considerable power.'

I should have begun this instruction years ago, he thought.

'Wait!' Talon said.

The emir turned to her.

'You're a generous man, too,' she said hesitantly. 'You're planning to end your life when this is over, give back your endowments – aren't you?'

'Let us just say,' he answered, 'that if you see me fall in battle at the end of the fight, do not come back to save me.'

'Do you think that that is what Siyaddah would want?'

'I think that she would be hurt,' the emir said, 'but in time she would think of me less and less often.'

'I think that some pain can never die,' Talon argued.

'Whatever happens to me,' the emir said, 'tell her that I died valiantly, in battle.'

'What if I don't want you to die in battle?' Talon asked.

Tuul Ra had no answer for that.

He rose, and climbed up from the cattails at the edge of the brook. He went beside the small fire. Little smoke came from the dry wood, and it was being dispersed by a light wind and by the trees.

In fact, the wind was strong enough that the flames sputtered with every gust, as if the fire would go out.

He had always felt uneasy around fire. He'd always been aware of how it pulled at his sanity, sought to command him. But today he felt more wary than ever.

He had learned what kind of man he had been on the shadow world – faithless, brutal, an enemy to all of mankind.

Of course, that's not me, is it? That was someone else, in another life.

But somehow it felt like him.

Fire was the connection. Fire was always there, at the

edge of his consciousness, calling to him: Use me. You need me. You are not whole without me, and I am not whole without you.

I was the most powerful flameweaver in the history of the shadow world, the emir thought. And I could be the most powerful in mine.

Yes, the fire seemed to whisper, its bright tongues speaking to some primal part of the emir's soul, piercing the base of his brain. You could be powerful. The world needs you to be powerful, to give yourself to the flames. How else will you conquer the wyrmling hordes?

How else indeed? Tuul Ra wondered.

It is a small matter, the fire whispered. Step into the flame. Give yourself to me.

It was a temptation. It had always been a temptation. Tuul Ra often suspected that his skills could blossom if he but let them. He'd dared imagine himself fighting the wyrmling horde, striding into Rugassa with a ball of sunlight balanced in his hand, one so bright that it would make the wyrmlings' eyes sizzle in the backs of their heads.

They are an evil people. Someone needs to destroy them.

The emir knelt in front of the fire, as if before an altar, and gazed into the flames.

Filled with curiosity, Talon, Daylan Hammer, and the Cormar twins all gathered around him.

The emir had long been able to bend smoke to his will. It was a talent he had noticed in childhood. And he could make flames rise up and dance like snakes at his command. But it was not a gift that he lusted for, or that he took pride in.

He studied the flames now. His pair of grouse was cooking unevenly. He sat staring at the flames, tried to twist them upward and to the south, so that the birds would cook more evenly.

But after what seemed like several moments, nothing happened. Fire was aware of him, of that he felt certain. He was drawn to it, as it was drawn to him. But it would not bend to his will.

'You can't just force it,' Daylan Hammer said. 'Fire always requires a sacrifice. Go fetch some wood. Try building it up.'

'I'll get some,' the Cormar twins said in unison, and they glanced at each other, laughed maniacally, and then leapt up and raced into the brush, each step choreographed, each move perfectly matching the other.

The emir considered waiting for the wood. But he knew that wood was not the only sacrifice that might be given. He reached up to his neck and pulled at a leather cord so that a sheepskin pouch popped out from beneath his ring mail. He opened the pouch and dumped a lock of hair into his hand, black and shiny.

He tossed the hair in, watched the fire consume it greedily, tiny flames flickering green and blue as they consumed the oils in the hair.

It had been the last memento from his dead wife.

In the hissing of the flames he heard the words 'Serve me.'

'I will feed you,' he replied. 'You may have my service, but not my soul.'

18

A GATHERING OF HEROES

Joy is the object of our creation. When one is united with a wyrm, it produces an abundance of joy. Therefore, always conduct your affairs in a way that makes you worthy of a wyrm.

—From the Wyrmling Catechism

Once Talon and the others had finished eating and broken camp, the emir kicked the coals from the fire off into the nearest bushes; seemingly with a thought the fire raced among some dry leaves and began licking the trunks of the nearest oaks.

What good will it do him, she wondered, to give himself thus to Fire? All it will do is warn the wyrmlings. They'll see the smoke.

Daylan watched the flames for a long moment and said softly, 'It is written that Raj Ahten fed his fires day and night, burning entire forests. I suppose that such sacrifices must be made if you are to gain his powers.'

'It is not much of a sacrifice,' the emir said. 'There is a blight upon the land. The trees will be dead within a month anyway, I fear, and then the first spark would set this whole land alight.'

'Sooner than a month,' Daylan said, 'unless we can break the wyrmlings' hold upon the land.'

Talon did not have any idea how that might be done.

She wasn't sure that Daylan knew. How were the wyrmlings even poisoning the land? Was it some sort of rune lore, like the reavers had used at Carris in her father's day?

The Cormar twins laughed at some private joke, then sprang off along the road, their steps perfectly matched, their arms swinging in unison.

We can't be far from Rugassa, Talon thought, though she could see no sign of it yet.

They raced on with renewed fury, running forty miles in the next hour, until sweat weighed down Talon's tunic. They stopped to drink at streams along the way, but each time it was only a gulp, stolen quickly, and then they were off again.

Soon, a mountain began to loom in the distance, dark and forbidding, its coned peak looking blue at first, and then gaining definition as the heroes neared.

From time to time, they continued to pass villages – all of the houses broken and destroyed.

We're near the town of Ravenspell, Talon realized, consulting a mental map.

It was late morning when they reached it, crossing a fine stone bridge into a walled city. The walls here were not high, only twenty feet or so. The gates of the city had been broken down, and like the villages before, the houses had been demolished, their thatch roofs pulled off, their doors smashed.

Talon had no desire to inspect the ruins. But as the three sprinted through the city streets, rushing at forty miles per hour, it was as if her mind was storing pictures – a burned hovel, a dead man sprawled on his belly while a buzzard flapped heavily into the air, a frightened dog rushing into the ruins to hide.

Suddenly they rounded a corner in the market section of town, and there she was – a girl of five or six with long blond braided hair there at a market stall, hunched over a pile of cloth.

She must have heard the noise, for she turned and shrieked, peering at them briefly in terror but not really seeing them.

The girl leapt over the counter of the market stall to hide.

The company came to a halt, and all of them stood for a moment, panting, each wondering what to do.

'Looks like the wyrmlings missed one,' the emir said. He peered to Talon, then to the others. 'What shall we do with the child.'

The Cormar twins laughed mirthlessly at some private joke, then said in explanation, 'We're not carrying her into battle.'

'We can't leave her here,' Talon said. 'She'll starve, if the wyrmlings don't find her first.'

'Nor can we take her with us,' the emir said. He looked about helplessly. 'All we can do is pick her up on the way back. If all goes well, we will be done with our business before dark.'

'She has managed to hide from the wyrmlings well enough for at least three days,' Daylan Hammer said. 'She should manage well enough for a few hours more.'

But Talon could not leave it at that. The girl was terrified. She had seen it in the child's face. That kind of fear can turn a person into an animal. If nothing else, Talon needed to soothe her mind.

'Stay here,' Talon said.

She approached the market stall quietly. The roof of the building was made from pine poles draped with red linen curtains. The curtains were ripped and bloody, flying like banners in the wind.

Approaching cautiously, Talon called out, 'Little girl? Little girl? Are you all right?'

She went and looked over the plank counter. There was a pile of cloth beneath it. The girl was hiding there beneath some rumpled cloth, trembling, so that the whole pile shook.

'Do you have a name?' Talon asked.

The girl was shaking frightfully. Talon could only see a portion of her leg.

'My name is Talon. I'm here to help you. I'm with friends, Runelords. We're going to go kill the monsters that attacked the city.'

'You're monsters!' the girl cried. She pulled the wrinkled

fabric away but merely sat there, in a fetal position, too frightened to do anything but look. Her eyes roved over Talon's face.

She sees the ridge bone on my face, and the nubs of my horns, Talon realized. I don't look human to her anymore.

'I'm not like those monsters. They're called wyrmlings. They're larger than me, and they're very evil. If I'm a monster, I'm a good monster.'

'How can I tell?'

'If I was one of them,' Talon said easily, 'I would have taken you already.'

The girl thought about this, but kept trembling in fear.

'Do you have a family? Is anyone else alive in this city?'

The girl shook her head no both times.

'Do you have a name?'

The girl shook her head no again, and shrank back against the wall of her little cupboard.

'I think you're teasing me,' Talon said. 'Everyone has a name.'

The girl turned her face to the wall, and just stared at it.

'I'm going to have to go fight the wyrmlings now,' Talon said. 'I don't want to leave you alone, but I have to. I'll come for you when I get back. I'll take you to safety. You can wait for me, can't you? You can be brave until then?'

The little girl did not answer.

Talon turned to leave.

I can track her by smell if I have to, Talon told herself. She hesitated, and whispered, 'Be well,' then walked away.

'No!' the girl shrieked. Talon turned as the child came leaping over the counter of the little market stall. Then the girl grabbed her by the leg and held on, terrified that Talon would leave.

'Come here,' Talon said, reaching down and grabbing the child.

'Don't leave me!' the girl shouted. 'Don't ever leave!' She peered into Talon's face, stricken. The girl's eyes were bloodshot from lack of sleep, her face dirty. She smelled of dog hair and sweat. But she was a pretty thing, in a common sort of way.

Daylan and the others came over, stood at their side. 'You can't take her with us,' Daylan said in the tongue of the warrior clans. 'We go to save a world. We cannot wait upon this child.'

Talon gave him a reproving look.

'She can't just leave the girl,' the emir said. 'Her mothering instincts are too strong.' He grimaced and looked down. 'Nor can I leave her. What kind of men would we be to do so?'

'Wise men?' the Cormars said as one.

Daylan grabbed the girl and gently pulled her from Talon's arms. He set her on the ground. 'We'll be back for you,' he said sternly. 'Go find a place to hide until then.'

The girl lurched toward Talon, but Daylan reached down, grabbed her by the forehead, and pushed her onto her butt.

'Stay there,' he warned. 'I don't have time to be nice about this.'

The child looked at him, terrified, and while she was frozen with indecision Daylan said, 'Let's go.'

The emir took Talon by the sleeve and whispered, 'Hurry. Don't look back.'

Talon ran, but her heart grew heavy as her legs stretched, carrying her away from the town. They raced through empty streets, where elms lined the path, and they leaped over another quaint stone bridge. She could hear the child screaming behind her, 'Come back! Come back!'

What would I do if that were one of my own little sisters? Talon wondered. How would I want her treated?

And then she knew. She would want the soldiers who were out to save the world to turn a cold shoulder to her little sister. She would want them to fight all the more valiantly to avenge her. She would want them to do their job.

'Come back!' the girl called as they raced into the fields beyond the edge of town. Talon's keen hearing let her detect the sound two miles away.

I will, Talon promised. I will.

They had not gone ten miles when they spotted another Knight Eternal all dressed in red, flying from the south. They were walking along the road at the noon hour when they saw it coming over the treetops, not a mile behind.

'Flee!' the emir hissed.

But Daylan just stood for a second, gazing up at the Knight Eternal. It came hurtling toward them so swiftly that Talon almost didn't have time to draw her weapon.

'Fear not,' Daylan cried. 'It is only our friend Rhianna.'

The robed figure landed before him in a flutter of wings, and Rhianna pulled back her crimson hood, her red hair spilling out in a tide. She smiled at them, and the emir and the Cormar twins all stepped back and gasped.

Much had changed. Rhianna shook her hair loose, and it seemed as if it was full of light. Her eyes gleamed like stars in a night sky, and seemed to beg for all to gaze upon their glory. Her skin had grown softer and more radiant than before. She was like some great queen of legend, so beautiful that she would turn men's knees weak with desire.

'Don't be afraid,' Rhianna said. 'It's only me.' Her voice was as pure as water, as mellow as a woodwind.

Daylan peered at her angrily. 'So, they're wasting forcibles on endowments of glamour nowadays?'

Rhianna looked down, embarrassed. 'The horse-sisters gave them to me. It encourages others to do the same.'

'How many?' Daylan asked. 'How many of glamour, how many of voice?'

'Perhaps twenty in all,' Rhianna said.

'Or thirty or forty?' Daylan suggested.

Rhianna shot him an angry look. She was obviously embarrassed. She had wasted forcibles taking beauty when she could have used them to boost her strength and stamina. 'The people have been generous,' Rhianna argued. 'They've granted me more than three hundred endowments in the past day. How many were you given?'

'Did they give them,' Daylan demanded, 'or did you steal them?'

Rhianna glared at him but held her silence.

'You know the law of the Ael. Taking another's glamour is forbidden!'

'I'm not Ael,' Rhianna shouted, 'and I never shall be. Your grand folk in the netherworld wouldn't even let me stay a season there. I'm a Runelord, and I'll do as I please. I'll do what I must!'

Talon glanced from face to face. She knew what Daylan was afraid of. He was afraid that Rhianna's beauty would corrupt her.

And maybe it shall, Talon thought.

'Let's go kill wyrmlings,' Rhianna growled. She looked north. 'I have a convoy of horse-sisters from Fleeds ahead. I saw them from the sky. They're only three miles from here. They have a wyrmling with them, a girl who can lead us to the dungeons.'

The moment of tension eased.

'Why would she do that?' Daylan asked.

'She wants to fight the wyrmlings,' Rhianna said. 'In the binding, two of her shadow selves were bound – a wyrmling and an Inkarran. The Inkarran had been one of Gaborn's chosen ones.'

Talon wondered at that, wondered how many more Inkarrans might be bound into the wyrmling horde, wondered how many of them Gaborn might have tried to sway.

'We saw your handiwork on the road a hundred miles back,' Talon said. 'Good job, that. Did you get many forcibles?'

'A few thousand. I couldn't let them reach the wyrmling horde.'

'Some got through anyway,' Daylan said. 'We saw Knights Eternal flying north not an hour ago, carrying cargo. We must fear for the worst.'

Rhianna bit her lip.

'We'll release the wyrmling girl,' she said, 'a few miles from the fortress. She can go to the doors, beg for mercy. The wyrmlings will take her to their dungeon for torture. I can track their path by smell. I promised that I would go in for her in less than an hour.'

It did not seem like much of a plan to Talon. She wanted things locked down better, more secure. But it was the first and only plan that had been introduced so far.

Daylan Hammer said, 'And once we get into the fortress, what next?'

'We kill anyone who stands in our way,' Rhianna said, all business.

Talon could not help but hear the ghost of the Bright One's warnings. Erringale had told them to spare the enemy, be as lenient as possible, lest they stain their own souls.

Almost Talon thought to object to the plan.

But why should I bother? she wondered. The wyrmlings have been a scourge upon the earth for far too long. They've all but destroyed my people, and if left to their own ends, they will exterminate us. We are strong. The six of us could wipe out the whole wyrmling horde.

She looked to the Cormars, saw that they grinned, their smiles obscenely identical. There was a glint of madness to their eyes.

Yet Talon couldn't imagine engaging in slaughter. There were innocents among the wyrmlings too, children and babes. There might be more wyrmling girls like the one that Rhianna had found, people who longed to be free and who were willing to fight for it, to die for it.

'I go to Rugassa to free my friend,' the emir said, 'not to wash in wyrmling blood.' He said it in Rofehavanish. His accent was thick, his words unsure, but he managed to say it. Talon was surprised that he could speak the tongue at all given their short conversation. Then he switched to the tongue of the warrior clans. 'Take a life if you must, but only if you must.' There was rage on his face, a temper barely under control. 'We are in dire straits,' he said, 'but I swear, if any of you take an innocent life, you will have me to deal with.'

Daylan Hammer translated his words for Rhianna, then gave him an appreciative look and added, 'And me.'

Talon admired their courage. 'And me.'

The Cormar twins peered at them with glinting eyes, and Talon could read their thoughts. We could take them, they were thinking. We could kill them all, and then kill the wyrmlings.

Suddenly they both laughed, each chuckle precisely synchronized. Daylan glanced at Talon, giving her a look of warning.

They've lost themselves, Talon realized. Somehow in twinning their minds, they've lost themselves. We should go to battle now, before they go completely mad.

'Let's not argue,' she said. 'We've got a job to do.'

So they plotted their attack. Rhianna related what intelligence she could, telling of her bargain with the horse-sisters and her overthrow of Beldinook. She told of the dangers she had faced at the Courts of Tide, and her hopes that the warlords there might form a diversion. She repeated reports of reavers surfacing near Carris, and relayed how the horse-sisters' scouts warned that they were marching in a northeasterly direction. She told how the wyrmlings at Caer Luciare had begun taking endowments, and described where she had hidden the forcibles that she'd stolen from the wyrmlings – news that was important, should she fall in battle.

Talon related all that had happened to her, including Erringale's vision of Borenson sailing to their aid upon a white ship.

It seemed as if they spoke for an hour; but all of them had taken endowments of metabolism, so in truth not five minutes had passed before Rhianna leapt into the air and flew north to meet the horse-sisters.

Then the company began their race again, sprinting down the broken road to Rugassa.

Holding a blanket over her head to protect her bleary eyes, Kirissa scrambled down out of the forest and over the uneven black paving stones into Rugassa, a fortress built into a tall volcanic cone of black basalt, smoothed on its slopes so that one could see where hundreds of towers and walkways and air shafts had been carved.

She had hoped never to see the fortress again, but the Earth King's words resounded in her mind.

The time was coming when the small folk of the world would have to stand up to the large.

But he didn't say that I'd live through it, Kirissa realized.

She stumbled, her toe catching on an uneven stone, and fell to one knee, then climbed up carefully.

The defenses of Rugassa were all underground. From the outside it looked as if you could just walk in. There were no tall walls with guards walking them, as you would see in a human castle. The wyrmlings didn't like being so exposed. No, the defenses were all inside, underground, so well concealed that those who managed to breach them never got back outside to tell how far they had gone.

So Kirissa walked across the dark stones with the sun blazing above her, a bit of sandalwood perfume upon her heel, until she reached the south tunnel.

Deep within its recesses, fifty yards from the entrance, guards were waiting. A great iron door stood closed before her, and the guards peered out through a slit, so that she could see only their white eyes.

They did not ask her questions. They only opened the door, winching it slowly, until the guards stood before her, great brutes in armor of bone.

One guard lunged for her, grabbing her in a stranglehold, then threw his weight against her so that she fell to the floor. He landed on her ribs, forcing the air from her sharply, so that she could not breathe. Two other guards grabbed her from behind and began feeling through her clothes, ostensibly searching for weapons.

One of them hissed, 'I would have thought that you would be smart enough to stay gone.'

'I came back,' Kirissa grunted, 'to serve the Great Wyrm. I was wrong to leave. I know that now.'

'Oh, she *knows* that now!' her strangler mocked. The others laughed harshly as his grip tightened on her throat. Kirissa gasped for air and struggled for all that she was worth for fifteen seconds.

As her lungs began to burn, she went limp, feigning unconsciousness, but the guard kept strangling.

Don't let me die, she begged the Powers. Please don't let them kill me now.

Talon and the heroes waited on a pine-covered hill with the horse-sisters of Fleeds, a fearsome company of women upon blood mounts, red warhorses with red eyes, their flanks painted with mystic runes.

Though the horse-sisters' armor was light, consisting of boiled-leather cuirasses enameled in green and gold, their lances were sharp, and they wore fantastic enameled masks over their helmets – images of stags with antlers, and boars with tusks, and bears with long fangs, and the green man with leaves for hair – so that they looked more like fearsome beasts than humans.

The forty women were four miles from Rugassa. The pines grew thick around them, but not so thick that the company couldn't see the entrances to the fortress from here.

They could not go to battle immediately. They needed to give the wyrmlings time to take their prisoner into the dungeons.

If they take her to the dungeons, Talon thought.

There were no guarantees. Rhianna had warned that the guards might kill her outright.

Talon said, 'That girl is showing great faith in us.'

'Let us live worthy of it,' the emir agreed.

It was early afternoon, a perfect time to strike.

Talon took a few minutes to sharpen her sword, then her daggers. The others did the same. She got out her sunstones, and gave one to each of her companions. She had only five, and so the Cormar twins were forced to share.

But Daylan Hammer urged, 'Keep them hidden. Use them only as a last resort. If Vulgnash sees them, he will draw the fire from them and turn their power against us.' So Talon hid her sunstone in her shoe. It was uncomfortable, but it was a familiar pain. As a child she had often hidden coins in her boot when she went to the fair.

The memory made her smile, reminding her of more innocent days.

It seemed that the sun crawled through the sky. Talon saw the emir wander off into the trees.

She followed him, until they found a private place in a small glen.

He did not speak. He took Talon's hand and squeezed it. It wasn't that he had nothing to say, she realized. It was that he had too much to say, and words did not suffice.

So she kissed him again, and held him for a time.

'Don't die on me today,' Talon said.

He made no promises.

Am I not reason enough for him to live? she wondered. But she understood his math. He had taken endowments from people, and he needed to give them back. The happiness of the many outweighed the happiness of two.

At last, Rhianna gave a small shout. It was time to fight.

The two of them walked up the hill, hand-in-hand, until they reached its top.

Daylan Hammer and the Cormars were itching to go. The horse-sisters were all mounted, ready to ride.

'Good fortune to you in your hunt,' Sister Daughtry said.

'Are you going to ride to Caer Luciare now?' Talon asked her. Almost she wished that the horse-sisters would join the raid, but none of them had taken the number of endowments that would be needed for such a fight.

'Yes,' Sister Daughtry answered.

'Don't try to take it yet,' Rhianna said. 'You don't know what you'll find there. There will be Death Lords for certain, and Runelords. Find a place to camp for the night, and hide well. We will join you as soon as possible, if we can!'

'Well spoken,' Sister Daughtry said.

Raising their fists in salute, the horse-sisters urged their mounts forward one by one, and headed down the road to the south.

When they were gone, Rhianna leapt into the air and led the charge, flapping madly, flying low above the road, veering among the trees, building up incredible speed – until soon she was a blur, faster than a falcon.

She had volunteered to hit the gate first, take out the guards, and leave the way open for the others.

The five stood upon the hill, watching her fly, and in moments she was lost in the trees. Just as Talon began looking for her, suddenly Rhianna was there at Rugassa, rising up out of the forest and hurtling over the wall. She could not have been visible for two seconds before she disappeared into the fortress, choosing a huge black gaping tunnel at the southern-most face.

'Good hunting,' Talon prayed, as she raced to catch up.

'Come, and see this, my friend,' Lord Despair said to his visitor. 'Forces are coming to attack the fortress. I believe that they are humans, empowered by runes. You should enjoy the spectacle.'

The creature beside him was covered with coarse dark hair, and stood nine feet tall, but the vast wings at his back rose even higher. He smelled like a storm, and normally would have wrapped himself in clouds and darkness, drawing all light from the room. But here in Rugassa, he felt at home. He was a Darkling Glory from the netherworld, but he was more than that. There was a wyrm feeding on his soul, a powerful wyrm named Scathain, the Lord of Ashes. For nearly twenty years now, Scathain had been feeding upon the Darkling Glory.

Despair was filled with nervous energy. Hundreds of endowments he had been granted this day, sent through various vectors. He had not wasted his time attending the rites. He'd been too busy negotiating. He'd taken so many endowments of stamina, he almost felt as if health and vitality must be radiating from him, bursting like beams of sunlight from every pore. His endowments of brawn were so great that he felt as if he was hardly touching the floor. His own weight seemed insignificant, as if he floated above the ground instead of walking. It was all that he could do to restrain himself, to keep from running.

Scathain followed at his side, walking in a hunched manner. Lord Despair said, 'The attackers will come down this very tunnel.'

'How can you be certain?' Scathain asked.

'My Earth Powers,' Despair said. 'Some of my chosen servants are down the corridor. I sense the danger coming.'

Lord Despair could see the attackers' path in his mind's eye. They would leave a trail of dead – all the way down to the dungeons, if he did not stop them.

'Yes, they will come,' Despair said, his anticipation rising pleasurably.

'Would you like me to deal with them?' Scathain asked.

'No. My wyrmlings will handle the intruders.'

'Yes, Great One,' Scathain said. Despite his size, the Darkling Glory walked lightly.

Despair had ordered a certain member of the High Council to watch the southern passage. That was how he knew exactly where the enemy would enter. He could feel death approaching the fool. But Despair dared not use his Earth Powers to warn him. If the wyrmling lord warned others, it could cause a panic. People would flee, defenders might gather. Despair could not allow that. The enemy could not suspect that he had set a trap.

But what is the source of the attack? he wondered. Most likely it was humans, since they were attacking in the early afternoon, when the sun was the brightest.

It could be the Fang Guards coming from Caer Luciare, he decided. But wyrmlings would traditionally travel at night. Still, he supposed, if it were members of the Fang Guard, they might have taken enough endowments of stamina to resist the sun's burning powers.

But something else came to mind. What if the Fang Guards had discovered some other way to abide the daylight?

What would happen, Lord Despair wondered, if a wyrmling took an endowment of sight from a normal human? Would he suddenly be able to withstand sunlight better?

What a fearsome thing that would be, Despair considered – a wyrmling that can abide the light.

He sent a guard to tell his facilitators to test the theory.

Or perhaps, he wondered, it is neither the folk from Caer Luciare nor the Fang Guards. His warriors had been harrying the small folk on his borders now for three nights running. Perhaps some of the small folk had found some blood-metal ore and taken endowments. Perhaps it was a contingent of these that were coming, a band of Runelords who planned an attack for reasons of their own.

He was so in tune with the Earth Powers, he could almost count the seconds until the attack. It would come at the southern gate, in only a few moments.

Running now, Lord Despair charged up the stairs to his chambers, three steps at a time, until he found himself in his rooms. He went to his parapet, and crouched there in the shadows in his black robes beside the gargoyles, watching to see what enemy would come.

Scathain raced up to his side, and knelt like a great black gargoyle himself.

The sun stood still in the sky, and the air was almost perfectly calm. Only the slightest afternoon breeze played across his brow.

With his endowments of hearing, birdsong seemed to rise in a chorus from the forest in every direction – the cooing of wild pigeons, the ratcheting of jays, the chirps of songbirds.

The plains before the gates of Rugassa were empty now.

In the nights, the fields would come alive as his minions toiled by the tens of thousands, a dark mass of wyrmlings coming to feed the city: huntsmen bringing in handcarts piled with carcasses to feed the empire; skirmishers leading bands of small folk in chains, to be stripped of endowments; woodsmen tugging carts filled with cordwood for the cooking fires; wyrmlings bringing animal skins for clothes, and ingots of iron from the mines, and all other manner of goods.

In such a throng, it would have been difficult to spot intruders. They might have hidden among carts or worn disguises.

But the plains were empty now.

Despair saw no armies in the distance. With a dozen endowments of sight taken both from wyrmlings and from the small folk, he would have spotted them across the miles.

Yet alarms blared in Despair's mind. 'Death is coming. Tell your chosen one to flee.'

At last something caught his eye on the horizon to the south: a flash of red in a shaft of light – the crimson robes of a Knight Eternal.

It was hastening toward the fortress, flying low through the pine trees that ran along the road.

Kryssidia? Lord Despair wondered. What is he doing out?

The Knight Eternal that flew toward the castle had endowments, it was obvious. He was flying at tremendous speed, perhaps two hundred miles per hour, making toward the southern entrances.

'Flee,' the Earth Spirit said. 'Warn your chosen to flee. Death is coming.'

Could it be Kryssidia? Despair wondered. Dismay filled him. If his Knights Eternal were to turn against him . . .

Then he spotted movement in the distance – too far for the city guard to see. But a handful of warriors was also racing toward Rugassa in the midday sun.

Humans. So, the heroes had come to rescue Fallion.

Death was imminent for the High Council member at the south gate. The Earth Spirit seemed almost to be thundering in his ears. The attackers on the ground were still miles away when the Earth screamed its final warning, and it took a great of amount of discipline for Lord Despair to withhold aid.

So the flier is just the vanguard, Despair realized.

Kryssidia would not be in league with humans.

It is one of them – a human with stolen wings and a Knight Eternal's robes.

'The flier is one of the attackers,' Despair told the Darkling Glory. 'But others are following.'

'The enemy flies swiftly and well,' the Darkling Glory said. 'I would be honored to fight that one.'

Despair smiled.

When death came to the High Councilman, Despair felt a cruel sense of loss, as if his very heart was torn from him. It was the Earth Spirit, punishing him for allowing the murder. Any other man would have crumbled to the floor and wept bitter tears, so overwhelming was the loss.

But Despair simply whispered to the Earth, 'Patience, my dear friend, patience. The one who died was a fool, and therefore worthless to me. I repent that I ever chose him. But I have others that I value more.'

The Earth did not answer. Despair felt its spirit withdraw, and worried that it might flee him forever.

'We must hurry,' Despair said to the Darkling Glory. 'I have prepared a most special welcome for our guests.'

Talon ran through the forest toward Rugassa, heart pounding, and watched for Rhianna's signal. Talon was still two miles out from the city, probably too far for the wyrmling guards to see. But she felt exposed here. The black volcano rose up from the plains, looming above her. As she drew nearer she could descry thousands of dark holes in the basalt, windows and air vents for the wyrmling labyrinth. And at each one, she knew cruel eyes might be watching.

Rhianna had hardly touched down in the tunnel when her signal came – three bright flashes from a sunstone at the mouth of the tunnel.

She had taken out the guards.

Now the race began in earnest. The Cormar twins led the way, giggling at some private joke, followed next by Daylan Hammer, the Emir Tuul Ra, and last of all by Talon.

Each of them had copious endowments of metabolism; now the Cormar twins sprinted at breakneck speed, matching each other stride for stride, fifty miles per hour, sixty.

They raced under the pines, through the shadows thrown by the midday sun.

Even a wyrmling can't see us yet, Talon thought. The sun is in their eyes, and we are all in shadow.

So she tried to comfort herself with reassurances of her own lack of visibility until at last the comrades exited the woods, passing a great basalt wall some forty feet high, and ran now through barren fields, subject to the scrutiny of any who might be watching.

It was still a mile to the gate, black and yawning ahead.

She waited for some alarm, for surely, she thought, someone is aware of us by now.

'Run faster,' Daylan cried.

The less time that we are exposed, Talon thought, the less chance that we will be seen.

At sixty miles per hour it would take nearly a full minute to cross the open plains. Only the greatest stroke of luck would let them make it unseen.

They would have to rely upon their own speed and fighting skills to get them to their destination.

Before she ever reached the gate, a gong sounded. It was a bell more massive than any she'd heard before. The tolling of it sent a thrill through the ground.

Twelve seconds later, the company burst into the tunnel and were soon at an iron gate that had been thrown open. Guards lay dead and bloodied, while Rhianna stood over their corpses, a black long sword in hand.

She pocketed her sunstone, waited a heartbeat, then turned and led the way into the fortress.

The Cormar twins charged in at her back. Suddenly both of them cackled and raced to take the lead, sprinting down the corridors in unison, cutting down any wyrmling that stood in their way.

There was no resistance. None of the wyrmlings had endowments as far as Talon could tell. Some had time to register a look of shock. Some warriors even had their hands stray toward a weapon. But the battle was over before it ever began, with the Cormar twins artfully hacking the defenders down, one man swinging high, another low, so that heads and legs came off at the same instant.

It felt too much like murder. Talon could hardly stomach it.

We have that right, Talon told herself, after all that they've done to us.

Talon was in the rearguard, and as such she kept a lookout behind. But her job, it seemed, consisted mainly of trying not to slip on the trail of blood left by those who blazed the path ahead.

As she ran, she had time to notice the little things – the glow worms grazing on the walls, wyrmling glyphs painted in white to mark the doorways. The air was warm and sultry inside the tunnels, stuffy and filled with the acrid scent of sulfur and the stench of a million wyrmlings. She saw kill holes and spy holes in the walls – and in one she glimpsed an eye, the pure white iris of a wyrmling, gazing back at her in fear.

She had no idea how to reach the creature. Surely some hidden corridor would lead her there, but she did not know which byways to take, or how many turns she might have to pass.

They're watching us, she thought. They know everything that we do. We can only hope that they don't have enough power to do anything *but* watch.

She lunged toward the spy hole and thrust her blade through before the wyrmling had time to back away or even blink. Her blade slid through the eye socket and clunked as it hit the back of the wyrmling's skull. The blade came out covered in gore.

Talon raced down the tunnel, following her comrades. They had not gone far when she heard a tremendous rattling. She turned and peered back in the gloom. A huge iron portcullis was dropping, gravity bearing it inexorably down. It looked as if it weighed several tons, and the whole tunnel shook. If she had not had endowments, it might have seemed to fall instantly, but with her speed it seemed to take a pair of seconds before it slammed into the ground with finality.

Our exit is blocked. There's no way out!

Her heart raced, but Talon realized that there had to be a path out. She'd seen thousands of windows and air holes. Surely there was more than one exit.

No one else seemed to worry. They battled on.

Only once did Talon provide any real help. They were following the scent of sandalwood on Kirissa's trail, but even with endowments of scent, the others could not be sure which way to go.

'Are we heading down the right tunnel?' Daylan called.

'Yes,' Talon shouted back. Her voice sounded stressed, frightened. She realized that from the time they had entered the labyrinth, almost no one had spoken.

Suddenly the corridor ahead darkened and a great red shadow filled the hallway. Talon saw wings rise up, and realized that a Knight Eternal stood before them, barring the way.

There was a nervous cry of warning from Rhianna. She raised her sunstone and squeezed it so that it sent out a piercing light. The Knight Eternal squinted a bit, then swiftly raised a hand.

The sunstone flared impossibly bright. A whirling torrent of fire went streaming out from it into the Knight Eternal's hand, and the sunstone shattered in Rhianna's fingers. Fragments went scattering like hot sparks across the stone floor.

'It's Vulgnash himself!' Daylan shouted, and Talon felt her bowels quiver.

The Cormar twins cried out in anticipation, like dogs eager to attack. But their perfectly choreographed moves ceased. In their haste, one of them stumbled.

They're fighting each other for control, Talon realized.

The stumbler regained his feet, and the two bounded forward; one swung low while the other went high. But their movements seemed slow, jerky, uncoordinated.

In a heartbeat Vulgnash leapt and ducked at the same instant. He did not seem faster than them. Indeed, he barely seemed to escape alive.

Then he went on the attack.

His own black blade swung and lunged and swung again with such ferocity that the Cormars were driven back. He pressed the attack, rushing forward, and in the dim light had some advantage.

He has endowments to match our own, Talon realized, maybe even more.

Out of the darkness at Vulgnash's back, specters appeared – a pair of shadows clothed in the ragged black robes of Death Lords.

The air suddenly chilled, the temperature dropping and becoming numbingly cold. The air fogged from Talon's mouth. Then the Death Lords shed their robes. They became indistinct shadows in the darkness.

No mortal blade could kill a Death Lord. Their very touch would freeze a man's soul, leaving him paralyzed.

The Cormars fought to fend off Vulgnash's ferocious assault, but the very sight of the Death Lords unmanned them. Vulgnash swung mightily. One Cormar tried to block with his axe, but Vulgnash's great sword landed with such ferocity that there was a snap.

Tun Cormar's arm shattered.

Instantly Vulgnash leapt, his wings flapping once, so that he flew over the young man's head – and kicked, sending Tun into the wall.

Tun's head hit with a smashing sound, and he began to slump to the ground, leaving a bloody red streak.

No endowments of brawn could save his bones from such abuse.

His brother Errant cried out in anguish, and leapt at Vulgnash's back, arms flailing in an unrestrained attack.

Tun is dead, Talon realized. His brother feels the loss of a Dedicate.

But the Knight Eternal ducked beneath Errant's blow, stepped backward, and clubbed the young warrior with an elbow.

Errant Cormar was thrown backward – into the arms of the Death Lords.

They took him, black shadows clawing at his face greedily as they consumed his spirit.

Errant's scream rent the air, and he kicked in vain.

Talon could not see what happened next, for Vulgnash raised

his wings high, so that they spanned the entire corridor. He lifted his sword in salute, inviting the next challenger.

Something's wrong here, Talon realized. Vulgnash is toying with us.

She wondered if he had more endowments than it seemed. 'Run!' Daylan cried. 'To the right!'

There was a doorway to their right, just behind Talon, a large corridor with an arched roof. Talon was rearguard, so she whirled and raced down the corridor with only glow worms to light her way.

She did not like the smell of the room ahead. It tasted of blood and putrefaction, like a slaughterhouse.

The emir was at her back. He reached into his own pouch and grabbed his sunstone, held it up and pinched it. The sunstone flared into light.

They were standing in a huge room, circular in shape. There were high walls all around them, twenty feet perhaps. And above those walls were seats.

We're in a coliseum, Talon realized, a place for blood sports.

'Welcome,' a man called out, 'to the Arena of the Great Wyrm.'

Talon halted, heart hammering, and saw a man standing before them in fine robes at the very center of the ring. At his side stood a dark creature, hairy and winged. Talon had never seen such, but she recognized it from her mother's description. It was a Darkling Glory.

Behind the man, a pair of burly guards were holding the wyrmling girl, Kirissa.

'Areth,' a voice cried at Talon's back. 'Areth Sul Urstone!' The Emir Tuul Ra sprang forward, confusion thick in his voice, as if he wanted to embrace his old friend but suspected that he should flee.

'Areth Sul Urstone no longer exists,' the swordsman said. 'I am the master of this house. I am the king of the Shattered Earth. I am the Great Wyrm that haunts your nightmares. I am Lord Despair.'

At their back, Talon could hear heavy feet. Vulgnash and

the Death Lords had stepped in to block the company's
escape.

The emir looked crushed, confused. He staggered forward,
as if he might embrace Areth.

But Daylan warned him back. 'Hold, my friend. This is not
the Areth that you so loved.'

'Areth!' the emir shouted in a near panic. 'Resist him. You
can resist evil. Resist it, and it will flee from you!'

Despair laughed. 'No, there is not much left of him in here.
What remains is hardly aware. Like a mouse stung by the
venom of a scorpion, he is torpid. Yes, that is it, a mouse. He
is a mouse hiding in my skull, a frightened mouse shivering
in the recesses of my consciousness, dreaming of escape. He
cannot resist me.'

'But, Areth,' the emir cried, 'we're here to rescue you.'

'Too late,' Despair said. 'You should have come years ago,
fourteen years ago. You could have offered ransoms. You could
have fought valiantly.'

'There is no coin that we could have paid with,' the emir
objected. 'There is no chance that we could have won.'

'Ah,' Lord Despair said, 'that is where you are wrong. You
could have fought. It is true that you would have died, and
Areth would have been saddened for a moment. But he would
have also been comforted by the depth of your love. The
knowledge of what you had sacrificed might even have steeled
him, so that he could endure all of our torments. But alas,
we'll never know. All he felt for you in the end was hurt and
betrayal.'

'That's a lie,' the emir said. 'Areth knew that I loved him as
a brother. I would have come for him years ago. I would have
come and died. But the wyrmlings would have destroyed our
people in the backlash. Areth knows that, too, I am sure. And
he would have suffered for an eternity rather than see that.'

The smile that crept across Lord Despair's face was terrible
to see. It was cruel beyond torture, and it mocked all who
beheld it.

'He held on to such noble sentiments for as long as he could,'

Despair said. 'But here in Rugassa, we have perfected torment, and in the end, pain drove all such thoughts from his mind.'

The Emir Tuul Ra attacked then; with a cry of anguish he drew his blade and lunged. Talon felt sure that it was a last desperate attempt to rescue Areth Sul Urstone, to free his soul, to save him from what he had become.

With the strength of a Runelord, the emir leapt thirty feet, blinding in his speed.

But Despair blurred into motion himself, easily batting aside the emir's weapon, and then landed a crushing blow with the butt of a dagger to the emir's head.

The emir fell to the ground with a crash, his sword clanging to the arena floor, then ringing as it spun away.

Talon almost charged next, but Daylan warned her back. 'Ware! Ware! He has more endowments than we do, and he has the powers of an Earth King besides.' There was fear in Daylan's voice, and regret and horror.

Lord Despair studied the fallen emir, as if dissecting him with his eyes.

'Fourteen long years Areth waited for you,' Despair said. 'Fourteen years of torture. Let's see how well you bear up as you suffer his fate.'

Then he turned his cold gaze upon the rest of the company. He glanced at Kirissa, who struggled in the grasp of her wyrm-ling guards.

'Fools,' Despair said. 'Why do you even bother to resist?'

'Ah,' Daylan said, 'and that is where you are wrong. We are not fools. The rules I live by are not the rules of this physical world. They are the rules of the invisible world. By abiding by those laws, Despair, we gain power that you never could comprehend, nor control.'

Despair dismissed him with a flick of his eyes. 'If you insist,' he said. 'But what has all of your power gained you? Yes, you resist me, but your efforts are of no consequence.'

'Until now,' Daylan said. 'Your time is coming to an end. The True Tree has been reborn. The Torch-bearer has returned. The Restoration of All Things is at hand.'

'The remains of the True Tree are rotting away at Castle Coorm,' Despair said. 'And the Torch-bearer writhes in my dungeon, and shall soon be joining me.'

Without blinking, Despair must have uttered some silent command, for from the corner of her eye Talon caught a movement. She whirled with her weapon in hand just in time to see specters hurtling toward her silently, as insubstantial as a mist. In their shapes, she thought that she saw the remains of their forms – skulls shrunken and meatless, with pits for eyes. A ghostly hand reached out to touch her with fingers of bone.

She cried out and tried to lurch away, but the finger brushed her hand. Instantly it felt as if the blood froze in her veins, racing up her arm, and her entire right side went numb.

The icy sensation swept up her arm, paralyzed her shoulder, and stopped her heart with its piercing cold. She heard Rhianna cry out and a rush of wings as the woman leapt into the air.

'Run!' Rhianna shouted.

But Talon could not stagger a step. The wight had taken her by the hand, and she could not break free. Even with the strength of a dozen warriors of Caer Luciare, her knees suddenly felt too weak to hold her, and she collapsed to the arena floor.

19

THE FLIGHT

Thus sayeth the Great Wyrm: I am your god. Above me there is no other. Thou must serve me or perish. The dumb man seeketh to disobey, and the fool seeketh flight.

—From the Wyrmling Catechism

With a glimpse of the shadow wights rushing up behind her, Rhianna leapt into the air with a shout of warning, and flapped up into the darkness. The arena was about one hundred and fifty yards across and had a high ceiling, but in the darkness she could not be certain how high.

She glanced below. A wave of wights had rushed in behind Vulgnash. Talon whirled to do battle, but it was in vain, for a wight merely took her hand, and its paralyzing touch drove her to the floor.

Daylan Hammer sprang forward, bringing his war hammer to bear on Lord Despair, raining blows upon him like a human cyclone. But Despair merely danced back, parrying every blow with his great sword, until after a dozen blows from Daylan's weapon a wight leapt into the air and grabbed him from behind, arms locked about his throat in a death grip, and rode him to the ground.

With her companions all either dead or paralyzed, Rhianna had no choice but to seek escape.

She flew up, circling the arena like a bird that had flown

into a house through an open door. She flapped higher and butted her head against the ceiling, a blow that nearly sent her reeling to her doom.

In the darkness she could see little, even with her endowments. Glow worms had not been placed up here, and apparently found little to eat upon the stone. She spotted doors at both ends of the arena, doors for wyrmling spectators to gain ingress, but the misty forms of wraiths streamed into the arena, blocking her escape. She could not get past them. There was no room.

She flapped about, peering down, and the wraiths stared up at her hungrily, eager for her death.

'Take her!' Lord Despair shouted, and Vulgnash leapt into the air, too. The Darkling Glory at Despair's back roared in mirth to see her predicament. There was not enough room for her to elude Vulgnash for long. All that she could do was to fly in desperate circles.

Nor can I fight, she realized. Vulgnash is under the protection of an Earth King, a twisted Earth King, but an Earth King nonetheless.

Her heart pounded with terror, and she was so frightened that she almost missed it. She felt a sudden updraft.

An air vent, she realized. The arena had an air vent at its top.

Vulgnash was hot behind her. Rhianna flapped harder, pressing in her need, and he fell back a few paces.

I'm faster than he is, she realized.

Whether it was because she had taken more endowments of metabolism or because she had taken more strength, she could not be certain, but Vulgnash fell behind.

Rhianna wheeled, then folded her wings and dropped into a dive. She swept low, just over the heads of the wights, and drew steel, as if to whack one with her blade, then rose up in the air.

She peered hard, looking for the air hole, and finally saw it – a thin circle of gray in the stone, where light shone down a long narrow shaft.

She flapped her wings hard and rose. Vulgnash wheeled

with a shout, and came screaming toward her, trying to block her escape.

Is the hole wide enough to let me through? she wondered. It will have to be.

Rhianna burst upward, reached the air shaft.

She folded her wings tight, letting her momentum propel her upward. She found herself in a narrow chimney, no more than two feet wide. Her shoulders were so large that she almost could not fit. Up above, she could see sunlight not sixty feet away.

I'm a Runelord, she told herself. I can make myself fit.

She dropped her blade and contorted her shoulders, bringing them together in a way that no human should. With a dozen endowments of grace, it was not hard. Then she clawed her way up the hole, scrabbling as quickly as possible.

Vulgnash grabbed her heel, and she considered kicking him, trying to knock him back, but some blind instinct drove her upward.

Claws of iron seemed to be wrapped around her foot, and Rhianna kicked, struggling to break free. His claws raked her, drawing slick blood, and suddenly Vulgnash lost his grasp.

Quick as an eel, Rhianna snaked up the hole.

Vulgnash roared in anger, and Rhianna reached sunlight, grabbed the lip of the hole and threw herself out, just as a fiery blast shot through the chimney.

She stood in broad daylight for a second, wondering if Vulgnash would be able to squeeze through the hole, wondering if there was any way to go back down and save her friends.

But she could not think. She heard growls and scrapes in the air shaft. Vulgnash was coming up. He had taken endowments of grace, too, and though he was larger than her, it seemed that he would fit.

In a blind panic, Rhianna realized that whether he made it up the shaft or took some other route, Vulgnash would be after her soon enough.

In a mad rush of wings, she launched herself into the sky. She flew up and up, then peered back to see Vulgnash charging after her, rising up from below, his massive red wings pumping furiously. He was horrifying in his persistence, inhuman. Somehow, he had managed to squeeze through the chimney, and now he peered up at her, blinking in pain at the sunlight, and gave chase.

I'm faster than him, Rhianna told herself. I have to be. She flapped madly, hurtling away from Rugassa as fast as possible.

Vulgnash was on her tail. Like a crow chasing a starling, Rhianna thought. He is larger and more ponderous than me. He cannot hope to follow for long. The sunlight blinds him.

But from the vent below, she saw a second form emerge, black and sinister. The Darkling Glory was joining the chase.

Rhianna pumped her wings furiously, terrified. The creature was an unknown. She could not imagine how it got through that hole.

How fast can it fly? she wondered. How well can it see in the daylight?

Suddenly the sky went dark from horizon to horizon.

Rhianna had only heard of such things in legend, from tales of her mother's time. Only the most powerful of flameweavers could do that. Fallion was able to draw heat from a fire, but he couldn't yet bend the very light to his will.

Is Vulgnash doing that, Rhianna wondered, or the Darkling Glory?

A glance revealed that it was Vulgnash.

Ropes of light began to weave together above her, whirling from the sky in streams of fire, tornadoes of white-hot flame. She veered to avoid one of the tornadoes.

He's catching the light in his hand, she realized. He's going to try to burn me out of the sky. He'll take aim and then hurl a ball of fire. In that instant, I must change course.

The darkness fled, and Rhianna peered down, but could see little. There was a mist of shadow beneath her, impenetrable to the human eye. Within it she could see only parts of the forms of creatures, struggling toward her. A fireball suddenly roared from the mist.

She banked hard to the left and folded her wings, going

into a vertical dive. The fireball roared overhead, expanding and slowing. The heat of it gave her a thrill of fear, for it was like standing too close to a forge.

Rhianna unfurled her wings and flattened her trajectory, then flapped all the harder.

She peered back. The mists of darkness followed, but could not match her pace. She veered to the right, lest another ball of fire come at her, and drew farther away. She veered up suddenly, heading toward the sun.

Increasing her speed, Rhianna raced ahead, mile after endless mile.

She had headed south by instinct – toward the horse-sisters, toward help. But she realized the danger in exposing the position of her troops. Better to lead her pursuers away from her allies.

So Rhianna veered to the west, so that the demons would have the sun slanting into their eyes.

She consulted a mental map. There was little in the way of human settlements here for many, many miles.

Vulgnash and the Darkling Glory slowly receded into the distance, becoming nothing more than a dark blur on her trail, miles behind. Soon, the Darkling Glory gave up the chase.

Yet Vulgnash clung to her trail. Perhaps he feared to displease his master, and it was fear that drove him to mindlessly follow. Or perhaps he thought that he was like a hound, and she was a fox that could be run to the ground.

Rhianna soared over what had once been Mystarria – lush lands with rolling hills, rich with farms and towns along the rivers, and sweeping fields and forests elsewhere.

But all was in ruins. Entire cities had been battered down and laid to waste.

Juxtaposed over this was the landscape of the wyrmlings' shadow world: occasional fabulous ruins, weathered and beaten, what had once been 'human' cities; monolithic towers and columns, all white as bone, were covered with obscene scrawls in the wyrmling tongue.

After fifty miles, Rhianna saw more interesting signs. A

contingent of Queen Lowicker's troops were on the move, unaware that their queen had been vanquished. Or perhaps they had heard and just did not care. In any case, a long column of knights was riding east toward Rugassa, as if to do battle, their lances raised to the air. But there was no one nearby for them to fight. The wyrmlings had razed their cities and then faded from the land for the day. They would be hiding in some dark hole where warhorses and lances would do no good.

Rhianna kept flying, winging into the wilderness as the sun continued to slant toward the horizon.

She flew over a desert that should not have been there – a rugged place of rock and sand – and on its borders she saw herds of shaggy elephants being trailed by packs of dire wolves and great hunting cats.

Three hundred miles from Rugassa, her sharp eyes descried something interesting – a cloud of dust to the south. At first she thought that it might be a great herd of shaggy elephants, but the formation was too tight. It could only be caused by vast forces marching in the wilderness.

But whose?

She veered toward it, hardly changing her course at all. Five miles later she was able to descry what troops marched there.

It was reavers, tens of thousands of them, marching roughly toward her. In the distance, they looked like great black beetles, though Rhianna knew that they were not small. Each reaver weighed more than an elephant.

As she neared, the sound of their marching feet made the earth tremble and groan; the clashing of their carapaces against the ground was like weapons clanging upon shields.

Rhianna had never seen a reaver. They were the stuff of legend, creatures that lived deep in the Underworld. She wanted a closer look, and with Vulgnash following, she wanted him to get a good look at them, too.

The reavers are marching in almost the right direction, she realized. In a day they could well be at Rugassa's walls. What would the wyrmlings make of the threat?

Rhianna swooped lower, dropping within a hundred feet of

the ground, and winged toward the reavers. The cloud rising from the ground smelled of dust and some strange musky scent.

Each reaver had four legs for walking, and two heavy arms that they used to bear weapons – great long hooks called 'knight gigs,' or enormous swords that could flatten a horse and rider with a single blow. Most of the reavers were gray-black in color, and thus were common fighters. But here and there among the hive she spotted smaller reavers, reddish in color, carrying bright crystalline staves. These were the scarlet sorceresses.

Other creatures marched near the ends of the line – enormous spidery creatures that carried packs upon their backs, and enormous white wormlike creatures that she recognized as 'glue mums.'

The reavers are coming for a full-fledged war, Rhianna realized. She had an almost primal fear of reavers. It was the fear of such creatures that had driven her ancestors to develop their rune lore in the first place. It was the fear of them that had caused the Runelords to build their vast fortifications.

It was tales of the depredations of reavers that had kept her awake with nightmares as a child.

So she swooped low above the reavers, and watched as the creatures raised their heads and hissed.

The reavers had no eyes in their heads. But that did not mean that they could not see. They had phillia dripping from their chins and from their bony ridge plates, and with these they sensed her presence, by scent and motion. The hissing noise came as they raised their abdomens and sprayed odors into the air, smells that they used to warn their neighbors.

She flew above the reavers, redoubling her speed, for fifteen miles. That is how long their column was. She estimated their numbers at fifty thousand strong.

How will Vulgnash like this? Rhianna wondered.

She kept flying, looking over her shoulders.

Vulgnash still followed, his blood-colored wings flapping

vigorously, but he seemed to slow into a glide above the reaver horde, and finally wheeled about.

It was still midafternoon when he began to recede quickly, racing north-east toward distant Rugassa.

Her hunter had turned back.

For a long hour, as time is measured by the sun, Rhianna continued to wing away from Vulgnash, lest he renew the chase. To her, it felt like six hours or more.

At last she reached the Alcair Mountains, and flew to a huge white pine that had been taken by lightning.

The skies above were the perfect blue of a summer afternoon, and the world at large seemed as it should be. The starlings and wild pigeons that flew up from the pines sang their songs, seemingly unaware of Rhianna's desperate plight.

What will I do? Rhianna wondered.

My love is still in the dungeons of Rugassa, in the hands of the wyrmlings.

Rhianna felt sick with anguish.

There seemed to be only one place to go – to the horse-sisters. But what could they do? Grant more endowments?

Despair had more than she did, and he had the powers of an Earth King besides. She could not slay him. She dared not even try.

She felt overwhelmed by doubt.

She wondered if the Wizard Sisel might help. Daylan had said that he was abroad in the land, traveling to commune with the True Tree.

He's had all day to find it, she thought.

But it was a long hike. A man of the warrior clans was expected to run a hundred miles in a day.

If Sisel left from Cantular at dawn, he'll make it there by sundown.

The notion of going to see him pleased her. She longed to go to Castle Coorm and seek refuge beneath the One True Tree, and throw her problems upon the shoulders of the wizard and his guest from the netherworld.

But what can they do? she wondered.

The Bright Ones had never shown her any kindness as a youth; their laws forbade them to interfere in the affairs of lesser creatures like her – the so-called *shadow people*.

Appealing to the folk of the netherworld would do her no good, and while the wizard had strong protective magic, he had never gone into battle.

Worse than that, she had no time to seek his aid. The reavers were marching toward Rugassa.

By tomorrow this time they could be there, Rhianna realized. What if they attack? They could kill Fallion.

I have to get him out of there, she thought.

But how do I kill an Earth King? Or failing that, how do I defeat one? What weaknesses does he have?

Rhianna thought back to the day that the Earth King Gaborn Val Orden had died. She had never been chosen by him, had never been put under his protection. But Fallion and Jaz had, and they had often recited the words that they had heard in their own minds during Gaborn's final moments. It was part of the creed of the lords of House Orden: 'Learn to love the greedy as well as the generous. Love the poor as much as the rich. Love the evil man as ardently as the good. And inasmuch as is possible in this life, when you are beset upon, return a blessing for every blow.'

In that instant, Rhianna felt almost as if Gaborn stood at her side, comforting her. She thought about Kirissa.

Could it be that he really had known that some Inkarran child would someday have to face the Wyrmling Empire?

She felt certain that he had.

Rhianna wondered about the Earth King. What were his weaknesses?

Borenson had said that it was his compassion.

Certainly, Lord Despair will not have that weakness.

And suddenly the answer hit her. Gaborn himself had given her the key.

I can't face an Earth King, she thought. I should not even try. With his power, he'll sense the danger. Which leaves only one alternative: return a blessing with every blow. So long as I present no danger, Despair cannot be forewarned of my attack.

Rhianna wondered, could she really free Fallion without harming a living soul?

Despair would not suspect such a bold move. Indeed, he was probably incapable of thinking of it. 'Of course any intruder would kill the guards.' That is how he thought.

But Rhianna knew of at least one air vent that was not guarded.

She had great strength. She had the speed. She had the key to the wyrmling dungeon on a thong around her neck.

I have to try, she told herself.

With that she took to the air, heading for a brief stop in Beldinook.

20

DESPAIR

The Great Wyrm shall put down all enemies. No weapon created by man can prevail against her.

—From the Wyrmling Catechism

In the fortress at Rugassa, wyrmling guards furtively dragged Despair's captives across the floor of the arena, laying them side by side, face up, arranged from largest to smallest, much as a fisherman might display the salmon that he had caught.

The wyrmling guards were terrified. The Death Lords hovered over the bodies, specters of shadow garbed in black robes of such thin weave that they were almost insubstantial. The Death Lords' lightest touch had devastated even the most powerful of the Runelords, leaving them paralyzed and half-dead.

Even now, the Death Lords radiated an icy aura that seemed to penetrate even Despair's thickest cloak, for it was not a cold that chilled the body so much as it chilled the soul.

The touch of a Death Lord was the touch of the grave. Had they wanted to, the Death Lords could have slain their victims with that touch. But Despair had warned them to keep the people alive.

Yet the nearness of the victims, the tastiness of their souls, tempted the wights to feed. They were like dogs upon a hunt, scenting blood while the bloodlust is at its height, unable to forbear when a spear brings down a stag.

Thus, the wyrmling guards cowered, lest they brush up against the hunger-maddened wights.

For their parts, the wights loomed above the fallen ones, trembling with anticipation.

'What shall we do with them, Great Wyrm?' a wight asked, its voice a hiss.

Despair approved of their lust, for it served him well.

'Leave them to me,' Despair said.

'But . . . we hunger,' the wight complained.

In touching mortal flesh, the wights had tasted their victims' spirits. For the wights, gazing down upon their victims would be like a man standing over a tremendous feast – where fresh loaves of warm bread filled the room with their scent, while delectable meats and pastries and puddings begged to be eaten – and being told that one might only have a single nibble.

'You have served me well,' Despair told them. 'Go to your chambers. We have fresh captives from the wild – small folks whose souls are sweeter and more succulent than any wyrmling. The guards will bring some shortly.'

The wights scattered at his command. A wind seemed to rise, and they floated away upon it, their black garments fluttering.

Despair bent over his victims and studied their faces. Each of them had gone as white as a wolf's tooth. Each of them bore a wound – a single place where a Death Lord had touched them. All breathed shallowly, and were in danger of dying.

But they were young and strong, and had endowments of stamina to boot. It was difficult to know if their stamina could keep them alive, for the touch of a Death Lord wounded the soul more than the body.

Most likely, Despair decided, they will each wake in a few hours, feeling more dead than alive. In time, even a wound to the spirit can heal.

'My lord,' a guard asked, 'shall we execute any of them?'

Despair peered at his captives, wondering how best to use them. He recognized some of them. Despair had taken over Areth Sul Urstone's body, and thus could access the prince's memories.

The Emir Tuul Ra had been Areth Sul Urstone's most beloved

friend at one time. The emir's people had been destroyed, and thus Despair considered that he might be of little worth as a political prisoner. Yet one never knew. Who ruled the folk of Caer Luciare now?

Vulgnash had killed their king, and Areth was his heir. That meant that they had no king at the moment. Had the people chosen the emir to act as regent?

It would have been a wise choice, Despair considered.

Thus, the emir had possible worth as a political prisoner. The folk of Caer Luciare might offer bribes for his release. But there was a greater hope.

Why had the emir come? To save Areth Sul Urstone alone? Or could he have, in his short span of time, forged some kind of bond with Fallion?

That was the question that nagged Despair. Who among these would Fallion value most? Who might he want to save?

Daylan Hammer of course had lived for an eternity. Despair had killed him time and time again, but his spirit was strong, and within days of his death, he would re-corporate.

How much has Daylan taught Fallion? Lord Despair wondered. What kind of bond have they forged?

He studied the girl that they had captured, leaned over her. She was petite for a girl of the warrior clans, and her hair was unusually dark. Most of those in the clans were redheaded, but her hair was a deep chestnut in color.

Despair reached down to her tunic, opened it slightly. She had runes of power branded there, just below her neckline.

Vulgnash had said that Fallion was traveling in company with two girls and a young man, another of the small folk. So Despair had suspected that one of his companions might come to his rescue, but he had not expected the two girls.

What luck! he thought. I have one of the girls, and Vulgnash will capture the other. Surely he loves one of them – perhaps both. What would he give up, in order to save them from the tormentors?

He reached down and stroked the girl's cheek. Such a precious thing.

'Keep them all alive,' Despair said, 'until I have a chance to question them.'

'Even this one?' a guard asked, kicking the wyrmling girl. Her guards had let her break free for just an instant in the battle, so that a wight might take her.

Despair considered. Of them all, it seemed least likely that Fallion would have forged a relationship with a wyrmling. But one never knew.

In the binding of the worlds, many folk had merged with their shadow selves – humans as well as wyrmlings. Had Fallion known this girl's shadow self? Is that why the girl had turned against her own kind?

'Keep her alive, too,' Despair said.

'Will our dungeon hold them?' a guard asked.

'The cells were made to withstand even the toughest wyrmling warriors,' Despair said. 'And though some of these may have the strength of ten men, their bones are as brittle as ours. They won't be able to batter down the iron doors, and even the smallest of them could not squeeze between the bars.

'Still, put only one captive to a cell. Search them thoroughly and remove any weapons. Then chain them securely; allow none of the guards to get near their cells. Vulgnash alone will be their jailer.'

At that Despair hesitated. Vulgnash was off chasing the winged woman, and would soon return either with or without her. Despair hated consigning Vulgnash to such a mundane task as guard duty. But prisoners such as these demanded his skills.

Despair dared not let common troops near the Runelords.

Yet . . . there were other duties that Vulgnash needed to attend to. There was the uprising at Caer Luciare, where the foolish Fang Guards were taking endowments from their kin, believing that they could best Despair.

They had to be punished. Despair considered sending his troops, captained of course by his chosen warriors. But the Earth warned against it. None of his lords could withstand the new powers that had arisen at Caer Luciare – none but Vulgnash.

So Vulgnash would have to go. Despair needed to regain control of the blood-metal mines, for he sensed a coming danger. Not today, not even the next. It might be days away – a week. But an attack was coming.

There was nothing for it. Despair needed Vulgnash to pull double duty.

The guards lifted the prisoners and carried them down to the dungeons. Despair followed, to make sure that none of the captives woke or tried to escape.

Once they were all stripped of weapons, and shackled in their cells, Despair stopped to check on Fallion.

He was dead asleep, with the frost still riming his lips. The room was bone-numbingly cold.

Fallion cried out in his sleep, 'No! Not that!'

Despair smiled and wondered what the tormentors were doing to the boy's Dedicates. Fallion had been given another hundred endowments of compassion. Right now, the tormentors were in the process of removing the excess body parts from Fallion's Dedicates. Despair had told the tormentors that in his opinion, any body part on a Dedicate was to be deemed 'excessive.'

'Sleep, my little friend,' Despair whispered. 'All too soon, we will wake you to your horror.'

Lord Despair left the prisoners to their cold cells, took a thumb-lantern, and went stalking to his throne room with his head bent, his brow furrowed, to await Vulgnash's return.

The glow worms that adorned the ceilings and walls did not give enough light for his all-too-human eyes.

In his throne room he took reports from his facilitators. Despair had garnered his allotment of a thousand endowments, and Fallion had been given his. A test had been run on a wyrmling, to learn if by taking an endowment of sight from a human, he might abide the daylight. The results were good, but not impeccable.

This pleased Despair. He ordered more endowments, but found that his supply of blood metal had been exhausted, so he sent his chief facilitator away, promising to get more ore soon.

Afterward, he went to his map room and brooded.

If my enemies are taking endowments, he realized, they must have Dedicates. All that I need to do to ease the danger is to send my troops to slaughter those Dedicates.

He considered the map, but it was of little use. So much had changed in the binding. His scouts were going out by night, telling of cities that had sprung up where none should be. His troops had already vanquished everything that they'd seen. But a hundred miles from Rugassa, all was unknown.

He did not have enough Knights Eternal to scout the lands nearby.

Lord Scathain will lend me some aid, he thought. A few thousand Darkling Glories should suffice.

His earth senses warned of dangers far off. That news gladdened him. Nothing would disturb his preparations for days.

Or is the danger really so far away? he wondered.

By sacrificing one of his chosen, he had disappointed the Earth Spirit that loaned him its powers. He knew that. He had felt the spirit withdraw from him, and when it came time to fight, he had felt it difficult to advise Vulgnash of danger.

It was a warning from the Earth Spirit itself. If Lord Despair did not submit to the Earth's wishes, he might lose his protective powers.

He could not let that happen.

In the future, I cannot let one of my chosen people die, Despair decided. I must heed Earth's every whim for the time being, regain its trust. I must act the perfect Earth King.

But it galled him. Lord Despair was on the verge of seizing control of worlds. Who was this Earth Spirit to tell him what to do?

It was late afternoon when Vulgnash returned, with the Darkling Glory at his side. The two seemed to have become fast friends. Quietly they approached Lord Despair's throne.

The throne itself was a massive thing, with a back that rose ten feet in the air. It was carved from the bones of a world wyrm, and thus was yellow-white, the color of aging teeth.

Vulgnash strode into the room, head down. His wings were raised in salute, but Lord Despair noticed that they were not raised to the full. He looked weak, submissive. The Darkling Glory stood at his back, glaring.

'I have failed you, my master,' Vulgnash said. 'The girl escaped. I followed her as far as I could, until I began to go dayblind.'

For a long moment, Lord Despair sat in disbelief. He'd felt certain that Vulgnash would catch the girl. In part he felt that way because he had supreme confidence in Vulgnash's abilities. In part he'd felt certain because he sensed a complete lack of danger.

The girl *could* be a threat, but he cast his mind about, and once again he felt sure that his empire was secure. There would be no attack upon him for days.

'Do not worry,' Despair said at last. 'There is no harm done.'

'The girl could pose a danger,' Vulgnash objected. 'She is a powerful Runelord. She could gather an army and return.'

'If she does,' Despair said, 'we shall have another chance to catch her. Won't we?'

Vulgnash looked up, thoughtful.

Despair assured him, 'She will not attack soon – not today or tomorrow or the day after. Of that I am certain. She fears us.'

'But . . .' Vulgnash said. 'This one has taken many endowments.'

'Of course,' Despair said. 'And she will try to get more – which means that it is all the more important that we secure our ore at Caer Luciare. Right now, that is my greatest concern. The Fang Guards there have rebelled, and now refuse to send me forcibles. I want you to punish them, with finality.'

'I will leave at dusk,' Vulgnash promised.

'I have a better idea. Do you have any more forcibles?'

Vulgnash had been toying with them in his cell while he guarded Fallion, creating new designs for his master. It was he who had devised the rune of compassion. 'A handful is all.'

'Make a pair of forcibles with a rune of sight. Then force the small folk to grant endowments to you and Kryssidia.'

'My lord?' Vulgnash asked.

'The small folk see well in full sun. I had a facilitator do a test while you were hunting. Once a human gives an endowment of sight, our wyrmlings will be able to abide the daylight.' Vulgnash smiled, his huge canines showing.

'Thank you, master,' Vulgnash said. But he did not leave. Instead he dropped to one knee. 'There is another matter . . .'

'Which is?'

'While following the girl, we saw reavers, a great throng of them. They are a little more than two hundred miles from the fortress. If they stay their course, they could reach us tonight.'

'They pose no threat,' Despair said. 'Most likely they will turn aside. The Earth gives me no warning.' He was growing tired of worrying. 'Go to the dungeons before you leave, and make certain that our prisoners are secure, one last time.'

'Very well,' Vulgnash said.

The Knight Eternal rose from his knee and went stalking from the room, his wings raised more proudly. That left only the Darkling Glory there before the throne.

'Well now, my friend,' Despair said, 'let us go and have some dinner, and we shall consider how best to conquer a million million shadow worlds.'

21

A LITTLE VENGEANCE

All men should strive to be cunning and strong. The Great Wyrm will take vengeance upon those who prove to be weak and foolish.

—From the Wyrmling Catechism

Vulgnash felt a peculiar craving. The dead are not subject to most human passions, at least not to the same degree as humans. Hunger they feel as a primal craving for life force, one that makes every cell in their bodies ache with need, much as a choking man burns with need for air. But there is little place in them for lust, or vanity, or compassion.

So this craving annoyed him. It was an ache for vengeance. The human woman had escaped him, had shown him to be weak in front of Lord Despair.

Vulgnash had seen his lord's displeasure.

The dungeons again, he thought, as he climbed down the winding stone stairs. I will be forever in the dungeons.

He yearned to be off on some more dangerous assignment. Watching over the Wizard Fallion had its dangers, it was true, but Fallion posed little threat.

Vulgnash went to the dungeons, found Fallion there. The floor was rimed with frost, and now snow fans were forming on the bars and walls. Fallion was out cold. Sound asleep, nearly comatose.

The rest of the prisoners were much the same. Talon lay still, barely breathing. The wyrmling girl appeared to be dead. Daylan Hammer's breathing was equally shallow. Only the emir seemed to be breathing heavily, and he groaned in his sleep as if at a nightmare.

Vulgnash tried rattling the doors. They were solid iron and each weighed a thousand pounds. He could not move them. The locks were secure.

Vulgnash paid one last call upon the Wizard Fallion.

He was firmly chained by a leg to the wall.

Vulgnash decided to have some fun with him. He took a cot from another cell, and took some old rope, then bound Fallion's arms and legs so tightly that it would cut off the circulation.

Then he dragged a cot into the cell, laid Fallion upon it faceup, and held Fallion's head back so that he could not see his own body.

He gave Fallion just enough heat to warm him so that he began to revive. Fallion came awake, regaining consciousness in fits and starts, so that he muttered and shook, trying to rouse himself.

When consciousness reached him, Fallion simply lay there on the cot with growing horror on his face. He struggled and tried to move his arms and feet, but could get no feeling.

Vulgnash knew what he was thinking. Dozens of his Dedicates had been mutilated, their arms and legs removed, and Fallion could not tell if he had any appendages.

'Fool,' Vulgnash hissed. 'Without arms or legs, you look like a worm. Squirm for me. Squirm for your master.'

'No, please!' Fallion called, trying to wriggle, trying to see if he had arms.

Vulgnash merely set a foot upon his forehead and held his head back so that he could not see.

'You thanked my master for letting you feel the pain of his subjects. So as your reward, he has cut the arms and legs off of thousands of them, and he has let you feel their pain. Would you like to see them?'

Suddenly Fallion lashed out with his senses, tried to pull heat from the walls of the cell. But the stone was cold and held almost no heat at all. Fallion's was a pitiful attempt at escape.

Vulgnash pulled the heat from Fallion once again, sent him deep into a swoon.

That should hold him for a few more hours, Vulgnash thought. And he will dream . . .

Vulgnash stalked out of the dungeon, found Kryssidia, and took his last four forcibles to the chief facilitator. It did not take fifteen minutes for the facilitator to round up some small folk and rip the sight from two of them. The effect at first seemed minimal. He could not see any better in the darkness, but now the glow worms on the wall gave off a color he'd never seen – a dim green.

With the last two forcibles, Vulgnash took more endowments of metabolism, and told Kryssidia to meet him in his chambers.

Quickly Vulgnash raced up through the tunnels, climbing the stairs, like a caterpillar winding its way up a twig, until he reached his own spartan quarters, where his crypt lay.

The sun was dying on the horizon, a bloody thing dropping toward its grave. Red clouds scudded along the sky line, promising a coming storm.

For the first time in his life, Vulgnash looked out upon a world of color – blues and purples in the sky, grays and tans and greens in the forests.

So this is what a human sees, he thought in wonder.

The endowment had worked well enough. The daylight annoyed him, but it did not hurt as much now. It was bright enough so that the idea of flying repelled him, but darkness would be here soon.

He went to his closet, got a fresh red robe, and strapped on a sharpened long sword as black as obsidian.

He halted for a moment near the door to his own parapet and glanced longingly at his own tomb.

Ah, he thought, to sleep, perchance to dream.

Vulgnash felt at peace. Torturing Fallion had salved his wounds, fed some of his need for vengeance.

But more than that, he felt secure knowing that he would be going into battle with Despair at his side.

As a Knight Eternal, Vulgnash had never been truly alive. He had no soul, and could not harbor or feed a locus. Thus, there was no way that he could communicate across the leagues with Despair, as the Death Lords did.

But now Lord Despair was displaying some new power.

He can speak to my mind, Vulgnash realized, with the powers of an Earth King, though he cannot hear my thoughts.

This development delighted Vulgnash. It almost made him equal to the Death Lords, and it raised his value to the master. At the same time it afforded him some privacy.

But an onus was upon Vulgnash. His master would be angered if he took too long to punish the Fang Guards.

Kryssidia came shortly, and the two of them raced to the nearest window and leapt from the tower, unfolding their crimson wings and taking flight.

They swooped low, so that the shadows of distant mountains covered them, and flew madly above the trees, careering this way and that, using their own momentum to hurl them forward faster and faster.

Day faded to dusk, and dusk surrendered to darkness.

As he flew even with Kryssidia, the Knight Eternal apprised him a little better of the situation at Caer Luciare. The Fang Guards were taking endowments, and they thought themselves powerful enough to challenge the empire. They were led by an egotistical fool named Chulspeth who did not know yet that Despair had taken physical form and now dwelt at Rugassa. Nor of course would Chulspeth be aware that Despair had gained unheard-of powers, the protective gifts of an Earth King.

Vulgnash knew Chulspeth. He was the leader of the Fang Guards. Vulgnash had personally chosen the man for the honor of being the first to take an endowment of bloodlust.

Once again, Vulgnash thought, I have not served my master well.

Kryssidia grew hungry, and the Knights Eternal slowed their flight for a time, veering from their course as they hunted. They found a small settlement where a little smoke from evening cooking fires hung in a haze.

It was a guard post of some kind for the small folk, a mountain village with nothing but a wall made of wood. Guards paced about in towers.

The Knights Eternal swept into the village, dodging arrow fire as they came. They spotted children playing in the street, children that leapt up in terror at the cries of their parents.

Vulgnash swooped low and scooped up a toddler on the wing, and Kryssidia did the same. The parents screamed frantically and chased after them, shaking their fists and hurling curses.

We are like jays, robbing the nests of lesser birds, Vulgnash thought as he placed his hands over the squirming boy's face and began to drain him. Child or adult, the spirits of these creatures provided the same amount of nourishment. So he and Kryssidia drained their prey, then let their corpses, their empty husks, rain from the sky.

Moments later, he heard his master's voice in his mind. *When you finish punishing my enemies, return with all haste. Bring back more blood-metal ore for forcibles.*

'Yes, Lord,' Vulgnash whispered to the wind, for he knew that his master could not hear him.

As they neared Caer Luciare, Vulgnash heard his master's voice in his mind once again. *Careful, my friend. Careful. The enemy has set a trap. When you land, they will attack. It is not with a sword that you can win this battle.*

Vulgnash signaled to Kryssidia with a slight tremor of the wing, and both of them veered to the left and landed in the woods.

'Our master bids us go in with fire,' Vulgnash said, and without preamble he kicked a few dead leaves into a pile, along with some wind-fallen twigs, then used a portion of his own body heat to give birth to a small flame.

He let it lick at the leaves for a few moments, growing in

power and might, then twisted the flames so that they took a small alder. A warm breeze nourished the flames until soon they raged and leapt up the tree, and from there began to spread through the detritus on the forest floor.

Vulgnash strode into the midst of the burgeoning inferno and basked in the heat, like a lizard in the morning sunlight, until the inferno did not just warm him but permeated his flesh.

Then the two Knights Eternal rose into the air and went winging up the mountain.

The dead wyrmlings from the recent battle were strewn about, littering the ground where they had fallen. To be left upon the battlefield was considered a great honor, and it was the wyrmling belief that any warrior left thus would rise up from the battlefield, weapons in hand, on that day when the Great Wyrm made flesh cleave to rotten bones and brought forth her honored warriors for the last great battle at the End of Time.

The three great arches of Luciare were no longer lit by the spirits of the human ancestors; vulgar glyphs now adorned the bone-white walls, signaling that this was wyrmling territory.

No proper guard seemed to be watching the doors. Perhaps there was no one left who could. Kryssidia had described the scene inside while on the wing – fallen wyrmlings strewn about the great hall, each with an endowment wrung from him, until few were left standing.

Never had Vulgnash heard of such abandonment, such debauchery.

Vulgnash settled on the ground at the mouth of the central arch, and called out, 'Chulspeth, come!'

No one stood at the door, but after a long moment, a voice cried out, high in pitch and fanatical.

'Am I a cur to be commanded so?' From the sound of his voice, Chulspeth had taken too many endowments of metabolism – perhaps twenty or more. Though he tried to slow his speech so that it might be better understood by common folk, it sounded squeaky and high, with strange lapses.

'You're not a cur,' Vulgnash said, hoping to sound reasonable, hoping to lure his enemy into the open. 'I honored you, and respected you. You were the first of our master's servants to taste the kiss of the forcible. It is rumored that you now crave it like wine, and you have lost all composure. I have come to reason with you, to offer you a chance to serve our master once again. You could be his most valued warrior.'

'I would rather serve a bull's pisser than our craven emperor!' Chulspeth squeaked. Still there was no sign of movement from within the fortress.

'The emperor no longer rules Rugassa,' Vulgnash informed him. 'Despair has taken flesh, and now walks the labyrinth among us.'

The news should have inspired a proper sense of religious awe in Chulspeth, or even fanatical zeal. Instead, there was only a yelp, followed by a snarl and a threat.

'I do not fear Despair!' Chulspeth cried. 'What are you, Vulgnash, nothing but a serving boy, bringing your lord dinner one moment, then pleasuring him the next? You should have a place of honor beside your lord, not groveling at his feet.' Now Chulspeth tried the inevitable bribe, one that Vulgnash had heard a thousand times before, though it varied in particulars. 'You, Vulgnash, should dwell with us. You would be welcome here. You would have honor among us, and be a great lord. The finest food would be yours, the finest women.'

A soft chuckle rose from Vulgnash, cool and deadly.

'I do not desire such things,' he said. 'And it would not be an honor to be counted among you. Lord Despair has come among us, and he has strange powers, unheard of among mortal men. I fear that if I were among you, he would crush us all beneath his heel, as if we were mice.'

Chulspeth roared in anguish.

Attack! Despair's voice raged in Vulgnash's mind. Vulgnash raised a hand, prepared to unleash a fireball.

Suddenly, from the recesses of Caer Luciare, Chulspeth

rushed from the shadows. Never had Vulgnash imagined such speed. Chulspeth came sprinting from the darkness, running at well over a hundred miles per hour, a black iron javelin in his hand.

Vulgnash hurled a fireball, white-hot and roaring in its fury. It was the size of his fist when he hurled it, but as it traveled it expanded in size, so that it was a dozen feet in diameter when Chulspeth came bounding through it.

For a heartbeat, Vulgnash imagined that his foe would simply race through the flames unscathed, like a child leaping through a campfire.

But Chulspeth hesitated an instant before it struck, long enough to hurl his iron javelin.

The javelin hurtled through the flames faster than any ballista dart. With hundreds of endowments of brawn to his credit, Chulspeth's attack was devastating. The javelin struck Vulgnash in the chest at dead center and hit with such force that it passed cleanly through him.

No matter, Vulgnash thought. This flesh will knit back together in time.

Then Chulspeth bulled through the fireball.

He might have done better to dodge it.

Perhaps Chulspeth did not imagine that the flames would be as hot as they were. Or maybe with so many endowments of stamina coursing through him, he imagined himself to be invincible. Or it might have been that the endowments of bloodlust he had taken had merely driven him mad.

For whatever reason, Chulspeth leapt through the fire and came roaring out the other side, his flesh blackened and oozing, his clothes blazing like an inferno. The fire wrung cries of agony from him, yet he charged toward Vulgnash, half-sword drawn, eager to battle to the death.

Flee! the Earth King's warning came.

Vulgnash flapped his wings, lunging into the air like a bolt of lightning, and though Chulspeth leapt to meet him, the bones of his legs snapped from the exertion, and he fell far short of his desired target.

Soaring high, Vulgnash left the High Lord of the Fang Guards there on the ground, sputtering and burning.

Now Vulgnash dove toward the central arch of Caer Luciare, where the remains of his fireball had blackened the pale arch-ways and melted the gold foil.

Time to finish this, he thought.

He worried that he might meet strong resistance inside, but no warning from Lord Despair sounded in his mind.

He landed in the archway, and gathered heat once again. Kryssidia marched at his back. Together they strode into the tunnel, and there found the fortress as Kryssidia had described it: wyrmling warriors lay sprawled upon the floor in heaps as if they had fallen during drunken revelry, arms and legs spread akimbo.

They had not fallen from wine, but rather from granting endowments. Even now, some were rising to their feet, regaining the precious strength, stamina, and speed that they had granted to Chulspeth.

Vulgnash was sickened by this waste of power. The fools in the Fang Guard had not realized what they were doing. They were leaving Dedicates unprotected, perhaps unaware that if a Dedicate was slain, then its master would lose the use of its attributes.

If the humans had tried to return and take the fortress, Vulgnash thought, they would have found it an easy target.

Ahead, down the hall, he suddenly saw some Fang Guards ready to oppose him – half a dozen warriors standing shoulder-to-shoulder.

Their faces were filled with fear and rage in equal measure, and every muscle in their bodies seemed strained, ready to spring.

Yet they were not eager to fight.

'Are you such fools?' Vulgnash cried. 'I could kill you all more easily than I dispatched Chulspeth. I should leave you to the mercies of the humans. But I will need force warriors to guard this fortress against the day of their return. Oh, and they will return – soon, and in great numbers. They left a mountain of blood metal behind.'

Vulgnash's words decided them. Seeing that there was hope of forgiveness, one warrior hurled his battle-axe to the floor in a clatter, then dropped to his knees to do obeisance.

In seconds, the rest of the Fang Guards followed suit.

Kryssidia went striding forward, into the midst of them. 'Cower before me,' he cried. 'For the Great Wyrm has chosen me and made me a lord over you. The Great Wyrm has come in the flesh, and now rules Rugassa and the world. But here, here in Caer Luciare, I shall be your emperor, and you shall be my people.'

With the battle won, Vulgnash set to work on his next chore. He demanded blood metal, and the wyrmling troops showed him to a foundry, where hundreds of pounds of forcibles had already been poured into molds.

Vulgnash smiled. His master would be well pleased, and Vulgnash imagined that he would be rewarded with more endowments.

Beyond that, Vulgnash had gotten something that he had wanted this day – a little vengeance.

22

ONE TRUE TREE

In the world to come, every tree shall be thrown down, and nature itself shall be humbled by the Great Wyrm.

—From the Wyrmling Catechism

It was late evening when the Wizard Sisel and Lord Erringale reached the One True Tree. All through the day they had marched, and Erringale was witness to the rot and filth of the shadow world, the blight that afflicted the trees, the frequent ruins abandoned by the defected warrior clans, and the bitter scent of death.

He had never witnessed such things before.

'I thought that things were harsh in my world,' he said at one point in the journey, as they hunched inside the ruins of an old inn. 'I have seen places like this in the Blasted Lands, but never have I seen destruction so unrelenting.'

'There is a whole world of ruins here,' Sisel had said. 'Beyond the mountains to the south, they are mostly covered by vines in the jungle. But far to the east there are fresher ruins, vast fortresses, elegant and strong, that are no more than tombs, filled with the bones of their defenders.

'Our battles against the wyrmlings have been long. For five thousand years have we fought. Sometimes we would prevail for a few centuries, and then our people would grow complacent, and the wyrmlings would strike in greater numbers. Other times, we lost vast expanses of land, never to regain it.'

Lord Erringale listened soberly. 'Daylan told me that the Great Wyrm has brought foul creatures from other worlds to boost his armies. What can you tell me of them?'

So the Wizard Sisel described what he'd seen. The folk of the netherworld knew some of the dangers: the Darkling Glories were their mortal enemies, but Erringale was horrified to hear of strengi-saats that filled the wombs of children with their own eggs so that when the young hatched, they would have fresh meat to feed upon.

'Where did they find such fell creatures?' Erringale wondered aloud.

'I do not know,' Sisel said. 'Yet I am surprised that your people withhold weapons from us.'

'If we gave you superior weapons,' Erringale said, 'the wyrm-lings would simply take them, and in time your fate would be worse than at first.'

'Ah,' the wizard argued, 'so you think it wise to withhold your knowledge from the shadow worlds. Tell me, if one of your own people were dying of thirst, would your law forbid you from telling him where to find an oasis?'

'Of course not,' Erringale said.

'So what is the difference? One man needs water to survive, the other needs a weapon.'

Erringale fell silent and did not speak for many miles. Instead he bowed his head, consumed in thought.

The sun was setting beyond the hills like a red pearl gently falling into a bed of rose petals. The wood doves were cooing out in the oaks on the hills, while cicadas sang in the fields.

The Wizard Sisel strode through a meadow with Erringale by his side, feeling at ease. As an Earth Warden, he had been granted a special gift. He could move through the woods and meadows unnoticed by enemies and friends alike, if he so chose. Now he did so, and a rabbit beside the trail paid no more notice to him than if a fly had landed on its ear. A stag had come to drink from the still waters of the moat, and as the two men passed, they never caught its eye.

So the two reached Castle Coorm at sunset and found the drawbridge thrown down. There was no sound of dogs barking or children playing in the castle, no singing of washwomen or an old man calling his children home for dinner.

It was obvious that the castle was empty. Its inhabitants had fled.

The men crossed the planks of the drawbridge, their feet thumping lightly. Even their shadows upon the water did not frighten a trout that was lying below the surface.

Just within the wall, they found the object of their desire. There was a roundabout in the courtyard, so that wagons could maneuver onto various roads as merchants brought their wares. At the center of the roundabout was a wall made of stone, about four feet high. It was filled with earth and rocks, creating a garden; a raised planter. At the pinnacle of the rocks hunched a stone gargoyle, a man with wings covering his face, tongue thrust out. Water poured from a spigot in his mouth.

There at his feet was the base of the True Tree. Above the gargoyle the tree's leafless branches arched in surreal beauty, as intricate as a fine piece of coral.

Never had the Wizard Sisel seen a tree so blasted. It was a marvel to behold. Every leaf was down, and fungi in colors of cream and canary covered it thicker than hoarfrost. Almost it seemed as if it were layered in snow. The setting sun painted it all in shades of rose.

The pungent odor of rot filled the courtyard, so overwhelming in intensity that Sisel raised his sleeve to cover his nose.

Erringale studied the tree. 'It's true,' he said. 'The One Tree did burst forth on a shadow world. But it is dead now – all gone to rot.'

'Yes,' Sisel said, 'but this is not a common rot. This tree is under a powerful curse.'

The sight of it was so overwhelming that it smote Erringale, and the Bright One leapt up onto the rock wall, strode beneath the tree, and then fell to his knees, just peering up.

'It's dead,' he said at last. 'There is no voice left in it. I had hoped to commune with it, but it has fallen silent.'

He peered down at the dead leaves. The land was scorched here under the tree, as only a few bones of leaves were scattered here and there. 'Perhaps there is an acorn,' Erringale said hopefully. He began poking among the ashes that lay thick around the bole of the tree.

'An oak does not begin to shed acorns until it has lived more than twenty seasons,' Sisel told him. 'This tree is much like an oak. I think you will not find any acorns. I visited here at Castle Coorm twelve years back, and this tree had not yet sprouted.'

Erringale's heart seemed to break at that moment. He climbed up off the ground and pulled at a twig from one of the lower branches until it snapped and broke free. 'A branch from the True Tree,' he said. 'My people will revere it.'

Sisel peered hard at the tree. 'Perhaps we can find some life in this tree yet. Legend says that it is strong in healing powers, and therefore strong in life.'

Erringale glanced back at him, as if he were daft. 'How could there be life here?'

'When a man falls into freezing water,' Sisel declared, 'he often dies a kind of death. His life hides deep within. He ceases to breathe, and his heart stops beating. But there is life within him still, and if you are patient, you can revive him.

'A tree is much the same. It dies a kind of death with the coming of each winter. Its thoughts grow dim and torpid. And this tree is suffering as if through the coldest blast. But there may be life in it – not in leaf or limb, bole or branch, but down deep, in its roots.'

Sisel raised his staff, blew upon the tree, and whispered a blessing:

> Root, bole, limb and bough,
> be strengthened now, be strengthened now.

He pulled back and peered at the tree, as if hoping that leaves might sprout green from the dead twigs.

'There,' Sisel said. 'That should stop the rot, to keep it from further damage. Now let us see if we can find any signs of life.'

With that, the two men went and searched through the town until they found the tools that they needed – a mattock and spade. Together they began to dig.

'Sisel,' Erringale asked when their hole was three feet deep. 'Why would the wyrmlings try to kill the tree?'

'Because it is a thing of beauty?' the wizard guessed.

'That does not suffice. The wyrmlings are infested with wyrms. It is the Great Wyrm herself who guides their hand. Certainly she needs the tree as much as we do – if she hopes to bind the worlds into one.'

Sisel stopped digging and thought for a long moment. 'Now, there is a mystery,' he said. 'Perhaps the Great Wyrm plans to try to bind the worlds without the tree. That would be her way – to try to twist the Powers to her own ends.'

'Or perhaps,' Erringale said, 'she fears the tree. She may fear its protective powers. Or maybe she fears what it does, for it calls to men and urges them to be better, to seek personal perfection, and thus it is an enemy to the Great Wyrm.'

Sisel followed that line of reasoning further. 'It also calls men into its service, inspiring them and filling them with hope and wisdom, in return for what little it requires. You may be right. The Great Wyrm sees it as a rival for her people's affections.'

'That which Despair cannot control,' Erringale said, 'she feels the need to destroy.'

'That is certainly the way that she feels about us.'

'Or perhaps,' Erringale said, 'the Great Wyrm herself cannot resist its allure!'

'Aaaaah,' Sisel said, smiling at the thought. 'I see several reasons for the Great Wyrm to destroy it, but that most of all rings true.'

Erringale wondered aloud. 'I don't know. I'm not sure that

I understand. The Great Wyrm tried to kill the tree, and now she holds the Torch-bearer captive – the only man alive who might have the skill to bind the worlds. It sounds almost as if she is trying to keep him from binding the worlds together at all.'

Sisel had no answer to that. The workings of the mind of the Great Wyrm were devious.

Erringale swung his mattock a few more times; then Sisel bit into the ground with his spade.

In a moment, in the darkness, Sisel reached down into the dirt and pulled out his prize – a tiny knot from the taproot, twisted and malformed. It easily fit into the palm of his hand.

Sisel quickly took it to the gargoyle fountain and let clear water run over it. Afterward he held it up in the starlight and inspected it.

'The rot runs through and through,' he said, his voice filled with dismay.

Erringale peered at it doubtfully. 'Are you certain?'

'I'm certain,' Sisel said. 'The sorcerer who cast this spell was powerful indeed. There is nothing here to be saved.' He tossed the root to the ground, shoved it into the loose soil with his heel, and peered up at the tree.

Erringale stood for a moment, his heart breaking. 'Is there nothing you can do?'

'I suppose,' Sisel said, 'that the Earth Spirit will provide a new tree when the time is right. All that we can do is wait.'

Erringale said softly, 'But we have waited for a thousand thousand years for the tree to be reborn!'

'You will have to wait a little longer. Even if one does come again, how do we know that it will not be destroyed in like manner?'

Erringale peered into the wizard's eyes in the soft evening glow, lit by stars and a new rising moon. The Wizard Sisel thought that he saw a hardness growing in Erringale's eyes that he had not witnessed before.

I wonder what it would be like, the wizard thought, if

Erringale goes to war. What powers would he bring to bear? What arms might he muster? What allies can he command?

'There is an evil brewing here beyond the understanding of men,' Erringale said. 'But I mean to find out what is going on.'

23

IN THE DUNGEON OF DESPAIR

Every man is born in a cage. The size of it is deter-
mined by limits of our ambitions.

—*From the Wyrmling Catechism*

Rhianna sped across the miles, flying with all haste. She kept
an eye out for Vulgnash, and watched his gray cloud on the
horizon. She reached Beldinook before sundown, the castle's
white towers and ramparts gleaming like fiery coral in the
setting sun.

Rhianna flew straight to the palace, and found the horse-
sisters' facilitators taking the last of the endowments. Their
thousand forcibles were nearly gone.

Standing among the crowds in the town square Rhianna
made a heart-felt appeal.

'People of Beldinook,' she said, 'I must go to Rugassa in all
haste. Give me your metabolism, I beg of you, not for my
sake, or the sake of the man I love, but for your own sakes,
for your children, your families, and your kingdom.

'If I fail, the sacrifice that you make will not be for long –
an hour at the most.

'But if I succeed, minstrels shall make a song of it, and your
names shall be sung forever!'

She did not have to say more. She had taken so many
endowments of glamour that she probably had not needed

to speak. She had taken enough endowments of voice that her words smote the potential Dedicates and softened their hearts.

'I will be pleased, milady,' a young man cried out, and soon a dozen people were offering similar thoughts. Rhianna did not wait for the endowments. She nodded to her facilitator, then went to the great room for dinner.

She was famished. She had flown four hundred miles in hours, and though she had the brawn and stamina and metabolism to meet such a goal, she did not do it without a price.

Her body seemed to have dropped twenty pounds during the day. Much of it had been sweat, she was sure, but she could clearly see the bones in her wrists, white and protruding through the skin.

So she fed, eating as much as her stomach could hold, drinking until she felt well.

Then she burst into the sky and went winging toward Rugassa at a more relaxed pace.

She had a problem: Vulgnash.

How will I get past him? she wondered. With the facilitators vectoring metabolism to her, she would be faster than he.

But will I be fast enough? she wondered.

She had no choice but to risk it.

So she flew over the darkening lands, her wings flapping steadily. She crossed a river, gleaming silver in the starlight. Great flocks of bats had flown up from the trees along the river's bank, and now they dipped and skimmed the water for drinks.

Rhianna dropped and tried it, surprising herself when water sprayed up and splashed her face and the front of her tunic. She could taste grit and bugs in the water.

I have become a bat, she thought.

Then she hurried on toward Rugassa, and the world seemed to slow even further as endowment after endowment of metabolism was added to her. At last Rugassa's dark cone rose up in the starlight, black and foreboding.

The wyrmlings will be awake, Rhianna thought. They'll be at their most active. Perhaps I should wait until tomorrow.

But she dared not wait. With every passing minute, the enemy would be taking more endowments, becoming stronger.

So she winged above the plains surrounding Rugassa at night, and saw the land filled with wyrmlings – troops by the tens of thousands marching to war, great armies of hunters heading out with wagons to harvest meat, loggers and miners and who knew what else – hundreds of thousands of wyrmlings toiling in a great mass.

She hurtled toward her entrance at two hundred miles per hour, a blinding blur. Many a wyrmling looked up to behold a flash of red in the night sky, crimson wings and a blood-red cloak – just a lone Knight Eternal flying to his tower. It was a sight that they had seen a thousand times.

With so many endowments of wit, she did not have to hunt for the entrance. She knew where it lay.

She hit the airshaft and eeled down headfirst, then opened her wings wide as she plummeted the last few yards to the floor of the coliseum.

Wyrmlings working in the arena seemed astonished by the sight, but Rhianna's hood was pulled tight and she whisked out through the exit, following the sandalwood-scented trail of Kirissa at a dead run.

With twenty endowments of metabolism, Rhianna was but a blur, a crimson figure with vast wings racing down the tunnel at nearly a hundred miles per hour.

I have taken my death in taking so many endowments of metabolism, she thought. In four more seasons, I will die of old age.

But she could not mourn her fate. She had chosen it, and it was only her endowments of metabolism that might allow her to rescue Fallion.

She could have gone faster, but she found that her momentum made it hard to turn corners, so she kept her speed low.

She found surprisingly few wyrmlings in the hallways. Perhaps it was too early for some of them, or perhaps they were already working.

But as she passed each one, Rhianna made sure to do no harm. She would duck past one, leap over others. Those who saw her did not have time to react.

She heard wyrmlings roar in blind challenge on several occasions, but Kirissa had taught her a couple of curses. Rhianna found that when she roared a curse and raised her wings, the wyrmlings often fell over themselves in their haste to make room.

Thus she put her endowments of voice to the test, perfecting her illusion. The wyrmlings did not even know what they saw, she suspected.

So she raced in dark tunnels while glow worms lit the ceiling of the labyrinth like a sky full of stars, following tunnel after tunnel until she reached the winding stair and descended, down, down, with a key made of bone in her hands.

Talon was the first to waken in the prison. Perhaps it was because she had more endowments of stamina than the others, or perhaps it was because a wight had only touched her lightly on the hand, but she woke, dazed and trembling, to find Rhianna standing over her.

'Up,' Rhianna called. 'Quickly. Get up or die!'

There was water on Talon's face. Filthy water. That was what had awakened her.

'Where? Where am I?' she asked. But Rhianna was too busy to answer. She had taken a guard by the throat and was shoving him into Talon's cell. In an instant, Rhianna had him chained to the wall.

Talon raised her head, blinking. Her right arm ached. She could feel ice in her veins, running straight to her heart, and it seemed to put a strain on her, as if her heart might stop beating any second.

'Help me,' Rhianna pleaded. 'The others are all asleep, and I can't wake them. I've come to rescue you. Vulgnash was gone when I got here, but there is no telling how soon he will come back.'

Rhianna was moving with tremendous speed, at least twice

as fast as Talon could. She rushed back out of the cell, and moments later came back with a second wyrmling guard, a hulking brute, dragging him over the floor as he kicked and screamed.

Talon climbed to her feet. She had so many endowments of brawn that she did not feel as if she weighed anything at all. Yet she was wounded to the core of her soul, and she felt terribly ill.

Rhianna urged her from the cell, and together they slammed a huge iron door, locking the guards inside.

An instant later, Rhianna had the door to Fallion's cell open. They found him lying upon a cot, unconscious. Strips of cloth bound his legs and arms tight against his body. There was an unholy cold in the room, and his lips had gone blue. The bars to his cell were crusted with frost, and ice fans had formed upon the stone walls.

'Try to get him warm,' Rhianna said. 'I don't think that a wight has touched him. Vulgnash just drained all of his body heat.' Rhianna began unwrapping his bindings.

Talon considered lying down beside him to get him warm, but remembered her sunstone. It was still hidden in her boot. The wyrmlings had taken her daggers, her belt, and her leather tunic. But they had left her boots.

She pulled off the boot and dumped out its contents. The sunstone fell and lay gleaming upon the floor. She squeezed it hard and held it up to Fallion's cheek.

He lay there for a long second, still barely breathing, and suddenly he began to rouse. The effect of the heat was astonishing. His breath had been agonizingly shallow one instant, and he suddenly gasped.

Blindly, he reached up with his right hand and tried to grasp the sunstone, but he missed it – or seemed to. His hand bypassed the stone, but in that instant the light seemed to flash in response to his need, and a stream of fire as golden as a wheat field flared from the stone.

The sunstone was so hot that Talon dropped it, her hand smarting from a savage burn. It left a white welt on her fingers.

But the fire streamed out of the stone and into Fallion, and he took no harm.

He opened his eyes, coming awake in an instant. Flames seemed to be dancing in them, and they were full of light. He peered up at Talon and Rhianna, obviously invigorated. Yet there was no relief in his face. His cheeks and brow were haggard, lined with pain.

Rhianna finished unbinding him, and now she used the guards' keys to unlock his shackles, then went racing to another cell. Iron doors began to creak open in rapid succession. She called out to the emir, Daylan, and the wyrmling girl.

She came back an instant later. 'I can't get anyone else to wake,' she said. 'They're barely breathing.'

Fallion had risen to a sitting position, but he moved with infinite slowness, like an old man burdened by the years. 'What's – what's going on?'

'Daylan Hammer and the emir are here with us,' Rhianna said before Talon could get a word out. 'They were touched by wights.'

Talon was still holding her own right hand. She couldn't feel her fingers, and she worried that at any moment she would faint.

'I see,' Fallion said. He thought for a long moment, as if he were still partly dazed, and said, 'There are some wounds that only Fire can heal.'

He took the sunstone from Talon, raised it in his palm, and began to draw a bright steady flame from it. Suddenly light seemed to burst from his every pore. The light filtered through the whole room. He turned into a glorious being, and he peered deep into Talon, then took her wounded hand.

Talon looked into Fallion's eyes, and felt as if she had never really seen him before. There was so much compassion in his face, so much sorrow. And here he stood ministering to her, shining like some Bright One out of a legend.

He's one of them, she thought. He's more than a mortal man.

Talon had always thought of him as a brother, a child that she had wrestled with, and played with, and worked beside. She'd never seen him like this before. She'd never imagined that he could be like this.

She felt herself warm. It began at her heart, which had felt cold and often skipped a beat. She felt a mellowness in her chest, as if beams of summer sun shone upon her naked bosom, and her heart responded by beating more easily. Then the sense of vigor and well-being began to move down from her heart, to her extremities. In a matter of twenty seconds, the warmth spread to her shoulder, then down her arm, until even her hand felt warm.

Fallion finished ministering to her.

Then he just held her eyes for a long second, as if peering into her, seeking other hurts to mend.

When he was done, he turned away, went stumbling into the other room. Talon followed and found him still shining brightly, the sunstone raised in his hand like some talisman, as he bent over the emir.

The sunstone flared again, casting a soft golden glow through the room, a glow that was softer than the pure white light that issued from Fallion.

He stood above the emir, simply shining over him, and the glow centered on the emir's chest. Talon began counting, to see how long it would take to rouse the man, while Rhianna rifled through keys and unlocked his manacle.

It was a full three minutes before the emir suddenly coughed and reached up in the air, scrabbling as if to grab something.

Fallion stood over him, growing brighter. 'He took a sore wound,' Fallion said, intent on his healing.

The emir coughed again and climbed to his elbows. He was half in a daze as he gazed around the room, trying to regain his bearings. 'What happened?' he croaked.

'We got caught,' Talon said. 'Rhianna came for us.'

'We have to get out of here soon,' Rhianna said, peering toward the doors. 'I got in here without killing anyone, but I hear bells tolling. The wyrmlings will be on my trail.'

Talon listened. She couldn't quite hear the bells. She translated Rhianna's warning for the emir.

'Tell her to take Fallion and go,' the emir said. He tried to climb to his feet, but he staggered and staggered and lost his balance. He looked up, saw them all sitting there. 'Go!' he demanded. 'I'll be along. He's the only one who matters.'

'He's not the only one,' Talon said. She knew what the emir was doing. He wanted to give his endowments back to his daughter. He hoped to die nobly.

The emir glanced up at her. 'Of course not,' he said, peering around. 'We must also get Daylan out, and the wyrmling girl.'

Fallion went to Daylan's cell, and began ministering to him. The emir climbed unsteadily to his feet, jutted his chin toward Rhianna. 'Your winged friend here is the fastest. She has the best chance of escape, and her charge matters more than we do. Please, tell her to go. I cannot save the father, but perhaps we can help save the son.'

Talon translated the emir's thoughts. By the time that she was through, Daylan Hammer was sputtering and moaning in the other room.

But suddenly the golden glow of the sunstone faded, its light all but dying. Fallion came from the room. Twisting the stone around, Fallion studied it. It shone like a dull ember. 'The fire is all but gone from it. Do you have another?'

Rhianna looked to Talon. Rhianna's had been destroyed, and Daylan's and the emir's sunstones had been taken.

'That was the last one,' Talon said.

'Go,' Talon told Rhianna. 'Take Fallion with you. He can do no more good here, and we'll just slow you down. We'll follow you out as soon as we can.'

'It won't be easy to carry the wyrmling girl,' Rhianna warned. 'Perhaps we should leave her.'

'I can't,' Talon argued. 'Besides, we'd have to carry her regardless. Without endowments, she's nothing but dead weight.'

Rhianna hesitated, as if trying to think of a sound reason to stay with them, but reluctantly she nodded her agreement. She'd take Fallion. 'Remember, kill no one. So long as we pose no threat, their false Earth King will not know where we are.'

'That may be easier said than done,' Talon argued.

Then Talon rushed into the wyrmling girl's cell and lifted her gently. With Talon's eight endowments of brawn, the girl seemed bulky, but not too heavy to bear. Talon's real concern wasn't that she would tire, but that under so much weight one of her bones might snap and she would be left hobbling about, unable to bear her charge.

She left Daylan Hammer and the emir to help one another.

So they began their journey, racing as fast as they could through the labyrinth, toiling up the winding stairs. The emir led the way, followed by Rhianna, who had Fallion clinging to her back. Without endowments of metabolism, he couldn't even begin to keep pace with the others.

The distant tolling of bells must have called the wyrmlings out. The company met them in the corridor at nearly every turn. Each time that they did, Rhianna would simply roar at them like a Knight Eternal sounding a battle cry. With her flawless memory, she knew the call well. With her endowments of voice, she could mimic it perfectly.

The emir shoved aside those who did not get out of the way. With his speed and brawn, the smallest push sent the wyrmlings toppling.

And as they moved through the hot corridors, Fallion began to recover his strength completely. He drew heat from air, channeling it into himself so that he glowed brightly. The wyrmlings roared in pain at the sight of him and backed away.

Rhianna reached the top landing, and charged down a wide corridor. Talon could hear the toll of the warning bell clearly now.

Ahead, a contingent of wyrmling soldiers marched toward them, four abreast. There were perhaps thirty in all. They cringed from the light, and Rhianna roared, but she did not give them time to withdraw.

She flapped her wings once and leapt, went soaring above their heads; some troops turned to engage her. In that instant, the emir and Daylan Hammer rushed in among the wyrmlings.

None of the wyrmling soldiers had endowments, it seemed. The emir and Daylan shoved the wyrmlings aside, half to the right, half to the left, so that they fell in tangled heaps. They'd cleared a path for Talon.

She rushed through, trampling over the few fallen wyrmlings who tried to rise.

We're lucky that there were no Death Lords among them, Talon thought. But her hope was that the Death Lords would be slow to come.

The emir grabbed weapons from the fallen soldiers – a few daggers and a pair of heavy axes.

They reached a great archway, and suddenly Talon knew where she was. They'd reached the Arena of the Great Wyrm. Talon could smell the fetid air inside.

Rhianna bypassed it and led the way down the tunnel toward the southern gates.

Talon recalled the great iron doors that had fallen behind them earlier; she worried that she and her friends might still be locked in.

The warning bells were tolling heavily, making the walls vibrate with every resounding gong.

The company sped through in haste now, and as they sprinted ahead, Talon saw the great iron doors beginning to fall. Rhianna reached the spot and ducked beneath, but Talon was lugging the big wyrmling girl and could not match her speed.

I'm not going to make it, she thought.

The emir raced to the door and rolled under, while Daylan dropped to his belly and skidded.

For an instant Talon feared that they had all left her behind.

But then the door slammed to a halt, and she saw what had happened. Two wyrmling axes had been placed beneath the door, their pommels in a groove in the floor, their heads up forming a T.

The emir had paved the way for her escape.

Talon reached the door, dropped her charge, and rolled under. By the time that she got to her feet, Daylan and the emir had pulled the wyrmling through, and the emir urged Talon, 'You go ahead. I'll give you a rest.'

Talon realized what he was doing. She had far more endowments than he. She might well be needed if it came to a fight. She didn't dare waste her energy being a pack mule.

So she went charging down the corridor, now racing ahead of Rhianna. Wyrmling troops were suddenly thick in the tunnels, and Talon had to shove each of them aside, gently, as if she were only practicing moves for a sparring match.

Suddenly she reached the exit, smelled open fields and pine trees, and went charging out into the night. The sky seemed to yawn wide overhead, and stars powdered the heavens. Off to the east, the slender crescent of a new moon was just clearing the mountains.

Down below her, tens of thousands of wyrmlings filled the courtyard.

Lord Despair was in his private quarters, dining with Scathain and making plans for the future, when he heard the warning gongs. Scathain raised a brow, giving Despair an inquisitive look, and Despair wondered what had happened. He felt inside himself, seeking the counsel of the Earth Spirit. There was no attack. Neither he nor any of his chosen lords were in danger, of that he felt certain.

'Probably one of the tunnels has collapsed,' Despair told his visitor. 'That is a constant danger when living underground. In the recent binding of the worlds, the ground here has been destabilized. A couple of small sections of tunnel have collapsed in the past few days. It is probably nothing.'

It took several long minutes for the captain of the guard to bring word, interrupting dinner.

'Lord Despair,' the captain cried as soon as he entered the door, 'the prisoners have escaped!'

Despair stared blankly at the man for half a second, unsure if he believed his ears. This was a terrible embarrassment.

'Impossible,' Despair said.

I chose my prisoners' guards, he thought. The earth should have warned me if they had been killed.

He looked into his heart, felt for the guards in the dungeon. His earth senses let him pinpoint their location.

They were alive. They were well. They were at their posts still.

Suddenly Despair laughed at his own folly.

'That clever girl,' he told his guest. 'She came in right under our noses and stole my prisoners – without taking a single life!

'But it will do her no good. Fallion is one of my chosen ones. I can sense his whereabouts.'

He felt the young man, fleeing swiftly from the fortress.

Despair rushed out to the parapet of his tower, and in one mighty leap he was atop one of his stone gargoyles, peering down from it, using its head as his vantage point.

The Darkling Glory raced up behind, flew atop a gargoyle beside him.

Down below were his prisoners, streaking out across the plain. Fallion was glowing brightly, a brilliant and unearthly white.

The prisoners were racing away so fast that Fallion looked almost like a comet streaking across the dark plain. Wyrmlings fell back from the light by the score, and Rhianna roared in warning, so that his people cleared a trail for the prisoners. In seconds they were beyond the wall and off into the brooding pines that surrounded the fortress now, and then Fallion let his brightness fade.

The Light-bringer lives up to his name, Despair thought.

Despair considered going down among the fools, doing battle. He felt no fear of his enemy's champions. The Earth did not warn against it, and he knew that they could not slay his body.

But Fallion had a power that no other flameweaver had ever displayed. He could shine so fiercely that he could slay a locus, incinerate it.

Would the Earth Spirit warn me of such danger? Despair wondered. No, it wouldn't. A locus is not a human. The Earth Spirit would not value its life.

I dare not try to take them alone, he thought. I need Vulgnash.

But Vulgnash was hours away, and his quest was of tremendous import. He had to win control over the blood-metal mines, and until he was finished, he could not be spared nor distracted.

And what harm does it do to let them run? Despair wondered. None of my servants was killed. My enemies only deceive themselves. They believe that they have freed Fallion, not knowing that he can never escape.

The guard had rushed in at Despair's back, and now he begged, 'Shall I have men give chase?'

'You can't catch them,' Despair said. 'And if you did, it is not in your power to take them.'

But Despair had a servant who could. He sent a thought to Vulgnash: *When you finish punishing my enemies, return with all haste. Bring back some blood-metal ore for forcibles.*

'Would you like some help?' Scathain said. 'I can have a murder of Darkling Glories here within minutes.'

Lord Despair smiled.

'Get them. It's time that these fools get a demonstration of what will come.'

The Darkling Glory did not walk back into the tunnel. Instead he leapt from the gargoyle's head and went winging up the mountain, toward the cone of the volcano, where the door to the netherworld stood open.

Despair turned to the captain of the guard. 'Tell the tormentors to get to work upon Fallion's Dedicates. I want him reeling in agony.'

24

TWILIGHT

*At the End of Time, darkness shall cover the world, and
gross darkness shall fill the hearts of men.*

—From the Wyrmling Catechism

Just outside the walls of Rugassa, the Emir Tuul Ra halted long
enough to steal a vehicle. It was a simple wyrmling handcart
– two wheels and a tiny bed, with a couple of long poles to
use as handles. The handcart was empty, and the wyrmling
woman who was pulling it never knew what hit her. A simple
tap from behind sent her sprawling into the dusty road, and
the emir had her cart.

The emir knew the wyrmling tongue well. He had not
wanted to hurt the woman. There were no words to make
apologies in the wyrmling tongue, so he called out, 'We have
great need. Be well.'

He urged Talon to throw Kirissa into the cart, and Rhianna
dropped Fallion on the back, and off they went, racing down
the road, running at sixty miles an hour.

By the time that the wyrmling woman recovered enough to
climb to her feet and hurl some curses at the thieves, the cart
was far, far up the road.

Rhianna led the way, clearing the trail before them. The
emir pulled the handcart, while Talon pushed it from behind.
Daylan Hammer could not match their speed, and so they

asked him to jump aboard so that they could make better time.

The green around the fortress had been clogged with wyrmling foresters and hunters, miners, and soldiers, for many in the great horde had come out to work for the night, but it was not yet an hour past dusk, and two miles from the fortress the roads were clear.

So Rhianna, Talon, and the emir ran.

After five miles, they topped a wooded hill and gazed back toward Rugassa. The trees overhead covered the company like a cloak, making them feel warm and safe. The woods were filled with the buzzing of cicadas.

They stopped only for a moment to catch their breath, but the emir felt sorely famished, more than he had ever felt in his life.

He wasn't sure why. Perhaps it was the touch of a wight that had done it. The hurt to his body had been tremendous, but he felt that its touch had been even more devastating to his soul.

Or maybe in part it was simply because he had taken so many endowments of metabolism, and he had been asleep, paralyzed, for hours, after running for hundreds of miles.

'I don't suppose you had the foresight to bring along any food or drink?' the emir asked Rhianna, for the wyrmlings had stolen their packs down in the dungeon.

'Food is for the weak,' Rhianna said, then laughed, shaking her head.

She peered back over the road behind them. The great volcano rose up, black and dominating in the distance.

Rhianna had enough endowments of sight so that she could see the road well enough under the starlight.

'There is no sign of pursuit yet,' she said after a moment.

'That won't last,' Daylan Hammer said with certainty. 'We have stolen Lord Despair's prize, and he will spare nothing to retrieve it.'

The emir looked to Rhianna, but told Talon, 'She should take Fallion to safety. She should leave us. The Knights Eternal

will be on our trail all too soon. She'll have a better chance
of escaping if we do not slow her down.'

'I'm surprised that the Knights Eternal are not already in
pursuit,' Daylan said. 'The emir is right. Rhianna should take
Fallion and go.'

Talon translated for Rhianna.

'Where would you have me take him?' she asked. 'Where
shall we meet?'

The emir could think of nowhere. There was nowhere in
the world that felt safe anymore. Rhianna had mentioned the
horse-sisters of Fleeds, but they had little in the way of fortifications.

'We should take him back to the netherworld,' the emir
said. 'If he is to fight Vulgnash, he will need proper endowments, powerful weapons, and time to train.'

The emir looked to the others for comments. Rhianna just
shrugged, as if the destination did not matter. Talon was willing
to concede the argument, for she seemed to have none better
of her own. But Daylan Hammer knew the folk of the netherworld better than any of them, so the emir looked to him
most of all.

'I do not know,' he said. 'The Bright Ones understand all
too well what kind of danger he will bring. We cannot hide
there forever.

'And yet,' he continued, 'Fallion brings hope with him, and
Erringale's folk might easily welcome him.

'I suppose it could not hurt to ask his permission.'

That gave them a destination. Erringale and the Wizard Sisel
had gone to gaze upon the One True Tree.

At that very moment, lightning flashed in the sky behind
them at the crown of the volcano. The emir glanced back and
saw a roiling mass of darkness there, obscuring the volcano's
crown. It was as if clouds had sprung forth from it in a matter
of seconds, and he worried that the volcano was about to blow.

But the clouds were strange in shape – oddly flattened on
top, so that they circled the volcano's crown like a great wheel,
and the mists that had suddenly risen were rapidly expanding,

blotting out the stars. Lightning flashed again and again, sending percussive booms over the land, and from those clouds he could hear strange sounds, peals of evil laughter and terrifying cries.

A bear roared in the forest nearby, and night birds began to peep and call out in terror.

'Well, I don't think that we have to worry about the Knights Eternal coming for us any longer,' Daylan said. 'It looks as if the Darkling Glories will beat them to the task.'

Over the tree-covered hills the party ran. Rhianna raced to the back of the handcart and began to push, urging the group forward. The emir was forced to sprint as fast as he could, stopping only for a drink from an occasional brook. They cast their eyes back furtively many a time, and watched as the storm around the volcano's cone intensified, the clouds growing thick, the lightning flickering wickedly, storming in the night.

For ten or twelve minutes, as common men count time, the storm intensified, until the crown of the volcano was hidden from sight.

During that time, the heroes ran, covering another dozen miles or more.

The emir sprinted beside the cart. It bucked and leapt over the broken road, and after only a few miles the wheels began to squeak. He worried that the cart would hit a rock too hard and suddenly explode on impact.

But it was a stout thing, made for wyrmling workers, and it held together.

Each time that he glanced back, he peered at the growing cloud, and he was able to take some comfort in the notion that the Darkling Glories had not set out after them – that they were only gathering, like a great flock of crows.

But as he peered back, time after time, he noticed that Fallion was gripping the side of the handcart as if afraid that he might fall off. His face had been sickly pale, but now his head lolled, and he seemed barely conscious.

He has taken some terrible wound, the emir thought.

There had been blood on his tunic, matted and dried, and the emir wondered if that was the cause of Fallion's distress.

The emir glanced back at Rhianna. She was pushing the cart, her face drained of emotion from fatigue. But she didn't seem to fear the Darkling Glories. The object of her fear was right in front of her. Fallion had taken ill.

'What's wrong?' she called to him at last.

Fallion's voice came softly, slowly, and as always Talon offered a translation. 'My Dedicates . . . the wyrmlings are torturing them.'

'What?' she asked, for his words made no sense.

The emir could not help but note the alarm in Rhianna's voice. She loved the boy. He could hear it in her every word. He drew the cart to a halt.

At that, Fallion reached up to his tunic, pulled it open. Strange runes were branded on his chest, dozens of them, larger and more intricate than any that the emir had taken in his own endowment ceremonies.

'What are those?' Talon begged.

'Compassion,' Fallion said. 'They're runes of compassion. I can feel the pain of others – their loneliness, their love, their horror. I feel when a foot is severed, or an eye gouged out. The wyrmlings are punishing me now through my Dedicates. Lord Despair is letting me know – I can never go free.'

The emir gazed at the runes, dumbfounded.

'I can go back,' Rhianna said. 'I can find those Dedicates, release you from your pain.'

'Certainly Lord Despair has chosen those Dedicates personally,' Daylan cut in. 'If you try to kill them, he will be ready for you.'

'Don't try it,' Fallion begged. 'They're innocent people – women and children. You cannot kill them without forfeiting your own soul. Even if you succeeded in freeing me, once you came back, you would not be the woman that I have grown to love.'

He peered up at her then, pleading. There were tears of

pain in his eyes – pain that he could not run from, pain that he could not bear.

'How many endowments did they give you?' Rhianna asked, as if she might charge into Rugassa and murder his Dedicates anyway.

Fallion shook his head in anguish. 'Dozens,' he said. 'Hundreds maybe, through those who act as vectors. Despair said that he will give me thousands of them, millions if he has to: until I break, until I become him.'

Immediately the emir cast his mind about, seeking a solution, but very quickly he realized that there was none. No matter what they tried, Despair would win. Fallion could not run from the pain, and they could not free him.

'What can we do?' Talon asked.

'Don't take me anywhere,' Fallion said. 'It only puts you and others at risk. Send me back.'

'I have killed myself to save you,' Rhianna said. 'I'm walking dead. I won't let you go.'

Fallion took her hand, squeezed it tightly, and just peered into her eyes. She was a Runelord now, powerful and beautiful, swift and deadly, with so many endowments of speed that she would never again be able to relate to those in the mortal world.

'You've saved me,' he whispered. 'Your love has saved me time and again, and if you desire, I will stay.'

In the distance, lightning began to flash brighter, and the sound of thunder was a solid roar. The ground was trembling beneath the soles of the emir's boots. It felt like the end of the world.

A blast of wind struck. The trees that had been sitting in silence all suddenly bent beneath a gale, and the leaves hissed like a distant sea.

'The Darkling Glories are coming,' Fallion said. The emir peered back toward Rugassa; the ring of clouds and lightning was expanding outward in every direction, and he suddenly realized that it was not one vast cloud that covered the crown of the volcano but dozens or hundreds of smaller clouds.

Within each, a form moved, a single Darkling Glory. They were separating now, winging away from the volcano in every direction, though a large contingent of them was heading south.

Talon whispered to the emir, 'In my father's time, a single Darkling Glory wreaked great havoc upon an entire kingdom. He was unstoppable. Now we must face an army of them.'

'It's not an *army*,' Daylan said. 'It's called a *murder* – a murder of Darkling Glories.'

'We should hide,' the emir suggested. 'We should get underground.'

'They'll check every building, every tunnel,' Daylan said.

'The Wizard Sisel can hide a warhorse behind a wheat stalk,' Talon offered.

'If you can get to him in time,' Rhianna said.

She looked at Talon and the others.

'We must get our forcibles,' Rhianna said, 'take them with us. Without them, we cannot fight the coming darkness.' She was speaking of the forcibles that she had hidden to the south. It was not far. But to retrieve the forcibles *and* then reach the True Tree sounded nearly impossible.

The emir looked into Talon's eyes, and knew instantly that they had to try.

Immediately Rhianna grabbed the handles of the wyrmling handcart and raced away. It was all that the emir could do to keep up.

The gale was gaining in intensity, and now the trees shuddered under the impact of blasts of wind, their leaves hissing and branches swaying.

Talon raced at Rhianna's side, glanced back at the darkening sky. 'If they get too close, take Fallion and go.'

Rhianna shot back, 'Run fast enough, and they won't get too close.'

The company charged south a few more miles and entered a familiar town, barren and broken.

With a start, Talon cried, 'The girl! We must get her.'

The emir had nearly forgotten about the child. He peered

about blindly, searching the rubble for a sign of the child. He didn't have Talon's many endowments of sight and smell.

Talon raced ahead, veered to the right and dodged into a ruined hovel. She came out with the girl in her arms, the child clinging to her as if Talon was her long lost mother. The little girl was weeping in relief.

In moments, Talon set her in the bed of the wagon, throwing her own tunic over the child as a shield against the night.

What have we saved? the emir wondered, peering over his shoulder at the advancing storm. The Darkling Glories will have us all.

Over hills and through fields they went now, running for what seemed hour after hour, though the moon on the horizon and the stars in the sky moved hardly at all.

The Darkling Glories filled the heavens. The emir imagined that with his endowments, he was running sixty miles per hour. But even on the wing the Darkling Glories could not keep pace. They were falling behind.

Forty or fifty miles per hour, he realized. That is all they are doing. The creatures were flying slowly, searching the ground methodically.

After what seemed to be a run of six hours, they came upon the site of Rhianna's slaughter the day before, and chased off a few wolves they found feasting upon wyrmling carcasses.

'I'll get the forcibles,' Rhianna said. 'Stay here.'

She leapt into the air and sped off, winging to the west. In moments she was lost from sight as she sped just above the treetops.

Every eye in the group kept peering back to the north, toward the flashes of lightning that flickered beneath the starry sky. The company had pulled ahead of the Darkling Glories. But soon the emir knew that the heroes would have to veer east, and then the Darkling Glories would gain on them.

Talon paced about near the handcart watching over the child, who had fallen asleep. Talon looked like a nervous wreck.

She has never been tested in battle, the emir realized. If

she were one of my men, I would go whisper words of encouragement.

He went to her, took her hand. Talon stopped pacing, and her eyes riveted on his.

'The girl is safe now,' the emir said. 'I think she has not slept in days. We'll be all right. Your friend Rhianna will be back soon. She knows how much is resting upon her.'

Talon didn't answer. Instead she threw her arms around him, hugged long and hard.

'This war isn't over, is it?' she said. 'It's hardly begun.'

'No,' he said, unsure what she was getting at. 'It isn't over.'

'You can't give back your endowments. Your people need you. You're as trapped as Fallion is.'

Then he understood what she was saying. She was rejoicing that he was alive, that he would be forced to stay alive for a while longer.

She kissed him, and he held her and kissed her in return. He felt guilty for taking his daughter's endowment, for being forced to keep it. He felt lucky to be alive and to have won Talon's love.

They broke apart for a moment, and the emir caught Fallion watching them.

What does the boy think of me? he wondered. I am an old man, holding and kissing his little sister.

But there was no disapproval in Fallion's eyes, only pain from the torments he suffered. Fallion flashed him a small smile, as if in gratitude.

He spoke something in his own tongue. The emir's few lessons in Rofehavanish were not enough to let him translate.

Talon translated for him, 'He said to me, "I have often wondered if there would ever be a man in the world worthy of you. At last you have found love, Little Sister. Congratulations."'

The lightning drew closer, and the mass of darkness beneath the stars was growing uncomfortably close by the time that Rhianna returned, lugging the forcibles – four chests, small but heavy. She had to flap her wings furiously, and sweat was coursing down her face when she landed. She gently laid the forcibles into the back of the handcart.

With the Darkling Glories looming near, there was no time to waste.

The company headed south for another fifteen miles, then Rhianna turned onto an older trail that climbed into the hills, a road that had been built by the folk of Caer Luciare ages ago, and most likely would lead into ruins.

'Are you certain this road goes where we need it to?' Talon asked.

'Yes,' Rhianna replied. 'I saw it from the air.'

So they raced up into the mountains, heading due east for fifteen miles. The Darkling Glories were rushing southward like a storm front, growing ever closer.

But as the company ran east, it became obvious that the vast majority of the Darkling Glories were heading south, following the road.

From the peak of a hill, the companions were able to peer east and see the murder of Darkling Glories now drawing even to their course. There were two or three hundred of the creatures following the highway.

Suddenly the whole flock came to a halt and began diving to the ground, as if to attack something unseen.

'What are they after?' Daylan wondered. 'The horse-sisters?' The emir wondered.

'No,' Talon said hopefully, thinking aloud. 'We warned them to hide well by night. There must be some other threat abroad in the land.'

Rhianna grinned wickedly. Horns began to sound, bursts long and deep of throat. 'Warlord Bairn, from the Courts of Tide, those are, his horns. I told him that a mountain of blood-metal was on the road north of here. He must have come looking for it. Too bad for him. If he hadn't tried to kill me, perhaps he would not have met such a miserable end.'

The heroes turned their attention elsewhere.

Farther to the north, spanning in every direction, were smaller storms where single Darkling Glories searched. Time and again, the emir could see them dipping to the ground or rising up, like fireflies among the bushes.

They're hunting, he realized, dropping down to check out every empty farm cottage, every pile of stone ruins.

Daylan pointed to the front, to the murder. 'They're going to Caer Luciare!'

'To get blood metal,' the emir said with conviction. 'Despair will have thousands of pounds of it before dawn.'

The emir's heart thrilled with battle hunger. He felt the urge to fight back, and glanced at the others.

'Maybe I can stop them,' Rhianna said. 'I can outfly them. I'm faster.'

'Can you outfly the lightning bolts that they'll rain down upon you?' Daylan asked. 'Don't even try.'

'We can't let Despair get those forcibles,' Rhianna said.

'We can't stop him,' Daylan said. 'Let it go. Let it go.'

Rhianna peered to the south, toward Caer Luciare. 'Look,' she said, 'here come the Knights Eternal!'

The emir peered hard, but could see nothing. He didn't have the endowments of sight to match Rhianna's.

'Where?' he asked.

'There, about thirty, maybe forty miles to the south.'

He squinted, but in the starlight could see nothing but hills and forests and barren patches of grass on the treeless plain.

'Well, at least we know now why Vulgnash has not been on our trail,' Daylan said. 'Most likely, he was fetching more blood metal for his master.'

Luck, the emir thought. It is only by luck that we are still alive.

'Vulgnash flies swiftly,' Rhianna said. 'In half an hour, he'll reach Rugassa. Ten minutes after that, he'll be on our trail.'

The emir calculated. The Darkling Glories had to stop to search every nook and cranny where the company might hide, and so they did not present an imminent threat. But Vulgnash had mastered arcane spells known only to the Knights Eternal. He would find them, eventually.

Our only choice may be to flee this world forever, the emir thought.

With that, the company dropped from the crown of the hill, down into the shelter of the deep woods, and raced for a time quickly, peering over their backs again and again.

In a few minutes they were out of the trees and onto a starlit plain. The road here was nonexistent. Grasses had grown over it, tall and golden.

The bent grass will give away our trail, the emir realized. It will make a road for the enemy to follow.

The others saw it too. 'Quickly now!' Talon shouted. 'There is no time to waste!'

Twenty-seven minutes later, Vulgnash reached Rugassa and met Lord Despair upon the parapet outside of his room. Vulgnash landed and dropped a chest of forcibles at his master's feet.

Despair smiled grimly. 'Vulgnash, my friend,' he said, 'Fallion and his companions have escaped. I want you to retrieve him for me.'

'Escaped?' Vulgnash asked.

'They will not elude us for long,' Despair said. 'Fallion Orden is one of my chosen. I know precisely where he is headed – toward Castle Coorm, and the One True Tree.'

'He shall find no comfort there,' Vulgnash said.

'No, he won't,' Despair answered. 'He will find you there. I'm sending a great graak with you, with guards to bind and secure the prisoners. You will return them to me . . . so that they may be properly punished.'

25

THE STRUGGLE CEASES

All who struggle against the Great Wyrm struggle in vain.

—From the Wyrmling Catechism

It seemed to Rhianna that she had been running for days when they neared Castle Coorm. Darkness still enveloped the world. With twenty endowments of metabolism, she knew that the darkness would stretch on endlessly. Ten hours of darkness would seem like two hundred, and she would suffer beneath the pall.

Then the sun would come out, and every day would feel like an endless summer.

But she feared that Fallion would never see a summer again. He was growing worse by the minute. He lay in the back of the wagon, his face blanched with pain. Sometimes when Rhianna glanced in, she saw him staring up at some private horror.

There is no escape for him, she thought.

They were sprinting across the grasslands, heading toward a line of trees, when they met the Wizard Sisel and Lord Erringale. It was as if the two appeared out of nowhere. Rhianna had a dozen endowments of sight, and should have seen them miles away, but the wizard and his charge seemed to spring up from the oat stubble magically, not twenty yards in front of them.

'Halt!' Sisel cried, smiling in greeting. Rhianna realized that he had been using his protective magic to hide himself as he moved. In the distance to the north and west, lightning flashed, though the stars overhead shone brightly and there was not a sign of clouds. She realized that the Darkling Glories had found their trail over the plains. 'There is no need to go to the tree,' the wizard said mournfully. 'The enemy has struck it down.'

The wizard's words seemed painfully slow. Rhianna's thoughts raced so quickly, she could hardly stand to wait for him to speak.

'Let us leave this world then,' Daylan Hammer said, 'for there are Darkling Glories on our trail – or worse.'

Rhianna could see the 'or worse.' Miles and miles away, on the horizon, a dark knot winged toward them. An enormous graak, its elongated body looking like a black worm, undulated through the sky. Pale riders sat upon its back, no less than a dozen of them – wyrmling warriors in their armor of bone.

To either side of the graak, a pair of fliers came, crimson wings flashing in the pale moonlight, hurtling above and around the slower graak, like starlings harrying some ponderous owl.

Rhianna jutted her chin. 'Vulgnash is coming. I see him, miles away. He's heading straight toward us.' She hesitated. 'He's flying fast. He has taken endowments.'

'I don't understand,' Fallion said. 'How can he take them? Endowments are gifts from the living to the living.'

The Wizard Sisel said, 'Life and death are a matter of degree. A man who is dying can be less than half alive. Vulgnash is not a living creature like you and me. It is said that he has no soul – yet I am forced to wonder . . . He animates a body, emulates life. To me this indicates that he does have a soul, a powerful and gifted soul.'

'It sounds to me as if there is a contradiction here,' the emir said, 'fit to baffle a wizard.'

'At the very least,' Sisel said, 'he does have a body, unlike the wights that he serves, and so our Vulgnash can take endowments . . .'

A sudden light filled Sisel's eyes, as if some insight filled his mind, but rather than voice it, he held silent, and pondered.

Talon looked stricken. She peered north, and said, 'So soon? How does he know where to look?'

The others only stared blankly, but Rhianna's thoughts spun ahead. 'If he were following our trail, he should be coming from behind us. He knows exactly where to look.' She turned to Fallion. There was no accusation in her voice, only regret. 'Lord Despair has chosen you,' she told Fallion. 'That's the only explanation. I don't believe that Vulgnash is coming this way out of dumb luck.'

Fallion looked crestfallen.

'Is that true?' Sisel asked. 'Did he choose you?'

Fallion looked around blankly, his face lined with pain. 'I, I don't know. I was unconscious much of the time. I sometimes woke to pain and torture, and I recall seeing Despair standing over me, grinning down at me. But I don't remember him choosing me. I don't recall anything at all. But . . .'

'What?' Rhianna asked gently.

'A while ago I heard a voice,' he said, 'Despair's voice – or thought that I did.' Fallion looked to the ground. 'I thought I was just hearing things: it was a warning. I was told not to fight. I was told that if I surrendered, Despair would not take vengeance upon you.'

Now there was no doubt in Rhianna's mind that Fallion had been chosen. If I were Lord Despair and I wanted to keep track of a prisoner, I would choose him, she thought. Then Fallion could not escape, could not take his own life, without me being warned.

Daylan turned to Lord Erringale. 'Milord,' he said humbly, 'I beg your help.' He then explained all that was happening – how the Darkling Glories had come to this world, the danger that Fallion was in, and the greater danger that he posed. 'We need sanctuary. I ask that you grant it for a little while, upon your world, if you can.'

Erringale frowned and looked to the ground. In the distance, there was a rumbling and flash of light to the east.

'You propose to hide Fallion upon my world?' Erringale asked.

'Yes,' Daylan answered.

'Won't this false Earth King be able to find him?' Erringale asked. 'How do we know that Fallion won't bring danger to all that love him?'

'It is a chance that we must take,' Daylan said.

'No!' Fallion said vehemently. 'I can't go with you, Daylan. Too many of my people would be made to suffer for my sake.'

'Then what do *you* want to do?' Rhianna asked. Fallion was the one in pain. She wanted to save him. She would do anything that he asked.

'Send me back,' he said. 'I won't put my friends in jeopardy.'

'You can't go back,' the emir said. 'Despair will continue to torture you. Just when you think that it could get no worse, it will. No one can bear such torment forever. In time, Despair will either drive you mad, or win you and make you his tool.'

Fallion shook his head. 'Having seen Despair, how could I ever consent to become like him?' He looked to Lord Erringale. 'You were there: you know how Despair was formed. The more that Yaleen felt others' pain, the more she hated them. But I'm different. The more I feel their pain, the more I care for them.'

For once, Talon's thoughts outraced Rhianna's. 'Fallion, if you return to Despair,' Talon said, 'all that you have hoped for will be lost. You will never be able to bind the worlds into one.'

Fallion considered his response thoughtfully. His face was filled with pain and anguish. Despair almost had him. 'How can I hope to bind the worlds now,' he begged, 'after seeing what horrors I have wrought?'

Perhaps I should kill him, Rhianna thought. Despair has already won. I could put him out of his misery.

And if I do, she realized, what will happen to Fallion's Dedicates?

The pains that he now bears will return to them in full – the horror of their mutilations, their grief and terror.

Fallion knows that. He stands between them and their pain. He can't give it back to them.

No true man would, she thought. For then Despair, in his fury and petulance, would subject them to unspeakable horrors.

Rhianna considered the arguments, and she knew that she could not kill Fallion anyway, even to save him from his torment. She was a strong woman, but she didn't have that kind of strength.

'There may be a way,' Erringale suggested to the group, hope rising in his voice, 'to turn the tables on Lord Despair – if we dare try it!'

Erringale looked to Fallion. 'To resist evil, we almost never need to resort to bloodshed. Let me ask, could you teach *another* how to bind the worlds?'

'Perhaps,' Fallion said uncertainly. 'It would be hard, but I could try. It would have to be a flameweaver of great power, but in time, yes, I think I could teach someone.'

Erringale's eyes shifted, focused upon the emir. 'There is a flameweaver among us, one who has come to help you. Upon your world, his shadow was the greatest flameweaver your kind has ever known, but upon his world he has shunned such power. Fallion, I would like you to meet the shadow of Raj Ahten.'

Fallion peered up at the emir, and his eyes went wide.

Rhianna knew what he was thinking. There was distrust written plainly upon Fallion's face.

'He's a good man,' Talon said. 'He's nothing like the Raj Ahten that our fathers slew. He's risked his life for his people time and time again, proven himself over and over. If there is anyone you can trust with your secret, it is Tuul Ra.'

Fallion shook his head, unconvinced. But he had little in the way of choices.

'The enemy will be here soon,' Lord Erringale said. 'We must be prepared to meet them. Come with me, Fallion, Tuul Ra. Let us prepare.' Lord Erringale nodded toward the hill nearby, covered with oaks and elms.

'We won't have time,' Fallion said. 'It might take days or weeks to teach him what he needs to know.'

'Trust me,' Lord Erringale said. 'You two will have all of the time you need.'

Fallion shook his head. 'I can't walk that far. The pain is too great. Every muscle in my body is cramping.'

'I'll help,' Erringale said, and he went to the wagon and began to help Fallion down.

Rhianna wondered, What is Erringale plotting?

The Wizard Sisel strode forward a pace, his russet robes whispering in the dry grass, and peered north hungrily. So often, Rhianna had seen him with a serene smile on his face. She would have thought that nothing could remove it. But now he glared toward the skyline like one eager to do battle.

'I think that Erringale is right,' the wizard said. 'There are ways to resist evil without resorting to bloodshed. The time has come for me to deal with Vulgnash.'

Vulgnash spotted his prey ahead, saw Fallion standing in a field near the tree line on a wooded hill, miles away.

Fallion was hunched over, arms folded over his stomach, in almost a fetal position. His face was gray and haggard from pain, and his hair was unkempt. The journey had taken its toll on him. He looked weaker than a kitten.

For the past half hour, Vulgnash had had endowments vectored to him – metabolism, sight. Vulgnash's endowments of sight were a marvelous thing. For ages, he'd seen all of the world in shades of gray, with an occasional splash of red. He'd never seen the world through a human's eyes.

But suddenly he could espy colors that he'd never dreamed existed – skies of deepest blue and undiscovered stars of gold glimmering above, powdering the heavens.

He suspected that if he took a human body in the future, he might see colors even more vividly.

Never again, he thought, will I take a wyrmling's body. From now on, when I need to commandeer a new shell, I will always take a human form.

He could see other advantages. It wasn't just the sight. The human fliers, with their smaller weight, were faster than him.

Vulgnash hastened forward, wings flapping in a rush. He heard a throaty *grooak*, and peered back. The enormous graak had fallen far behind.

I need them not, he thought. The wyrmling warriors had their place. They could bind the prisoners once Vulgnash secured them.

Yet Vulgnash worried about a trap. He saw Fallion waiting in the grass ahead, but not the woman who had rescued him.

Even as he worried about her, she came swooping up over the hill, speeding toward him, faster than any falcon, her wings blurring.

She moved at a frightening pace. Before he realized it, she was overtaking him – two miles out, then one.

But Vulgnash had more than endowments to his credit. He stretched forth his hand and drew starlight from the sky. From horizon to horizon, darkness suddenly stretched, while a thin light whirled like a tornado out of the skies, and landed blazing hot in his palm.

When the darkness faded, he peered ahead, but saw no sign of Rhianna.

She has dived into the trees, Vulgnash reasoned. Smart girl.

He peered down and ahead, where a copse of elms rose beside a stream, their canopy of leaves shielding the ground from view.

He searched for signs of movement, hoping that she had veered into a tree, that its swaying branches would betray her.

But he saw nothing. Dimly, he became aware of shouting far behind. Wyrmlings were roaring frantically.

He craned his neck, looking back. The girl was behind him!

She redoubled her speed during that moment of darkness, he realized.

And now she was winging toward the giant graak, like a falcon to the nest of a dove.

Now we shall see how the wyrmling warriors fare! Vulgnash thought. He had hated bringing them. They and their mount only slowed him down. He longed to see them fail, these fierce champions rife with endowments, all under the protection of their master.

But Rhianna did not dare engage them. She flew straight toward their graak, hurtling in with an astonishing burst of speed, and then dropped as she neared. The warriors hurled battle darts.

She fell, dodging missiles, and the enormous black graak snapped at her as she passed.

Then Rhianna's wings unfolded and she was rising again.

Vulgnash saw a flash of silver as her blade struck the monster's right wing, slicing the leathery membrane between its bones.

The huge graak roared in pain; instantly it began to fall, unable to bear its weight. The graak dropped, flapping frantically, spinning out of control. Wyrmling warriors cried out and fought to hold on, though some tumbled from their mount, raining from the sky.

After downing the graak, Rhianna went soaring upward, wings flapping so quickly that she made a vertical climb.

The girl has learned to fly well in two days, Vulgnash realized, better than I would have imagined.

Some of that had to do with her endowments of wit, he suspected. She would learn much more quickly, when she recalled every twinge of every muscle.

Part of it was her small size. The large wings gave her greater lift than a wyrmling, and allowed for acrobatics that Vulgnash would never master.

But he suspected that there had to be more to it. The girl had tremendous reflexes. In part she might have been born with them, but they had also been trained through years of battle practice.

Yet she did not press the attack. She hurtled around him in a wide circle, and went winging off into the distance.

She fears me, Vulgnash suddenly realized. She is nothing.

She didn't dare get near him. She was hoping that he'd give chase. She was only seeking to distract him, delay him.

He whirled and peered forward. Sure enough, Fallion and the others had fled the clearing and gone into the trees.

Vulgnash growled in frustration, and redoubled his speed, racing toward the meadow at the base of the hill.

As he neared, he spotted movement in the trees.

The Wizard Sisel hid there, between the boles of two mighty elms, with Fallion at his back.

The ground was clear beneath him, except for a carpet of desiccated leaves. The wizard raised his staff in hand and held it at one end, swinging it in great arcs like a club, muttering an incantation.

He hopes to cast a spell of some kind, Vulgnash realized, but Vulgnash had no fear. Vulgnash was under the Earth King's protection. If Sisel were going to attack, Vulgnash would have heard his master's warning.

The old wizard knew many tricks, but his spells were all about healing and protection. At the best, he might hope to avert Vulgnash's fireball.

Vulgnash glided toward the pair warily, like an eagle on the wing.

He could hear the wizard shouting his incantation:

> Bright flows your blood.
> And hale are your bones.
> Your heart is no longer a heart of stone.
> Light fills your eyes, and brightens your mind
> with longings common to all mankind.

Suddenly the wizard whirled and pointed his staff, and though Vulgnash was still a quarter of a mile away, too far to hurl a fireball, the effects of Sisel's spell were devastating.

A *force* smashed into him, like a powerful wave that smote him and washed through him. The blow was minor, not much greater than he'd feel if a gust of wind hit him.

But in an instant, the world changed.

Vulgnash suddenly felt a powerful need for air.

In five thousand years, he had never drawn a single breath, and it was as if his body recognized this fact, and filled him with a singular craving.

At the same time, he was assailed by a consuming hunger. He had never eaten as humans do. He had always drawn his life force from others when the need arose. But instantly he realized that his belly seemed to be clinging to his backbone.

More than that, there was a tremendous pounding in his chest as his heart burst into motion, and every sense came alive. He felt warm wind streaming through his hair, and every follicle of it was alive. For the first time he tasted the smell of the earth – the rich humus of the forest nearby and the drying grasses of the fields below.

His own robes held the cloying scent of death, of decaying flesh, and he'd never recognized his own reek.

A tremendous thirst overtook him, for he had never tasted water, and suddenly the mucus in his throat seemed drier than sand.

In shock, Vulgnash peered ahead and saw that the spell had cost the Wizard Sisel dearly. Where once his robes had been russet and burnt umber, the colors of dying leaves, suddenly they had gone as white as snow, while his beard and hair had turned to silver.

He now leaned on his staff, gasping, as if he had just run a tremendous race.

The pain that Vulgnash felt was more than he could bear. Vulgnash wailed in torment and lobbed the fireball from his hand, sent it careering toward the wizard. But he had thrown too soon. The fireball raced forward a hundred yards, then began to expand, growing larger and larger, and slowing with every second. By the time it reached the trees, it had become nothing more than a cloud of burning gas, and the wizard turned and fled, disappearing from sight.

Vulgnash went wheeling down to the earth, slamming into a tree, then falling in a tangle.

He hit the ground, and such an overwhelming feeling of illness coursed through him that he was reeling with pain.

I'm alive! he realized. I'm mortal.

He climbed to his knees and peered at his hands, as if he'd never seen them before. There were holes in his arm where maggots had burrowed into his flesh, and everywhere that he had a hole, the pain was white-hot and magnificent.

Lying on his belly, Vulgnash collapsed among the dead leaves on the forest floor, smelling the rot of decomposing humus, the scent of mold and soil.

Blood had begun to flow from the wormholes in his arms, welling up unexpectedly.

Vulgnash folded his arms in close, and sat for a moment, rocking back and forth, mind racing.

I'm mortal, he realized. I'm undone.

His heart hammered with excitement; emotions that he'd never felt before assailed him – dread, hopelessness, fatigue. He'd never realized how powerful and incapacitating human emotions could be.

I'm mortal.

It was like a slow poison.

I might live for a few years, he realized, but I will surely die.

In fact, he wasn't sure that he could live even a few hours more.

How old am I? he wondered. He had existed for five thousand years, given a semblance of life from the time that he was a stillborn child, strangled first, then stripped from his mother's womb.

No human lived so long, and indeed he had sent his consciousness through hundreds of corpses.

So if he had suffered a mortal's fate, he would have died of old age by now.

How old is the body I've taken?

He did not know. He had taken the corpse from a tomb, where it had lain rotting. The hands looked old – with thick veins and dark patches of liver spots.

How had it died? Vulgnash wondered. There were no wounds upon the corpse, no gashes from an axe, no broken bones. Vulgnash had checked for such things before taking it.

Had it died of disease – a hacking cough, a weakness of the heart?

He had no way of knowing.

Whatever killed the previous owner could kill me, Vulgnash realized. I could die any second.

Few weapons had ever been formed that could slay a Knight Eternal. Now Vulgnash felt vulnerable.

A voice rang out from the trees. Vulgnash peered up, but could not find the source of it. It was as if the woods spoke to him, not some man. Yet it was a human voice, the crowing voice of the Wizard Sisel. 'Vulgnash,' he shouted. 'How does it feel to be mortal?'

'Why?' Vulgnash screamed, peering this way and that, trying to find the source of the call. But all that he saw were the gray boles of trees, spotted with lichens and moss.

'You have taken countless lives,' Sisel called. 'And the thought occurred to me – how can he value that which he has never owned?'

Vulgnash tried to clear the phlegm from his throat, for it was thick and crusty. He wanted to shout some curse, but a great weariness was on him. He had not slept in days.

'So,' Sisel said, 'consider now your allegiance. You were a servant of death. Your masters fed you till you grew strong by consuming innocent souls.

'But think: there in that empire of death, what can they offer you now?

'I invite you to join us, to switch your allegiance. I can heal your wounds, help you.'

There were no words to express Vulgnash's outrage. He knew curses that he could hurl, but they would do no good. He peered about frantically, searching for some sign of the wizard, but the woods were still and empty.

He peered up, realizing that the voice might have been coming from above.

At last, panting from weakness and despair, Vulgnash roared his defiance. 'Never!' he cried. 'I come for you, by all that is unholy I shall have you!'

Cramped with pain, Fallion Orden hugged Rhianna good-bye. They stood in the deep woods not two hundred yards from where Vulgnash roared, hidden by little more than the Wizard Sisel's spell. Behind Rhianna, a door to the netherworld yawned wide.

It was a solemn moment. Fallion did not know if he would ever see his friends again.

For her part, Rhianna stood before him, shaking, looking so weak that he thought she might swoon. All of her endowments had failed her. None gave her the strength for this moment.

'I love you,' she said. 'More than you can ever know.'

Fallion hugged her hard. His body told him that he was being torn apart – that teeth were shattering in his head, that ears were being stripped into ragged bits, that skin was being pulled from his face by some brute who wielded powerful tongs.

But he also felt Rhianna's yielding flesh, and knew that her fierce love was true. That memory would have to suffice. It would have to be something he held on to in the weeks and years to come.

'I should have married you by now,' Fallion told her. 'I should never have waited, or entertained other thoughts. I should have seen that you were my destiny.'

Rhianna wept bitter tears on his shoulder, and kissed him good-bye. It did not seem like a long kiss. Had she had a week to hold him, it could not have been long enough.

She has twenty endowments of metabolism, he realized. To her it seems long enough.

Grimacing in pain, Rhianna reached up and covered her belly with one hand.

'What's wrong?' he asked.

Rhianna shook her head in anguish, then apologized. 'I think that some Darkling Glories just found my Dedicates.'

There was such sorrow in her face that Fallion wished that he could take one more endowment of compassion, take upon himself all of her pain.

Talon stepped forward and hugged him briefly with one arm. She'd taken the little girl from the wagon, and now held the sleeping child.

'At least we have saved something from this world,' Fallion told her.

Daylan clapped him on the shoulder, and offered a bit of advice. 'You cannot break free, but here is something that might help. The emperor's daughter, Princess Kan-hazur, will weaken over the coming days. While in our prison at Caer Luciare, she was poisoned with red-wort. Its effects can kill her as she withdraws from it. I know that you cannot break free, but perhaps this information will be of use to you. You may be able to barter for favors – for leniency toward your Dedicates.'

Last of all came the emir. He did not speak. He did not need to. They were more than brothers now, for they were joined with a special bond. Each of them bore the scars of a fresh endowment of wit. Fallion's own scar was upon the heel of his right foot, where he hoped it might never be seen.

I will be with you, my friend, the emir whispered into Fallion's mind. *Through all of your trials, I will be there to advise you, to console you.*

And I will guide you as best I can, Fallion offered in return, *when you seek out the Seals of Creation, and bind the worlds into one.*

The emir clasped Fallion on the shoulder, and nodded.

Moments later, Fallion's friends were gone, stepping one by one into a brighter world, where the wind blew sweeter scents.

Fallion turned and walked through the brush, partly hunched and racked by pain, until he found Vulgnash there in the leaves, driven to his knees.

Fallion dared not fight him. Fallion had his skills as a flameweaver, skills that Vulgnash could never match. But they did not lend themselves to battle. Besides, Vulgnash was a powerful Runelord.

'I'm ready to return to your master,' Fallion said.

Vulgnash glared at him with murderous eyes. The great wyrmling in his red robes looked different now. His gray skin had fleshy hues to it, and there were emotions in his eyes that Fallion had never seen before – rage, self-pity, hurt.

'Where are the others?' Vulgnash roared.

'They've gone where you cannot find them,' Fallion said.

Quicker than a snake, Vulgnash reached out a hand and stripped the heat from Fallion's body. He felt himself falling, falling, as if into a sea of ice.

Back in Rugassa, Lord Despair stood upon the gargoyle outside his rooms. He peered down upon his minions, toiling in the dark fields, and smiled.

Lightning flashed above Mount Rugassa, and thunder pealed.

All was right with the world. The city of Rugassa lay beneath a dark cloud, one that would never lift. The Darkling Glories had put a pall over the city, so that for miles around, the night would never end.

Thousands of the creatures were streaming through the world gate, eager to hear his command, while the Thissians instructed them.

To the south, armies of reavers were marching toward him. Yet Lord Despair felt no fear. He had sent a Thissian ambassador to communicate with them, to invite them to join him, and the reavers would bow down to him and obey.

The Earth Spirit whispered peace to his soul, and Despair had no fear.

Only the small folk of the world presented any threat now, and that threat was dissipating too.

Darkling Glories were already flying in every direction, hunting down the small folk, looking for those who might have given themselves to his enemies as Dedicates.

Within a matter of days, the entire world would be under his sway.

The little mouse in the back of his skull fretted and squeaked its imprecations. 'Your dying amuses me, Areth,' Despair whispered. 'Draw it out for as long as you like.'

Despair smiled. He could sense Fallion. At this very moment, the young man was on his way home.

extras

extras

about the author

David Farland began writing at the age of seventeen, and in the years since has published over forty fantasy and science fiction novels for both adults and young adults.

Over the years, he has worked the typical writerly jobs – as a missionary, a prison guard, a meat cutter, an editor, a contest judge, a writing professor, a video game designer, and as a movie producer.

He currently lives in Saint George, Utah, with his wife and five children, where his hobbies include hiking, fishing, and working-out.

To contact the author, email davidfarland@xmission.com. To see news of the series, visit his site at www.runelords.com.

Find out more about David Farland and other Orbit authors by registering for the free monthly newsletter at www.orbitbooks.net

if you enjoyed
THE WYRMLING HORDE
look out for

MONUMENT

by

Ian Graham

1

Thus it commenced, on a cloudless night,
A clothes-maker of the south
Of Meahavin
Received the word of the creator-god
And vowed to do His bidding.
Abandoning all worldly goods, he left
His home and became a Most Holy Pilgrim . . .

Extracted from the unexpurgated, forbidden account
of the Pilgrims by Mascali, the Ninth Witness

It was a foolish fashion, thought the big man. A mixture of vanity, bluster and juvenile stupidity.

Across the common room, a group of stonemasons sat at a long table. They were young men, sinuously muscled from long hours of labour. White dust caked their skin, hair, eyelashes – they seemed much less men than phantoms granted flesh. They were drinking ale, jesting, and waiting for the whores to arrive. The big man objected to none of these things. Alcohol, laughter and women were sensible pursuits. But he found absurd the manner in which the stonemasons wore their purses.

Each purse hung from its owner's belt on a two-inch braided leather strip. Some strips were brightly coloured, reds interwoven with greens and blues. Others were darker: a sombre plaiting of blacks, browns, and dried-blood ochre. The purses dangled from these strips as vulnerable, and as tempting, as ripe apples. The most cack-handed thief could've snatched one.

And that, supposed the big man, was precisely the point.

Like any young men with hot red blood in their veins, the stonemasons wished to appear confident, strong, dangerous . . . exactly the type of men who could fearlessly expose their valuables to theft. For no one would dare steal them. It would be akin to snatching food from a lion's jaws: an act of suicidal lunacy.

The big man lifted a wine flagon to his lips.

Since mid-morning, he had been in the tavern. He had scarcely budged from his corner table − except to use the pissing yard and purchase fresh drinks at the bar. He had imbibed enough alcohol to float a warship. Whisky, gin, rum, ale, wine . . . all had sluiced into his stomach. He had drunk enough to make most men fall violently sick. Enough, perhaps, even to kill those of an under-developed constitution. But the big man was immeasurably resilient. Effortlessly, he could drink ten times as much as most men.

And *looked* like he could.

Drink had bloated him. Over his belt sagged an ale gut − a flaccid drum of flesh, straining against his tunic. His face was swollen. And never a handsome man, he now resembled a boar. His nose had been broken so frequently in drunken brawls that it had crumpled to a snout. His beard − thick, tangled, lice-thronged − was the dull black of a tusker's pelt. His slightly hunched shoulders, barrel chest and lumbering movements added to his porcine appearance. Only his eyes looked fully human. Set in watery, bloodshot whites, the green irises were sharp, attentive. They glittered insolently.

The big man's name was Ballas.

It was time, he decided, to get himself some money.

He dropped his wine flagon deliberately and watched it shatter on the floor.

Startled by the sudden noise, the stonemasons glanced over.

'Clumsy bastard,' shouted one − a red-haired youth, his skin still blemished by childhood freckles. His brown eyes were cold and cruel; they burned with a type of habitual resentment. He gazed intently at Ballas. 'Look at the state of him,' he urged his friends, pointing. 'There is dried vomit on his shirt. His hair bristles with lice. I'd wager piss stains daub his breeches. Tell me, fat man: when did you last take a bath?'

Ballas shrugged.

'You seem untroubled by your own filth,' said the youth. 'And by your stench. Do you go whoring, eh?'

Ballas nodded.

'I take it the girls hold their breath? I take it they struggle to keep down their gorges? For you're more likely to provoke nausea than desire.'

Ballas shrugged once more.

'You have no self-respect, fat man,' said the youth. 'If I ever hit low times and live as you do, I'll kill myself. Sweet grief, I'd slit my throat. I'd slice off my balls. I'd do anything to bring about my death. No matter how painful, no matter how degrading.' He turned to the other stonemasons. 'Promise that one of you'll butcher me, if ever I take on the fat man's aspect. Go on: we are all loyal to one another. I'd do the same for you. It'd be a true act of friendship. A mercy killing. Surely you wouldn't deny me?'

The red-haired youth's purse dangled from a plain black strip. Its burden of coins strained against the fabric. Ballas eyed it for a moment like a snake eyeing a mongoose.

He stooped to pick up a shard of flagon glass.

'No, wait,' came a voice.

A serving girl hurried over. 'I shall do that. You'll only cut yourself, and then I'll have to mop up blood as well as wine.'

Kneeling, she used a short-handled brush to sweep the shards into a heap.

'You have been here since we opened,' she said, glancing up. 'It is a rare thing, to see someone drink as much as you. You have guzzled a river, sir. You are not going to turn foul, are you?'

'Foul?' murmured Ballas.

'You know: *rowdy*. This is a peaceful tavern, more or less. We don't want trouble.'

'You'd reckon it best if I left?' asked Ballas. His deep voice rolled with a Hearthfall burr.

'No,' said the girl quickly.

'A serving girl doesn't ask a man if he's going to go rotten,' said Ballas. 'Not if she wants him to stay, and keep drinking. I've spent a purseful here—'

'You misunderstand me,' interrupted the serving girl.

'I misunderstand *nothing*,' said the big man, rising. 'I'm not welcome here, right? So I'll just piss off, then. There're finer places in Soriterath – places where a man can drink, *and* be well treated.'

Edging around the table, Ballas swayed. The floor seemed to tilt like the deck of a tide-shaken ship. Gripping the table's edge, Ballas steadied himself. He was drunker than he had expected. Taking a deep breath, he started towards the doors.

He took ten paces, tripped – and crashed into the red-haired stonemason. The stonemason fumbled his tankard; the vessel clanked on to the table, and an ale pool spread over the surface. With an angry shout, the stonemason sprang to his feet.

'You bloody *oaf*!' he snapped, his eyes blazing. 'Can't you even walk properly? Look what you have done!' He pointed furiously at the spilled ale.

'Accident,' mumbled Ballas. 'I'm drunk. Every step is an adventure. Forgive me.'

The stonemason wrinkled his nose. 'Close to, your stink is even fiercer than I imagined. You reek worse than a tanner's shop!' He pushed Ballas away.

Surprised by the youth's abrupt move, Ballas stumbled over a stool and fell to the floor.

The stonemason stood over him. 'You owe me a tankard of ale.'

'I've got no money,' said Ballas, slowly. 'I've got . . . nothing.'

'No man without money can get as drunk as you are . . .'

'No man as drunk as I am,' replied Ballas, struggling to his feet, 'can possibly have any money *left*. I've supped enough to bankrupt a Blessed Master. To settle his account, he'd have to pawn the Sacros.'

'Do not lie to me,' said the stonemason. He advanced on Ballas.

'Aiy!' The serving girl glared at them from across the room. 'Do you want me to summon the tavern-master? He has a wolfhound as big and ill-tempered as a bull: would you like him to turn it loose on you?' She looked sharply at Ballas. 'Go on: do as you promised – *leave*. The first time I saw you, I knew you were bad.'

'Is that so? Then you're smarter than you look,' said Ballas. He glanced at the stonemason. He considered insulting the youth. He knew exactly what to say. The youth was embarrassed by his freckles. In every other aspect he was a man, full-grown and strong. Yet he still bore the faint leopard-markings of a child. Alternatively, Ballas could ridicule his acne: it sprawled over his chin, each spot a sore red hue, and pus-laden.

Ballas said nothing. It was wisest by far simply to leave. Turning, he shambled outdoors.

It was mid-afternoon. Bright autumnal light fell from a clear blue sky. The big man stood in a thoroughfare of half-frozen mud. On either side, there were taverns constructed from pale grey stone. Many appeared to be half-derelict: the wooden eaves were rotting, mosses and moulds blotched the brickwork, and paint had long since peeled from the doors. Ballas had been in Soriterath for only a few days, yet this particular area was one of the shabbiest he had encountered – not only in this city, he reflected, but in all of Druine. Soriterath was the Holy City, the city where the Pilgrim Church leaders dwelled. But it was not a place of splendour. In the opulent areas, there were grand buildings, true enough; but mainly the city was like many in Druine: a place of creeping squalor, of houses, taverns and shops constructed from tired stone and mouldering wood, packed tightly together, as if to confine as many souls as possible to the smallest space. And, like many such cities, it had a distinctive smell: a combination of decaying vegetation and decomposing flesh. The greengrocers dumped their unsold produce in the streets, and when any of the city's feral animals – a rabble of rats, cats and dogs – died, their carcasses were left to rot where they lay. A similar fate awaited many human corpses; others, weighted with rocks, were dumped in the Gastallen River. In an effort to control the diseases emanating from such corpses, the Pilgrim Church had erected communal pyres throughout the city. During times of plague and famine, Ballas had heard, the air over Soriterath grew black with the smoke of burning flesh.

Soriterath might have been the Holy City, but it frequently had a hellish aspect.

And when common room pessimists spoke of the country's decline, of Druine's gradual slide into moral ruin, they often held up Soriterath as an example.

When Ballas arrived here, he had felt instantly at home.

An icy breeze swirled along the thoroughfare, stinging his cold-cracked skin.

He shivered. Then he grinned.

'Let me see what I have here,' he said, unfurling the fingers of his left hand. Upon his palm crouched the stonemason's purse. It had been easily stolen. When Ballas had tripped – deliberately – into the young man, he had cut the purse from its strip with the shard of flagon glass. He had performed the operation with a conjuror's dexterity.

The purse was full.

'When night falls,' murmured Ballas, 'I shan't be dossing on the streets.'

Then he noticed that the purse felt light. *Too* light, for a purse burdened with coins.

Frowning, he rubbed it. He felt what he had previously observed: coins' hard edges, straining against the fabric.

Yet the lightness persisted.

Was the wine playing a trick on him? Could it make heavy objects seem near-weightless – just as it made ugly women appear beautiful?

He emptied the purse on to his palm. And cursed as a dozen discs of plain wood tumbled out.

He hurled them to the ground.

'Pissing eunuch,' said Ballas, as if the stonemason was present. 'Freckled, pimple-crusted eunuch. I ought to castrate you, and complete the effect.'

A door slammed open. Echoes raced along the thoroughfare.

The stonemason stepped from the tavern. Two others stood beside him.

'You idiot,' said the red-haired youth, pacing toward Ballas. His fingers probed the strip, dangling purseless from his belt. 'Did you imagine I wouldn't notice? Did you suppose that, like you, I am so insensible that I can suffer an indignity without realising?'

'What are you talking about?' said Ballas, lamely.

'Oh, come now – don't feign innocence. You stand with my purse in your hand, my coins spread about your feet. You know fully what I speak of.'

'It was a jest, nothing more—'

'As is this, my friend.' Springing forward, the stonemason swung a flagon against Ballas's head. Dazed, Ballas staggered. A second blow landed on his cheekbone. Then the stonemason kicked him in the crotch.

There was a heartbeat of terrible expectation – then a choking pain surged from Ballas's testicles to his throat.

Sinking to his knees, Ballas vomited. The stonemason ran forward and kicked him in the face. The impact knocked Ballas on to his back.

Kneeling beside him, the stonemason punched him in the mouth. Then he brought down the flagon on Ballas's head – again and again, until the vessel shattered.

Then the real violence began.

The stonemason's friends kicked Ballas in the chest, legs and stomach. They used their fists, too, and delivered blow after muscle-jarring blow. Ballas felt like a fox set upon by hounds. His body jerked this way and that. The stonemason struck him repeatedly in the face, as if determined to disfigure him . . .

Eventually, exhausted, the three men grew still.

Silence fell.

Then came a splashing noise. Something showered on to Ballas's face.

Grimacing, he cracked open his swollen eyes.

The stonemason was urinating on him.

'Is it not apt that one who belongs in a sewer should be wetted by liquid destined for a sewer? Is this fluid not your true habitat? Aren't you as at ease in piss as a fish is in water?'

The stonemason laughed; his companions laughed, too.

'A warning, fat man. If I ever set eyes on you again, or catch your stench, you are dead. Understand? I've been merciful. But next time, I'll drag down lightning, and blast you from this world into the next.' He spat at Ballas. Then, turning, he walked away.

His friends followed him, vanishing back into the tavern.

Ballas sat upright. Over his body, bruises blossomed: his skin throbbed as blood spread beneath it. Tiny spasms rippled through his muscles. Lifting his fingers, he touched his nose – and gasped: it had been broken yet again. Right now it felt like nothing more than a plug of bloody gristle.

'Bastards,' he grunted. 'Pissing bastards . . . But now, let me see.' He gave a blood-clogged laugh. 'Maybe it is not all bad news.'

Within his left hand nestled a second purse. This one also belonged – *had* belonged – to the stonemason. Like the first it was stuffed full. Unlike the first it felt heavy.

Ballas upended it. Out on to his palm tumbled twelve copper pennies. A week's wage for an apprentice stonemason.

'Well, young man,' he said, 'the purse hanging from your belt was a cheat. But this one . . . Ha! Little boys have much to learn. Treat this as a lesson.'

Getting to his feet, Ballas limped away along the thoroughfare.

Several hours later, Ballas clambered from a pallet-bed and pulled on his leggings.

From the purse he rummaged two pennies, tossing them to the plump whore beneath the blankets.

He had visited a different tavern – he could not recall its name – immediately after the beating. He had drunk a flagon of Keltuskan red. Then, his ardour roused, he had purchased a few hours of the whore's time and taken her upstairs.

She had expressed surprise that someone so recently beaten could possess carnal inclinations. In her experience, they flowed away with a victim's blood. Ballas insisted that, in his case, that was not so. The whore had believed him.

To her credit, she had treated him gently. She had performed the more strenuous motions of coupling, allowing Ballas to remain immobile, grunting like a pig happy at the trough. Contrary to the stonemason's expectations, his sweat-odour had not offended her: on the windowsill a bowl of herbs smouldered, their fragrance filling the room and masking any other smell.

Ballas put on his shirt and boots.

Opening the shutters, he observed the night-cloaked Soriterath streets. He felt drunk, satisfied, tired – and thirsty. He was a stranger in the city. But he recalled that, a few streets away, there was a tavern that sold a sweet white wine, which would provide a gentle end to a trying but satisfactory day.

He left the chamber and went down a flight of steps into the common room. There was noise here: every table was occupied, and laughter shook the rafters. Ballas crossed the floor and stepped out into the night.

Reaching back, his gaze on the darkened street, he tried to shut the tavern door. It moved a few inches – then halted.

Grunting, he tugged harder but it would not budge.

He glanced back.

And exhaled.

In the doorway stood a tall, thin figure. He had small dark eyes, a pimple-spattered chin – and freckles.

He gripped a cudgel in his right hand.

'We have hunted you all evening,' he said, very quietly. 'Your persistence amazes me. You steal from us once, and get beaten.

Then you steal from us again. Truly, I believe drink has destroyed your mind. The Four preached abstinence. I always thought that it was over-pious nonsense . . . But now, I see the hazards of the bottle.'

The stonemason's friends appeared.

Ballas opened his mouth. But the stonemason said, 'Do not speak. At the moment of his death, a man ought to tell the truth. And you utter only lies.' Leaping forward, he slammed the cudgel against Ballas's cheekbone. The big man fell. Before he could move, the stonemasons were once more upon him.

2

On the eastern coast, in Saltbrake town,
A Chandler received the creator-god's word
And became a Pilgrim, and upon a road
Of Suffering and Enlightenment, he would learn
The true natures of Good and Evil . . .

'Will he live?'

'Oh – he might.'

'You sound uncertain . . .'

'Years ago, I tended a farmer who had been stampeded by a herd of bulls, and I doubt strongly he would have traded his injuries for this fellow's.' The voice, that of an old man, paused thoughtfully.

There was a long sigh.

'Look at him,' the voice continued. 'There is scarcely a square inch of flesh unbruised. From head to toe, he is caked in dried blood. I dare say many of his bones are broken – and the Four only know what more, ah, *subtle* damage has been done.'

'Subtle damage?' echoed the other voice – that of a much younger man. He spoke softly, but with great urgency. As if fearful a moment's laxity would exact a terrible cost. 'What do you mean, Calden?'

'Damage to his innards,' replied the old man. 'To his lungs, heart, liver. They are fragile things. It isn't always obvious when they are injured. They may bleed, and no one – neither patient nor physician – will know. And there are other maladies that do not loudly proclaim their presence. A blood-taint, for instance, kills as readily as any poison. Yet it will not be detected until it strikes.'

'But you *will* treat him – as best you can?'

'Of course. But Brethrien, observe him closely. It may be necessary – despite my ministrations – to give him the Final Blessing.'

Ballas lay perfectly still. He had already attempted to open his eyes. But the surrounding flesh was too swollen. His body felt at once strange and familiar. Strange, because the beating had covered it with contusions – and, as the old man had suggested, many bones were probably broken. Familiar, for Ballas had been beaten many times. He had grown accustomed to the terrible foreignness of how his body felt when freshly thrashed.

He wondered where he was. He tried opening his mouth so that he might ask. But his lips too were swollen, and stuck together with blood.

'His Blessing,' said the younger man, 'has already been administered. I delivered it in error. I came upon him in the street, covered in blood – and *frost*: I found him at dawn, and he had been outdoors overnight. I presumed he was dead.'

'An understandable mistake,' said the old man.

'When the Papal Wardens tried to load him upon a cart, so that he might be taken to the city's pyres, his wounds bled afresh.'

'So his heart was still beating . . .'

'I could scarcely believe it. I sent for you straight away.'

Something splashed into a bowl of water.

'Well, his wounds are clean,' said the old man. 'As for the blood covering the rest of him, we shall leave it be. It will do no harm.'

There was a wet grinding noise, slow and rhythmic. A pestle pulverising something in a mortar.

'Knitbone?' queried the young man.

'Yes, and a fine thing I brought plenty of it. A meadow's-worth would be hardly sufficient.' The grinding paused.

Ballas sensed the old man leaning close.

'He has been drinking. From his breath, it seems he has downed a lively mixture: whisky, ale, wine, rum . . . He has varied tastes.'

'I found him on Vintner's Row,' explained the young man. 'A place of taverns, gambling rooms and . . . ah . . .'

'Brothels,' finished the old man. As if the younger man would have problems speaking the word. 'I know of Vintner's Row. And that urges me to ask: what do *you* know of your patient?'

'Know of him? Well, nothing. I merely found him, in a poor state. It was my duty to help him. I have sworn an oath. I cannot ignore a distressed soul.'

The old man muttered something.

'Pardon?'

'Be wary,' repeated the old man, loudly. 'No decent-minded man takes his pleasures on Vintner's Row.' The grinding noises stopped. 'Unroll that bandage, will you? My thanks.' A squelching noise followed. As of a paste being smeared.

'I will grant him the benefit of the doubt.'

The old man laughed. 'The doubt? What is there to be doubted? You find him in one of Soriterath's most disreputable quarters, stinking of liquor, beaten halfway to the Eltheryn Forest . . .'

'I must grant him shelter,' said the younger man firmly.

'For how long?'

'Until he heals. Assuming such an event . . .'

'. . . Such a minor miracle . . .'

'. . . Occurs,' finished the young man.

The squelching stopped. Something cool and sticky was draped over Ballas's chest. A poultice. For a heartbeat the sensation was nearly pleasurable. The unguent numbed Ballas's flesh, and cooled it.

Then a gentle pressure was applied, to fix the poultice.

Pain swept through Ballas's body. He felt as if a lightning bolt had struck him. He imagined white heat crackling from rib to rib, then erupting from his pores. Every sinew tightened. Every muscle clenched.

He gasped.

'Ah, a response – did you see it?' In the old man's voice there was a note of surprise. 'That is encouraging.'

If the old man spoke again, Ballas did not hear. Garish scribbles of light sizzled behind his eyes. The pain steadily increased, until Ballas thought he would burst into flame.

Then: a swirling numbness. A delicious resignation engulfed him. He found himself spinning gratefully into warm black oblivion.

After a few days – because he was constantly slipping in and out of consciousness, he was unsure how many – Ballas opened his eyes. He found himself in a small white-walled room that had a single shuttered window and a fire blazing in the grate. The floor was bare stone, and there was a table laden with an array of medicinal items: bandages, swabs, yarn and needles for stitching wounds, herbs that could be ground into poultices.

The young man was a priest. No older than twenty-five years, he glowed with pious devotion. His fair hair was short-cropped into something resembling a monk's cut. His dark blue robes hung loosely on a slender frame. This, coupled with his pale skin, lent him the appearance of someone recovering from a serious ailment.

Yet he was animated by holy urgency.

Even the smallest tasks – the bringing of food and water, the examination of Ballas's wounds – seemed of the utmost spiritual importance.

Often, while changing Ballas's dressings, he asked, *Who are you? Where are you from? Will anyone be worried about you – ought I tell someone where you are?*

Ballas never replied.

The questions irritated him; his life was his own business, not some tender-hearted priest's.

But if he *had* answered, he would have revealed only that he was a vagrant and so hailed from everywhere and nowhere. No one in Druine would be concerned about him. Not the tavern-masters who sold him wine, ale, whisky. Not the whores who caught his mouldering seed.

The small room depressed Ballas. The persistent fire-smoke, the colourless walls and unguent-scent made him restless. He wanted to breathe clean, cold air. He needed to experience sensations other than warmth.

More than anything, he needed a drink. The priest had administered many medicines – except for those he craved most strongly.

One afternoon, Ballas felt strong enough to rise. Swinging his feet from the pallet-bed, he stood. A constricting pain seized his chest. As if an iron band was bolted tightly around it. Swearing softly, he waited for the discomfort to pass.

He was naked, he realised. Except for dried blood. It covered his body like a second skin. Grunting, he flexed his left arm. Where the flesh creased, blood-flakes cracked loose, drifting to the floor. Where had the blood come from? he wondered. A stab wound? A bottle-slash? It did not seem so. Inspecting his body, he found no sharp-edge injuries. Only jagged tears, where blunt objects had struck forcefully enough to split his skin.

Bruises covered his chest; they had ripened from black to a mix of metallic greens and golds. Murmuring, he touched his face. A nose shattered still further, a grotesquely swollen jaw, lips split open like sausages left too long upon the grill – these were the things his fingertips encountered.

Grunting, Ballas spat on the floor. A gobbet of red-tinged saliva quivered on the stone.

A heap of clothes lay in the corner. A brown tunic, soft cotton vest and black leggings . . . They were not Ballas's clothes. Yet they were intended for his use. Ballas tugged on the leggings. They were a comfortable fit. But the vest was slightly too tight. And the tunic couldn't easily accommodate Ballas's ale gut, which stretched the fabric almost to breaking point.

The boots were exactly the correct size. As they should have been: for they were Ballas's own, scrubbed clean of blood and vomit. The ripped stitching had been repaired, too.

'Holy man,' murmured Ballas, 'what are you, eh? A conscientious soul? Or a meddling toe-rag?'

Ballas left the room, stepping into a long corridor. At the far end stood a door, half ajar. Beyond, there was a kitchen. On a shelf rested wooden cups and bowls. There was a fire enclave but the stacked logs were unlit.

The priest Brethrien sat at a table.

Writing on a parchment, he wore an expression of rapt concentration. An illuminated edition of *The Book of the Pilgrims* lay open in front of him. Around his neck, he wore an elongated brass triangle: a miniature of Scarrendestin, the holy mountain.

'These are not my clothes,' said Ballas, entering the kitchen. His voice was naturally loud, with a growling note.

The priest jerked, startled. A blob of ink dripped from his quill-tip, splattering the parchment. Turning his face to Ballas, he blinked.

'These are not my clothes,' repeated the big man. 'Where are the clothes you found me in? I want them back.'

'You walk very quietly,' stammered the priest. Nervously, he fingered his Scarrendestin pendant – as if it were a protective amulet. 'I did not hear your footfalls . . .'

'For the last time, where are my clothes?'

'They had to be burned,' replied the priest.

'Burned?' asked Ballas darkly.

'They were infested,' explained Brethrien. 'Every manner of crawling thing inhabited them. They were, ah, *unhealthy*: unless one were a blood-feasting parasite – a louse or a grip-worm, say. They were threadbare, too. I suspect only the wildlife held them together.' He gestured to Ballas's new apparel. 'I apologise if I have taken a liberty. But, truly, your old clothes could not be saved. And those that you presently wear – they are of better quality. The wool is soft, yes? As soft as when it lay upon the sheep's back. Your old tunic was as coarse as a hair shirt.'

He laughed uneasily. 'Saint Derethine suffered many self-imposed tortures. But I dare say even he would have shrunk from your tunic.'

Ballas stared balefully at Brethrien.

'I, ah . . . Do you hunger?'

'For days, I've eaten piss-all but soup,' grunted Ballas. 'Of course I hunger.' His gaze alighted on a shelf of wine flagons. 'But my thirst troubles me more.' Grasping a flagon, he started tugging out the cork.

Alarmed, the priest sprang to his feet. 'No!'

He seized the flagon, trying to wrest it from Ballas. 'Please – you cannot drink that! It is forbidden!'

'Why so?' Ballas lifted the flagon to the window. 'What's inside, holy man? I reckoned this to be wine. But perhaps it's something else. The piss of a martyr, perhaps? Better still, that of a Blessed Master?'

'Holy wine,' said Brethrien. 'You are holding holy wine. The Brandister monks made it; and the Masters bless it in accordance with the strictest rituals – rituals transcribed by the Pilgrims . . . by the Four: may they lead me safely to the Eltheryn Forest . . .' He faltered. 'Holy wine can be imbibed only as part of a church service. Morning, noon, eveningfall – it matters not *which* service; but the wine can be drunk then, and *only* then. To do otherwise is sinful, and will bring only misfortune. Please – give me the flagon.'

'D'you have any wine I *can* drink?' Ballas allowed Brethrien to take the flagon. '*Un*holy wine, perhaps?'

The priest shook his head.

Ballas scowled. It was typical of his ill luck that he should be in the care of such a man.

Brethrien cradled the flagon as if it were a baby. Then he set it gently upon the shelf.

'What do you have to eat?' demanded Ballas.

'Many good things,' said Brethrien. 'Porridge oats, potatoes, carrots—'

'What about meat? Beef, pork, venison . . .'

'The Four forbade the consumption of animal flesh,' said

Brethrien. 'So I abstain from anything that has eye, ear or mouth. My larder is bare of all except the soil's produce.'

On the table rested a linen-draped cheese block. Drawing back the covering, Ballas lifted the morsel to his mouth – and bit down. His lip wounds reopened, streaking blood over the cheese. He chewed carefully, wary of shattered teeth. The stuff was watery, tasteless.

'Pathetic,' muttered Ballas, tossing it back on to the table.

The priest stared, his blue eyes glinting anxiously.

'A problem, holy man?' asked Ballas.

'I—' Brethrien faltered, as if his true feelings were difficult to utter. He sighed. 'If you crave meat, you may purchase some from the market.'

Ballas laughed – an ill-humoured snort. 'Do you reckon I'm a man of money? I haven't got a penny to my name.'

From within his robe, Brethrien produced a purse. 'Two pennies ought to be enough,' he said, proffering the coins.

Ballas gazed at the copper discs nestling in Brethrien's palm. Then he glanced at the priest.

'Go on,' said the holy man. 'Take them, if you truly crave meat.'

Shrugging, Ballas did as he was told. You're a trusting soul, he thought, eyeing the priest. Or a stupid one.

'You are bleeding,' said the priest, gesturing at Ballas's tunic. Blood soaked the sleeve. Scarlet drops pattered from the cuff. 'Are you certain you are well enough to visit the market?'

'I'll find out soon enough,' said Ballas.

'Yes, I suppose you will.' Brethrien blinked rapidly. 'I was, ah, wondering if you might do me a favour. It is but a small thing—'

'Have you tended my injuries,' said Ballas, 'so you might use me as an errand boy?'

'Of course not!' exclaimed Brethrien, fiddling with his triangular pendant. 'I nursed you because . . . because you were injured and I am a priest, wishing only to do the Four's work. That is all. I was not trying to . . .' he groped for words '. . . strike a contract with you. Far from it.'

The holy man's edginess irritated Ballas. Every gesture – every blink, every anxious touch of his pendant – scraped upon the big man's nerves. The holy man was as timid as a dormouse. It was understandable that he should harbour a certain unease: he had, in his home, a bruised, bloodied stranger whose temperament inclined towards surliness and who, even after a period of abstinence, still smelled of alcohol.

Yet the priest's response seemed excessively nervous. He had the demeanour of someone almost fearful for their life.

It wouldn't remain a problem for long. Already, Ballas had decided to leave the priest-home. He did not belong in such places. Not even as a guest. Only brothels and taverns brought him pleasure. Better not to linger in the stale air of Brethrien's abode.

'W-will you perform my errand?' Brethrien rummaged again in his purse. 'It is, as I said, only a small thing.' He plucked out three more pennies. 'There is a man, Calden, who applied the first poultices, and who taught me how to look after you. He is a fine soul. Sharp-witted, yet compassionate: he has not cultivated his mind at the expense of his heart. It will be—'

'What do you want me to do?'

The priest faltered.

'Come on!'

'He supplied many things that aided your healing,' blurted Brethrien. 'Herbs, physician's tools . . . I must repay him. He is not a wealthy man.'

'You are mistaken,' said Ballas sourly. 'I've yet to meet an impoverished physician. Like their leeches, they are parasites. One sucks blood, the other money. What does a physician leave behind? Just a healthy bankrupt. They get fat and happy on our suffering.'

'Calden is not a physician,' explained Brethrien. 'Rather, he is the curator of the museum on Half-moon Street. Go now, and you will find him there. I expect he will be pleased to see you. And surprised: he did not believe you would recover, let alone so quickly. You have a strong constitution. He—'

'I'll do as you ask,' interrupted Ballas, taking the coins.

'You know the way to Half-moon Street?'

'Are there taverns close by?'

'I believe so.'

'Then I'll know Half-moon Street.'

Five pennies – he felt them in his palm. Enough for an evening of wine. Of ale. Of whores.

If only all thefts were so simply done, thought Ballas. What an easy world it'd be, if every man were as gullible as this priest.

'Give Calden my best wishes,' said Brethrien.

But Ballas had already crossed the kitchen and was leaving the priest-home.

Ballas walked slowly through Soriterath. After the priest-home's warmth, the outdoor chill bit him deeply. He had half-forgotten that winter was approaching. Soon, a layer of crackling frost would cover Druine. Snow would fall. The land would be blizzard-struck; and the streets, where Ballas slept, would be heaped with frozen white.

For twenty of his forty-five years, Ballas had lived as a vagrant. He was painfully well acquainted with the bitter cold of autumn and winter. If asked, he could describe times of exceptional suffering. On Kranstin Moor, he had slept in a ditch; the nocturnal cold had been so profound that when he woke he found himself bonded to the ditch soil. His clothes were stiff, as if carved from thin wood; his fingers' skin stuck to blades of grass. Once, in Genhallin Town, after a night's drinking, he fell into a pond; and for the next two weeks his wet clothes glinted with ice shards. And on the road from Coarthe to Falrannan, wind and hail-blasted, he had near perished from exposure. A passing merchant had saved him. He gave Ballas fresh clothes, and food, and whisky; he stacked wood and lit a campfire, and rubbed warmth back into the big man's limbs. The gesture surprised Ballas. Not enough, though, to stop him robbing the merchant at first light, knocking him out with a lump of firewood for good measure.

Ballas couldn't clearly recall how badly, during those times, the cold had hurt. But he knew that he was uncomfortable now. The chill seemed to originate *inside* himself: it spread out through his flesh, as if radiating from his bones. He did not believe that the cold itself was notably severe. He simply felt it keenly. Perhaps the priest-home had softened him. Maybe his damaged body had become suddenly sensitive to a lack of heat.

More likely, Ballas was underdressed for the weather. The holy man had not given him a cape. Leggings, vest, tunic – *they* had been provided. But a warm woollen cape, with a fur-lined hood? The priest's generosity had limits, it seemed.

Scowling, Ballas moved onwards.

He wandered through the narrow streets, thinking of the coins in his pocket, scarcely caring where his footsteps took him. After a while, he found himself in familiar surroundings. He had last been here . . . how many nights ago? It did not matter. Everything had been cloaked in darkness but even now, in daylight, the taverns remained familiar. One in particular had a place in his memory. Over the doorway hung a sign: a stumpy, rivulet-encrusted candle burning with a red flame – an indication that the tavern also contained a brothel. Ballas briefly recalled his time there, and the whore he had rutted with in a room on the second floor. He smiled at the memory of her warm, fleshy limbs. And the ginger-and-cinnamon scent of her hair.

Then his gaze lowered to the thoroughfare. His smile faded.

This was where he had been beaten. What name had the priest given this place? *Vintner's Row*.

Ballas halted, shuffling uneasily from foot to foot.

He did not want another encounter with the stonemasons. He fleetingly imagined their surprise at setting eyes upon him; and discovering that despite their best efforts, he was still alive. This surprise would quickly darken to anger – as if Ballas had insulted them by staying in the world of the living. They would want to rectify matters. They would want desperately to finish, for once, a job that they had begun . . .

Ballas hastily went down a side-street, and walked west-wards until he emerged into a large city square.

It was market day. The square was crowded with wooden stalls, and Ballas walked amongst them, his eyes open for anything he might spend the priest's money on. Most items did not appeal to him. He had no desire to buy jars of herbs and spices, or jewellery carved clumsily from oak and mahogany. Similarly, he had no use for cooking pots and cutlery. Or for religious tokens, such as verses from *The Book of the Pilgrims*, etched into beech wood, or quilled upon scrolls of fine parchment.

He passed through a cluster of fishmongers' stalls. Their outspread wares, a jumble of cod, salmon and rainbow trout, glinted as if fashioned from silver. He walked by the butchers' stalls, offering ragged cuts of pork, beef, venison and gammon, all oozing in their own bright juices.

Only when he reached a cooked meat stall did he stop. He ravenously eyed minted lamb cutlets, roast pork encased in a thick layer of crackling, grilled steak awash with gravy . . . The big man deliberated for a few moments, before choosing a honey-glazed chicken. It had been roasted that morning, and though it was now stone-cold, this did not bother Ballas. He ate the chicken greedily, swallowing mouthful after mouthful, until only the pale bones remained.

Wiping his hands on his leggings, he wandered to a stall selling spirits and wines. It was a cold morning, and he felt in the mood for whisky. He bought the cheapest flagon he could find, caring less for its taste than its potency. Leaving the market, he began to walk further across the square.

After a few steps, he realised precisely *which* city square this was.

There was an oak tree at the far side of the square. A huge oak tree, its trunk was twice as broad as that of any other oak he had ever seen. Its hue was so dark brown as to be almost black; and its branches groped outwards, like a mass of thick black serpents.

There were human heads nailed to those branches. Three, all counted. They were too far away for their features to be clearly seen. To Ballas's eyes, they were scarcely more than dark lumps, hanging there like baubles. Curious, the big man strolled over, uncorking the whisky flagon as he went.

Gradually, the heads became clearer. One belonged to an old man. His tiny green eyes were stretched wide, his mouth open as if he were in shock. On another branch, there was the head of an adolescent boy. His eyes were bright blue in colour, and his skin was pale, delicate. Between his eyebrows, the stub of a nail glittered; underneath it, dried trickles of blood marked his nose and cheeks. Against the youth's pallor, it seemed as garish as a cheap whore's lip-daub.

Ballas took a sip of whisky. The hot fluid swirled down his throat. He gasped, feeling a pain that was both pleasurable and reassuring.

His gaze drifted to the lowest branch.

The head of a young woman was nailed there. Her eyes were deep brown, her hair auburn and curling. She was pretty in a vulgar, peasant-like fashion. Ballas looked at where her neck ended; where the skin and muscle terminated and there was nothing except empty air, and he found himself wondering what her body had been like. Probably, it had been voluptuous; a thing of softness and warmth, a treat to hold. Exactly the sort of body Ballas savoured the most.

What had been her crime? he wondered. Witchcraft? Seership?

The details were not important, Ballas realised. She had been nailed to the Penance Oak: that meant her crimes had been unholy. She had not offended her fellow man. Rather she had, in some way, defied the Pilgrim Church. Perhaps her crime *had* involved magick. For those who practised the forbidden arts were often found upon the Oak. It did not matter whether their skills were used benignly, or with genuinely wicked intent. Magick was outlawed as contrary to the Four's teachings and as such, those who used it had to be punished.

But those who did not practise magick also found their heads nailed upon the Oak's dark branches. Those who blasphemed in a holy place; those who spouted heresies; those who sought the services of a magicker . . . All of these people offended the Church. And all of these people warranted retribution.

A crow flapped down on to the young woman's head. It loitered there for a moment; then, hopping lower, it set its spindly-toed talons around her bottom jaw and, perching there, started to jab its beak into her left eye, attempting to prize it out as if it were a pearl inside an oyster.

Murmuring, Ballas raised the flagon to his lips.

Then someone called: 'Dare you drink so near to the Oak?'

Ballas ignored the voice.

'Citizen,' it cried again, 'do you not understand that the Oak is holy, and your actions are a blasphemy?'

Your actions are a blasphemy. The words' formality disturbed Ballas. They were not like those used by the common folk. He turned round.

Two Papal Wardens approached. The Realm's keepers-of-law, the foot soldiers of holy justice. They wore jet-black tunics, each with a narrow blue triangle stitched into the chest. Each man bore a sheathed sword and a dagger. Their helms were polished black iron. Beneath these hung chain-mail ventails.

A young Warden put out his hand. 'Give me the flagon,' he said. 'It is forbidden to drink in Papal Square.'

'I am not drinking,' said Ballas easily.

The Warden's gaze hardened. 'The flagon holds whisky – I can smell it from here. And you are pouring it down your throat. So you're drinking, citizen. Now stop this nonsense and give me the flagon.'

'It's whisky, true enough,' said Ballas. 'But I drink it as a *medicine*.'

'A medicine?'

'It stops me freezing to death.'

'I have no time for such games,' said the Warden, tightly. A tawny fringe poked out under his helm. He was twenty-five years old. Certainly no older, thought Ballas. Who was this pup, to confiscate his whisky?

'Give me the whisky,' the Warden repeated.

'What if I refused? Would you nail me to the Oak? Would you claim that the Four – the virtuous, forgiving Four, who love every living soul – those Pilgrims, who traipsed this wondrous land, so we might be forgiven – will you say they demand my execution, for drinking a little liquor?'

Ballas realised he was slightly drunk. He had drunk the whisky flagon half-empty.

'We'll make a bargain,' he continued. 'I'll keep my whisky. I'll find a doorway, somewhere or other, and finish it off. Then we'll both be happy, aye? I'll be warm and drunk. And you . . . you'll have restored order to the Square.'

Turning, he ducked under the Oak's lowest branches.

'Halt! Stay right where you are!'

Ballas ignored the command.

A hand grasped his shoulder. The grip was relatively gentle, meant only to restrain. But it sent pain flaring through Ballas's bruised flesh.

Crying out, Ballas spun round – and reflexively lashed out at the Warden. The movement was clumsy. The big man's open hand struck the Warden's cheek – a blow that was neither punch nor slap. The Warden stumbled, surprised. Then he sprang at Ballas, slamming a fist into his face.

The impact burst open Ballas's lips.

Stepping closer, the Warden doubled-punched Ballas's chest. Gasping, Ballas felt rib grate against cracked rib. Another punch drove into his stomach. Ballas groaned and sank to his knees.

The Warden moved closer. But the second Warden restrained him.

'At ease, Janner,' he said. He was much older than the first Warden and sported a grey moustache. On his tunic's shoulder he bore the two red stripes of a Warden Commander.

'He struck me!' shouted the younger Warden.

'This is holy ground,' said the Commander. 'If he were in an alleyway, you could treat him however you liked. But not here. Not so near the Oak. Not so near the Sacros.'

At the northern edge of Papal Square there was a wall of white, faintly gleaming marble, thirty feet tall. It was so neatly constructed that the individual bricks could not be seen; instead, it looked as if it had been sculpted from a single, enormous block. It encircled a large, pyramidal building, fashioned from scarlet stone. Its height was almost dizzying; two, perhaps three hundred feet tall, it loomed over the Square, and the marketplace, like a blood-coloured mountain. It seemed scarcely possible that it had been erected by human hands; rather, its scale gave the impression that it was the work of the creator-god Himself. There were windows set into the brickwork, arched and shadowed; their frames were crafted from some bright golden metal, possibly brass, but in all likelihood, gold. The walls were traversed by narrow ledges of black stone, upon which a scattering of crows roosted.

Around the main building, there were four towers, each five hundred feet tall. Each of these towers, Ballas knew, represented one of the four Pilgrims. Upon every tower's red-tiled spire, there fluttered a flag symbolising the occupation of a Pilgrim: a loom for the clothes-maker Pilgrim, a ship's sail for the sailor, a candle for the chandler and a flensing knife for the tanner. In the day's strong light, the towers spread weak shadows across Papal Square.

The Warden Commander gestured toward the building. 'We have to be careful,' he told the younger Warden. 'If we misbehave, and we are seen . . .' His voice trailed off. He had no need to say anything else, realised Ballas. The edifice beyond the marble wall – the Esklarion Sacros – was home to the Blessed Masters. The seven highest-ranking clergymen in Druine; the seven men who, garbed in scarlet robes, governed the Pilgrim Church.

And because there was no power in Druine *except* the Pilgrim Church, they governed Druine itself: every acre of forest and farmland, every mountain and every pool and every river, was under their control. And the life of every living thing.

'Should we drag him to an alleyway?' asked the younger Warden. 'Then we could—'

'We will leave him be,' said the Commander. 'He has learned

his lesson. Do you live in this city?' he asked, turning his gaze on Ballas.

'That is not your business,' replied the big man.

'Vagrancy is a crime,' replied the Commander.

'I *had* lodgings,' muttered Ballas. 'But I've abandoned them. As I shall abandon this city. It's brought me only ill luck.'

'We have all endured bad fortune,' said the Commander, with unexpected sympathy. 'From your condition' – he gestured towards Ballas's blood-sodden garb – 'you have suffered more than most. Perhaps it was warranted. Perhaps it was not. But I will offer you a few words of advice. Return to your lodgings. Do not leave the city. Vagrancy is vagrancy, whether here or on the road to somewhere else. Wardens can distinguish between a traveller and a tramp. You will be arrested. Besides, you are in no fit state to travel. Winter is almost here. You will freeze.'

'Not if I have whisky,' said Ballas.

The Commander took the flagon from him. Ballas was in too much pain to resist.

'Watch your step,' said the Commander.

Turning, he strode away, followed by the young Warden.

'Bastards,' muttered Ballas.

Grunting, he tried to stand. Nerve-splitting pain surged through his body. With a yelp, Ballas sagged against the Penance Oak. He coughed up a splash of bile. A breeze swept over him. He began shivering – as if the gust had blown unabated from the Frozen North. He had never felt so sick. So frail. So vulnerable.

This feeling – painful, unfamiliar – appalled him.

Growling, he grasped the Oak and dragged himself upright. His legs buckled. He dropped once more to his knees, heavily.

A few passers-by stared. A courting couple, a gang of children, an aged, stern-eyed woman . . . they watched him, half disgusted, half amused.

'What do you want?' shouted Ballas. '*What do you want?!*'

This outburst hurt his ribs again. He groaned. The children laughed. Angry, Ballas thrust out a hand at them. They sprang back, as nimble as squirrels, elusive. Ballas overbalanced, falling on to all fours.

He lifted his head slowly, like a wounded animal.

'You should follow the Commander's advice,' said the aged woman. 'Gaze upon yourself, and you will see he has spoken sense. You are a wretch. You are drunk, injured, incapable—'

'Shut up!' shouted Ballas. 'Let me alone. All of you – be gone!'

Yet there was something in the old woman's words, Ballas conceded.

Leaning against the Oak, feeling nauseous, he realised that he was not strong enough to leave Father Brethrien's care. A single night on the streets could kill him. He might freeze to death. Or his open wounds, exposed to disease-infested vermin – the rats, dogs and cats that wandered the city – might get infected with a blood-taint.

The holy man's fluttering manners annoyed Ballas. But if he were to stay alive, he had to remain in the priest-home a little longer.

And that meant performing his errand.

Leaving Papal Square, Ballas shuffled to Half-moon Street. Several times he paused to catch his breath, or to vomit. When he arrived at the museum, his ribs were throbbing and bile blotched his tunic front.

Stooping through a set of arched doors, he found himself in a large, high-ceilinged chamber of oaken display cases. Ballas scarcely glanced at the exhibits. Out of the corner of his eye he saw pottery, clothing, weaponry, carved idols – each item either from the past or from some region far beyond Druine – or both. But he took no proper notice. History was a futile passion, a bloodless sifting of bones and dust. Only the present mattered. For only in the present did fleshly joys exist. A whore's rutting room was more beguiling than an ancient queen's bedchamber. Common-room gossip more fascinating than intrigues of court. A cockfight more exhilarating than an account of a long-forgotten war.

Ballas passed through the chamber. Then another. In the third, he heard voices – they came from a small doorway in the wall to Ballas's left.

Stooping through the doorway, Ballas found himself at the top of a flight of steps. He followed them down, halting a few steps from the bottom.

Ahead stretched a long candlelit vault. Dark stone slabs paved the floor. From the walls shelves jutted. Upon some, animals' skulls rested. There were deer, bull, wolf and ram skulls, each one white and criss-crossed with faint fracture lines. But there were also skulls of unrecognisable origin. A snout bone extended from one; from another's pate jutted a curving, sharp-tipped horn, surrounded by inch-long spikes. Another skull had an absurdly heavy and protuberant jaw. Another had only a single eye socket, staring emptily from the forehead. Jumbled bones were heaped beside the skulls: a pale mound of fibulas, tibias, ribs, vertebrae.

Other shelves held ancient vases, statuettes, graven images . . . objects like those exhibited in the chambers above.

An old grey-robed man stood in the vault's centre. Alongside him was a second man, of middle years and with a crumpled, wind-scoured face.

'So,' asked the old man, 'how are things at the Academy? The institution – it is thriving, hmm?'

'It is thriving,' said the second man. 'As far as anything can thrive with the Church's boot planted on its throat.'

'The Blessed Masters are proving troublesome?' It was the voice Ballas had heard in the priest-home, when his injuries were first tended. 'They are interfering, yes?'

'Every day, they place tighter limits on what we may study. They are suspicious of certain disciplines. They mistrust Linguistics, believing it may expose as counterfeit the testimonies of the Nine Witnesses. I do not understand how it could do so – the testimonies' authenticity is beyond doubt. Yet the Church remains wary. And wary, too, of history: our historians are permitted to teach only a single Church-approved version of the past: one that acknowledges the Four's existence, but does not delve deeply into Their lives – or even the age in which They lived.'

'Including the Red War?'

'From the blood spilled during our conflict with the Lectivins,' said the other man, 'Druine, and the Church's power grew. There must be no reappraisal of that time. The foundations must be seen to be secure. The Church thinks it wisest to blindfold those scholars who would look closely.'

'What do they fear, I wonder?' said Calden, softly.

'Fear? I do not believe the Masters *fear* anything: for there is nothing of substance *to fear*. There are hundreds, *thousands* of accounts of our conflict with the Lectivins. From the arrival of the Lectivin ships upon our shores, to our obliteration of the Pale Race, everything has been transcribed innumerable times. There is nothing new to be discovered.' He sighed. 'I think the Church worries that if people study the Lectivins, the Lectivins will cease to seem . . .' He paused.

'Extraordinary?'

'Extraordinary,' agreed the other man. 'In our hearts, the Lectivins were demons, djinns, *cohkaris* – we know this is not so, but our hearts believe it nonetheless. However, our hearts will grow sceptical if our minds insist often enough that, in truth, the Lectivins were merely a different species. And in that, they were no more extraordinary than dogs, birds or fish. Or ourselves. The Church cannot permit this.' He grew quiet. Then, as if uttering a dangerous secret, he said, 'Have you heard about the archaeological dig in the Galdirran hills?'

'A few rumours have floated my way.' The old curator nodded. 'Lectivin relics were unearthed, were they not? Then the Church closed down the excavations.'

'You would imagine the relics were of a great and terrible nature. A nature that could shake the Church to its core . . .'

'But they were not?'

'The archaeologists unearthed bowls, spoons, eating daggers – that is all. Simple objects, in design similar to our own. And therein lies the problem. The Lectivins were not hugely unlike ourselves. Our appearances differed. But, like us, they prayed, crafted churches . . . and ate with cutlery.' He laughed softly. 'Such tiny details destroy any air of mystery. It is hard to imagine a real demon using a spoon. To preserve the Lectivins' traditional image, the excavation was, as you said, terminated. The relics were confiscated, the ground filled in.'

'And the archaeologists?'

'I do not know for certain. But they have not returned to the Academy. Perhaps, when the site was earthed over, they too were buried. This is a dangerous era in which to be a thinker.'

The two men were silent for a long time.

Eventually Calden asked, 'I take it *your* subject has not been forbidden?'

'The Masters have yet to find geology objectionable,' replied the other man. 'I suspect they actually approve of it: they have a taste for fine, glittering objects, mined from the soil.'

'I have something that may interest you,' said Calden, moving towards a shelf.

Muttering to himself under his breath, bored by the two men's talk, Ballas almost descended the final steps into the vault. Yet he paused. Something had changed in Calden's manner. Drawing out a wooden casket, the old man seemed excited. And infused with pride – as if he was about to amaze the geologist with something clever. Or unexpected.

Maybe the casket contained nothing of interest. A pottery fragment. A famous warrior's rusted dagger handle. A quill used by a revered philosopher. Any article that, despite its drabness, would thrill a scholar.

But maybe it held something better.

Ballas stepped back into the gloom at the stairwell's base.

Calden placed the casket on a wooden desk, then opened it with a key strung around his neck.

'This is why I sent for you,' he said, taking out a black iron disc, about four inches across. In the centre nestled a blue gemstone, measuring an inch from side to side. Near the disc's edge, four more stones – blood red, this time – were inset at the cardinal compass points.

'What do you think?' asked Calden, passing it to the geologist.

'It is pretty,' said the other man. 'What is it?'

'I have yet to deduce its function. Perhaps it is a mere ornament. Or maybe a talisman of some description. Several weeks ago, a scholar of some eminence passed away. He bequeathed me a collection of items, of which this was one. I believe its origins were as unknown to him as they are to me. Now,' he moved slightly closer, peering himself at the disc, 'tell me what the gemstones are.'

'Those on the outside appear to be rubies.' The geologist touched a fingertip to them. 'Yes – rubies.'

'And the gemstone in the centre?'

'Opal,' replied the geologist. 'No, wait. It is too dark. Diamond, perhaps. Stones of a similar shade have been brought from Gohavi.'

'It is not a diamond.'

'How can you be so certain?'

'Hold it to a candle flame,' said Calden, 'and tell me if any diamond in history has behaved like this gemstone.'

Crossing the floor, the geologist lifted the disc to a candle burning in a niche. From his position on the steps, Ballas could not see the effect of the flame's light on the gemstone itself. But what he could see surprised him. Startled him, even.

A wash of blue light poured from the gemstone, illuminating the geologist's face. The light was strong; blinking, the geologist tilted his head. Then he frowned.

'Calden,' he whispered, 'I have never seen such a thing.'

'A marvel, is it not?'

'Never have I witnessed such a play of light within a gemstone's depths. It does not merely glitter; it . . . it . . .' Words failed him briefly. 'Those flecks, drifting and falling, like sparks in a furnace . . . each flaring like a fragment of gold . . . like sunlight in a rock pool's shallows . . . You said it was left to you, by a scholar of note. Where did *he* obtain it?'

'I do not know. He travelled widely, within Druine and beyond. He could have found it anywhere. I have consulted the major texts. Bahane's *Catalogue of the Earth-Bright*, Tharkannan's *Minerals Universalis* . . . Of such a stone, there is no mention. Perhaps—'

'—It is unique?' finished the geologist.

Calden nodded.

'Perhaps it is indeed one of a kind,' said the geologist thoughtfully.

'If you wish to study it properly,' said Calden, a touch hesitantly, 'you may borrow it. If you promise that, in your hands, it will be safe.'

The geologist lowered the disc. The candle flame no longer lit the gemstone. The blue light vanished.

'It will not be safe,' said the geologist plainly.

'You fear the Church might confiscate it?'

'The frame-piece has a primitive look; the Church might believe it was a religious item, from the age before the Melding. They will not permit such items to circulate. And my students – they are interested less in scholarship than in drinking and whoring. Such pastimes are not inexpensive. Every now and then, a few items are stolen from the storage rooms. Such a piece as this,' he touched the disc, 'might prove a great temptation. It is best not to place shining things within the sight of magpies. Now, Calden, I must go; I have to deliver a lecture on Catharrian emeralds. In themselves, they are truly beautiful. But compared to that gemstone? Ha! They might as well be lumps of coal. Fare you well, Calden.' Turning, he walked towards the door.

Spinning on his heel, Ballas jogged noiselessly up the steps, unseen by the geologist and the curator.

Ballas returned to the priest-home. In the kitchen, a fire blazed. Warm air curled over the big man as he stepped inside.

Father Brethrien was kneeling at the hearth, prodding the fire with a brass poker. 'Did you pay Calden?' he asked, glancing up.

'Aye,' replied Ballas truthfully.

'Was he happy to see you? You are, in part, a testament to his skills as a physician. He must have found it gratifying to—'

'We did not speak. I merely paid him and went.'

The curator had wanted to talk. When Ballas gave him the coins, he had asked some question about the big man's health. Uninterested, Ballas had ignored him.

Now he treated the priest the same way. Striding past him, Ballas went to his sleeping-room. He uncorked a whisky flagon, stolen from the cart of a market-stall owner. Taking a long swallow, he thought of the iron disc. Of the four glinting rubies. Of the blue gemstone.

He remembered the geologist's awe. He heard again the talk of drifting golden sparks . . . of uniqueness . . .

'What am I,' murmured Ballas, 'but a magpie? Enjoy your bauble while you can, curator. Soon it will be gone.'